RULES OF WAR

ALSO BY MATTHEW BETLEY

Overwatch

Oath of Honor

Field of Valor

RULES OF WAR

A THRILLER

MATTHEW BETLEY

EMILY BESTLER BOOKS

—

ATRIA

NEW YORK   LONDON   TORONTO   SYDNEY   NEW DELHI

EMILY
BESTLER
BOOKS

ATRIA

An Imprint of Simon & Schuster, Inc.
1230 Avenue of the Americas
New York, NY 10020

First Emily Bestler Books/Atria Books hardcover edition May 2019

EMILY BESTLER BOOKS/ATRIA BOOKS and colophon are trademarks of Simon & Schuster, Inc.

For information about special discounts for bulk purchases, please contact Simon & Schuster Special Sales at 1-866-506-1949 or business@simonandschuster.com.

The Simon & Schuster Speakers Bureau can bring authors to your live event. For more information or to book an event contact the Simon & Schuster Speakers Bureau at 1-866-248-3049 or visit our website at www.simonspeakers.com.

Manufactured in the United States of America

10 9 8 7 6 5 4 3 2 1

Library of Congress Cataloging-in-Publication Data is available.

ISBN 978-1-5011-6202-2
ISBN 978-1-5011-6203-9 (ebook)

For Sergeant Terry O'Hara, 9/11 responder and NYPD officer (1976–2017);
Betsy Harrigan, retired NSA employee and author (1945–2017);
and Joan Digani, mother, wife, sister, and aunt (1950–2015).
While their fights are over, the battle wages on.
As Terry said every time I talked to him, "Fuck cancer." Amen, brother.
Someday, we'll all dance on the Big C's grave.

PROLOGUE

Calvert County, MD

Charlie Reker didn't care for county officials. As far as he was concerned, the local politicians were just as power-hungry as the corrupt parasites that occupied the Capitol twenty-five miles to the northwest. Many a day he'd half-heartedly hoped that some lucky terrorist might figure out a way to blow up Congress and the morally bankrupt people it contained. The only reservation he had—the one that mattered most to him—was the innocent loss of life that would result. And that was something he couldn't abide, no matter how bitter he was toward the federal government.

A fifty-three-year-old mechanic with a rough face, short grizzled beard, and cropped black hair, he owned a four-bay, full-service garage in rural southern Maryland. But thanks to the moronic lawmakers and the last president, his income had significantly declined over the past several years due to the Affordable Care Act, *which was a fucking lie of a name, if there ever was one, hand to God,* he thought. In addition to his lowered earnings, he'd also been forced to lay off his best mechanic, a young man who had a talent for quickly identifying any problem that plagued an engine, no matter how small or complicated the cause. The kid had been excellent—not as good as Charlie, but still great, nonetheless.

But the cost of the limited health-care plans in Maryland had shot up exponentially, and the financial burden had been more than he could bear. As with every other ill-conceived government plan, there'd been one more unforeseen effect: he'd had to increase the number of hours he worked every week just to make ends meet. It infuriated him, but he knew there was nothing he could do about it. *The septic tide would turn at some point, God willing.*

It was also why Charlie didn't care that he'd violated the law six ways to Sunday in the middle of summer for the past three years, hunting for deer with a Stryker Katana 360 crossbow, the easiest hunting weapon he'd discovered and come to love as much as he loved anything. *I dare them to come out and find me. Fucking park-ranger Rambo wannabes. I've been playing in these woods longer than those baby-faced Ranger Ricks.* He hadn't even put on an orange vest for safety. *Who the hell else would be out here, anyhow?* The nearest neighborhood was two miles away. He figured the biggest risk he had was getting bitten by a snake or having another tick lodge itself in his nether regions, the way two had done last year, scaring the living daylights out of him when he'd showered after a twenty-four-hour period in the woods. Unfortunately for Charlie, he was wrong.

The dense woods were hot and humid, alive with the midmorning sounds of insects and small, energetic animals. With the canopy of shade from the thick pine and oak trees, the heat was tolerable on the forest floor. He felt a sharp, not-so-mild pain as one of the region's aggressive deerflies landed on the back of his neck and bit into his sweaty flesh.

"Goddamnit!" he swore, releasing the front of the crossbow to swat at the angry creature. His green-gloved hand hit the flying annoyance, and he turned around and looked down to see the large deerfly struggling on top of the leafy underbrush. He brought a brown boot down on top of it to stop its flailing. *Great. Hope I don't get that stupid disease that rhymes with anemia,* he thought, not able to recall the exact name of the rare disease transmittable to humans and fatal if left untreated.

A movement through the trees twenty yards to his right redirected his attention, and he placed his left hand on the foregrip, lifting the weapon. *What the hell?* There was a sudden noise from behind him, and he whirled on his heels, adrenaline pumping.

"Whoa! Whoa! Whoa! Don't shoot," a man said, wearing a full-blown 3-D tree suit like the ones Charlie had seen advertised in Cabela's magazine. His face was darkened with green shades of camouflage paint, disguising his features other than the whites of his eyes. He wore a backpack that blended in with his tree suit, but he also had a rifle slung across his back.

Is that an AR-15 painted brown? Charlie thought. It wasn't the first time he'd seen someone hunt with an AR-15, *but at this time of year?* It was one thing that he was out here with a crossbow—he wanted to be quiet while he stalked through the woods—but an AR-15 would draw attention immediately, no matter how far the nearest neighborhood was. *Someone always hears the shots.* But then he saw the suppressor at the end of the barrel, angled toward the ground for easy access. His mind registered the pistol in a thigh rig, which was when he heard another noise to his left, and a second figure emerged from behind a tree, triggering alarms in the back of Charlie Reker's mind.

Charlie raised the crossbow, the tip of the bolt subtly shifting to the feet of the first intruder, which was how his mind cataloged the two men. "Who the hell are you? Why are you out here?"

"I could ask you the same question, friend," the first man replied, a hint of amusement in his voice. Another noise from Charlie's right coincided with the appearance of a third figure, a man in similar hunting garb—*That's not quite right; it's tactical clothing, like those boys in the military wear that I saw on the History Channel*—who now stood silent next to a dying oak tree, blackened and mortally wounded by a bolt of lightning.

"Who the hell are you people? You're not from the county, are you?" Charlie asked, the hairs on the back of his arms and neck vibrating in alarm.

"I'm afraid not," the man replied, a hint of regret underpinning the words. The man looked to Charlie's right and nodded.

Charlie sensed the movement and tried to turn, and panic gripped him as he swung the crossbow to his right. He heard two sounds like loud mechanical bangs, and his momentum faltered. He looked down and saw dark wetness spreading in two places on the right side of his chest. Weakness slammed into him like an invisible hand, and he collapsed to his knees, the crossbow falling to the dark, dank earth.

Charlie Reker suddenly felt tired, and he realized the end of his life was at hand, but rather than let it slip away, he felt a brief, burning sense of fury course through him. He'd been a fighter his entire life, and he wasn't about to go out with a whimper. His killers would hear his voice before he died. He turned back to the first man, even as the edges of his vision dimmed. "Why?"

"Because you were here," the man replied matter-of-factly. "Nothing more. I'm sorry, if it's any consolation. I promise you one thing: we'll make sure your body is found so your loved ones can lay you to rest."

Because I was here? "Damn you to hell," Charlie coughed, with precious seconds left in life. "Murderers always pay, and you will too." They were the last words he uttered, and a moment later, his lifeless form toppled sideways, coming to rest next to a pile of leaves from the previous fall.

"I'm sure you're right," the man responded to no one in particular.

"What do you want to do with him?" Charlie's executioner asked, the suppressed AR-15 slung across his back once again. He bent down, picked up the two empty cartridges, and placed them inside a cargo pocket on the right side of his tree suit trousers.

"Nothing," the first man replied. "We leave him here, and when our mission is over, we notify the authorities. I just made a promise to a dying man whose only misfortune was to cross our path, and I intend to keep it."

"Agreed," the third man said.

"Good. Now let's get going. We still have a mile before we get to our assembly area. Then the hard part begins," the first man said.

"What's that?" the second hunter of men asked.

"The waiting," the first man replied. "It's always the goddamned waiting. Now let's move."

Without another word, the three men in full tactical gear formed a single Ranger file and moved silently through the trees, leaving Charlie Reker in his temporary resting place deep in the Maryland woods.

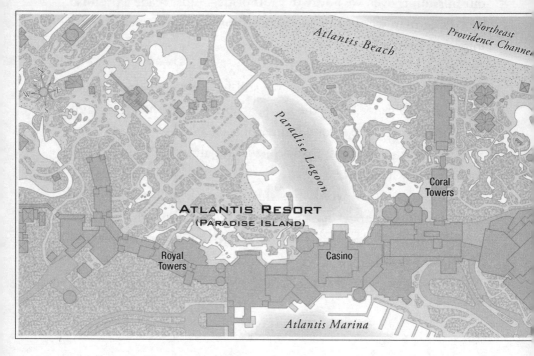

PART I

SHARKS AND MINNOWS

CHAPTER 1

Caracas, Venezuela

The pain of his little girl was all that mattered. He knew he would likely die if he did what they asked, but it didn't matter. All that mattered was saving her.

Chief Inspector Santiago Rojas of the Counterintelligence Direction of the Bolivarian National Intelligence—known as the SEBIN—stared across the rectangular wooden table at the two older men; one he knew, the other he only recognized from Venezuelan television and politics. At thirty-nine and the head of a special domestic unit charged with preventing internal threats, he'd been summoned to the meeting at a clandestine safe house that the SEBIN used for staging operations and other low-level tactical planning on the northern outskirts of the city at the base of the Venezuelan Coastal Range mountains.

An executive to one of the men had approached him at home and notified him that they needed his help in a sensitive, dangerous matter and that they'd be willing to help his daughter in return. *She is everything to me. No matter what they want, no price is too high if they can help her.*

"If you do this," the older of the two men now said in Spanish, white hair loosely falling across his forehead, "we will do everything we can to save your daughter, starting this very moment. Do we have an agreement?"

The second man, bald on top with black hair shaved neatly to the skin on both sides of his head, sat quietly, studying Santiago.

The irony is that either one of them could have ordered me to do this, but instead, they're bribing me. Whatever this is, it's not for official channels. But he knew better than to raise his questions. *Men of power always have their reasons.*

"We do, sir," Santiago replied calmly, and looked both men directly in the eyes. *Please, God, let the treatment work.* "Myself and my men are at your disposal."

"No. This is for you alone. Your unit must never know. Ever. Do you understand?" the seventy-year-old politician replied. "This mission is too sensitive, Santiago," he said, using the chief inspector's given name. "If you utter a word of it to anyone, you put us, yourself, and most importantly, your daughter, in serious danger. This mission must not be compromised."

What have I just agreed to? Santiago thought, his black eyebrows furrowing momentarily above sharp eyes and angular dark-brown features that women paid attention to when he was near. *Whatever it is, you're in it now.*

"Gentlemen, *what* exactly is the mission?" Santiago asked, genuine interest in his voice.

The two men looked at each other, and the white-haired man opened the leather bag in front of him, pulled out an 8.5" x 11" high-resolution color photograph, and placed it in front of Santiago.

Looking off to the side toward something Santiago would never see was a figure he instantly recognized as a man of purpose with an indefinable aura of danger around him. Staring into the unknown was a strikingly handsome American with a slightly tanned complexion, short brown hair, and a faint scar that ran down his left cheek. But it was the eyes that the hidden photographer had captured that drew him in—bright-green pools of intelligence seemed to dance on the thick, glossy paper in front of the inspector. They shone with calculation, but Santiago sensed there was much more to him, that this formidable man was capable of great violence.

"It's not a 'what.' It's a 'who,'" the white-haired man replied and jabbed a bent, aged finger onto the face of the man. "And *he's* now your primary target."

Santiago was quiet as he studied the photograph a moment longer, before finally speaking. "Tell me who he is," he said, and committed himself to a course of action from which there was no turning back.

For my daughter, Santiago thought one last time, and proceeded to listen to what the director of the SEBIN and the president of Venezuela's Supreme Tribunal of Justice had to offer.

CHAPTER 2

Atlantis Resort
Nassau Island, Bahamas
Saturday, 1100 Local Time

Logan West studied the great hammerhead sharks as two of the three twelve-foot-long fish circled and chased each other in the middle of Predator Lagoon. A warm Bahamian breeze blew in from the north, and the faint scent of the ocean ran through his nostrils with a sense of weight from the high humidity. It was a typical sunny summer day on Paradise Island, and Logan was entranced by the low thrum of the other patrons at the Lagoon Bar & Grill, the wind, and the air, all of which combined to create a soothing, trance-like effect. *This place is amazing. Sarah and I need to come here, preferably before she gets too pregnant to fly.*

The luxury resort of Atlantis occupied the central portion of Paradise Island, an oddly shaped strip of land just north of New Providence Island, connected to it by two bridges. Multiple hotel room towers, interconnected walkways, restaurants, shopping areas, lagoons, and water parks lay sprawled across the island canvas in an endless array of adult and children's entertainment. The most identifiable features were the two Royal Towers connected by the enormous Bridge Suite that spanned the buildings at the seventeenth floor. Featured in every commercial and multiple movies, it reportedly went for more than twenty-five thousand dollars a night. *Should have put that on the government credit card,* Logan thought.

A sudden splash broke the calm surface as one of the hammerhead sharks suddenly charged the other, which accelerated and fled from its attacking lagoon mate. *Predators will be predators, even among their own kind,* Logan thought, and refocused his attention on his menu. *Twenty bucks for a drink? That's highway robbery, even for something called an Atlantis Punch. Thank God you're sober,* the recovering alcoholic in him commented. *Otherwise, you'd be broke already. And I wouldn't care about why I was down here,* Logan reminded himself, bright-green eyes scanning the lunch crowd for potential threats.

From his seat at the open-air bar under the enormous seashell roof that covered the entire outdoor restaurant, he had an unobstructed view in all directions, except through the low wall of top-shelf liquor that faced him. He smiled briefly at the realization that now with more than two and a half years of sobriety, he wasn't even tempted by the alcohol buffet laid out before him. One day at a time had turned into one month and now one year at a time, and he had no desire to return to the lifestyle that had nearly destroyed his marriage and his life.

Cole should be here in ten minutes or so. I'll order us some pulled chicken Caribbean sliders in the meantime, and then we can figure out the next move while we wait.

It had been nearly two weeks since the vice president of the United States had orchestrated his own "kidnapping" in order to deceive the public and flee North America, a traitor to the Constitution and his country. According to retired Marine Corps Commandant General Jack Longstreet, also the chief of security operations for Constantine Kallas, the head of a multibillion-dollar international shipping conglomerate, Vice President Joshua Baker had escaped to South America. Complicating matters was the fact that only Task Force Ares, comprising Logan West, his team, and selected others in the government—including the president and the directors of the CIA and FBI—knew the truth. All other US law enforcement and even the Intelligence Community thought the vice president had been kidnapped by a Montana-based militia. *How long that ruse holds up is anyone's guess,* Logan thought.

Once Constantine Kallas had died, violently, at the hands of very powerful members of the clandestine international Organization that he himself had spent decades building and operating, Jack Longstreet had vowed to hunt down and eradicate the traitors who had betrayed his employer, friend, and mentor. The killing had started with the director of the National Security Agency, and Logan suspected Jack and his team of former operators were somewhere in South America, even though Jack wasn't exactly checking in with Logan. *Retired generals will do what retired generals will do.*

It was Jack who had called Logan and notified him of the location of a high-ranking member of the Organization known as the Recruiter. At the orders of the president, Logan and Cole Matthews, the former head of the CIA's Special Activities Division, had kidnapped, interrogated, and executed the conspirator. They'd then sent his body to the bottom of the Chesapeake Bay for the crab and other aquatic parasites to feed on. But before he died, he'd provided the location of a meeting at the Atlantis Resort he was to have with multiple facilitators of the Organization who had participated in the rebellion. They were the Recruiter's tour guides to his final destination—which hadn't been disclosed to him before he died—in South America.

And hopefully, once we identify the targets, they'll lead us to other members of the Organization and the ultimate prize, the vice presi-

dent. They're all going to burn, Logan thought as he felt the presence of a man who suddenly sat down in the empty bar chair to his right. *Jack better get us new intel, or this is going to be the shortest vacation I've had. At least it's better than Iraq,* he thought. *Come on, Cole. Where are you?*

"Who's winning?" the newcomer asked.

Logan glanced at the widescreen TV mounted on top of the wall above the rows of liquor bottles. A soccer match played out on one of the Fox Sports channels broadcast to the island from Miami. He looked to his right and was greeted by a handsome man with short brown hair and a light-skinned complexion he couldn't place.

The man spoke in an accent to the bartender, a resident of the island who'd been watching the game quietly from the other end of the bar. "Just a rum and cola, please."

"You got it, sir," the bartender replied, and the man turned to face Logan.

"Honestly," Logan finally answered, "I'm not sure. I was just watching the sharks while waiting for a friend."

The man nodded. "They are impressive, no? My daughter told me that they like to swim in schools during the day, and then turn into solitary predators at night."

Like a lot of creatures, Logan thought, *although I always prefer a pack.*

"How old is your daughter?" Logan asked, sensing a sincerity to the man, who appeared to be in his midthirties and fit, at least from what Logan could tell through the man's light-blue poplin button-down short-sleeve shirt and khaki bathing suit.

"Nine," the man said. "This vacation is for her. Her mother passed away two years ago. Cancer. She's handling it as well as can be expected, but who can really know what's in her head?"

Or anyone's, for that matter, Logan thought.

The man briefly looked at Logan before quickly turning away.

"I'm sorry. It's probably more than you needed to know. I'll leave you to wait for your friend," he said, and started to slide down a seat to the only other empty spot at the bar. The bartender placed a glass of dark liquid in front of him, as if luring him back to his seat.

Before Logan could catch himself, he said, "It's okay. Feel free to stay, at least until my buddy gets here."

The man considered for a moment, and then stuck out his hand. "I'm Alejandro. Thanks. If you don't mind, I will."

Logan shook the man's hand and said, "Logan. Nice to meet you."

It must be the fact that Sarah's pregnant. I normally wouldn't introduce myself to some stranger, his mind cautioned him. *Then again, he's where you could be someday, and he's already been where you're going. Cut him some slack.*

"No problem at all," Logan replied. "My buddy, Carl, and I just came down for the weekend to check out the resort, enjoy the casino, and maybe do some deep-sea fishing. This place is breathtaking, and I realized while sitting here that I could spend weeks and not discover everything it has to offer," he said, sweeping his right hand in a semicircular motion to emphasize the point.

"It's a modern masterpiece. I agree. And my daughter loves it, especially the Dig," Alejandro said, referring to the world's largest open-air aquarium, set at the base of the east Royal Tower and casino. Underground passageways adorned with exhibits and artifacts wound along the base of the aquarium through ruins intended to replicate the lost city of Atlantis.

"It is," Logan said. "I walked through it earlier this morning. So how long are you here?"

"Another few days, and then back home," Alejandro replied.

"Which is?" Logan asked nonchalantly.

"Colombia," Alejandro replied.

"Really? I've never been, but it seems like a beautiful place," Logan said.

"It is, but we're still recovering from the damage the drug cartels did to the country. It's better than it was under the Medellín and Cali cartels, but when you create a void, something always steps in to fill it," Alejandro said.

"I'll drink to that," was all Logan said, knowing that Colombia was still the world's largest producer of cocaine. *But there's no need to insult the man.* "If I may ask, what do you do?"

"I'm a police officer," Alejandro said.

Really? Now that's interesting, the former Marine thought. It was no surprise that many law enforcement officers—local, state, and federal—in the US were former Marines. Many Marines who left the Corps often replaced one lifestyle of discipline and honor for another. *Marines are Marines, no matter what uniform they wear.* "Is it dangerous?"

"I'm in a small town outside of Bogotá. So it could be a lot worse, but honestly, I'm happy with it, since my daughter is all that matters."

Logan hoped that soon he'd feel the same way, although how he was going to square the circle that was his professional life with a baby eluded him at the moment.

"I just found out before this vacation that my wife is pregnant," Logan replied.

Alejandro looked genuinely surprised but then smiled and clapped a hand on Logan's shoulder. "Congratulations! That's excellent news, my friend. Trust me when I tell you, your life *will* change, and absolutely for the better. When you have a child, it's like you step through a door to a different reality, and then you realize something."

"What's that?" Logan asked, genuinely interested.

"That there are only two kinds of people in this world—those with kids, and everyone else," Alejandro replied sincerely. "And those without, they'll never, ever understand what it's like to be a parent, no matter what they say or do. It's just a fact. It's not their fault. It just is." Alejandro smiled at Logan. "You'll see."

Logan nodded and turned back to the soccer match. "I actually never wanted kids, but now that life has somewhat stabilized for me and my wife, I can't think of anything else in the world that could brighten our lives more."

Alejandro was quiet, and Logan sensed a subtle shift, as if his new friend were contemplating something significant. *Something touched a nerve, but don't be your typical self and press him,* Logan heard his wife say inside his head.

Alejandro's phone vibrated, and he lifted it from the marble-patterned bar, spoke something in Spanish, and ended the call moments later. "Well, Logan, my daughter is up, and she's eager to hit the water park," Alejandro said, pointing across the enormous Paradise Lagoon to the west side of the resort where several slides emerged from a large facsimile of ancient ruins.

"Sounds like you have your work cut out for you. It was a pleasure, and enjoy the rest of your vacation," Logan said, and raised the Diet Coke from the bar.

Alejandro clinked his drink to Logan's, downed the rest, and said, "Congratulations once again on joining the club. No matter what, you won't regret it. Having said that, enjoy your time here. Once your baby comes, you won't have it anymore." He smiled mischievously. "It's part of the package. Take care, and God bless."

"You too," Logan said, and watched his new friend disappear down the circular set of stairs in the middle of the restaurant that led to the underwater viewing area and a tunnel that wound along the bottom and through the lagoon in a glass-enclosed viewing tube.

Logan captured the server's attention, and moments later he placed an order in anticipation of Cole Matthews's arrival.

How am I going to bring a child into this world? Logan thought.

Everything he'd told Alejandro was true, but he was still terrified. *I just hope I can be the kind of father I know I should be.*

"You daydreaming again, killer?" Cole Matthews suddenly said from beside him.

Logan smirked at his friend and fellow member of Task Force Ares. Tanned, with chiseled features and black hair swept back but trimmed neatly on the sides, Cole turned nearly as many female heads as Logan. *Nearly*, Logan thought, acutely aware of his own looks, as well as his ego.

"Definitely. Just not of you, D-boy," Logan shot back, referring to Cole's past with the world-renowned Unit, more commonly referred to as Delta Force in movies and on television.

"Ha," Cole said, and sat down on the barstool Alejandro had vacated moments earlier. "Did you order?"

"As a matter of fact, I did," Logan replied.

"I knew I could count on you for something," Cole said drily, aware of the irony, as Logan West had saved his life in Sudan six months previously in a hellhole black-site prison. *Actually, that was a team effort.*

"By the way, tough guy, you're five minutes late," Logan said. "Even by my standards."

"Cute, but now that I'm here, let's get down to business," Cole said seriously and quietly. "We have a problem."

Logan turned, looked at his friend, saw concern in his brown eyes, and said, "Don't we always."

CHAPTER 3

Coral Towers, 3rd Floor
Saturday, 2000 Local Time

Santiago Rojas was in a position with which he was not familiar—indecision. After his first encounter with Logan West, he'd spent the day contemplating his next move.

At first, he'd been hesitant to execute the "coincidental encounter" with West, even under the cover of an alias, as he knew that West would likely detect even the slightest hint of subterfuge. It was why he'd kept the conversation on a topic for which he could not feign insincerity, even if he tried—his daughter. And when the conversation had ended, he was certain he'd made the right choice, especially after West had disclosed the fact that his wife was pregnant. *There was no way he was lying about that. I could tell it in his voice, as a father.*

The sun was in the final moments of setting to the west directly out the window of his lagoon-side room, which provided a view of the entire north side of the resort, as well as the Caribbean waters to his right.

You don't have much more time. The director of SEBIN had

informed him earlier in the day that the meeting Logan West was here for was now scheduled to occur tomorrow morning at Mosaic, a casual fine-dining restaurant in the Cove Beach section of the resort on the other side of the Royal Towers. And that was the crux of the issue—to let Logan West and his partner take the meeting, or intervene beforehand. The risks were high with either option. If he chose to act, it would have to be tonight.

He averted his gaze from the sunset and walked over to the powerful HP ZBook 17 G3 laptop that sat on a small, round glass table near the patio sliding door. He sat in the oversized cream-colored chair—one without arms, which he thought was odd—and swiped his finger across the sensor built into the screen. A password field appeared, he typed in the code, and a moment later, he stared at a live-camera video feed of a grand suite on the fifth floor of the east wing of the towers. The room was still empty. *Where had they gone?*

Two days ago, he'd handsomely paid a young local named Freeman who worked the concierge desk after the SEBIN had provided a quick background on the man, his family, and the fact that he was barely making ends meet on the hotel's salary. Freeman had agreed to the proposition, and he'd provided an additional electronic room card to Santiago. More importantly, Freeman had notified him when housekeeping had confirmed that West's suite was vacant. Santiago had then taken that opportunity to enter the room and place a very powerful wireless, battery-powered miniature camera that used the resort's wireless internet to send an encrypted feed to his ZBook. He'd placed the camera in the far corner of the room at the end of a curtain rod on the back side so that unless one stood directly in front of it, it was nearly invisible.

Santiago rewound the live feed until he found what he was looking for—West and his partner leaving the room fifteen minutes ago. *Where are you and your friend?*

A sudden knocking on his door broke his train of thought. *This isn't good.*

He quietly approached the door, a large kitchen knife held blade down and away in his right hand. He'd been unable to smuggle his FN HP 9mm sidearm into the country, but then again, he hadn't thought he'd need it.

Santiago looked through the peephole, studied the scene outside his room, and slowly exhaled. His decision had been made for him.

"Hold on a second," he said through the door, and pushed down on the levered handle.

As soon as the door cracked open, Logan West hit it with his right shoulder, the suppressed Glock 19 9mm pistol he held in both hands aimed at the floor. The door swung swiftly inward, and Logan felt it strike a soft target, slowing the heavy door's momentum.

He pushed through the widening gap, and Cole Matthews followed him into the room, his own suppressed Glock 19 raised and pointed into the interior.

Once he'd cleared the door, Logan stopped and looked down at the sitting figure of the man who'd joined him at the Lagoon Bar & Grill briefly before lunch. The handsome South American sat still, his forearms resting on his elbows, even as Logan pointed the Glock 19 at his face. An expression of slight amusement met Logan's gaze, which was hostile and aggressive.

Cole pushed past Logan, his Glock 19 searching for targets.

"The only question I have is this—how did you two get weapons onto the island? Your embassy?" Santiago asked curiously.

What the hell? This guy's got a gun pointed at his head, and all he asks about is my Glock? "That's not your concern," Logan replied calmly. "What should concern you is that we're here, we've got guns, which you apparently don't, and unless you tell me who you *really* are, we're likely going to use them."

Santiago stared at Logan and ignored the threat.

"It's all clear," Cole said, reappearing from the bathroom and moving to close the blinds. "We're alone," he said as he shut the taupe-colored drapes. "Get him up and over to the couch."

"You heard the man," Logan said. "Up and at 'em."

He transferred the Glock to his left hand and shut the door with his right, using his right leg to close it completely without turning away from Santiago.

"You know you can put those away," Santiago said as he rose. "I'm not armed. Unlike you Americans, *Venezuela*—not Colombia; that's where I'm really from—doesn't have an embassy I can use to smuggle weapons."

"Well, that answers the first question," Logan said, the Glock 19 following Santiago. "But if you think we're putting these away, you're out of your mind."

"Do as you want, but why don't you ask some more questions so we can get right to the point and bypass all of this nonsense?" Santiago said, facing Logan and Cole from the middle of the maroon couch.

Nonsense? This guy is way too calm for this situation, Logan thought.

"Something feels off here," Cole said. "Not we're-all-about-to-die kind of off, but off nonetheless."

"I know," Logan replied curtly.

"Well, if you want to play twenty questions, then let's get started," Logan said to their captive. "And we're going to do this rapid-fire. So try to keep up."

"Fire away," Santiago said, "although not literally, please."

Cole couldn't help himself, and he laughed. "Great. Another jokester. John would probably love this guy and try to recruit him."

Logan ignored his friend. "First question—are you a member of the Organization?"

Without hesitation, Santiago replied, "I have no idea what that is, but I'm pretty sure the people who sent me here do."

Goddamnit. He's telling the truth, Logan's gut told him.

Ignoring the response, Logan said, "Next question—what's your real name and what do you *really* do?"

"Santiago Rojas, and I'm a chief inspector in Venezuela with the SEBIN."

No signs of deception. Just straight answers, which raised the hair on Logan's arms. *This is way too easy. Try this curveball, asshole.*

"Shouldn't you be killing protestors or oppressing your citizens?" Logan replied with aggressive condescension, referring to the current chaos, protests, political violence, and economic collapse underway in Venezuela.

"That's not who I am, although I'm not going to deny what's been going on in my country," Santiago said.

He's not even trying to deceive us. "Did your wife really die of cancer two years ago?" Logan asked quickly.

A flash of pain swept across Santiago's face and disappeared just as quickly. "Yes, and here's some more harsh reality for you: my daughter, the one I told you about, she's dying of cancer as well."

Logan was silent.

"This is the easiest interrogation we've ever had," Cole said quietly. "No drowning, no removing fingers. I'm not sure how I feel about this." Cole spoke directly to Santiago. "You sure you don't want to try and resist? Do something? We're just not used to the easy way."

Santiago ignored the sarcasm. "Ask your questions. We're running out of time."

"Time for what?" Logan asked.

"Why you're here," Santiago said.

"Which is?" Cole asked, curious as to what the answer might be.

"To try and find the vice president of the United States," Santiago said matter-of-factly.

Good God. He knows everything. Logan paused. "More importantly, why are you here?" Logan asked, suddenly quiet, suspecting the answer that had been unspoken.

"Now we're getting somewhere, gentlemen," Santiago said, and smiled genuinely. "I'm here for *you.*"

CHAPTER 4

"Me?" Logan asked, although he'd already begun to suspect that was the case, and lowered the Glock 19 involuntarily several inches. "Why?"

"Because we have mutual interests," Santiago responded.

"I find that hard to believe," Cole injected. "Like my friend here just said, you work for a tyrannical dictatorship that's currently oppressing its people, which is pretty much the *opposite* of everything we hold dear in our country."

Irritation flashed across Santiago's face. "Don't lecture me about democracy. Your politicians, while self-righteous and sanctimonious, are just as corrupt. They just hide it better. Otherwise, you wouldn't *even be here looking for your lost vice president.*"

No one spoke. The words lingered in the air like ominous accusations.

"Damn, Logan. You kind of can't argue with that," Cole said.

Logan stared at Santiago, green eyes assessing the man before him. *Sonofabitch is telling the truth. Anyone with a grade-school understanding of politics knew how hypocritical and corrupt politicians in America had become.* "No. You can't. But I still can't wait to hear what kind of 'mutual interests' two agents of the United States and an agent of a South American socialist dictatorship have in common."

Santiago opened his mouth to respond, but the conversation was interrupted.

Knock. Knock.

Logan and Cole exchanged glances.

"He's alone. I confirmed it with Jake earlier," Cole said quietly, referring to Jake Benson, the director of the FBI and one of the senior members of Task Force Ares.

"Great. More variables," Logan said softly. Events were happening faster than they'd anticipated. *And we still don't know where the meeting is supposed to be tomorrow,* he thought to himself. *But I bet your new friend does.*

"You didn't order room service, did you?" Logan said, hoping beyond all hope that was the case, even though it would be one of the worst decisions a covert operative in a foreign country could make—invite company to your ad hoc base of operations.

"Of course not," Santiago said, slightly offended.

Logan nodded at Cole and holstered the Glock 19 in an inside-the-waistband Kydex holster inside his khaki lightweight trousers, the suppressor extending farther down than was comfortable. The dark-blue polo hung over the pistol grip, concealing the weapon. Cole followed suit, as Santiago sat quietly, watching the two men.

Knock-knock-knock.

The sharp thuds increased in tempo, heightening the tension in the room.

"I didn't think so," Logan said. "Here's how this is going to play out." The moment he said it, part of his brain rebelled, reminding him of the countless times his plans had gone off the rails the second the tactical train had left the station. *Good luck with that.*

———

Santiago looked through the peephole and blinked, as if in disbelief at what he saw. *It can't be.* For the first time during his time on the island, a brief moment of panic burrowed itself into his gut, and then it faded. *So be it.* He exhaled, closed his eyes, and opened the door.

Two smiling Venezuelan faces that masked the cold personas beneath met his gaze through the gap in the door. "Hello, Santiago," a forty-something handsome man with short brown hair cut in a flattop said. While his lips were spread in a smile, his dark eyes were hostile, malevolent intent dancing in them.

"What brings you this way, Hugo?" Santiago said to the SEBIN chief inspector in charge of the immediate action unit responsible for counterguerrilla operations inside Venezuela. Notorious for a streak of cruelty fully expressed in bodies and blood, his presence sent a wave of dread through Santiago. "This is *way* outside your area of responsibility. If you're here, you obviously know what I'm doing here and who sent me."

Hugo pushed his way into the room, and the door swung back against the wall to the right, forcing Santiago backward into the room, almost adjacent to the bed. He was followed by a young man no older than twenty-five. He was at least six feet tall with dyed blond hair that reminded Santiago of one of those pop artists he'd seen his daughter watch on Hispanic TV. While Hugo at least feigned a bad attempt at pleasantries, his protégé had not learned the subtle art of deception. He glared down at Santiago—two full inches shorter—with contempt as he entered the room and positioned himself next to the bathroom door, which was slightly ajar.

Hugo stopped several feet inside the room and paused as if contemplating whether or not to fully enter the room. "I do, but like you, someone very powerful sent *me* to stop *you*." It was stated as a matter of resolved fact, devoid of doubt.

"That's not going to happen, Hugo," Santiago said.

The painful grimace vanished instantly from Hugo's face. "Do you think you actually have a choice? Why do you think my young friend, Eriko, is here?"

At the sound of his name, the Venezuelan wannabe pop star withdrew a matte-black knife with his right hand from the back of his brown trousers. As Santiago examined the blade with his eyes, Eriko smiled and ran his finger across the serrated back of the straight four-and-a-half-inch blade.

"Is that supposed to be for me?" Santiago asked, a tone of amusement in his voice.

Expecting fear or acquiescence and surprised by the absence of both, Eriko glanced at Hugo for reassurance and started to take a step forward.

"You really should have thought this out a little better, young Eriko," Santiago said.

The words forced the young man to pause, momentarily ceasing his forward momentum.

From within the darkened bathroom, an arm shot through the opening, followed by the imposing figure of Logan West. As his left hand latched on to the back of Eriko's wrist, Hugo's eyes widened, a reaction that was cut short as the closet door less than a foot away to his left slid open like two panels of an accordion, and Cole Matthews launched himself at the SEBIN chief inspector.

The plan was to take them alive, and Logan raised Eriko's arm upward, rotated toward the younger man, and delivered a solid punch to his rib cage. He felt the man gasp in surprise, and he hit him again. Eriko buckled slightly, but he held on to the knife, refusing to release the only advantage he had.

Rather than waste another upper body blow, Logan swept his left foot forward behind Eriko as he grabbed his right shoulder and pulled him backward. His properly executed move knocked the man off balance as his right foot was swept out from underneath him. Eriko, with only one leg to support him and Logan pulling him backward and down, crashed into the nightstand, his upper back slamming into the upper edge. The nightstand was propelled into the wall, and the impact sent the lone night lamp into a violent wobble.

Logan grabbed Eriko's wrist with both hands and kicked him in the ribs, hoping the pain would uncurl the death grip on the knife. *Come on already, kid. Let the fucking knife go.* He bent his wrist backward and adjusted his feet, so that he was leaning toward Eriko, hoping to break his wrist and secure the knife.

Had Eriko just released the blade and sat still, he likely would have avoided calamity. Unfortunately, Hugo had selected Eriko for his athleticism and willingness to unleash it on anyone that his superiors deemed enemies of the state. He was a violent young man not known for his tactical prowess or excellent judgment. A tough decision for Eriko was whether to wear a brown belt with black shoes, not how to execute a complicated hostage rescue mission. In this case, his decision-making doomed him.

As the lamp toppled over and off the table, Eriko pulled his right leg in, kicked outward at Logan's shin, and released the knife. He pulled his arm backward in a last-ditch effort to grab the falling lamp and wield it as a weapon.

In his mind, he saw himself smashing the lamp into the side of his attacker's head, picking up the knife, and killing the second man in the room, proving himself to be the hero his twisted logic told him he was.

Unfortunately, the kick knocked Logan off-balance, and he fell forward, holding the knife, which was aimed at Eriko's throat. *Oh no,* Logan thought, and tried to redirect the point of the blade. All that did was guide the point of the knife directly into the right side of Eriko's neck, slicing his carotid cleanly and cleaving a bloody gash along his neck.

Blood spurted into the air in a warm gush and across Logan's face, burning his eyes and filling his nostrils with the smell of copper. He dropped to his knees, and his left hand kept him upright as the right hand still held the knife that he'd pulled out of the dying man's neck. Eager to see, he rolled to his right, sat on his haunches, and rubbed the blood out of his eyes.

The image before him sent a flash of the Sudanese prison through the window of his mind, the knife penetrating the wounded monster's neck, and the final twist for all to see that ended his evil existence. *Great fucking memories, for sure,* he thought, temporarily sickened.

Blood pumped out of the side of Eriko's neck as his eyes fixed on Logan's, his body spasmodically jerking in its final moments. His eyes blazed intently in defiance, as if cursing Logan. His pupils suddenly dilated, and his eyes went vacant, leaving the glassy-eyed expression that Logan knew too well. *Nothingness.*

He felt a slight twinge of guilt, but then his warrior's mind reminded him, *He pulled a knife. He wasn't going to use it to taunt Santiago. He was going to kill him. He made a bad choice, like all the others before him.* His hardened resolve back in control, he started to stand when a single gunshot roared across the room.

When Logan had ambushed the young killer with the knife, Cole had blindsided Hugo. He'd crushed him into the wall and slammed his own right shoulder into the man's left side, but to his surprise, Hugo had absorbed the blow, turned toward Cole, and delivered an uppercut that glanced off Cole's jaw. Momentarily stunned, Cole had turned his head away and reached out. He'd locked his hands behind Hugo's neck and delivered a powerful knee to the Venezuelan's midsection.

His knee had struck something solid—*metal*—and he'd looked down to see Hugo attempt to withdraw a black compact pistol from inside his waistband. Cole's tactical mind had changed his thought process from subdue to survive, and reflexively, he'd released his left hand from the back of Hugo's head, reached down, and grabbed the barrel of the semiautomatic. He'd yanked the pistol up and away from his face. For a reason unknown to Cole, Hugo had already placed his finger inside the trigger guard, and the movement of the weapon caused his finger to pull backward on the trigger.

Bam!

Cole's ears rang from the proximity of the shot, but it could've been worse. He glanced up into the face of Hugo, which was now missing the lower back right half of his jaw as the round had shattered it on its path into his brain, killing him. Blood and bone speckled Cole's tan polo. *Damn. Should've worn a darker color.*

He yanked the pistol out of the dead man's hands, let the body slump to the floor, and turned to see how Logan had fared against the other man.

A thick, viscous pool of blood lay on top of the nightstand, and blood still flowed—although at a slower rate—from the man's destroyed neck. The lower half of Logan's face was red as if covered with Native American war paint.

"Jesus, man. Did you have to do that?" Cole said, out of concern not for the loss of the young man's life but for the mess it had created in the room. "No way housecleaning is going to go for this one."

"Whatever you say, Mr. Glass House," Logan said, and nodded behind Cole.

Cole turned and saw the mess of blood and tiny chunks of flesh that had covered part of the wall. "Damn. Guy had his finger on the trigger. Who does that?"

"Someone looking to use it immediately," Santiago said, speaking for the first time since the violent encounter had begun. *Who are these two men?* They seemed too disconcertingly comfortable with the level of violence they'd just perpetrated on two men they didn't know. And then he realized the glaring truth of his mission:

there's a reason you were sent to find Logan West. He instinctively knew that the scene that had just played out inside his room might be only the tip of the proverbial iceberg when it came to the two Americans.

"Who were they?" Logan asked, placed the knife on the bed, and reached for his cell phone from his left rear pants pocket. "I need to know, and I need to know now, but I also need to call our embassy before we all end up in whatever passes for jail down here. I don't do well behind bars."

"That's a fact," Cole said, remembering how they'd been incapacitated and held—temporarily—in a Sudanese prison that didn't officially exist.

"SEBIN, like me," Santiago replied, "but much more ruthless and cruel."

"You might have some explaining to do back home, in that case," Logan said as the other end of the line started ringing.

"More concerning is how they knew I was here," Santiago said. "I literally only spoke to two—"

Bang!

The hotel door flung inward as parts of the lock shattered. Cole instinctively dove backward into the room, lifting his newly acquired FNS-9 compact 9mm pistol toward the new threat.

A third man stood at the entrance, and at the sight of Hugo's corpse, lifted his own FNS-9 and opened fire as Cole Matthews did the same midair.

Crack-cr-cr-crack-crack!

The series of shots was deafening. Two rounds shattered the sliding glass door, but Cole's return fire strayed high. He slammed on to his back with a thud, ensuring his finger was off the trigger to prevent a negligent discharge.

Just as quickly, the man disappeared down the hallway to the left, even as Logan darted for the door in pursuit.

Logan reached the door as Cole scrambled to his feet and followed, shouting at Santiago, "Stay here. We'll be back." There was no time to argue.

Logan looked left and then glanced right, and saw a second figure fleeing down the opposite hallway. He turned to Cole and said, "Another guy just went this way. You get him. I've got the shooter." He vanished out the doorway to the left.

Here we go again, Cole thought, as he dashed out of the entrance and turned right.

CHAPTER 5

Logan sprinted down the hall, but his quarry had a head start, hitting the T-intersection at the north end of the Coral Towers. In a flash, the man in the dark-green polo and tan chinos fled left around the corner. Logan ran harder, twenty yards from the end of the hall. He heard a door slam as the fleeing man hit the opener on the stairwell door. *If he makes it to the ground floor, he's gone,* Logan thought, remembering the endless paths and buildings the man could use to easily disappear.

Logan reached the corner, slowed down only as much as necessary to avoid barreling into the hotel room across the intersection, and sped up, the stairwell door closing twenty feet away.

Within seconds, he covered the distance, blew through the door, and bounded down the steps two at a time. He heard another door slam open at the bottom. *Move faster, or he's gone.*

His body responded, and a moment later, he arrived at the bottom floor and crashed through the door into the warm, humid, relaxing breeze of the Bahamian night. The man was nowhere to be seen. He forced himself to be still, inhaled to control his gasping lungs, and held his breath.

The faint *thwap thwap thwap* of soft-sole shoes fleeing down a path to his right into the illuminated network of walkways reached his ears. *That's all I need,* he thought, and started running once again.

It. Never. Fucking. Ends, he thought in between controlled breaths, closing in on his prey.

For Cole Matthews, having the gun only added a layer of chaos and complexity to the foot pursuit. His target had run to the southern end of the hotel, turned left, and disappeared into the stairwell.

A hotel room door fifteen feet ahead of him opened up, and an older, distinguished-looking couple dressed for an evening of dining and entertainment stepped into the hallway. The woman, attractive with graying hair and a sparkling gray-sequined dress, let out a quick gasp at the running figure of Cole Matthews holding a gun and covered in blood.

"Sorry, folks, but I'm actually the good guy," was all he thought to say as he dashed past them, hit the intersection, and followed the only way out. *I'm sure that calmed them down and allayed all their concerns, idiot,* his mind snapped.

Like Logan, Cole hit the door, pursued the man down the stairs, and found himself outside on the east side of the tower, facing another network of walkways that led to numerous pools, the conference center, the Beach Towers, and golf course. *Where the hell does this guy think he's going?*

A flash of movement to his left disappearing around a curve into the overhanging palm trees caught his attention. He followed, lampposts faintly illuminating the way ahead. Fortunately, foot traffic was relatively light on the east side of the hotel, as most of the vacationers were getting ready for a night at the restaurants, shops, and casino. The absence of people also cut down on the ambient noise, allowing him to follow the footsteps trying to evade him. *Good luck with that.*

Less than a minute later, he emerged into an opening, and he realized he was at one of the many kids' pools. A giant, round, vertical water fountain resembling a mushroom on a ten-foot stalk that poured water onto enthralled children below during the day stood like a sentry in the middle of the abandoned pool. A statue of the upper body of Neptune, trident in hand, reaching outstretched for the heavens, rested on top of the fountain. *Cool trident,* Cole thought, and recalled the voice of Brick from Ron Burgundy, *"I killed a guy with a trident."* *Well, I hope it doesn't come to that here,* Cole thought, and ran through the deserted pool and down another walkway.

He realized he was headed toward the beach and the villas when he heard a shout from twenty yards in front of him, and he redoubled his efforts, moving quickly through the gloom of dusk.

Logan ran through the maze of walkways, trees, and lampposts and emerged at another decision point. He heard the footfalls of the shooter, closer and from his left, but a much louder sound reverberated throughout the area—*waterfalls*—and he realized where he was, the rope bridge at Predator Lagoon.

Spanning the north side of the lagoon was a wooden 110-foot rope bridge just above the water adjacent to the man-made waterfalls that served as a barrier between the resort and the sandy beach beyond. It was a woven latticework of rope and wood that formed a tube across the lagoon, its sides rising more than seven feet above the surface to prevent the wayward tourist from plunging over the side into the predator-filled water.

Logan saw the east entrance to the bridge and the fleeing figure already ten feet across it. He kept running and hit the bridge, gaining ground. The bridge swayed in the breeze from the pounding of the two men dashing across its suspended boards. The sensation was slightly unsettling, but the cargo netting sent Logan back momentarily to the infamous obstacle and combat endurance courses at Officer Candidate School. *At least I don't have to go through the fucking Quigley again,* he thought, remembering the claustrophobia he'd first experienced when his foot had become stuck going into the submerged, narrow concrete tube. He'd been upside down on his back, muddy, cold water filling his lungs at the first sensation of panic in the dark before his boot had dislodged itself. *The good old days, when you were young and stupid . . . and hadn't killed dozens of men, justifiably or not.*

"What the hell, man?" Logan heard an angry American male shout ahead of him—*can always pick out the sound of American outrage overseas*—and he watched as the fleeing man barreled into a young couple out on an evening stroll. *Must be nice,* he thought, reminded briefly of his beautiful pregnant wife, Sarah, back in Virginia.

The young woman, a short brunette, was knocked to the planks, and her husband fell against the side of the cargo net. But it was Logan's quarry, reckless in his haste to escape, who took the brunt of it, bounced off the Americans, spun, and fell to the boards face-first.

Oh no, Logan thought as he realized what was about to occur and covered the remaining fifteen feet as quickly as possible.

The blond American regained his footing and moved aggressively, oblivious to the real threat that lay before him.

You fool, Logan thought, and prepared to act as events escalated.

His target suddenly spun on his back, the black pistol he'd fired into Santiago's hotel room aimed upward at the American, a look of savage hatred on his face. The American faltered, the realization of the imminent danger stopping him in his tracks like an invisible wall. The Venezuelan, a man in his midthirties with a spiderweb scar on his right cheek and jet-black hair, smiled at the man's fear and moved his finger from the trigger guard to the trigger. But then he saw the moving shape of fury that was Logan West, and he hesitated—just long enough—before deciding to shift the weapon to his pursuer.

Logan launched himself at the man's arm, dove on top of him, and pushed the pistol with both hands up and away from the young couple. He braced himself for the shot, a loud *crack* that temporarily stunned both men by the proximity of the gun to their heads.

The report echoed off the rocks, a warning to all who heard it that something out of the norm was unfolding on the island resort.

His ears ringing and muffled from the noise, Logan pressed his weight on top of the Venezuelan and struck him in the jaw with his right elbow, both hands securely holding the pistol. He spun left so that his back was on top of the man's chest, and pulled upward with both hands. The gun broke free of its owner's grasp, and Logan rolled to his right, intent on subduing the suspect at gunpoint.

The Venezuelan had his own plan, and he lashed out with a roundhouse kick that struck Logan's wrists perfectly, and the gun clattered to the wooden walkway. It slid through a gap in the cargo net and fell into the lagoon below with a barely audible splash. *Great. Now I have to do this the hard way,* Logan thought, and stepped toward the man, who rolled backward and on to his feet before Logan could grab him.

"Okay, asshole. You asked for it," Logan said, and attacked, not caring if the man understood English or not.

Cole found himself under a lamppost on a small, circular island near several cabanas that sat along the southwest side of the large, irregular-shaped pool on the west side of the Beach Towers, an affordable alternative to the high-end Royal Towers. The pool had a sandy beach on its north end that merged with the actual beach that descended into the clear blue waters of the Caribbean.

Dozens of vacationers lounged around in recliners, drinks on tables next to them. *The party never stops here. Where the hell did you go?*

He turned his head slowly, eyes absorbing every feature of the nighttime scene, trying to detect anything that seemed out of place. *He has to be hiding here. There's no way he got away that fast.*

From a few hundred yards away on the other side of the new additional tower adjacent to the beach, he heard the shot that Logan had just experienced at close range. He felt the pool admirers turn their heads as one, dismissing it. A gunshot at a resort like Atlantis was so out of place that even those who knew what one sounded like might mentally deny the reality. But Cole knew better. *Plus, I just killed a man.*

He decided to move closer to the Beach Towers, but he only made it two steps before he heard the rustle of movement from his right. He spun instinctively and brought his forearms up to protect himself, which was the only thing that saved his life.

He felt the blade slice past his right forearm, a faint pressure from the contact, and he thought he'd dodged the blade in time, even as he wrapped his left arm up and around the attacker's arm, securing it.

Thus, he was surprised when he heard the blood dripping to the stone patio below, and then the pain—and accompanying anger— hit him in the arm.

As a world-class expert in Krav Maga and someone who'd fought two evil, ruthless, armed attackers in a boxing ring in Sudan, killing both with a machete, Cole Matthews was outraged that he'd been cut by a blade. *Thanks, Logan. I'm blaming you,* he thought, even though he knew it wasn't his friend's fault.

Instead, he focused his anger on his attacker, intent on disarming him as quickly as possible. He raised his flat left hand up and placed it at the base of the attacker's wrist, and he slammed his right hand against the back of the man's fist. The sudden force bent the man's wrist, braced against Cole's left hand. The attacker's fingers uncurled, and the knife flew from his grasp, tumbling end-over-end until it skittered across the stone and over the edge, disappearing into the clear water of the pool.

Now, it's my turn, Cole thought, and smashed his left elbow up into the attacker's face, which he still hadn't seen. He was rewarded with a *crunch* as his elbow connected squarely with the man's nose. As he turned into the unarmed man, he felt himself smile briefly, satisfied at the initial damage he'd done as blood flowed down the man's face.

Cole faced the Venezuelan and was greeted by the image of an angry, experienced fighter who ignored the blood pouring out of his nose and mouth. Rather than put his hands to his face—the typical reaction when struck in the nose—the pale-skinned Venezuelan with thick brown hair cut to less than half an inch over his whole head counterattacked.

He swung his leg up in a short roundhouse kick that surprised Cole and struck him in the upper thigh. Cole ignored the pain and delivered a powerful front kick that landed right below the man's sternum, pushing *through* his target several inches. The man bent slightly at the waist, and Cole planted his front foot on the ground and transitioned into a spinning side-kick. The blow landed on the Venezuelan's sternum, and he was driven backward against a lounge chair. He flailed like a high-wire artist on the verge of plummeting to his death and fell backward over the chair.

Cole pressed the attack as the pain in his right forearm fueled him forward. He kicked the lounge chair backward, and the edge struck the Venezuelan in his left side. He staggered to his feet, and Cole Matthews, usually a pragmatic and deadly fighter, could not resist the sudden opportunity to act with a flair for the dramatic.

He leapt *onto* the lounge chair, careful to keep his left foot turned sideways to avoid sliding between the rubber slats, and jumped into the air, hurtling at his enemy. He cocked his right fist back halfway, and as he reached the dazed man, he struck him on the left side of his face.

The man fell backward and tumbled into the water over the large misshapen coral rocks that served as the edge of the pool.

The water was shallow, and the wounded combatant tried to raise himself laboriously to his hands and knees.

Cole jumped into the water, aware they were in a small section of the pool that wrapped around the island of cabanas and lounge chairs. Without hesitation, he dropped a knee on to the man's back and submerged him completely. Rather than give him a moment to come up for air, Cole slithered on top of him, put him in a choke-hold, and kept him just under the surface.

Cole felt the panic rise up in his captive, but he felt no sympathy. *Shouldn't have tried to come at us. This is all on you.*

He pushed the man's arm, which was trying to reach in desperation for Cole's face, away, and moments later, the man stopped fighting, fading into unconsciousness. Cole pulled the man up, at which point the Venezuelan gagged a mouthful of pool water and coughed uncontrollably.

Cole stood and dragged him through the water to the entrance that sloped into the pool from the island. "You speak English?" Cole asked.

The man nodded, too exhausted to answer.

"Good," Cole replied, stopped dragging him by the collar, and leaned down into his face. "Here's the deal, if you make any kind of sudden move, I'm going to break your neck, and there won't be a goddamned thing you can do to stop me. Do you understand?"

"Understand," was all the Venezuelan had the energy to mutter.

"Good," Cole said, when his foot brushed up against something in the pool. *My lucky day,* he thought, and reached down into the water. His arm emerged holding the dark blade with which he'd been cut.

He laughed, a short abrupt sound. "Finders, keepers," he said, holding the knife in his left hand. "Change in plans. You make a move, and I'll stab you in the throat with your own knife. Now get up and move, slowly. I'm tired of this pool. I didn't wear my bathing suit."

Logan struck the spiderweb-scarred man with a short jab, which glanced off his jaw as the Venezuelan turned his head left to diminish the impact. But rather than let his opponent counter, Logan instantly followed up the jab with a short right hook that landed on the left side of his face. His head was whipped around to the right, the blow dazing him momentarily.

Logan felt the steady *thump-thump-thump* as the couple he had saved fled back up the bridge, eager to escape the two men locked in combat.

Not much longer before security shows up. Logan was certain the confrontation had been captured on the camera system that constantly monitored the resort. He'd seen unarmed guards patrol at seemingly random locations and times, and he figured that they were ordered to maintain a low profile so as not to upset the guests. But he also knew that there had to be security protocols for an active shooter or terrorist attack, given the increased frequency with which the global jihad had conducted attacks in the past few years. Logan just hoped that he had enough time to end the confrontation before security arrived: he had one call to make, *or else we're all screwed.*

Logan assaulted the man with a body blow to his left side that dropped him to one knee, within perfect striking distance. He stepped in to deliver a knee to the scarred man but struck thin air. *Motherfucker duped me.*

The fighter had somehow adjusted his position, elongating his body to the right and kicking his left leg forward in a sweeping motion. He caught Logan off-guard, and his shin struck Logan's left ankle, which sent him crashing into the cargo net.

The Venezuelan realized he was outmatched in hand-to-hand combat, seized the moment, regained his footing, and dashed up the rope bridge in the opposite direction the couple had used.

Oh no you don't, Logan thought, and pushed forward on the cargo net, propelling himself backward and spinning at the same time. A moment later, he chased after the Venezuelan.

While the Venezuelan had a head start, Logan West was fast, world-class runner fast, and he'd proven it in combat time and time again. The fleeing man never had a chance.

As his combatant reached the edge of the rope bridge, momentarily convinced he was safe, Logan slammed into the running figure and shoved him violently in the upper back. The man lost his footing and tumbled out of control to the ground, rolling end-over-end off the wooden bridge and onto the cement walkway.

But rather than stay down, the black-haired man tried to stand back up, refusing to succumb to the damage he'd sustained during his fall. He managed to push himself onto his knees, wobbling in the darkening night, staring at Logan with resistance in his eyes.

No way. This ends now. "I'll give you an A for effort, but this is over," Logan snarled, frustrated at the man's determination and refusal to surrender. *He's a fighter. I'll give him that.*

Logan stepped in and launched a roundhouse kick that struck the man on the left side of his head. The kick temporarily dazed the Venezuelan, which was unfortunate for him, as he toppled sideways off the walkway.

Oh no, Logan thought, realizing his tactical mistake a moment too late.

As the man fell off the side of the walkway, Logan shot out his hand, trying to prevent the inevitable. His fingers extended, but he snatched nothing out of the air but the breeze of the Bahamas.

The spiderweb-scarred man tumbled down a short embankment of coral rocks and splashed into the dark water of the lagoon below.

Logan deftly climbed down the rocks to the water's edge, eager to help the man he'd unintentionally placed in grave danger, recognizing the irony even as he did so.

Now fully awake and alert from the impact with the water, rather than take the assistance of the man who had bested him in hand-to-hand combat moments ago, the Venezuelan made the worst possible choice he could have: he started swimming away from the rope bridge and across the middle of the lagoon.

"Stop right now or you're going to die!" Logan shouted as loudly as he could in an attempt to be heard over the waterfall behind him and the ambient outdoor noise of the resort.

The man ignored him, pressed on, and increased his pace, as if encouraged by Logan's words.

Logan took a step backward up the rocky slope, watched, and waited for the inevitable. *I just hope Cole didn't kill his guy. Otherwise, we've hit a literal dead end.*

The swimming man made it halfway across the lagoon when Logan spotted the first fin from one of the great hammerhead sharks that roamed the fenced-off Predator Lagoon. Normally not aggressive to human beings, the great hammerhead preferred to feed on smaller prey, although they were especially fond of stingrays. The problem for the Venezuelan was that it was dusk—the prime hunting time for the great hammerhead. Add to the saltwater mix the blood in the lagoon from his various wounds and the fact that there were three sharks, and the Venezuelan had unwittingly hit the Great Hammerhead Main Course Lottery.

Two more fins emerged from two other locations in the dark pool, forming the tips of a shrinking invisible pyramid as they closed in on their splashing and kicking prey.

At the sight of the fin of the first twelve-foot shark less than ten feet away, the man realized too late why Logan had shouted at him to stop. He screamed involuntarily, changed course . . . and swam directly into the path of one of the other sharks.

Logan imagined the fear the man was experiencing moments before his death, and a shudder ran through him as he recalled a similar swim he'd successfully executed last year in Sudan in the Nile River. The other man in the water hadn't been so fortunate.

The Venezuelan, fully panicked, turned one last time, which proved to be the fatal move. The second great hammerhead surged forward, its jaws opening and expanding. The shark bit the man fully on the side of the neck and shoulder, its several rows of teeth sinking into the man's soft flesh as its broad head covered him like a slippery shroud.

There it is, Logan thought, hearing the shriek he knew would come. He understood that some men deserved this kind of death, but he wasn't sure about the man he'd fought. Still, it was a brutal and fatal business in which he and his friends were engaged, and his opponent had just learned that in the most Darwinian of ways. *Only the strong survive.*

Blood surged across the top of the water and formed a black slick that glistened sinisterly in the dusk. The other two sharks attacked and seized the struggling man's upper right leg and lower forearm.

Logan watched as the great hammerhead with the man's neck in his mouth adjusted his bite, creating a new set of punctures that hurried the man's death, sending him mercifully into unconsciousness as the other two sharks joined the feeding frenzy.

Logan heard two horrified tourists begin to scream from the side of the lagoon along one of the stone pathways. *That's my cue,* he thought, and started walking west toward the central part of the resort. He pulled out his iPhone, hit the contact list, found the one he needed, and pressed it. *Come on. Come on. Come on.*

"Was that you with the shot?" Cole answered on the other end. "I've got my guy. Where do you want me to take him? We might not make it to the room, depending on how quickly security reacts."

"My guy is gone," Logan said. "He resisted, tried to kill me, and ended up in the lagoon. Needless to say, he couldn't outswim the sharks."

"Christ," Cole replied. "But you're okay? No one else is hurt?"

"I'm good. Tell your new friend that if he resists, what happened to his partner will seem like a life coaching lesson compared to what I'm willing to do to him. Try for the room. I'm calling the embassy to get us out of this mess. We should have some private time with our friend before the cavalry arrives."

"Got it. See you up there. I'll call you if we get stopped," Cole said, and hung up.

Logan ended the call on his end, found the second number he needed, and pressed it. The iPhone automatically connected. Seconds later, a man answered in a crisp voice. "Peter Cornell speaking."

"It's Logan West," Logan said. "I need help."

The chief of station for the US Embassy in Nassau had privately hoped he wouldn't receive this phone call, as he enjoyed the quiet life of a Caribbean station chief. But CIA Director Toomey, his ultimate boss, had provided him with a short list of names and one clear order *on behalf of the president,* no less: *If he calls, do whatever he says and give him whatever he wants. Do you understand?*

As a career covert case officer—*although who really is, these days*—he understood perfectly. "Tell me where you are and what you need."

CHAPTER 6

East Royal Tower, Room 527

The Venezuelan that Cole had captured sat in a dining room chair, his arms zip-tied behind his back, immobilizing him. His name was Juan Esteban Sanchez, and although he looked exhausted, he didn't look panicked. *He's regained his confidence,* Logan thought. *That's not good for us.*

Logan, Santiago, and Cole stood over the man. Santiago had fled his room before security could arrive and had been waiting for them when they returned to their suite. Out of the three, it was Santiago who'd taken the lead in interrogating his fellow countryman.

He spoke quickly in Spanish and then switched to English, which Juan used to respond. "Good," Santiago said. "Now that my friends here can understand you clearly, who sent you?"

The man scowled. His boxer's nose, which had been broken again, had swelled from the elbow Cole had landed, and his voice was thick from the congestion. "Only Hugo knew, and he didn't tell us. He only gave us the target—*you*—and told you you had betrayed our organization and our country."

"Hold up," Logan said. "What do you mean by 'organization'?"

The mention of the multitentacled shadow conspiracy threatening global stability raised alarms in his head.

Juan looked at him with confusion before replying. "The SEBIN, of course. What else would I be talking about?"

False alarm, Logan thought. *Just as the Founder intended, a generic name that could mean anything to anyone. Christ.*

"You know who I am. You know my reputation. Did you really believe that?" Santiago asked.

"Are you serious?" Juan asked. "You and I both know what happens when orders aren't followed. I don't want to mysteriously disappear. Do you?"

Santiago knew Juan had a point. Not even members of the SEBIN were immune to the paranoia of certain leaders in their country. Fortunately, Santiago and the men under his command had remained immune to the political oppression and targeting, mainly because his unit had uncovered an external plot by the Russians to fan the flames of unrest burning across Venezuela. While Russia was one of Venezuela's strongest allies, elements inside the desperate socialist government had explored opening backdoor channels to the US. The Russians, in an attempt to halt such discussions, had hatched a plot to assassinate three high-ranking members of the National Assembly and blame the Americans. Fortunately, Santiago and his unit had prevented it—unknown to the targets of the plot—which had brought him the attention and thanks of the director of the SEBIN.

"He's telling the truth," Santiago said to Logan and Cole.

"He knows something," Logan said matter-of-factly. "They always do."

Juan stared at the American, and an unsettling sensation washed over him. *He'll kill me. I can see it in his eyes.*

"You have sixty seconds to tell me something worthwhile, or I swear to you, here and now, you aren't leaving this paradise alive.

Do you understand me?" Logan said, and then turned to Cole. "Start the timer now, and hand me his knife."

Cole Matthews punched a button on his black diver's watch. "Done," he said, and handed Logan the knife he'd confiscated from Juan. "Let's see how this plays out."

Juan had no intention of dying, not after knowing what these two Americans and Santiago had done to the other three men on his team. "I swear to God I have no idea who sent us. The order came from Hugo."

"Not good enough," Logan said.

"Fifty seconds, Juan. Trust me. He's not kidding," Cole said. "I sincerely hope you understand that, and I think you do, from what I can see in your eyes."

Fear insidiously inserted itself into the pit of Juan's stomach. *Think. Think. Think. There was one thing.* "Your meeting—the one you were supposed to have tomorrow—it's canceled. I know that much."

Logan shook his head. "No kidding. There's a shock. After what you guys pulled, I didn't really think that was going to happen anymore. Try again." He paused. "You shoot with your right hand?"

What the hell? "Are you serious?" Juan asked, and realized the man was deadly serious the second he'd asked the question.

"I once watched a friend of ours cut off a man's little finger. Trust me. You don't want to go through it," Cole said. "Like my friend said, try again."

Juan's breathing increased rapidly. *They'll do it. I have no doubt of it. Have to give them something.* "You have Hugo's phone? There has to be something on it."

"Already got it, thanks to your coworker here," Logan said. Before he'd left the bloodbath in his room, Santiago had removed the dead men's wallets and cell phones and brought them to Logan and Cole. "Keep trying."

The week had been a blur. Juan and two members of his team

had been pulled off an assignment as soon as Hugo had returned from . . . *of course. That's it.*

"Twenty-five seconds," Cole said coolly.

"Stop counting and put the knife down," Juan said calmly.

Logan raised his eyebrows. He had to give it to Juan, maintaining a calm demeanor in the face of what he knew was a very real threat. *It's always the older ones with more maturity and experience that are the better operators.* He knew it was a truism across all branches of the US military and law enforcement as well. Logan didn't respond and waited.

"Hugo took a trip out of the city. I swear to God I have no idea where. He said it was a personal matter, and that he needed to resolve something. We knew better than to ask where. He said it was a family matter, which is all that matters, anyhow," Juan finished quickly.

You're on the money, there, Juan, Logan thought, a brief vision of his wife invading his thoughts. Logan looked at Cole and nodded.

Cole hit the timer on his watch and said, "Looks like you got a reprieve, my friend. So what now?"

A sudden knocking at the door elicited a smile from Logan. "The cavalry."

"I hope they're not on horses. Not sure what the hotel policy is on that," Cole said drily.

Logan ignored him, handed Santiago the knife, walked to the door of the suite, and turned the handle.

Three men stood at the entrance—an American in his late forties with a full head of brown hair that touched the top of his ears and what Logan presumed were two native Bahamians. The American's blue eyes squinted at the amount of blood on Logan's shirt, and he looked into Logan's face. "Logan West?"

"Peter Cornell?" Logan replied, and nodded in confirmation at the mention of his own name.

"I am." He handed his embassy credentials to Logan, who inspected them briefly, folded the black leather ID, and handed it back.

Logan stepped aside, beckoned the men in, and said, "Welcome to the party."

Peter walked in, nodded to Cole and Santiago, and glanced curiously at the man zip-tied to the chair. "Gentlemen," he said courteously, and turned to Logan. "This is Commander Edward Henderson, the head of the Central Division of the Royal Bahamas Police Force."

The dark-skinned man in his early fifties stepped forward and extended his hand. "Mr. West," he said in a slight Caribbean accent. "This is Ramon Sandibal, inspector and head of my security intelligence. We're here to help."

Logan raised his eyebrows and glanced at Peter. "No offense, but you trust them?"

Peter responded instantly. "Without hesitation. You and I both know whom we serve. I wouldn't jeopardize that in any way. Let's just say that I've worked with both of these men closely, on local crime issues involving narcotics, as well as possible threats to the US. After seeing how they operate, I have *no doubt* about their loyalty to their people, as well as to us." He paused. "Does that satisfy you?"

Logan thought about it for a moment. He knew that most men in the world wanted to do the right thing. He loathed the phrase "assume noble intent," but it was a universal truth. Family, security, honor, and service were global concepts, even if the ways in which they were carried out varied from culture to culture. The last two and a half years had shaken his sense of trust, but he'd still seen one thing over and over—good men doing good things, often at the expense of their own lives. He heard Sarah's voice. *You have to trust someone.*

"That's good enough for me," Logan said to Peter, and shook Inspector Sandibal's hand. "Because we need all the help we can get. But most importantly, we need to get our friend out of here and to the embassy as quickly as possible. Once we do that, I'm going to need you to contact Langley for some digital forensics support. I need to know *exactly* where those have been in the last week," he said, and pointed to three cell phones resting on the hardwood top of the dining room table.

"No problem," Peter said. "I thought you were going to ask for something difficult."

"Like what?" Logan asked curiously.

"An attack helicopter. Maybe a tank?" Peter said, smiling briefly. "I know a little bit about you, at least what's left in the various agencies' databases."

Cole laughed. "He just met you, Logan, and he has you nailed." Turning to Peter, he said, "Your suspicions are more than justified, Mr. Cornell. Trust me, as I've been rolling with this crew for the last six months or so."

Logan ignored Cole. "Not on this trip," Logan answered Peter. "Transportation will be plenty. And on that note, can we please get the hell out of here? We've got work to do, and I have a feeling we're going to need more than just a shuttle to the embassy once we get started."

Logan looked at Santiago. "In fact, I think we're going to need *your* government's travel services. Looks like your vacation is over."

CHAPTER 7

Northwest of Caracas, Venezuela
Monday, 1000 Venezuelan Standard Time

Lieutenant General Victor Ascensión Cordones, Commanding General of the National Army of the Bolivarian Republic of Vene-zuela, contemplated the news his aide had just delivered, or more accurately, the *lack of news*. The team he'd dispatched to Paradise Island to eliminate the Americans had failed to report back for the last two days, which meant one of two things—they were dead or captured. It was irrelevant. They were expendable, considering the stakes involved in his latest—*and final, at least as an official officer of the army*—operation.

The fifty-three-year-old general, black hair neatly trimmed and parted on the left side, stared out the window of the field office on top of the two-story building that he used as his command post at the temporary military base he'd built over the past year and a half. Nestled in the mountains ten miles west of Caracas on a large pla-teau at twenty-three-hundred feet elevation, the base was isolated and remote, surrounded by a thick canopy of mountain forest. The only ingress or egress was the railway that ran from the heart of

Caracas, up the mountain, across the plateau through the middle of the base, and ended at the west end of the plateau, where it split into three dead ends, a railway pitchfork. Several transportation rail cars and two engines were parked on the split tracks, waiting like slumbering beasts for the next load of personnel or equipment to be carried into the capital.

Scattered across the plateau were several weapons ranges, obstacle courses, temporary housing quarters that could accommodate a full battalion, a dining facility, and multiple smaller buildings used for planning and communications. *My own personal kingdom, complete with my own personal chariots,* he thought, glancing at the two Russian helicopters parked near the edge of the plateau.

The minister of defense had asked him during the initial stages of construction why he needed such a base, and his answer had been simple—to train and plan for asymmetric warfare, including the execution of a realistic, full-scale defense of the capital, including Miraflores Palace, the office of the president of Venezuela. He smiled at the recollection. *It was true, just not in the context that he had asked. But first things first.*

Before he could do anything, he had to secure the vice president of the United States of America, which would guarantee his physical and financial safety once he'd begun his operation. The irony was that the vice president wasn't even aware of his own unlimited worth, even as he sat on a private yacht, which would be arriving in two days after a trip from America to Mexico. Once he was on Venezuelan soil, a short convoy ride would have the vice president within his grasp, and the knowledge the American held would be his to wield.

Had it not been for the Russian ambassador to Venezuela, Victor would not have known about it himself. Unfortunately, knowledge of the Organization had come at a tragic and steep cost for him—the death of his son during an opposition protest that had quickly turned violent.

Daniel Mateo Cordones had followed in his father's footsteps, but instead of joining the military, he'd joined the SEBIN. As a young detective in the Counterintelligence Direction, he'd been directly involved in monitoring and countering the waves of violent protests that had swept through the capital once the economy had crashed because the price of oil had plummeted across the globe. Unlike his father, Daniel had sympathized with the protestors, a view that his father had scorned and chalked up to youth and naïveté. He'd been convinced that his son would learn the hard way that the opposition could be shown no mercy, that they threatened the very existence of the republic. He just hadn't anticipated in what form that hard lesson would be—a violent death at the wrong end of a machete wielded by one of the protestors, a teenager who'd been shot thirty-six times after he'd mortally wounded Daniel.

Lieutenant General Cordones had been at the Ministry of Defense at the time, in a meeting with the Russian ambassador and the defense minister, negotiating a new arms deal for upgraded fixed-wing support and motorized artillery. The meeting had been interrupted by the defense minister's secretary, who'd notified him that there had been an incident with his son. He would later discover that Daniel's friends and fellow SEBIN detectives had brought him to his father upon his dying request. Even in his last moments, he was told afterward, he'd asked for his father. His friends had known he was dying, and they'd followed his last wishes.

By the time Victor had reached the seven-ton truck parked inside the gates, his son was gone. The moment he'd seen him, he'd known, and something inside him broke, a void that engulfed him as he stared at and then cradled his dead son. It was a blur of torment, grief, and time stretched across an eternity of pain. It was minutes or hours later—he still wasn't sure—when he heard the Russian ambassador talking to him quietly, alone, even as he held his son, telling him he understood his pain.

Victor had lashed out, shouting in an agony-choked voice. "How could you possibly know what this feels like?"

The answer had been simple, concrete, and had brought him back from the edge of madness that he'd internally hoped would consume him: "Because my son died in Chechnya serving the Motherland. And I still feel it, every moment of every day, what you're feeling right now."

The two fathers had talked, left alone by Daniel's unit and the soldiers at the Ministry of Defense. A bond that only they understood had been formed on that day of tragedy. It was that common understanding of true pain that had persuaded the Russian to indoctrinate Victor into the Organization.

The day after he buried his son, Victor started planning, because that was all he could do. He'd realized too late that his son was right—that *he'd* been wrong. It wasn't the protestors who were to blame. They were only reacting to their circumstances, rats placed in an urban maze of ruin and poverty from which there was no escape. The real men responsible were the ones inside the government, men he served, men like the minister of defense and even the president himself.

Armed with that knowledge and understanding, he spoke openly of his plans with the Russian, who understood his desire for vengeance, who encouraged it. *And now, eighteen months later, it's all about to happen, and they'll never see it coming. If the American vice president keeps his word and can do what he says he can do, it's nearly a guarantee,* he thought, even though he knew that in his business there were no guarantees, only best-laid plans followed by ruin and destruction.

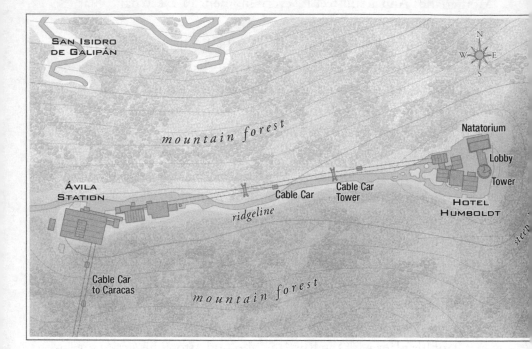

PART II

THE BEAR ON THE MOUNTAIN

CHAPTER 8

Logan West pushed through the magnetically sealed security doors once the keypad beeped and followed Santiago into the modern medical facility that occupied the top floor of a brand-new, five-story research building in the middle of the campus. Two guards in civilian attire sat at a desk on the right, staring impassively at the newcomers, black pistols worn in shoulder holsters *over* their dark-blue polo shirts. One of the men nodded at Santiago, who returned the gesture, pushing forward deeper into the space.

"Impressive," Cole said next to Logan as the breadth of what they beheld became clear with each step. They walked through a short corridor of patient rooms, which were partially occupied. The beds were new, the monitors and other equipment seemed to shine, and the rooms themselves were spotless.

"It is impressive, especially for Venezuela," Santiago said as they emerged into the central, rectangular hub of the floor.

Personnel in white overcoats and various shades of blue scrubs

61

scurried about, not urgently, but with a sense of purpose that Logan and Cole recognized and appreciated. In the middle of the hub was an area of desks, monitors, and charts arranged in an open-square configuration, positioned with the workstations and chairs facing outward into the surrounding hallways and adjacent rooms.

"It's just like any emergency room you'd find in any high-level hospital in the US," Logan commented, somewhat in amazement.

"I wouldn't know," Santiago replied, "but I was told it was modeled after precisely that. Believe it or not, I only found out about this place the day I found out about you."

"I thought Venezuela despised all things American," Cole commented sardonically.

"Not all things are always what they seem; not all Venezuelans feel that way," Santiago said.

The three men pushed past the core of the facility and continued down the hallway.

"Why are we here?" Logan finally asked.

After the events at the Atlantis Resort, Logan, Cole, and Santiago had spent Saturday night and Sunday morning at the US Embassy in Nassau. Commander Henderson had run point with local law enforcement and the security on Paradise Island. The official story was that the carnage in the room had been a rare robbery attempt gone wrong, which had spilled out onto the grounds of the resort and ended with one subject falling into the lagoon, to the dietary benefit of the three great hammerheads. The American couple on the bridge had provided a description of Logan to security, which Commander Henderson had personally obtained and then buried. No official report of Logan's presence existed. While the story was messy, it was good enough for the Bahamian government.

By Sunday afternoon, Santiago had been able to secure safe passage to a private airfield south of Caracas. The location was remote and guarded by a unit from the SEBIN. Various Venezuelan government agencies utilized it for discreet travel both in and out of the country. The fact that the Gulfstream jet—dispatched at CIA Director Toomey's request—was from the US hadn't even fazed the security personnel. They'd been there long enough to see aircraft from all over the world arrive and depart.

Once in Caracas, the team had established contact with the chief of station at the US Embassy, who had been personally briefed by the CIA director. It was full crisis-management mode, and analysts at CIA headquarters in Langley, Virginia, had been ordered to determine exactly where Hugo Sanchez had been the previous week. Until that intelligence was obtained, Logan and Cole were in a holding pattern, staying inside the US Embassy compound at a residence that was used by the ambassador for personal guests. It was also how they found themselves at the medical facility, invited along by Santiago for a purpose he refused to reveal until they were at the location. With little else to do but wait—the worst part of any mission, Cole had commented, more than once—they'd accepted.

Santiago stopped at a room with a light-colored oak door partially closed. A placard read ROJAS above room number 504. He turned to Logan and Cole, his features softening, and said, "This is why we're here. Be pleasant, and no foul language, understand?" He emphasized the point by raising his first finger in front of his face.

Logan suspected what lay inside, nodded, and followed Santiago into the room of nine-year-old Camila Rojas.

CHAPTER 9

Logan studied the beautiful little girl who slept peacefully on a slightly elevated hospital bed. A high-definition monitor displayed her heart and respiration rates, but there were no visible wires or electrodes. *Wireless monitoring? Impressive . . . and not cheap.*

The girl had shoulder-length, jet-black hair—like her father—sharp features, and a cute button nose that would one day drive boys crazy, at least Logan so hoped. An immediate wave of empathy engulfed him. Children were sacrosanct in his worldview, even though he knew thousands suffered horrible illnesses and death on a daily basis. There was no stopping it, a part of the cruel cycle of humanity, but in his opinion, there was no purer motivation than to prevent the suffering of children.

"This is why I found you," Santiago said, as he stood over the bed and brushed the hair off the side of her face, causing it to cascade across the pillow. "Her name is Camila, like her mother, who really did die of cancer two years ago, like I told you," he said, looking back at Logan. "And she's sick. She has acute lymphoblastic leukemia. She fought it once, with traditional chemotherapy, but she relapsed, which is usually terminal."

"I'm so sorry," Cole replied.

"You said 'usually,' " Logan noted.

"You are perceptive," Santiago said. "In Venezuela, due to the economy collapsing, medical care has become so poor that not even lifesaving prescriptions are available. I honestly didn't know what I was going to do. When the hospital informed me that her cancer was back, I was devastated. This is something I pray to God you never have to go through. I researched our options, which all lead to just one possibility—something called CAR T-cell therapy, which uses the patient's own T cells to fight the cancer. It's been successful in multiple studies, especially for Camila's type of cancer. I'd started to look at possible programs in Venezuela, but the trials and waiting lists were long. My supervisors at the SEBIN knew what I was dealing with. It was shortly afterward that I was approached by the director with an offer—find you, and they would begin treatment immediately."

Logan understood, empathizing with Santiago. He knew that given the same predicament, he would have made the *exact same choice* Santiago had made. It wasn't even a choice, not to any parent who felt the emotional pain of a suffering child. "Is it working?" he asked.

"This kind of stem-cell therapy takes several stages," Santiago said. "Before I left to track you down, they drew several pints of blood to separate the T cells. Those T cells are being genetically engineered, kind of like a computer program, the way it was explained to me, to produce a certain kind of receptor that will attack her cancer. Once they've finished the engineering, they then have to reproduce the cells into hundreds of millions. And once that's done, they'll be ready to infuse them into her body."

"How long will that take?" Cole asked.

"Normally weeks, but the doctors here have reduced the weeks to just seven days, which means that tomorrow they should be able to start the targeted treatment," Santiago said.

"When will you know if it works?" Logan asked.

"It depends on her body. It could be a week; it could be a

month, but regardless, it's the best chance she has, and this place was the only option *I* had," Santiago explained.

Logan watched silently as Santiago leaned down and kissed his daughter's forehead. "You did the right thing," Logan finally said. Patriotism, politics, and national security aside, Santiago had protected his family, *which says all you need to know about him as a man,* he thought.

"I know, and one day you will too," Santiago replied.

Logan's encrypted iPhone buzzed in his rear pocket. He slipped the phone out, saw the initials "JQ" displayed, and hit the talk button.

"How's your Venezuelan vacation coming along? Hit any night-clubs? Start any protests?" John Quick shot in rapid-fire succession.

"Hold on, smartass," Logan replied. He glanced at Santiago and said, "It's my work. I need to take this. I'm going to step out into the hallway and find someplace I can talk."

Santiago nodded, and Logan pulled on Cole's shoulder to indicate he should follow. They exited the room and entered the cream-colored hallway. An empty room lay directly across from Camila's, and Logan and Cole entered, leaving the door open in order to see the little girl's room.

"Okay. I've got Cole with me. We're in a secret medical facility for the rich and powerful in Venezuela. It's a long story, but we've got some privacy. What do you have?" Logan asked.

"No small talk? I get shot almost three weeks ago, nearly *died,* and there's no 'Hey, brother. How you doing? How you holding up?' Nothing. Always mission, mission, mission. You know what they say about all work and no play. So sad," John finished.

A little less than three weeks earlier, in an ambush by Vice President Baker's elite Secret Service detail at Task Force Ares headquarters on Marine Corps Base Quantico, John had been shot in the stomach. He likely would've died, had it not been for the FBI's HRT

Black Hawk helicopter that had arrived on-site to transport him to Inova Fairfax Hospital, which had a premier Level 1 trauma center.

"You're alive, aren't you?" Logan retorted.

"No thanks to you," John replied.

"Whoa, killer. *All* thanks to me," Logan said, reminding his best friend that he'd been the one to execute a kamikaze maneuver against an armored Secret Service SUV, a move that had ultimately saved both of their lives thanks to its brazenness.

"Fair enough. I won't argue the point. Okay. Let's get down to business. Here's what Jake just called to tell us that analysts at Langley discovered," John said. "Hugo Sanchez, also known as dead bad guy number . . . fuck it, I can't count that high." While it was meant as a joke, the truth was that the shadow war in which they'd been engaged for the past two and a half years had racked up a body count on all sides equivalent to a third-world insurrection. "Anyhow, Mr. Sanchez apparently traveled north of Caracas to El Ávila National Park. And here's the crazy part—he stayed for three days at the Humboldt Hotel."

"Why is that crazy?" Logan asked. "It's a hotel, right?"

"Because the Humboldt Hotel, what I could get from the wonderful world of the internet, has been abandoned and shut down for decades. It stands atop Avila Mountain, and supposedly, the government has been remodeling it for years. Bottom line—whatever Hugo was up to is up there. The analysts also identified an increase in HF and satellite communications activity, although they weren't able to break the encrypted signals. They sent it over to the boys and girls at Fort Meade," John said, referring to the National Security Agency, "but they had no luck either. Whatever encryption they're using is beyond our capability to break."

"Great," Logan said. "More unknowns."

"At least we—and by 'we,' I mean you—have a place to start. It could be worse," John said. "*And* it sounds scenic. I'm sure you'll love it. Take a selfie from the top. King of the world and all that jazz."

"And I'll post it on fucking Twitter and Instagram," Logan said.

"You have to start somewhere. Before you know it, you'll be the social media Taylor Swift of the spy world. You're so cool," John added for good measure.

"Go fuck yourself. Wonderful. A stroll up a mountain. Just what we need."

"Hey, at least you can get your cardio in. Stop complaining. Doctors told me no working out for several more weeks. Don't want to risk tearing the wound. The good thing is that Amira is here to take care of me," John said.

"I'm sure she's loving that," Logan said sarcastically.

"Could be worse. At least we're getting out of the city the day after tomorrow. We're having dinner at her dad's place." Amira's father, a retired DC homicide detective, had left the city after her mother had passed away and retired in the suburbs. "Should be a nice break from hanging out here all day."

Two men much older than Logan and Cole suddenly appeared in the doorway, stared at them, and turned to enter Camila's room. *That's our cue,* Logan thought.

"Brother, I have to go. Take it easy, no kidding. I need you back at full strength," Logan said to his fellow warrior and brother-in-arms. "Say hi to Amira for me." Logan paused for effect, surreptitiously hitting the speaker button. "And Cole sends his love. Says he misses you every moment of the day."

"Go fuck—" was all either man heard as Logan hit the end button.

"You know, sometimes you're as much of a child as he is," Cole said in mock exasperation.

"I know, but it's still fun. Let's go see who the new old guys are." Logan slid the iPhone back into his pocket and crossed the corridor to meet the newcomers.

CHAPTER 10

"Logan West, Cole Matthews, allow me to introduce the director of the SEBIN, Manuel Caballero, and President Oscar Silva, the president of the Supreme Tribunal of Justice of Venezuela, what you would call your Supreme Court," Santiago said.

"Chief Justice," Logan said, shaking the hand of the older, white-haired man first. He'd seen his picture in the news during the protests, aware of his precarious position occasionally in opposition to the president.

"Mr. West," Justice Silva replied. "I'm glad you were able to join us."

Logan nodded and turned to the director of the notorious SEBIN. "Director Caballero," he said, and extended his hand. The bald man with short-cropped black hair on the sides gripped his hand firmly, but there was something bordering on hostility in the eyes that assessed Logan and Cole.

"Mr. West," was all Director Caballero said.

As Cole repeated the exercise in formality, Logan spoke. "Gentlemen, your man here found us and relayed your message. I need to inform you both that our president is completely aware of where we are and what we're doing, as you must know, since the existence of our task force is only known by two groups of people—a very select handful inside the US government, including the president, whom we *work directly for*; and the rogue elements of the Organization, which we are systematically hunting down, dismantling, and destroying. More importantly, do you understand what that information means for the two of you?"

"As a matter of fact I do, and I'm glad to see you realized it before we had to tell you," the chief justice said.

"What's he talking about, Logan?" Cole asked.

"These two distinguished public servants either were or *are* members of the Organization," Logan stated.

"It's actually a little of both," Director Caballero said, his expression never changing as he met Logan's gaze.

"How so?" Cole asked. "The Organization doesn't strike me as the understanding type, especially of traitors. Just ask the former NSA director—former, of course, because the Organization had him gunned down in the middle of a highway."

A slim smile formed on Justice Silva's face. "Mr. Matthews, you are correct, but you're missing the bigger picture. Thanks to you and your associate here, right now *no one* is running the Organization. Your crusade and the Founder's death have triggered a protocol that he set up. Once he died, a message went across our global network, a message with one purpose—to instruct every member to temporarily cease and desist all operations, to go dark until further notice. As of two and a half weeks ago, the entire Organization went dormant, waiting for a reactivation order that only the Founder can authorize."

"But he's dead. He won't be issuing any orders from beyond the grave," Logan said, "which means his network should remain dead with him."

"Normally I'd agree with you, except for one thing," Justice Silva said.

"What's that?" Cole asked.

"When the network went dead and we saw the news out of your country, I became concerned," Justice Silva said. "The way the Founder died, the rebellion on the Council—it put all of us at risk. As a result, I asked the director here to target all of the Organization's communication links we either used or knew about. It was precautionary, more than anything else."

"And while our SIGINT methods may not be as robust as your NSA's, they are effective," Director Caballero interjected. "Like you, though, we thought the network would stay dark. But last week, one of the links, a satellite channel, went live again, and it's been active intermittently since."

"There are only two people I know of who could possibly have that kind of authority delegated by the Founder—General Jack Longstreet, the Founder's head of security operations, who is actually working with us, kind of; and our vice president," Logan said.

"That's exactly what we thought, considering whom the channel is dedicated for," Director Caballero replied.

"And who exactly is that?" Logan asked, slightly apprehensive at the possible answers. *It's got to be someone in power. I pray to God it's not the Venezuelan president. That will be a nightmare. I can only take on one traitorous executive branch member at a time.*

"Lieutenant General Victor Cordones, Commanding General of the National Army," Director Caballero replied, the weight of the words heavy on the hospital room air.

"That doesn't sound like a very good thing, not one bit," Cole said drily.

"We felt the same way, which is why I contacted a very sensitive source the SEBIN has inside General Cordones's inner circle," the director said.

"Wait a second. You have a source *inside* the army?" Cole asked, somewhat incredulously.

"I do, and be thankful for it," the director said defensively. "He told us that while he's not sure when, the general is expecting a very 'sensitive shipment' in the next few days. All he knows is that it's from North America, and that the general believes it's critical to Venezuela's national security."

"Does he know where or when?" Logan asked quickly.

"No. He does not," Justice Silva replied.

"Which is when we decided to reach out to you, Mr. West," Director Caballero said.

"But how the hell did you find out who we are? Who I am? You can't exactly find me or my team on Facebook," Logan said.

Director Caballero smiled. "Why, the Founder, of course."

"I don't understand. Why would he out us to you?" Cole asked. "It doesn't make any sense."

Logan laughed slightly, catching himself in order not to wake Camila, who had slept through the entire exchange among the four men. A perceptive man who had a preternatural talent for assessing a situation, he also reached conclusions quicker than most. "The smart bastard knew this would happen, didn't he? And he trusted you just in case. You're his fail-safe, aren't you?"

"You're right on all counts, Mr. West. Constantine said you were smart, and you don't disappoint," Director Caballero said, using the Founder's chosen first name. "For the same reasons that we decided to monitor all Organization communication networks known to us, he chose to tell me about you and your team. He suspected that once the rebellion on the Council began, it might spread, like a cancer, to other regions of the world. As a result, he chose one representative, for lack of a better word, for every major region of the globe, and I was his trustee for South America. He told me that the president had created a task force after the Cain Frost business two and a half years ago, a task force whose purposes had aligned with that of the Organization, even if that task force wasn't aware of it. He told me who was in on it, as well as who was running it. He said that if events reached a catastrophic tipping point, I should reach out to you, and you would ultimately help or die trying. You may not have known him, but he knew who and what you are, and he respected it."

Logan absorbed the information. *Damn you, old man,* he thought, amused, angered, and humbled all at once. Logan had to give him credit. The Founder must've anticipated endless scenarios, including his own death, and had set in motion circumstances that might counter the instability that would result from his absence. And Logan West and Task Force Ares had become one of his biggest counterweights.

Logan sighed. It was an alliance of necessity. If the preening politicians knew what he was about to engage in, they'd collectively have an aneurysm, *which might not be the worst thing in the world. Things might actually get accomplished in DC.* "Just so we're all on the same page, here's the bottom line—my mission and commander's intent, to put it in *my* terms: the commanding general of your national army has gone off the reservation and is likely smuggling our vice president, a traitor to his country and a threat probably to your country and the entire free world, into Venezuela in the next day or two. We have no idea how, when, or where. We also don't know what the hell the good general is up to, but if he's got positive control of the vice president, I'm pretty certain it's not good for anyone, here or anywhere else. And to top it off, you want us to help you stop whatever the hell that is. And our reward will be to reclaim that which is rightfully ours—our very own vice president. Did I miss anything?"

Santiago Rojas stared at the man who had just spoken as a peer—even a *superior*—to two of the most powerful men in Venezuela, men he'd never have dared to speak to in such a tone. *Who is this man?* He was starting to appreciate not only the gravity of the situation but the force of nature that was his new American friend.

"No. You did not," Director Caballero said. "And in case I don't get a chance to say this later, thank you for doing this."

"Sir," Logan said, suddenly respectful, "do I really have a choice?"

"All men have choices," Justice Silva said, "even when they don't. It's recognizing them that sets one apart from others."

Logan understood. Many men—Marines and other service-members he'd known—had faced choices like that in Iraq, choices which led to either death or cowardice. And every last one had chosen the former, preserving their honor over their lives.

Logan nodded.

A rustling from the bed disturbed the silence that had fallen over the room. A weak voice called out, "Hi, Daddy."

Logan turned toward Camila and watched as Santiago slid onto the bed, wrapped his little girl in his arms, and kissed her fiercely on the forehead. "Hey, princess. How you feeling?"

Logan felt a physical ache well up inside him, recognizing the love of a father for his daughter, knowing, *feeling*, that it was that love that would see them through this dark time, no matter what happened. *It could be you. Check that: it* will *be you,* he thought, which was almost too much to bear.

"Tired, but okay," Camila said. "Daddy, who are all these people?"

"Friends from work, honey," Santiago said. "Nothing to worry about. I've got you now." He squeezed his daughter tighter and closer.

"Come on, gentlemen, let's give them some privacy," Logan said. He started to leave the room, stopped, and turned back toward the bed, only to see Camila staring intently at him.

"Camila, you don't know me, but I just wanted to tell you that you have a very brave father, one who would do absolutely anything for you," Logan said. "I hope you get better soon." He smiled at her, green eyes sparkling with intensity. "I believe you will." He glanced at Santiago, nodded, and walked toward the door.

"Daddy, who is that?" Logan heard Camila ask.

"He's a friend, and more importantly, he's a good man," Santiago replied.

"I like him," Camila said faintly, as Logan walked into the hallway.

If she knew the other Logan West, she might think differently, his subconscious challenged. *But all that really matters is what a parent will do for a child.*

CHAPTER 11

Off the Coast of Venezuela

Former Vice President Joshua Baker—how he thought of himself after fleeing the United States, even if the rest of the world thought he was still vice president—was eager to have his journey of no return over and behind him. The last two and a half weeks had been grueling, even for the relatively fit man in his midfifties.

Exactly as his saviors had promised, after the gun battle at the National Cathedral in northwest Washington DC, they'd driven west toward the Blue Ridge Mountains and then worked their way southwest across the lower middle part of the country until they'd hit Texas. Their only stops had been at three hotels, where he, his driver—who asked him to call him Nick—and two other members of the Organization had each time changed vehicles.

Their final destination in the US had been just north of the border at Piedras Negras, where they'd waited for two days in a modest house on the north side of the city. Finally, a black Mercedes S-class sedan with diplomatic plates issued by the State Department had arrived, and the least enjoyable part of his trip had commenced, with him below the trunk in a specially designed hidden space with lighting and ventilation. For more than an hour, as the vehicle traveled over the pavement, he'd forced himself to remain calm, fighting occasional nausea from motion sickness caused by a lack of visual cues to center his equilibrium. He'd heard voices, the vehicle had completely stopped once, and then the sedan had driven away, until thirty minutes later, the pavement had transitioned into dirt. The sedan had halted, and Nick had opened the trunk, smiled, and said, "Welcome to Mexico. Come on, sir. Let's get you out of there." And just like that, he was no longer in the US. It'd almost been too easy.

A few days later, they'd boarded a 120-foot yacht—he never learned who owned it—north of Ciudad Madero and set casual sail east across the Gulf of Mexico toward Venezuela. The gulf had been warm and humid, and for brief moments he'd been able to forget—*almost*—that he'd left behind the only person he truly loved, his eleven-year-old son, Jacob. Saying goodbye to him at the cathedral had been the most gut-wrenching thing he'd done in his life, affecting him more deeply than the countless deaths he'd been responsible for, including those of his own Secret Service detail.

Their course had taken them between Cuba and Cancún, where they'd stopped for one day off the coast of Jamaica and then another near Aruba. Regardless of the vacation destinations, he'd never left the yacht, where he'd been in constant contact with General Cordones, the man who was planning the next phase of Joshua Baker's life, frustratingly without his input, at least at this stage.

The general had told him that there was something the vice president could provide that would help alter the course of his country's history, although what that was, he had no clue. The list that had been the cause of the chaos and mayhem in Washington DC a few weeks earlier had been destroyed. While he had some names and a few operational details on the Organization, once the Founder had died, Baker was fairly certain those details were no longer valuable.

He rubbed his right hip, which had been replaced a year earlier, and stood up from a chair in the main cabin of the yacht, eager for some fresh air. He walked toward the stern, slid a glass door aside, and stepped out onto a wooden balcony. Warm air enveloped him, and he inhaled deeply. *If only I could forget who I am and stay on this boat forever.* But he knew it was a pipe dream, a fantasy to entertain only in precious moments of solitude, lest he begin to believe it was attainable.

He was out of options, and the general was his last resort. If the Venezuelan could provide the protection he promised, then Josh would do everything he could to help the man, no matter what it was. He was a practical man, and his survival demanded practicality above all else.

And I do have one play left in the US, on the off chance that the president and his damned task force figure out where I am. But he knew that if he pulled that trigger, there was no going back, ever. *Desperate measures for desperate times,* he thought, and stared at the slowly rolling waves.

CHAPTER 12

San Isidro de Galipán
El Ávila National Park
Tuesday, 2100 Venezuelan Standard Time

Just north of Caracas along the central section of the Cordillera de la Costa mountain range lay El Ávila National Park. The park itself covered more than three hundred square miles of forested mountains and included areas for rock climbing, endless hiking trails, camping areas, and numerous zip lines. But it was the area at the top of the ridgeline at just over seven thousand feet that was the main tourist attraction.

Due to its remote location, the main mode of transportation to the ridgeline was the Teleférico de Caracas cable car system, which connected Ávila Station on top of the mountain to the city below for a scenic two-mile ride. The original system had had a second section that ran from an additional station in the park down the north side of the mountain to the coastal town of Macuto. But over time, the coastal cable had wasted away from a lack of maintenance and had stopped running by the end of the 1970s.

Open to the public during the day, the park contained several food stands and a market where residents of the small mountainside village of San Isidro de Galipán sold crafts to tourists and locals who took the cable car up the mountain for the scenic views, which included the sweeping urban landscape of Caracas to the south and the Caribbean Sea to the north in stunning contrast to one another.

At the east end of the park, six hundred meters from the cable station along a narrow cobblestone walkway that curved back and forth, stood the most visible landmark in all of Caracas—at one point, in all of South America—the Hotel Humboldt.

Built in 1956 under President Marcos Pérez Jiménez, the hotel was designed to unite Caracas with the coastal region through the cable car complex and tourist park. During its heyday in the oil boom of the 1950s, everyone who was anyone—including Fidel Castro—stayed at the luxury hotel. Unfortunately, once President Jiménez was overthrown, the hotel's first descent into disrepair began, and it closed in the 1960s, only to begin its solitary life of abandonment through several failed initiatives to renovate and reopen the iconic landmark. Currently, the government of Venezuela owned the hotel, and the rumor on the cobblestone street was that there were actual plans to recondition the hotel and rebuild the Ávila-to-Macuto cable line. But even out of commission, the hotel was a daily destination for tourists and locals eager to glimpse a piece of national history.

Visible from nearly every point in Caracas, the hotel stood watch as decades of dictators and history unfolded below. With a circular tower fourteen floors high that contained seventy guest rooms, the abandoned structure reminded Logan West of the Capitol Records Building in Hollywood, although he acknowledged to himself that the only time he'd seen that landmark was years ago at the end of a fairly decent action comedy that featured a crude comedian who'd had his brief time in the La La Land limelight.

At the base of the tower, a series of connected, vaulted-ceiling buildings with glass facades contained numerous social areas, an indoor pool, a restaurant, and a private cable car system that ran down the sloped ridgeline six hundred meters to Ávila Station.

Logan looked at his watch as he sipped the last of a glass of ice water that the owners of the outdoor restaurant kept refilling. He'd been surprised at the high quality of the food and the exceptional service provided by the couple in their sixties and their two sons who owned the mountainside restaurant. "It's time," he said.

A handful of other guests, who appeared to be all locals—*or at least not Americans*—drank and ate merrily as a Spanish radio station pumped out the latest dance and salsa music. The patrons were all cheerfully oblivious to Logan and his partners.

He glanced up the mountain, the guest room tower darkly silhouetted against the clear sky, the stars twinkling in the background against the black cloth of night.

Cole, Santiago, and a third man—Hector Salazar, a barrel-chested, squat human tank and Santiago's closest ally in the Counterintelligence Direction *and* godfather to Camila—scooted their chairs back in unison and picked up the heavy-duty hiking backpacks that lay on the floor next to their plastic green chairs. Dressed in dark earth-tone hiking attire, cargo pants, and fleece pullovers, at first glance the four men resembled a rugged advertisement for the North Face apparel and equipment company.

Logan pulled out four hundred bolívars and left the stack on the table, knowing that the owners would appreciate it, given the current economy and the domestic turbulence that had crushed tourism over the past few years. With the cost of living eighty percent lower than in the United States, he figured the Ares black budget could afford a forty-dollar South American dinner.

The owner's son said something in Spanish to the four men, to which Santiago replied with a laugh, pointed at the two Americans, and spoke briefly. The thin boy in his early twenties nodded, smiled, and began to clear the table as the group left the outdoor area and walked around the side of the restaurant along a narrow stone path.

"What was that all about?" Logan asked once they were out of range of any eavesdroppers.

"He thanked us for the generous tip, wished us well, and told us to watch out for any black jaguars," Santiago replied.

"Black jaguars? Are you kidding me?" Cole asked, concern suddenly in his voice.

"He was, as jaguars are an endangered species down here and notoriously rare, especially the so-called black jaguar, which is actually a regular jaguar with a color abnormality," Santiago replied. "He was being funny."

"I don't care if he thought he was the reincarnation of Richard Pryor. Big apex predators are not a laughing matter, *especially* at night," Cole said.

"Don't worry, brother. We're the only real predators out here tonight. I promise I'll protect you if things get scary in the big bad woods," Logan said.

"It's a mountain forest, jackass. Know your environment," Cole shot back.

"John really is rubbing off on you," Logan replied quickly. "Before you know it, you'll be doing stand-up and trying out for *America's Got Talent.*"

"At least I might have a shot. I'm pretty sure there's no room for serious, brooding former Marines," Cole said.

Logan smiled in the dark and ignored the jab, as the four men hiked away from the restaurant up the narrow, paved street that wound its way and branched out across the mountainside village. There was no vehicle traffic, as the residents were either secured in their homes or enjoying the night out at one of the many restaurants and bars. *I wouldn't want to stumble home drunk up here. One small slip, and you're taking a violent tumble that won't end well.*

A faint glow covered the village from sporadically placed lampposts, homes, and buildings. The cool mountain air was crisp, with the smell of the Caribbean Sea pervasive even at their elevation.

As they climbed higher, the hotel loomed above them several hundred meters away. The group reached a switchback at the far eastern edge of the village, and Logan stepped off the road into a dense growth of mountain forest. As he entered the shifting shadows, he softly said, "Remember, whoever they are, they don't know we're coming. I can't imagine more than a handful of men, no matter what. The more guns they have, the more suspicion they draw. This is simple: close with and incapacitate whoever is up there and try to find out what the hell is going on." He knew the other three members of his ad hoc fire team had heard him, and he pressed on.

Cole, Santiago, and Hector followed, vanishing into the forest and up the slope toward the Humboldt Hotel.

CHAPTER 13

Penthouse Suite, South Side
Guest Tower, Humboldt Hotel

Lieutenant Colonel Grigori Sokolov stared out through the space where large pane-glass windows had once shielded the suite and its occupants from the elements. Unfortunately for him and the additional seven men of his VDV Spetsnaz unit, that time had long passed, and the wind buffeted the tower, sending blasts of cold air throughout the upper levels. The only thing in their favor was that they'd set up their operations center on the south side, facing Caracas and out of the direct line of sight of the open windows. They'd also duct-taped sheets of opaque plastic in the presidential suite, leaving part of the last window uncovered. It was through this window that he studied the expansive landscape, the lights of the city that spread out in illuminated tendrils from the center mass in the valley below. The image reminded him of a virus—which he felt was appropriate—the fingers of light yearning to corrupt the untouched darkness just out of reach. *Corruption is one thing Venezuelans do well,* he thought, knowing that his role in the upcoming operation would be critical in balancing that scale in favor of the people.

The men were currently under strict noise-and-light discipline, and the assorted communications equipment and laptop computers had all been blacked out with both screen dimming sheets that prevented ambient light from escaping and black tape over the power switches and other functioning lights. On their first night in the hotel, once they'd established the communications links and relay receivers, including the satellite and HF antennas on the roof, he'd had his communications officer, Major Fedor Azarov, walk down to the abandoned park at two in the morning and see if he could detect any escaping light. He hadn't been able to, and Grigori was confident their presence would remain undetected for as long as they were here, which he expected would only be less than a week.

Too young to be a veteran of Afghanistan, he'd cut his teeth in the brutal campaign in Chechnya, part of a special forces unit dedicated to hunting Islamic extremists responsible for targeting civilians, both Russian and Chechen. A young officer at the time, his indoctrination into the full horrors of war had occurred when his unit had captured a young Chechen rebel on the outskirts of Grozny during the Russian siege of the city. His unit had suffered three KIA the previous day from an attack on their convoy as it moved around the left flank of the besieged city, and the major in charge of the unit had decided to send a message to the rebels.

As one of the Spetsnaz commandos filmed, one man held the rebel fighter—in reality, a boy no more than nineteen—by the legs, pinning him to the gravel road, while a second Russian stepped on his head with a boot. As the camera recorded, the major bent over, taunted the Chechen, and proceeded to cut his throat, working his way from the side to the front.

It was the gurgling screams and dying cries that had slammed home the reality of Grigori's situation, a reality he had learned in Chechen blood: it was kill or be killed. There was no quarter to be given to the rebels, no peace to be had. There was only death, but not for him and his fellow Spetsnaz soldiers. No. Death was for the enemy, regardless of the form it took.

Since that day, he'd led his men across several fronts, including Georgia and Crimea, with only one guiding principle—no mercy for the enemy. He was convinced it was why he'd survived every violent confrontation, every bullet that cracked near him, and every barrage of mortar or artillery fire. It was also why he was extremely cautious, especially in hostile territory. In fact, it was why the other seven men in the unit slept in three shifts and rotated patrols throughout the abandoned hotel. Armed with suppressed H&K 4.6x30mm MP7A1 machine pistols with reflex sights, they had more than enough firepower to handle any wayward Venezuelans who wandered past the chain-link fence that had been emplaced days before his unit had arrived. To provide an extra layer of protection, multiple motion-sensor-activated, night-vision HD cameras mounted on the third floor provided a bird's-eye view in all directions.

Staring at the city, he decided that in the morning he'd speak to the Venezuelan general to confirm the timeline, and he'd consider placing a call to the Russian embassy. Tired, he decided to grab some sleep, if only for a few hours, as he'd take one of the midnight patrols with two of the other men.

He walked back toward the center of the room, glanced one last time at the bank of monitors side by side on a table . . . and froze.

All thoughts of sleep were suddenly swept away, replaced by an urgent alertness as he grabbed the handheld encrypted push-to-talk radio from the table and pressed the talk button.

Logan knelt inside the tree line and waited, scrutinizing the angled glass surface of the building that housed the indoor pool. From the diagrams Santiago had provided, the pool building contained a second-floor walkway that not only overlooked the pool inside but also connected to the guest room tower. The building itself resembled one of the many Quonset huts scattered across the base operations area of the Mountain Warfare Training Center in Bridgeport, California, where he and his Force Reconnaissance Company Marines had conducted Mountain Warfare Survival and High-Angle Shooting training. *I just hope I don't have to capture and kill a rabbit on this trip. Bad guys, check; soft, fluffy bunnies, not so much. They're not all Monty Python monsters.*

From forty meters away, he scanned the building with a Bushnell night vision monocular that Santiago had provided. The SEBIN inspector had also equipped the four men with suppressed H&K 9mm MP5s with red dot reflex scopes and suppressed Glock 17 9mm pistols, weapons that both Logan and Cole were comfortable with from their Marine Corps days.

Outer layers now off and packed away in their backpacks, which they staged just inside the tree line in order to lighten the proverbial soldier's load before they entered battle, the four men were outfitted in black long-sleeve neoprene shirts, the lightest black Kevlar vests Santiago could find, and black tactical chest rigs for extra magazines. The Glocks were held in place on their web belts via gun clips that could accommodate the suppressors. Logan didn't expect heavy resistance, but if heavy resistance came at them, they were as prepared as possible for it.

The plan was simple—make entry into the pool building through the exit on the east side wall of glass, work their way to the second-floor walkway, infiltrate the guest tower, and move up floor by floor via the only stairwell on the north side of the tower. All hostiles they encountered were considered enemy combatants. They wanted to take at least one alive, but their safety came before that of the enemy's, especially an enemy that had aligned itself with the Organization. *They'll either surrender or die,* Logan thought, and put the monocular away.

Logan turned once and looked at each of the men. "Once we're in, we don't stop until we hit the roof. I don't want to give them a chance to destroy whatever's up there. We move fast—"

"Please say 'and furious,' just once," Cole quietly interjected.

Santiago and Hector exchanged a glance, and Logan ignored his friend.

"And *quietly.* I've got point. Cole, on my right. You two cover three to six and six to nine o'clock. Once we get up top, we'll see what we see. Just be prepared to call in that air support," Logan said to Santiago.

Their retrograde plan was simple. Once they'd secured the site and the intelligence, Santiago would call in the SEBIN Eurocopter AS532 Cougar the director had placed at their disposal. The pilot and copilot had been handpicked by the director for their discretion and aversion to questions. The only thing they needed to know was where to go.

Santiago nodded, Logan turned around, and the four men moved out of the tree line, two by two, toward stone steps that led up to the outdoor patio and exit door.

"All patrol members to the pool building," Grigori said in Spanish, another requirement all team members had for this mission. "I say again, all patrol members to the pool building. Four unknown threats with automatic weapons and tactical gear. Engage at once. They'll be inside within thirty seconds. I'm remaining up here until you have this situation neutralized. Alpha out."

Looking around the penthouse suite at the equipment and maps, the last thing Grigori wanted was to risk a compromise of the mission, although he immediately realized that at some level, the operation had already been compromised. *Otherwise, these men wouldn't even be here.*

As the commanding officer, it was his painful duty to wait and to protect the contents of the room. But if need be, he'd engage directly. *Any mission, any time, any place.* Grigori, an honorable and devoted Russian and a warrior who believed the words of the Spetsnaz motto, thought, *That time is now.*

CHAPTER 14

The four-man fire team led by Logan West reached the exit door
and discovered it propped open, the bottom two hinges broken
away, leaving the door to vibrate gently as it whistled in the wind.
Although no longer functional, it was still secured by a heavy chain
and a new padlock, which Logan had spotted through the monocular.

As the crisp night wind whipped around them, Santiago handed
a small pair of powerful bolt cutters to Logan, and within seconds,
the chain unraveled and fell to the patio, clanging loudly on the
stone.

No point in hiding now, Logan thought. *Ready or not, here we
come.*

He stepped into the mountaintop natatorium and was assaulted
by the smell of dust, decay, and mildew. *Guess those renovations haven't started yet.*

Logan moved forward, his objective the stairwell at the far end
to the left of a small building that contained restrooms and show-
ers. The second-story overlook walkway was directly in front and
above them. Stacks of boxes were scattered in random locations
underneath, and to their right, the empty pool sloped down and

away into the shadows. The pool had been dug so that guests could wade up through the shallow end to enjoy the view down the side of the mountain just past the outdoor patio, directly behind Logan. Clouds passed in front of the half-full moon, and shadows skittered ominously across the enormous empty pool, creating shifting shapes of deep black under the walkway.

Logan was stepping softly when the first sounds of movement reached him, followed by a distinct click above that he recognized immediately—the selector switch on a weapon being shifted. *Oh no,* he thought, even as he screamed "Move!" and dashed forward, diving under the walkway as the first bullets struck the large panes of glass behind them, shattering the silence and sending sections of glass cascading to the floor.

Cole, Santiago, and Hector reached Logan's location a split second behind him, and the four men huddled behind the large box.

"Hold on," Logan said, aimed upward, and fired several shots into the walkway over his head. He had no idea if he hit the shooter, but it was worth trying.

Loud high-pitched *thwacks* of suppressed weapons filled the space as more rounds struck the box they crouched behind for cover.

Logan glanced around the left side of the stack and spotted small, bright bursts of light from on top of the walkway that extended around and on the roof of the bathhouse fifty feet away. He saw no suppressed flashes on the first floor, which meant only one thing—they'd been ambushed by an enemy that held the high ground. *Never a good thing,* he thought.

"This is not good. Either someone told them we were coming, or they have surveillance cameras set up," Cole said.

"Fewer than five people in my country even know we're here," Santiago said, as Hector risked leaning out to the right and unleashed several rounds from his MP5.

"Doesn't matter. Nothing changes," Logan said sternly. "We just need to go *through* these guys. There are at least three of them. Hand me a grenade."

Hector, who had volunteered to carry two breaching charges and other explosives, pulled a grenade out of a loop on his chest harness and handed Logan a German-made Diehl DM51 fragmentation grenade. Logan pulled the pin but held the spoon in place. "On my signal, shoot the hell out of that walkway."

Incoming rounds struck the empty pool, the windows, and the box. Unfortunately for the three Spetsnaz shooters, they hadn't synchronized their gunfire, and all three weapons simultaneously emptied, leaving the sudden quiet unnerving and eerie.

Shuffling and scuffling sounds of movement reached them, and Logan heard the first empty magazine clatter to the floor as one of the shooters reloaded. "Now."

Santiago, Cole, and Hector unleashed a sustained volley of fire that shattered the glass railing and struck the glass wall at the other end of the pool house.

The enemy weapons went quiet as their operators went into the prone position on the rooftop of the bathhouse, suppressed by the crack of bullets over their heads.

Logan stood up to his full height, cocked his right arm back, released the spoon on the grenade, and hurled the weapon like a baseball. It soared over the empty pool and disappeared into the darkness. *Please be close.*

All four men ducked back behind cover just as the grenade detonated with a blinding flash, briefly illuminating the natatorium in a garish light, followed by a thunderous *BOOM* that shattered whatever glass hadn't been destroyed by the gunfire. Sixty-five-hundred steel balls encased in the fragmentary shell of the grenade tore through the space, as well as the three shooters on top of the walkway.

Two of the men were killed instantly, but the third rose to his feet, stunned, and staggered toward his fate.

Logan and Cole were already moving, MP5s raised and locked on the area on top of the bathhouse. As the figure materialized out of the darkness, Logan and Cole opened fire.

Several rounds struck the shooter in the chest, and he toppled over the railing, diving headfirst into the empty deep end of the pool, performing an involuntary forward somersault. There was a sickening sound as his head, neck, and shoulders slammed into the concrete of the deep end.

No one spoke, and the four men combat-walked forward toward the base of the open-air staircase to the left side of the bath-house, weapons steady and elevated in front of them.

Who are these men? Grigori thought. It was a question of professional curiosity, as he knew the answer was irrelevant. What *was* relevant was the fact that they'd just killed four of his soldiers, men he'd fought with on other continents, men he considered brothers. His men had even had the tactical advantage, yet one grenade and excellent marksmanship had neutralized that advantage. *How quickly tides of war turn,* he thought with a rising anger that yearned for justice for his dead comrades.

The last thing he'd seen from the mounted camera inside the pool house was one of his Spetsnaz plummet over the ruined railing to his death. The four intruders had disappeared under the walkway, but he knew which way they'd be coming.

"Sir, what do you want us to do?" asked Major Oleg Poroshenko. A second Spetsnaz soldier stood behind him, waiting for orders. When Grigori had issued his first commands, the two men had dashed into the room from the suite next door that they were using for billeting.

Grigori pulled himself away from the camera, grabbed his MP7A1 machine pistol, and clipped the push-to-talk radio to his web belt. "Oleg, you're with me. We try to delay them," he said in Russian, having reverted to his native tongue. "Fedor, I need you to execute the emergency destruction plan. Burn all the maps and then destroy all the computers and communications equipment. If you have time—and I mean if—head up to the roof and destroy the antennas. I don't want to leave that encrypted gear up there intact. Once that's done, get off this tower via the escape route and meet us at the station. This place is burned. Understood?"

"Yes, sir," Fedor Azarov replied. "Be safe, sir. Kill these motherless cowards for Mother Russia."

Grigori felt a wave of pride. *Professional to the end.* "For Mother Russia, Fedor. I hope to see you soon, but if not, it's been my honor."

"Likewise, sir," Fedor said, nodded to his commanding officer and then Oleg, and turned away to begin the destruction of every trace of their presence.

"Let's go avenge our fallen brothers," Grigori said to Oleg.

"With no mercy," Oleg replied, and the two Russian operators fled the suite into the hallway.

Logan led his fire team up the stairs, the acrid smell of gunpowder following them like an invisible cloak. The soft thud of their boots on the concrete stairs echoed off the circular-vaulted ceiling, the only sound lingering in the aftermath of the brief battle.

Halfway up, the staircase turned ninety degrees to the left, and they ascended, reaching the second floor in a section of the pool house set back from the larger overlook. Logan realized they'd emerged onto the connecting walkway between the pool house and the guest tower. Directly across from him, the glass walls and ceiling of the skywalk emptied into the pool house ten feet to his left. Logan could see through the glass wall to the curved glass exterior of the natatorium, but the darkness prevented him from seeing inside. "Cole, you and Santiago check on the fourth shooter. We don't need any surprises on the way out of here."

Santiago had come up behind Cole and turned left, which placed him closer to the pool house. He was a foot away from the corner, MP5 raised, when Logan thought he saw movement. *Just another shadow?*

"Hold on a second. I thought—" was all Logan managed to say as Santiago stepped out from behind the walkway's glass wall back into the natatorium.

Two bullets struck him squarely in the chest, and he crumpled to the floor with a grunt, falling sideways.

Logan and Cole fired simultaneously, with Hector following suit a half second later. Bullets shattered two large sections of the enclosed walkway, and additional rounds destroyed the remaining glass exterior of the pool house that faced the guest tower, providing a clear line of sight into the dark space. A shadowy figure stood on the walkway, dark arms extended toward Santiago.

Logan, Cole, and Hector continued to fire as glass plummeted onto the walkway, the ground floor, and the cement outside with a cacophonous tinkling sound like the world's largest wind chimes. The fusillade of fire struck the shadow, which jittered back and forth as if deciding to go one way and then reversing course, before choosing one last time and falling forward face-first, motionless.

Hector reached Santiago first and rolled him onto his back. Logan dreaded what they might see, and the image of Camila's beautiful young face, looking lovingly up at her father, suddenly filled his mind. *Please, God, let him be okay.*

Santiago rubbed his chest, a tremendous relief to the other

three. "Well, I guess these things really do work," he said a little too calmly for someone who'd come inches from death seconds before.

"They do, but you're still lucky he aimed center-mass," Logan said. "I thought I saw movement in the shadows through the glass, but you'd already stepped out. I was about to call out. I should've yelled sooner."

Hector helped Santiago to his feet. "Not your fault. Just the nature of this business. I got lucky, this time," Santiago said.

"Hey," Cole said, "I'm pretty sure that we've all been lucky once or twice. Sometimes, that's all that counts."

"Amen to that," Logan said. He'd heard enough stories about close calls and had experienced enough randomness in Iraq to believe in the power of luck. "Now, let's get upstairs."

The four men turned to leave the natatorium, when a flickering light from above caught Logan's attention. He looked up through tinted glass and saw the guest tower looming fourteen floors over him, a cylindrical black mass silhouetted against the sky. On the top floor, a yellow light flickered in and out of the empty windows, increasing and dimming in intensity. *Fire.*

"Goddamnit," Logan said, and transitioned into a sprint through the connecting walkway. "They're burning everything up there to cover their tracks." *No way we let them escape, whoever the hell they are.*

The team dashed up a darkened stairway at the end of the connecting walkway. Intermittent periods of moonlight pierced the windows as the men climbed frantically. Logan reached the top of the stairs first, his right eye searching through the red dot scope, his left looking past it, realizing they'd entered the lobby, a massive space that was shaped like a quadrangle that hadn't decided what it really wanted to be.

The walls ran away from him at angles, with the other end of the welcome area larger than the width of the entrance where they now stood. The front of the lobby was a wall of glass—*like everything else up here*—and beyond were the darkened shapes of additional buildings, which he knew had once contained restaurants, a spa, and even a ballroom. Shadows cloaked everything in varying shades of gray and black. *An ambush in every dark corner. Wonderful.*

Two dark shapes appeared from a doorway at the far end. Logan couldn't discern anything about the two new targets, which didn't matter in the great scheme of things, as subdued flashes and bangs of suppressed weapons moved across the lobby.

"Two targets, twelve o'clock," Logan said and dove to the right, eager to be out of the line of fire. "Stay on the stairs until I tell you. I've got this," he ordered the rest of his team, who crouched down in defilade on the stairs in relative safety.

Okay, assholes, this is getting tiresome. Logan scampered across the floor, halting behind a large couch in the middle of the lobby. The incoming fire ceased. He moved to the far right end of the sofa and peeked around the corner, confident that the two shooters didn't have a bead on him. *Unless they have night vision, in which case your next thought will be nothing.*

No shots came, as Logan squinted into the darkness, eager for a glimpse of shifting shadows. He thought he heard movement, the shuffling of feet, but the acoustics were deceptive. *Need a diversion to pinpoint their locations.*

He quickly glanced around his immediate surroundings and stopped on the long table between the couch and four leather high-back chairs in front of him. *You've got to be kidding me.*

On top of the table was an object immediately recognizable to most of the Western world. Like a relic of the seventies, a wooden bowl containing plastic fruit sat on the table. The presence of the bowl sent goose bumps dancing across the back of his neck as he realized how truly abandoned the hotel was, lost in a bygone era, cursed to stand above the city as a beacon from another time. Logan West didn't believe in ghosts, but if there were ever a place that might actually be haunted, he believed it could be this one.

Logan shuffled around the couch, grabbed the entire bowl, and like an amateur shot-putter, hurled the bowl and its contents to his left. As the assorted fruit salad sailed through the darkened lobby, Logan raised the MP5, transitioned into a kneeling position, and waited.

The pieces of fruit and the wooden bowl clattered loudly to the floor, disrupting the eerie quiet of the lobby.

More suppressed flashes and bangs appeared at the far end of the lobby, but the two shooters had separated, creating a space of at least forty feet between them. *Smart bastards,* Logan thought, as he took aim at the shape on the left and fired several times.

The only feedback he received that he'd struck his target was the sudden silence as the shooter stopped firing, the sound of a weapon falling to the tiled floor, and what he thought might be a grunt of pain.

Logan moved the scope to the right, but the second shooter had also ceased firing. He looked away from the scope and spotted the dark outline of a figure running toward a set of glass doors at the front entrance. The shooter opened fire, but not at Logan; instead, he fired several rounds that shattered the glass doors.

Logan fired hastily, but the figure dashed through the ruined doors, even as glass crumpled around him.

Logan turned around and screamed toward the stairs. "All clear! One escaped through the front entrance. I'm going after him: no one gets away. Santiago, on my six. Cole, you and Hector get to the penthouse and see if there's anything left to salvage. Rally back here, if we can. Go!"

He didn't wait for a response and started for the door, confident that Santiago would soon be behind him. Within seconds, he stepped outside and into the pale moonlight, the wind and clouds whipping around the mountain's ridgeline.

The fleeing figure was gone—*fucker's fast*—but another building stood across the courtyard, and a door stood open, swinging slowly. *Bingo.*

Glass crunched under his boots as he pursued his prey. *Like I said, no one gets away.*

Cole and Hector ran through the lobby, the knowledge that evidence was burning several stories above them spurring them forward. As they reached the far side, there was a low moan from the downed shooter lying on his side.

Before Cole could react, Hector stopped, raised his suppressed weapon, and fired a single shot into the man's head. The groan stopped.

Hector looked at Cole through the gloom. "No second chances for these men. If he somehow survived and ambushed us on the way out, your friends would never forgive me."

Cole briefly contemplated the response. As someone who had executed a traitor under the cover of darkness on the back of a boat less than three weeks earlier and then dumped the body into the crab-infested depths of the Chesapeake Bay—albeit at the direct orders of the president—he understood the logic of the split-second judgment Hector had made. It was always the same—*them or us.* "Fair enough. We're on the right side of this war," Cole said, and breached the darkness beyond.

He paused, pushed a button, and the SureFire LED flashlight mounted under the barrel illuminated the space. The two men found themselves inside a small foyer. A small hallway lay in front of them, but to their immediate left stood another entrance.

Cole lit up the space. *Thank God.* Stairs ascended away from the doorway. "Hope your cardio is good, Hector. We've got fourteen floors to conquer as quickly as possible. Don't be offended if I run ahead. Time isn't our friend right now. See you up there," Cole said, and sprinted up the steps two at a time.

Logan found himself in another building with a concave ceiling and another wall of partitioned glass on one side of the space. *Well, I found the restaurant,* he thought wryly. Tables and chairs were arranged neatly, as if patiently waiting for patrons that would never arrive.

He moved quickly through the space, even as he heard Santiago outside trying to catch up with him. *Sorry, friend. Need to catch this rabbit.* Another connecting walkway exited the restaurant in the far wall, and Logan ran into it, reckless in his determination to catch his quarry.

Five long strides later, he found himself in another building—*this place is a rattrap*—but before he could assess his surroundings, a mechanical whirring roared to life and reverberated throughout the area. *Of all the things they could've updated, they had to do the cable car first. Awesome.*

Built into the enormous far-side, two-story wall was a gigantic opening that led directly outside. Mountain air rushed into the arrival and departure area, cooling the sweat that had beaded on the back of his neck. One long cable ran in the left side of the mouth of the space, connected to an enormous concrete pillar with a rotary top, around which the metal cable wrapped before exiting through the right half of the opening.

A white, modern cable car moved around the pillar toward the opening, black gears on top of the pillar turning counterclockwise, propelling the car toward the dark night beyond the ledge of the wall.

Logan West, aggressive to the point of reckless abandon, launched into a sprint, only one thought in his mind—*stop the shooter from fleeing.*

The MP5 dangled across his chest as he accelerated, smacking his black Kevlar vest with each stride. He breathed hard as he closed in on the cable car, which had nearly escaped into the open air, lifting up to begin its voyage to the main station at the other end of the park.

This is not smart, Logan. But he didn't care. The purposefulness and determination that separated him from all others was in control of his actions. He locked on to his target and ran harder.

The cable car lifted out of the station, escaping its grasp, as Logan West reached the edge of the platform. *Please, God. Don't let me be short,* he thought as he leapt into the cold unknown.

For the briefest of moments, he thought he'd misjudged, and he wondered how far he would fall, either to the ground or to his death off the side of the mountain. But then his hands slammed onto the metal safety bar near the bottom of the white car. As he closed his fingers around the metal, he was yanked upward, feet dangling over the darkened walkway fifty feet below.

Great. Now what, genius? As he pondered his next move, a structure loomed in the distance, growing closer with each passing second as the cable car approached. The support tower was old, with a crossbeam at the top where the cable passed through and then another crossbeam farther below, creating a space through which the cable car could pass.

You've got to be kidding me, he thought, as real concern washed over him in the face of his new dilemma—find a way inside the cable car or be knocked off as it traversed the support tower. *This just gets better and better.*

CHAPTER 15

Cole and Hector reached the top of the stairwell after what felt like an endless climb but in reality only lasted a little more than a minute. They found themselves on a landing on the outer wall of the hotel, where a hallway to their left led toward the center of the circular floor.

Cole forcibly slowed his breathing, preparing for what came next. Based on what he'd seen, the layout reminded him of a big donut, with the doors to the suites on the inner ring. In the short hallway, a glow danced across the walls from a source unseen. Tendrils of dark smoke wafted toward them. *Great. It's my own personal towering inferno.*

"Let's go, and let's hope we don't burn to death," Cole said. "Believe me, there are much better ways to go." Cole Matthews had seen enough videos of hostages being tortured and burned alive for one lifetime. It wasn't like the movies, where a person caught fire, fell over, and died. In reality, it was a slow, excruciating, and suffocating death that lasted minutes, not seconds.

The two men started down the hallway, MP5s raised and bobbing slightly, ready to engage. The sound of fluttering flames reached their ears, growing in intensity and reminding Cole of the conflagration that had violently erupted inside Task Force Ares headquarters in Quantico less than three weeks ago. *This place is a lost cause. It just might go up in flames.*

They were pushing farther down the hallway when Cole heard a noise from his left and felt the rush of cold night air swirling around him. He turned his head and saw a small closet with a ladder in the middle that led upward.

Cole raised his hand in a fist, the universal hand signal—at least for those with training or military service or anyone who had seen a military movie from the eighties—to stop. He stepped into the room and looked up. Several thumps and a loud metallic clanging resounded through the access hatch in the ceiling. He turned back to Hector, and in a low voice he was certain no one other than the two of them could hear, said, "I'm going up. Someone's up there. You see if you can save anything from the fire. If you can put it out, great. If not, come back and get me, and we'll get the hell out of this death trap."

"Understood," Hector said, and exited the closet without another word.

Cole slung his MP5 across his back, pulled the suppressed Glock 17 from his web belt, and began to climb.

He reached the access panel, prayed there was no one waiting on the other side with a gun pointed at his head, and climbed through to the roof of the Humboldt Hotel.

No shots came his way as he assessed his surroundings. He was on the main level of the roof, but in front of him, two more levels like an oddly shaped wedding cake rose into the darkness. The outline of a large radio wave tower several decades old hung over him, creating a slight but growing sensation of vertigo, as if the tower might fall on him if he kept looking.

More noise came from above, and he crossed the outer ring of the roof, reached another ladder built into the side of the base layer of the roof structure, and ascended. As his head crested above the next surface, he saw the source of the commotion.

Directly in front of him, less than fifteen feet away, a figure stood over several pieces of communications equipment. The man swung away purposefully with an axe. *Take him quietly and disarm him.*

Cole Matthews, the former head of the CIA's Special Activities Division and onetime member of the elite Unit that resided on secured grounds at Fort Bragg, North Carolina, stalked quietly toward the man.

It wasn't anything Cole did wrong. It was just luck, bad luck in his case.

When he was within two strides of the axe-wielding man, the shadow stood up and turned. The man's eyes widened in surprise, and he reacted, forcing Cole to launch a full-fledged assault.

As Cole closed the final few feet between them, the axe arced up and toward him, reached its apogee, and came plummeting back down. He quickly sidestepped the attack, and the axe clanged loudly off the hard surface of the roof. Cole was suddenly reminded of the fight he'd had in Sudan where he'd faced off against two homicidal prisoners with a bat and machete in an Everlast boxing ring in a black-site prison in what had definitely not been a sanctioned bout. *This should be easier and with less buckets of bloodshed.*

Still holding the suppressed Glock, Cole stepped toward the man and struck him in the temple with the butt of the weapon. The blow sent the man stumbling backward, even as he regained control of the axe. Cole moved forward and grasped the axe with his left hand and yanked with all his strength.

Unfortunately, his opponent executed the one countermove Cole hadn't anticipated: he let go of the axe and shot both hands up to the Glock, which Cole had pulled back to use to strike him again.

With no counterweight to anchor him, his own strength pulled him off balance, and Cole fell to the left, the axe in his left hand.

The worst part was that as he fell, he lost his grip on the Glock, which remained with his attacker.

Smart motherfucker, Cole thought. In one flawlessly executed expert move, his opponent had managed to disarm him and switch weapons.

Cole landed on his hands and knees and sprawled forward, acutely aware that he likely had less than two seconds before the shooter properly gripped the pistol, aimed, and fired. *Think fast or die.*

And then the rumbling began, and the Humboldt Hotel, a decaying symbol of decadence whose mere existence taunted the oppressed and impoverished citizens of Caracas below with its watchful gaze, began to shake.

Logan's mind raced as he searched through a catalog of options. *Break the glass. Climb in. Get shot. No good. Hang on the underside of the car like Indiana Jones and hope for the best. No way.*

The clouds raced by overhead and taunted him with weightless speed. *You stay here, you're definitely dead.* He looked down past his dangling feet and wondered if there was someplace soft he could drop that wouldn't instantly kill him. He didn't see anything below him in the darkness that might break his fall, only his neck or back. He lifted his right leg and propped the heel of his foot on the far end of the safety bar, his left leg still dangling below him, hoping that when the impact came, he might only lose a leg, not his life. *This was a bad decision, Logan, and Sarah is truly going to be pissed if you die on this mountain.*

But then the mountain began to tremble. Logan recognized the familiar sound, although he was too disoriented to locate the source. He turned his head toward the city, as the cable car swayed on its journey.

A black shape suddenly rose up one hundred yards away, blotting out part of his view, and Logan West, hanging precariously from the cable car, one slip from death, smiled in the darkness.

Grigori's only thought was escape. Once Oleg had been shot in the lobby, his options had dwindled to two—stand and fight or escape to warn the general that they'd been compromised. While his Spetsnaz honor demanded that he stay, he knew that the larger mission was more important, and that required that he survive. So he did the only thing he could do—he ran, praying to the gods of war for his escape, thankful that his team had installed inside the cable car a remote control for the computer system that connected Ávila Station to the hotel. The Venezuelan government had ensured that the system was operational less than two weeks ago, and the remote was a simple system that transmitted operational commands to both ends.

When the cable car had left the hotel's station, Grigori had felt the car rock when his pursuer had leapt onto the safety bar. He wasn't sure if the man was still under the carriage, but his MP7A1 was trained on the rear of the car after he'd moved to the opposite row of red plastic seats, swathed in darkness. He glanced over his shoulder, saw the tower, and waited. *Whoever he is, he won't be there much longer,* Grigori thought. *Once he's off, get to Ávila Station, hop on the ATV, and head into the city under cover of darkness.*

He'd been through much worse than this, even if the men he commanded were now all dead or dying. *I'll make it. I always do,* he thought, remembering the lessons from Chechnya. But then the interior of the cable car was suddenly awash in a bright, garish light, and his thought process changed dramatically.

As Cole dove to the side, he fully expected to receive several rounds in the back from his own weapon. He was pleasantly surprised when he reached cover behind a large HVAC exhaust vent unscathed and still alive.

The rumbling intensified, and Cole glanced around the corner of the vent. The man was no longer there, but instead was running toward another ladder that ascended to the highest level of the rooftop, never turning around once to see if Cole was pursuing.

Where the hell is he going? Cole realized it didn't matter. All that did was that he pursued him until he either caught him or died trying. *Just another fun-filled day on Task Force Ares,* he thought, and galloped across the rooftop with the axe held in front of him.

As soon as the pilot turned on the light, Logan acted, realizing he only had precious seconds left. He unholstered the Glock and prepared to fire when the glass in the doors on the side of the cable car exploded outward.

Bastard is shooting at the helicopter, he realized, *not me.* And then the helicopter pilot did exactly what Logan expected—he fired back.

The pod-mounted 20mm cannon hammered the top of the cable car, and Logan felt the car shutter and rock with each impact from the large-caliber rounds, knowing that if whoever was inside hadn't hit the deck, his body parts had likely hit all the surfaces of the inside of the car. Logan had seen enough IR pilot footage of terrorists blown to white smithereens to know what a 20mm cannon did to the human body. He also knew the moment to act was upon him, and he aimed at the window above and fired in quick succession.

The window shattered, but Logan knew that the man inside probably thought it was incoming fire from the helicopter. *Now or never,* he thought, and reached upward with one hand and then the other, pulling himself over the lip of the bench seat and through the crumbling window, careful to avoid the jagged glass falling around him.

Logan fell onto the seat, aware that the 20mm rounds had suddenly stopped. His mind captured everything inside the interior of the cramped cable car in a quick snapshot. *Dark figure kneeling. Doesn't see me yet. Weapon pointed out.* And through the other side of the cable car, he saw the support tower looming closer in the darkness. *At least I won't get knocked off this thing,* he thought.

Unfortunately, two things simultaneously happened that ruined his optimism: a loud wrenching sound vibrated through the car, as if a tin can were being torn apart and the sound magnified by a thousand; and his target's head turned toward him in the darkened close quarters.

Logan lashed out with his right foot, and the black machine pistol was knocked from the shadow man's hands, clipped the top lip of the cable car doors where the glass had been, and careened through the empty space down to the mountainside below. *At least now I have a chance to take this sonofabitch alive.*

The man stood and backed away at the same time, the back of his legs stopping against the edge of the opposite seat.

"I don't know if you speak English, and I don't care. If you move, I'm shooting you in both legs. So stand still until we get to the station," Logan said. The man didn't respond, which told Logan he understood either his words or his tone. It didn't matter which.

Two loud pops echoed inside the car, and Logan's view of the world outside tilted crazily as the left side of the car dropped, sending both men plummeting to the floor toward the ruined doors and the darkness beyond.

Cole Matthews was not accustomed to good fortune, even when it presented itself to him in a nice little package, wrapped in a bow of irony.

Once he'd reached the top of the roof, he'd found no trace of the man who'd stolen his Glock. He'd been confused, refusing to believe his enemy had jumped from the rooftop to his death below. Cole hadn't seen a parachute on him. He acknowledged that one could've been staged on the rooftop, in which case his Glock and the man who held it were likely sailing down the side of the mountain like Batman through Gotham City.

But then he'd found the rope tied to the base of the radio tower, wrapped around a support beam, from where it trailed over the edge of the roof.

He stared at the man rappelling down the side of the building and smiled to himself. And he waited. *Should've kept the axe, asshole. This is what you get for stealing my Glock.*

The man passed the middle of the hotel and picked up speed. He kicked off the side of the hotel as he bounced his way down. Cole figured he'd be at the bottom in another fifteen seconds. *You're going to get there faster than you anticipated.*

He stepped back away from the edge, positioned himself, counted to five, and forcefully swung the axe over his head.

With a tremendous impact that sent vibrations shooting up his arms, the axe split the rope, and Cole either imagined or heard a faint scream that was abruptly cut off two seconds later. He smiled in the darkness, walked back to the ledge, and looked over the side.

A figure lay unmoving at the base of the hotel fourteen floors below. Cole didn't think he was dead, but he also didn't care if he was, not really. He'd roughly calculated to drop the man from two to three stories, his intent to break his legs and incapacitate him. *Better get down there just in case he wakes up.*

Cole turned, climbed down from the top of the roof one level at a time carrying his newfound favorite weapon, eager to link up with Hector to see if he'd been able to salvage any intelligence from the burning penthouse.

Logan's feet hit the steel bottom of the left door, and he found himself leaning backward against the floor at a forty-five-degree angle. The cable car rocked back and forth, even as it barreled toward the support tower, the motion sending a moment of panic racing through Logan as he realized a crash was imminent. *No way we make it through the gap between the beams now. Have to get off this thing or I'm dead. Other guy can fend for himself.*

Logan turned to his right as the man he'd pursued across the hotel, who'd also braced himself against the bottom of the right-side door, locked eyes with him and had the same epiphany— *Escape or die.*

Logan rotated and struck the man in the face with his left fist before he could react. The blow landed on the man's cheekbone, splitting the skin. He saw blood, glistening black in the darkness, flow down the man's cheek. The man raised his hands to defend himself, and Logan delivered a second blow, which sent the man's own fist crashing into the side of his nose. Hands in the air, Logan focused on the man's body, which had been the main target all along. It was just like boxing, except in reverse and for survival, not a championship belt. *Weaken the head to get to the body.*

Logan pivoted to his right and delivered a series of powerful blows to the man's rib cage. He felt at least one crack, and the man keeled over like a drunk outside a bar after a hard night of drinking.

Logan reached for the man's head when a tremendous crash roared as the cable car slammed into the bottom support beam of the tower. The impact sent him sprawling forward into the bent-over enemy, and both men hit the juncture where the floor met the bottom of the doors.

The car suddenly lurched up, as if the gears on top were going to grind it through the space, crushing the car between the beams. Sparks from the machinery above cascaded over the sides of the car, illuminating the inside with twinkling flashes of synthetic light. The car suddenly stopped its short ascent and dropped back down two feet, jarring to an abrupt halt as Logan felt a moment of weightlessness. The left side of the door was flung open, swinging wildly down and out—*like my luck,* Logan thought—and then everything was still. The two men were motionless, as if stunned by the violent turn of events. *I need to get the hell out of here,* Logan thought. *Have to climb out the door and up.*

Two loud metallic pops exploded above the car, and both men were spurred into action.

The man uttered something in Russian, and Logan cursed himself as he recognized the language. *It's always the goddamned Russians. What is it with these guys? Can't we all just get the fuck along?*

Apparently, the Russian did not share the same sentiment, as he tried to pull Logan's legs from underneath him, shouting in Russian at Logan.

Logan West was exhausted from the chase, but his adrenaline surged, along with the rage he'd been fighting for months after the death of Mike Benson. *This bastard is another shadow puppet in the Organization's play. No mercy, Logan. It's you or him. Climb or die,* he heard Mike say inside his head. *Damn straight,* Logan replied, and lashed out with his left foot, striking the Russian on the side of the jaw with his Oakley hiking boot. The man's head snapped backward, and he slumped to the floor, either dazed or unconscious. Logan didn't care which.

Now for the hard part, he thought, as he braced his left foot against the inclined floor and stepped up onto the bottom of the right-side door where the glass had been before being shot out by the helicopter, which now hovered one hundred yards away, as if waiting to attack again.

Logan didn't know what else to do, so he waved at the pilot, praying he wouldn't be torn apart by automatic cannon fire. The nose of the helicopter moved up and down slightly in acknowledgment, and Logan nodded, more to himself in relief than to the pilot. He turned and stepped up through the empty window, reaching for the safety bar above the doors. He grasped the bar, shoulder width apart, and said a prayer of thanks to the Marine Corps for the thousands of pull-ups he'd performed during his service. "Semper Fi, motherfucker," he muttered, and pulled himself up until his upper body was above the top of the cable car.

He found himself staring at the bottom of a J-hook curved metal arm attached to a large square frame connected to the top of the cable car. Half of the frame had been wrenched away from the top of the car, either from the cannon fire or the impact. The tower was mere feet away, stretching vertically above and below him, the support beam level with his head. *Get on the roof and jump to the beam.*

As Logan reached for the bottom of the J-hook, he watched in horror as two more rivets popped like gunshots, and the frame peeled away from the roof like the top of a soup can being ripped open.

The car shuddered beneath him, and Logan grabbed on to a metal bar covered in rubber that jutted from the bottom of the J-hook. Two more rivets let loose, and the car dropped several inches. *You have seconds, jackass. Move or die!*

Logan West scrambled to the roof of the ruined cable car, with only one thought, singular in purpose—*get off this death trap.* Ignoring the howling wind, the roar of the helicopter, and the dizzying height, he exhaled, focused on the support beam, and leapt from the roof of the cable car.

His chest slammed into the metal beam, and for a moment, he thought he'd bounce off and to his death below, but his arms held tight, and his boots found a footing on a crossbeam. He turned to look at the top of the car, wondered how soon before it fell to the trees and pavement eighty feet below, and was greeted by the face and upper body of the Russian, who'd regained his composure from Logan's blow and followed his lead up and out of the car.

The man screamed in Russian, and Logan replied, "English! I don't speak Russian!"

In a thick accent, the man spoke loudly, "Will you help me?"

Logan was transported in his mind to the Nile River, when he'd been forced to make a similar choice as a monstrous crocodile had silently stalked him and the man he'd captured in the river moments before. It had been startlingly simple—use the man for bait or die. He'd cut Namir Badawi across the chest and swum for his life. He'd made the right call, and the Sudanese intelligence chief had died a horrifically violent death. But Logan had survived, which was what had mattered.

But this was different: there was no crocodile. There was just a man, an enemy he'd just bested in hand-to-hand combat, asking for help before he died. Logan West was many things—husband, warrior, killer, Marine, soon-to-be father—but his moral compass was guided by the innate desire to help others, even enemy combatants. *And that's what this middle-aged man is. A warrior. I can see it in him, on his face.* His decision was made.

"Get on the roof and jump and grab my arm," Logan replied loudly. He wrapped his left arm around the top of the support beam, rotated his body so that he was perpendicular to the tower, and extended his right arm. "But if you try anything, I swear to all the gods that I will drop you. Do you understand me?"

The Russian nodded and scrambled to the rooftop and pulled his legs up behind him. He rested for a brief moment, his back

113

against the J-hook, but the moment was all it took for calamity to strike.

"Move it or—" were the last words the Russian heard as the remaining rivets on the frame exploded upward, freeing the cable car beneath it.

The Russian realized his death was imminent, that he'd run out of time, and he looked at Logan with a resolve that Logan recognized. *He's facing it like a warrior.* The Russian nodded, acknowledging that an enemy he didn't know had been willing to help him in his final moments, even if he'd failed, and then he was gone, plummeting to his death below on top of the ruined cable car.

The cable and J-hook, free of their burden, sprang upward, and Logan sidestepped to his left to avoid being slashed by the flailing metal. He gripped the crossbeam for dear life and waited.

A second later, the earth shook and the tower vibrated violently as the cable car crashed to the ground inches from the base. Logan prayed that the tower, as ancient as the hotel, didn't collapse, as he looked toward the helicopter and pointed down.

The pilot understood and slowly began to circle the area, spotlight flashing across the park grounds as it looked for an area with enough clearance for the rotor blades.

With no imminent threat to life or limb, Logan descended the tower, wondering if Cole and Hector had succeeded. *Don't want to think about it if they didn't,* he thought. Too much blood had been sacrificed on the mountain. *Just focus on your footing, one foot, then the other. The rest will sort itself out. It always does.*

Logan knew this to be true, and reached the ground safely. As he stepped off the tower, he was confronted with the remains of the cable car, which had crumpled inward at the impact. The Russian's body had been sucked back inside, and all that was visible were two forearms sticking up at awkward angles.

I tried. I'm sorry. But Logan knew a hard truth—not everyone was saved. Intentions had no place on the mountain. The Russian had chosen the wrong side, and he'd paid for it with his life. The finality of it crystallized the issue for Logan. *If you're not with us, you're against us.* And Logan knew that was a place that evil men did not want to be.

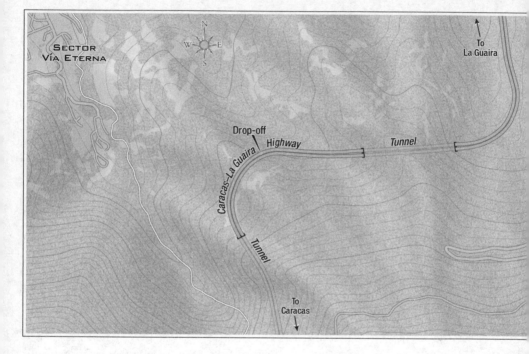

PART III

OLD FRIENDS

CHAPTER 16

The knowledge that he was standing in the most notorious detention facility in Venezuela, a place that housed political dissidents, criminals, and anyone else the regime deemed an enemy of the state, sickened Logan West. He knew Cole felt it too. While it was not as full of degradation as the Sudanese black-site prison that he and Cole had fought their way out of, it was still oppressive, intended to break a man's will and crush the human spirit. After only a few hours in the underground facility, he had no doubt it likely had a one hundred percent success rate.

It was widely reported by the press and family members of its captives that the facility, known as La Tumba—the Tomb—subjected its political prisoners to a constant barrage of inhuman conditions while in captivity. Cells were painted white, and bright lights were kept on twenty-four hours a day to induce a form of white torture that caused the prisoners to lose track of time. The only sounds were from the Metro Caracas railway cars that passed through nearby tunnels. Additionally, temperatures were freezing, cells didn't have individual toilets, and the prisoners suffered malnutrition and hallucinations.

Now, having been a witness to the real thing, Logan could confirm that the reports were all true. He was present in a place of evil and suffering, forced to choke back the waves of anger that relentlessly assaulted his conscience. He had the feel of being in the mouth of madness, a place suffocating and overwhelming, and he knew that if he spent too much time in it, it would threaten to consume a part of him.

Just breathe, Logan, he calmed himself, as he looked at the closed-circuit TV and listened to the conversation in the cell three doors down from the monitoring room.

As if reading his mind, Cole said, "Just the mission, brother. We're not here for anything else. He put himself in that room."

He's right, and you know it. Yet Logan also knew that they were on shifting moral sands on this one. Enemies had become friends, adversaries had become allies, and one had nearly died for their mutual cause. He'd had to shift his paradigm. The old ways and codes of conduct were gone. It was a different, merciless geopolitical world with new rules of war.

"That's true to a certain extent," Logan replied. "More precisely, the puppet masters that *ordered* him and his unit here are the real ones responsible. He was just doing his job, just like we were. The only difference is that we're much better at it than they are." *Because you've had too much practice in the dark art of bloodshed over the past two and a half years,* his psyche reminded him. *But I didn't ask for it. It came to my doorstep. Remember that.*

"And thank God for that," Cole replied. "In fact, the Russian major in there should be grateful for it. He's lucky to be alive, and I'm pretty sure he knows it."

After Logan had survived the chaos on the cable car, he'd linked back up in the lobby of the hotel to find Hector, Santiago, Cole, and the lone Spetsnaz survivor, Major Fedor Azarov, waiting for him. Even before Logan had run back up the cobblestone street, Hector had retrieved their packs from the tree line, and Cole had bound, gagged, and blindfolded the Russian to prevent him from observing others as he was transported to the Tomb.

Unfortunately, the fire in the penthouse of the Humboldt had destroyed everything inside the suite before burning out, preserving the historic landmark, but Hector had grabbed the remains of two shattered Toughbook laptops with Cyrillic keypads. Logan had no idea what the SEBIN's digital forensics unit was like, but he doubted that they'd be able to retrieve anything actionable in the near term, which was when he knew they'd need it. The FBI lab in Quantico was out of the picture, since it would take at least a day to get the laptops back to the States, too little, too late.

No. Whatever happened next would be determined by Major Azarov and the intelligence he was willing to reveal.

The conversation stopped inside the interrogation room, and Hector and Santiago slid their metal chairs back from the table, stood up without another word, and exited the room, leaving the shackled Russian chained to a thick loop on top of the table. Moments later, the two men entered the monitoring room.

Logan waited for Santiago to begin. It was his show, at least inside the Tomb, and Logan respected the professional boundaries.

"Major Fedor Azarov, second in command of an elite Russian VDV Spetsnaz unit that was ordered to provide electronic SIGINT force protection, as well as electronic communications jamming, as part of a mil-to-mil agreement between the Russians and the Venezuelan army," Santiago said. "They thought it was part of an exercise, but they'd been briefed by their commanding officer, the one you killed, that there could be a real threat by hostile forces unknown, which is why they had live ammunition and protective measures in place."

"That's a convenient cover story," Cole replied. "No way he thought that, especially as the second in command."

"You watched the interrogation," Santiago responded. "He might be lying about some things, but I believe he's telling some of the truth as well. He looks shell-shocked and devastated at the knowledge that we just wiped out his entire unit except him. He's in disbelief."

Logan nodded. He could relate. Both he and John had been in that *exact* emotional hole after their Force Reconnaissance platoon had been ambushed just outside of Fallujah, Iraq, at an insurgent compound. They'd been misled by a CIA officer into believing one of Saddam Hussein's HVTs had been using it as a bed-down location. There was no HVT, and most of Logan's platoon had been brutally slaughtered, killed in the initial mortar attack or executed by the insurgent leader as the Marines who'd survived the barrage lay dying. While Logan and John and the remaining Marines had fought their way out of it and killed every last insurgent, that day had led to Logan's separation from the Marine Corps and a downward spiral into depression and alcoholism. Fortunately, he'd come back from the brink when the Organization had brought their shadow war to his house in Annapolis, Maryland. But he knew how the Russian felt, and he could genuinely commiserate with him.

"Let me talk to him, while you translate," Logan said to Santiago. "Once he hears what I have to say, whatever he's holding back, he'll tell us. Trust me on this one."

Santiago nodded. Logan West was the reason his precious Camila had been given a fighting chance. And he'd already proven himself to be the fierce warrior and leader that Santiago had been led to believe he was. Whatever the American needed or wanted, Santiago would provide. "Let's give it a try."

"You're not going to go Amira on him, are you?" Cole asked, the subtlest concern in his voice. Amira Cerone had used one of her stilettos to slice off a Chinese prisoner's finger after they'd been ambushed in Khartoum. Logan and Cole had been kidnapped, and she'd gone straight to the most extreme measures, no small talk or niceties beforehand.

"No. He's been through enough, and I don't need to. Trust me on this, brother," Logan said.

Cole nodded. "Good luck."

Less than a minute later, Logan and Santiago sat across from Major Fedor Azarov.

Up close and under the bright white lights, combined with physical exhaustion and stress, the Russian looked ragged, the tolls of the earlier combat worn like a battle mask. No more than thirty-five, the man had short brown hair and a short beard, but like Logan, no matter how hard he tried to blend in with a civilian environment, the military and warrior mind-set shone through. It was always the eyes, alert, inquisitive, and prepared.

Fedor looked at Logan with a combined expression of hostility, interest, and concern, as if internally assessing whether or not the newcomer was a threat.

"Do you speak English, Major Azarov?" Logan asked, meeting the man's gaze.

"I do," Fedor replied in a thick Russian accent. "It's one of the unit requirements, especially for what we were and where we operated." The past tense was intentional, laced with contempt, but the implication was clear: they had been global.

"I figured as much," Logan replied, nodding in confirmation. "Do you know who I am?"

"The man responsible for killing my brothers, my friends. The devil in the flesh," Fedor answered, the anger spilling forth from him in a flurry of words.

Santiago sat quietly, waiting for Logan to respond, *to see* how he would respond to the verbal assault.

"That anger you're feeling, you're going to hold on to it. You're going to tell yourself that evil men killed your friends and comrades. At first, it's going to fuel you, like the world's worst, most poisonous energy. But you're going to welcome it, because it will remind you that you survived. You'll train harder, once your injuries heal, to make sure what happened to you never happens again. And you'll think that dark rage is your friend, focusing your mind, body, and soul. And you'll welcome it." Logan leaned forward, Fedor's attention fixed solely on the intense man in front of him. "But I know something you don't, and I would not lie to a fellow warrior, even on the opposite side of the battlefield: it's going to destroy you, corrupt you from the inside, erode your ability to think professionally, and chip away at the clear lines of your moral compass, until one day, you won't remember the man you were. And on that day, you will be so distraught that you will become self-destructive, maybe to the point of taking your own life, maybe not. But mark my words, it *will* happen."

"Why do you speak of such things?" Fedor asked after a moment, controlling the rage that seethed beneath.

"Because what happened to you happened to me in Iraq in 2004, when most of the Marines under my command were slaughtered by an evil butcher motivated by religious extremism and a thirst for blood," Logan stated bluntly.

"And how are you *different* from the man that killed your Marines?" Fedor challenged.

"I'm not motivated by religious extremism, greed, power, or influence. I don't care about *any* of those things. The only thing I do care about is stopping the chaos that has been spreading across the globe over the past few years, stopping innocent people from getting killed as a result of a shadow war raging between two sides of a secret organization, the *same* organization that sent your unit here," Logan finished, allowing his words to sink into the man's battered psyche.

Logan sat back, waiting. Santiago was motionless beside him.

"What are you talking about?" Fedor replied. "The colonel told us this was part of an exercise. I told him that as well," he said, nodding at Santiago. "That's the truth."

"No," Logan said. "That's the truth he wanted you to believe. I'm sorry to tell you, he used your unit, your *motto*, to control you. He may have been your leader, your comrade, your brother-in-arms, but he still used you. I know this to be true, as do you, even if you won't admit it."

The briefest of cracks appeared momentarily on the Russian's face, revealing the internal struggle at knowledge he wished he could deny. *It's not going to be that easy,* Logan thought. *Keep pressing.*

"Let me ask you something," Logan said, leaning across the table. "Did you talk to anyone in your chain of command, other than your colonel? And if not, was that normal?"

Fedor paused, but after a moment he said, "Usually we have a brief with our brigade commander, but for this deployment the colonel activated the team, and we left Kubinka the next day." More silence, before he added, "But that doesn't prove anything. The colonel told us that it was a last-minute request from the Venezuelan government, channeled through our embassy here. You know who we are, what we've done, where we go. While out of the normal, it wasn't unheard of."

Logan considered the response and knew that Fedor either believed the explanation or at least wanted to. Logan needed to hammer home the reality for him, to get him to break through his denial.

"I'm tired, Fedor," Logan said honestly, surprising the Russian. "I've killed more men than I care to remember. Do you remember the Russian unit operating in Alaska last year? It made international news after being leaked. Our government sucks at keeping secrets, but that's another matter. More importantly, your government disavowed knowledge of that unit and actually provided a dossier on every one of the team. They too, like you, had been sent on a mission, but not by your government."

"That was you, wasn't it, who killed them?" Fedor asked, the truth beginning to dawn in the dark crevices of his mind.

"It was, just like I killed your team tonight, or at least some of them," Logan added. "I didn't want to, but I didn't have a choice. Your comrades ambushed us, and no matter what, like you, *I will not fail my mission*." Logan paused intentionally for effect. *Come on, Fedor. Take the bait. Ask me.*

"What exactly is your mission?" Fedor asked.

Bingo. Gotcha. Game over. "To find the vice president of the United States, who has not been captured by a militia, if you've been paying attention to the news, but in fact has betrayed his own country, is responsible for the deaths of scores of people, and fled the US like the coward that he is."

For the first time, a look of concern washed away some of the hostility, as the real danger and the implications of this story presented themselves. "Why are you telling me this? What does this have to do with me or my unit?"

"Because whether you know it or not, the vice president is either here or on his way here, and you have been helping make that happen," Logan said.

Real anguish broke through the Russian's features, as the gravity of what he'd been a part of was laid bare for him to behold. He and his unit had been betrayed by their commanding officer and misled to their deaths. The emotional pain was palpable in the room.

Logan remembered the rage he'd felt toward the deceased CIA officer who'd done the same thing to Logan and his Marines, albeit under much different circumstances. While he empathized with the Russian, he didn't have the luxury of time. *Make him see it all for what it is, and give him the choice.*

"Here's the brutal truth, Fedor. I didn't want to kill you or your comrades. In fact, I tried to save your commander before the cable car broke free with him on top of it, sending him to his death. It's the truth. I have no war with you, but I swear to God as my witness, that I am at war with those that are helping our traitorous vice president, and I will stop at *nothing* to find him, literally. And you have unfortunately found yourself in my crosshairs, with only one choice left to make—and it's an easy one. Do you want to live?"

Fedor realized in that moment that he had no options. The American was a man possessed, and he would not be denied.

"One of two things is going to happen," Logan continued. "You are either going to tell me everything I need to know, no matter how small, after which you will be remanded to your embassy here when this is over, or you will spend the remainder of your days here in this hellhole. And trust me—this place will drive you insane. You can feel it, can't you?" Logan asked. "That's what it's intended to do, to break a man's spirit and will. I personally despise the fact that places like this exist, but like I told you, my mission comes first. So I ask you, one time—do you want to live, Major Fedor Azarov, or do you want to die slowly, quietly, as you sink into madness?"

Fedor answered in less than five seconds. "Before I answer, I have one question."

"Go ahead," Logan said, more out of curiosity than concern.

"What happened to the man who killed your men?" Fedor asked, legitimate interest in his voice.

When Logan answered, he spoke quickly in order to control the pain and anger that still resided just below the surface of those memories. "Myself, my platoon sergeant, and a handful of Marines survived the initial attack. We ambushed the insurgents as they tried to come inside the compound we were pinned down in.

We ended up flanking the remaining enemy, killing all of them, including their mortar teams, with fifty-caliber machine guns mounted on their own pickup trucks," Logan added. There was no doubt Fedor knew what a .50-caliber round did to the human body.

"What about the insurgent leader?" Fedor asked.

"I killed him myself," Logan said, an edge to his voice, remembering the moment he'd pulled the trigger of his Kimber Tactical II .45-caliber pistol. The insurgent leader had been lying on his back, hit multiple times from Logan's M4, but he'd executed the dying man for the evil he'd wrought. *And I'd do it again.* "Now, for the last time—and I won't ask again, just so we're clear—do you want to live?"

"Yes. I do," Fedor said, resigned to his fate and praying to himself that these men would honor their word. He thought they would, but regardless, it was now out of his hands.

Logan nodded, as if it'd been the easiest decision in the world. "Good. Then let's talk."

CHAPTER 17

"What now?" Cole said, weariness in his voice. "All we have is a time."

"Honestly, I don't know, but the only thing I can do is call Jake and have him talk to Director Toomey," Logan said, referring to the director of the CIA. "If anyone can shift national intelligence real-time resources, he can. Maybe we get a break; maybe not."

Fedor had told them about a force protection operation scheduled for 0900 the next morning. In addition to the communications equipment on top of the hotel, they had several SUVs with tactical SIGINT gear, which included equipment for SIGINT terminal guidance, electronic jamming to prevent the detonation of remote-controlled IEDs, and capturing data from nearby cellular devices. The plan was to rally at the Russian safe house in the Capital District and provide communications overwatch while a convoy transported its cargo.

Unfortunately, the only person who'd known the location was Colonel Grigori Sokolov, whom Logan had been unable to save.

Only two more seconds and he would've lived, and we'd know where the vice president would be in the morning. Come on, God. Throw us a bone.

"Santiago, get him in a cell and ask them to turn the lights off. He's been through hell. He deserves some sleep," Logan said.

"We'll take care of him until this is over," Santiago said.

"Good," Logan replied. "I want to keep my word. I don't want anything to happen to the major. There's no need for it, and he doesn't deserve it. He was doing his job, just like all of us."

"Understood. No harm will come to him," Santiago said. "I assure you. Even we can be men of honor," he finished, and left the room.

Logan's encrypted iPhone, which sat on top of the table, suddenly vibrated, startling him. Cole and Hector exchanged glances and looked back apprehensively at the phone.

"God, I really hate it when your phone rings, brother," Cole said. "It's either really great news, like you won the lottery, or something horrific and awful."

Logan ignored him, staring at the flashing "Unknown" on the Retina display. "Well, I guess there's nothing left to do but find out."

Logan picked up the phone, hit the accept button, pressed the speaker button, and placed it back on the table, ready for the full spectrum of news.

"Hey, Logan," retired General Jack Longstreet and former commandant of the Marine Corps said. "How's Venezuela treating you so far?"

Logan briefly squeezed his eyes shut, both relieved and pensive at the voice of his onetime commanding officer, a warrior and mentor he'd fought alongside with in Iraq in 2004 after their convoy had been ambushed on the way from the government center in Ramadi. More recently, after the events of three weeks ago at Con-

stantine Kallas's house and after learning about the role Jack Longstreet had played for the Organization upon retirement from the
Marine Corps, the pedestal upon which he'd once placed the man
had eroded significantly. He was still a man of purpose, a Marine,
and one of the alleged good guys, trying to right several wrongs he
and his former employer had wrought upon the world. But Logan
no longer considered him a modern-day Chesty Puller. Now, he
was a convenient ally in the struggle against chaos and instability.
Logan still considered him a brother-in-arms, but the luster in the
relationship had dulled with every revelation about Jack's involvement. Yet here he was, calling Logan once again.

"I thought you were off the grid, gone hunting for rogue Organization elements and all that," Logan said.

"I have been, but as you know, I go where the work takes me,"
Jack said.

"Let me guess," Logan replied. "Could you be in South America, say in a special socialist country in the midst of civil strife and
turmoil? A country that begins with the letter *V*?"

Jack let out a short laugh and said, "I always said you were
smarter than most."

"Thanks for the vote of confidence," Logan said, "but please get
to the point. It's been a long night, and I've got places to be, people
to shoot."

Hector, who'd been watching Logan throughout the conversation, glanced at Cole, who looked up at the white ceiling and
shook his head in mock exasperation.

"That's why I'm calling," Jack said.

"And?" Logan asked.

"I know *exactly* where you need to be, as well as why," Jack said,
a note of confidence and satisfaction in his voice.

"I'm telling you, Jack," Logan said, "one of these days, you're
going to make a promise you can't keep."

"Trust me. I can keep this one," Jack said. "And you want to know why?"

"Do I have to?" Logan said in a tired voice.

"Only if you want to capture that sonofabitch traitor and one-time vice president," Jack said.

And there it is, the carrot dangling before the stick, Logan thought, and listened as the thirty-sixth commandant of the Marine Corps told him where the vice president would be in a little more than seven hours. *No rest for the weary.*

CHAPTER 18

Lieutenant General Cordones ended the call after trying to reach the Russian Spetsnaz colonel for the third time in the last hour. His aide had awakened him per his very specific instructions once the aide had seen the breaking news story on Globovision, Venezuela's 24-hour news network.

Cameras and cell phones from across the city had captured a fire at the top of the hotel, as well as a helicopter circling the area for several minutes before landing and leaving the mountain. As soon as he'd seen the footage in his command post office, he'd summoned his communications officer and asked him to scan all local police and SEBIN networks they listened to, but after an hour, the seasoned major had come back with nothing to report. There'd been no police or military operation on the mountain, *at least none that had been officially sanctioned,* he'd thought at the moment.

Since then, he'd tried unsuccessfully to reach Grigori, and after the latest attempt, he accepted the fact that the Spetsnaz unit—or at least Grigori, at a minimum—had been removed from the field of play. By whom and why, he had no idea, but it was irrelevant. All that mattered was that Grigori had ensured that the Spetsnaz soldiers knew the time and route tomorrow for the vice president's convoy—*the one that I gave them, for this precise reason.* It was the bait that he'd planted at the hotel, a diversionary tactic he'd thought was a bit of overkill at the time. But here he was, in the middle of the night, thanking his methodical training and preparation for anticipating the possibility that the mountaintop communications team might be compromised.

He stood outside the entrance to his command post and stared at the black forest that encircled the plateau, breathing deeply and calmly as he listened to the cacophony of night sounds—the insects, the predators, the prey, the rustling of leaves—allowing it to calm his mind. The animals in the forest had adapted to the military installation, learning to stay away from the men with guns. He'd heard an occasional jaguar, but the big cats were smart, not suicidal.

Victor was confident that any trespassers—feline *or* human— would be dealt with quickly by the reinforced platoon of special forces soldiers he'd personally selected for the mission from the 509th Special Operations Battalion. Not only lethal experts in jungle warfare, they'd trained for months in the shoot house on the plateau, honing their close-quarter combat skills to a razor's edge. *And tomorrow will be the first time they get to cut into the corrupt flesh at the top of the country's ladder.*

In moments like this, his mind wandered to his lost son, a fresh stab of suffering and grief breaking over him in soul-crushing waves. But then he focused, breathed deeply, and exhaled, numbing the pain with the knowledge that by tomorrow afternoon, the political landscape of the country of Venezuela would be changed forever. Once he had the vice president secure, the rest would fall into place.

By this time tomorrow, I may be alive, I may be with my son, but no matter what, Venezuela will be better off than it is at this moment.

He looked up at the night sky, the stars burning brightly in the clear air, said a small prayer, and turned back to the barracks building that housed his quarters.

Tomorrow would be a trying day, and every minute of rest mattered, especially when he didn't know when the next sleep would come, and when it did, whether it would be the long, dark one.

CHAPTER 19

"Tell me again, are you sure of this, Jack?" Logan asked the barrel-chested former Marine Corps commandant who stood next to him. The two men stared down the side of the multitiered dirt-road hill above the curve in the Caracas–La Guaira Highway just below them. The morning traffic had lightened between Caracas and the main port of La Guaira, but vehicles sped past in both directions, oblivious to the men above them who plotted impending chaos. "This is the only lead we've had, and you know it. All we got from the Russian was a time and that the vice president is being transported via convoy along this route."

The portion of the highway before them was shaped like a question mark that lay flat on the ground, bracketed at both ends of the two-thirds-of-a-mile-long section by two tunnels. The short one to their right led east to the port, and the longer one to their left past the curve ran due south for more than a mile toward Caracas. The section between the tunnels was a natural choke point, if they successfully blocked off the four tunnel entrances.

"That's partially true," Jack Longstreet replied. "You have the time right. It's going to happen in ten minutes, but the how is what you have wrong because it's what the vice president and General Cordones *want you to believe*. This is the only way to get to Caracas from the Caribbean, at least without drawing attention."

"Your source had better be correct, or our last lead is going to be a dead end," Logan said, an edge to his voice. It'd been less than three weeks since he'd found out that his onetime mentor had executed the director of the National Security Agency in a brazen attack on the Baltimore–Washington Parkway. The fact that Marine Corps General Taylor was a true traitor to his flag and country was the only thing that had spared Jack from the president's wrath. *That and the fact that he's been helping you since. He owes you for Ramadi, and he knows it.*

"I'm one hundred percent confident in my source, Logan. Trust me on this one. It's personal for him, and he actually wants the vice president dead. Like I told you last night, this country is dying, and the people are bleeding out on the streets, literally and figuratively. You've seen the stories: the government and military are in bed with the cartels and organized crime lords, and the good General Cordones is using both of them for his own means," Jack said.

"In exactly eight minutes from now, a three-vehicle military convoy is going to travel west out of that tunnel. It's the decoy, intended to draw people like us to it like lemmings to a cliff."

"You got something against small, cute rodents?" Logan interrupted, even as his mind evaluated the approaching storm.

"I thought John was the funny one," Jack shot back. "Now shut up and listen," he added with a tinge of impatience. "Less than a minute behind the convoy will be a dark-green Land Rover with tinted windows. It's being driven by three members of a local cartel that's part of the *megabandas*, criminal groups involved in all kinds of bad things down here. In that vehicle will be the vice president. My source is certain of it."

"Because it's personal for him? That's all I get?" Logan pressed.

Jack paused. "This particular gang—they murdered the source's wife while trying to get to him. They killed her with a machete when they found her home while he was out. He found her mutilated corpse at their home in Maracaibo. He's not the same man that I knew several years ago. I don't think anyone would be. So if he says the vice president's in a green Land Rover, I'd bet my life on it. In fact, I have, as well as yours, Cole's, and your new friend's."

The evil that men do, Logan thought, not wanting to let his mind drift toward the dark place, the one where he saw himself in the source's shoes, imagining what he would do if something like that happened to Sarah. *It almost did. Once.*

"I still can't believe they won't fly him in a helo. Putting him at risk like this seems so much more dangerous to me," Logan said.

"It is," Jack said, "but apparently Cordones doesn't want to draw attention to himself in any way before his exercise kicks off. *And you know how dangerous helicopter rides can be.* If the vice president dies in a crash, whatever he has that's so important dies and burns up with him."

Logan's experience included enough close calls in helicopters—including one crash into the Euphrates River in Iraq more than two and a half years ago—to last a lifetime. As fearless as he could be, he was always aware that when he flew in a helicopter he was truly not in control. While the odds of a crash were low, after all the things that Logan had done in the Marine Corps, it was the one thing that had always unnerved him: he despised being helpless, and flying in a CH-46 or CH-53E across Iraq, hydraulic fluid leaking onto his pack, had reinforced to him just how much he was.

"Okay, then," Logan said, and looked across the highway and down the side of the hill to a neighborhood several hundred feet below them. "Let's get back to the SUVs and get our game faces on. It's about to get exciting."

"It always does with you," Jack added.

"Wrong," Logan said. "With us. Your retirement hasn't exactly had you sitting by the fire and reading history books or thrillers. You've got just as much blood on your hands as I do." *And if things go sideways, more is about to come.*

The plan was simple, as the best ones were. The only challenge would be the timing, but sixty seconds—if the Land Rover kept its distance from the three-vehicle convoy—would be plenty to work with on the road below. Logan and Jack had driven the road and had timed it between forty-five and fifty seconds to traverse the entire open length.

Once the three Tiuna multipurpose military vehicles exited the east tunnel, the hardest part of the operation would commence—waiting for the green Land Rover. When the target vehicle had been spotted, two things had to happen simultaneously: the three Tiunas needed to cross the open distance and enter the next tunnel, and the Land Rover had to be between the tunnels. When the Tiunas and the soldiers that they carried were no longer a threat, Jack's mercenary squad of former operators would use the three Russian communications tracking and jamming SUVs—with the jammers on to ensure reinforcements were not called—to block the entrance to the western tunnel, sealing the Land Rover in the linear ambush area.

While that happened, a group of the source's friends or gang members—Jack hadn't told Logan what they were, and at this point, Logan didn't care, as long as they did their jobs—on Chinese motorcycles would trail, pass, and then slow down in front of the Land Rover, using one of the city's major nuisances to their advantage.

Caracas was plagued by roving bands of motorcyclists, known

as *motorizados*, responsible for endless unintentional accidents, as well as intentional kidnappings and homicides. The opposition to the current regime viewed them as part of the criminal underworld, tied to the government, although most of the cyclists claimed they were just trying to earn a living any way they could, using cheap transportation to do so. Regardless of their true purpose, Logan had seen that the presence of the bikers, who obeyed only the traffic laws of chaos theory, created vehicular mayhem almost everywhere they rolled. The vice president's driver wouldn't think twice about a few reckless motorcyclists who pulled in front of him.

As soon as the driver of the Land Rover was distracted and in position, Logan, Jack, Cole, and Santiago would execute their phase of the ambush, secure the vice president, and move to the extraction point.

It always seems so easy in the planning stage, Logan thought, as traffic flowed by in both directions thirty yards in front of the gray, box-shaped 2018 Mercedes AMG G65 621-horsepower SUV in which he sat. He still couldn't believe that Jack had been able to acquire the luxury SUV beasts on such short notice, no doubt from someone engaged in some kind of organized criminal enterprise.

Jack sat in the passenger seat, and Logan looked past him at Cole and Santiago in the second Mercedes G-Class parked next to them. He nodded at Cole, faced front, and waited as the final minutes ticked down.

The two SUVs were parked on the south side of the highway, in a dirt-road area at the base of the hill they'd been standing on minutes before. Small buildings on both sides of the road contained equipment that controlled the tunnel's ventilation system. A few pickup trucks were parked farther down the dirt, but no one glanced twice at the two SUVs that faced the highway.

The handheld radio in Jack's hand erupted, and a disembodied voice said, "Three Tiunas just exited the tunnel, heading your way. Estimated speed sixty miles per hour. Stand by for target confirmation."

Something about the voice made the flesh on the back of Logan's neck prickle. He knew the voice, but he couldn't place it, even though it set him on edge. "Who is that? That's your source, isn't it?"

"Not now," Jack replied curtly. "There's no time for this."

Logan inhaled and knew Jack was right. Whoever it was, wherever he knew him from, it could wait. He exhaled and allowed the battle calm with which he was familiar to wash over him, focusing his senses and smoothing the edge off his nerves.

Three olive-drab military SUVs appeared from their right as the Tiunas came around the curve. Four soldiers were in each one, and Logan was certain that their weapons had to be within arm's reach. More alarming was the M60 7.62mm machine gun straight out of *First Blood* turret-mounted on the back of the middle SUV, its gunner facing forward and swiveling the barrel back and forth from ten to two o'clock. *Just another reason to trap these guys in the tunnel.*

The three Tiunas barreled around the curve, when the voice reported over the encrypted UHF radio channel, "Green Land Rover just exited the tunnel, heading your way. Looks to be moving a little slower than the SUVs. Stand by."

Both the target and the threat were in the ambush zone. *A few more seconds and we'll be clear,* Logan thought, anticipation building at the thought of capturing the vice president and ending his flight from justice.

The three Tiunas rounded the curve and entered the final straightaway before the tunnel entrance. The Land Rover was still beyond the curve, out of sight. One hundred more yards, and the vehicles would be gone, the biggest threat neutralized by a man-made feature.

As the three SUVs closed the distance, the earth began to shake, slowly at first, building in intensity. Logan looked at Jack, horror and determination dawning on the retired general's face. "You've got to be motherfucking kidding me," Jack said.

Of all the things to go wrong, Logan thought, and dismissed it just as quickly. *Time to adapt or time to die.*

The Venezuelan drivers recognized the imminent danger, and traffic immediately slowed in both directions on all four lanes with the approaching wave of vibration, sound, and fury. The earth shook violently, and Logan watched hopelessly, already anticipating what was to come, as the three Tiunas slammed on their brakes and stopped fifteen yards short of the tunnel entrance.

Logan grabbed the handheld radio from Jack, depressed the talk button, and said, "Plan B. Motorcycle team, delay the soldiers any way you can. We're going to find the Land Rover and secure the vice president. Santiago, call in the extract and tell Hector to meet us at the east end of the highway near the other tunnels. We'll see you there. Out."

Hector was onboard the SEBIN Eurocopter AS532 Cougar with the pilot and copilot from last night, both of whom had been extended on their temporary detail to provide any and all air support to Santiago and his American friends. They had the bird in an air overwatch position, minutes away from the ambush area at the north end of the city, when they received Santiago's message.

Logan threw the radio back at Jack, shifted gears, and slammed the accelerator to the floor. The Mercedes SUV rocketed across the dirt road, its electronic traction system instantly gripping the dirt and loose rocks. Cole followed closely behind him in the second SUV.

With each passing second, the Caracas–La Guaira Highway was

becoming a parking lot as panicked drivers and motorcyclists halted in the middle of the road with nowhere to go. Mother Nature was its own merciless force that didn't care about geopolitical warfare, corrupt governments, or treasonous vice presidents. She had her own agenda, and there'd been no way to account for it ahead of time.

CHAPTER 20

If we make it out of this one, I'm never coming back to Venezuela, Logan thought as the front tires of the Mercedes reached the pavement. Logan swerved around the nose of a stopped white pickup truck as the intensity of the earthquake increased. *This is going to be a bad one,* he thought, and recalled the devastation from a quake near Caracas in the late 1960s. *God help us all.*

Logan glanced left and forced himself to remain calm as the tunnel entrance in front of the Tiunas crumbled inward, sending a mountain of dirt and rocks as if thrown by the hand of God onto the pavement. The taillights of a car inside the tunnel disappeared in a cloud of dirt and debris, and Logan hoped the driver had floored it, escaping deeper into the tunnel for refuge.

He turned back to the road, which started to buckle, and slammed the accelerator to the floor, swerving into the second lane of eastbound traffic. He avoided a young man on a motorcycle who saw the approaching Mercedes and ditched the bike onto its side rather than take the brunt of the SUV. Logan accelerated through the gap in the traffic barrier and crossed into the westbound traffic head-on.

A small, old green sedan crashed into the right rear quarter panel of the SUV, pushing the back end of the Mercedes several feet to the left before the V12 engine rocketed the Mercedes past the smaller car.

"Jesus Christ, if the earthquake or the Venezuelan army don't kill us, you're going to," Jack said quietly through clenched teeth.

"Shut it, Jack," Logan said, and concentrated on the maze of nearly stopped or parked vehicles in front of him.

The air was suddenly filled with a deafening roar, and Logan glanced right, only to see the hillside they'd been standing on minutes before slide into the eastbound traffic and cover cars as the earth devoured its human and metal victims. The resulting cloud of dirt and dust rolled into the westbound traffic and plunged the entire section of highway into a hellish tan darkness. *It's like an Iraqi sandstorm, minus the flashes of green lightning,* he thought, as he focused more intensely and slowed to navigate the treacherous highway, even as the earth continued to shake.

Even though the air-conditioning was on and the recirculation button had been depressed, tendrils of dust filled the cabin and swirled inside like a floating invisible jet stream.

"We're in the cloud," Jack said into the radio. "Does anyone have eyes on the Land Rover?"

A garbled response was audible from the handheld radio, followed by the distinct sounds of gunfire. *So much for tactical surprise,* Logan thought, and inched between a black Toyota Land Cruiser and the median.

The sounds of a crash to his left in the disorienting dark cloud sent a lurch through his stomach as he prayed they wouldn't take a hit head-on. Screams mixed with the rumbles and turned Logan's blood cold. *This is hell on earth. Right now, at this moment, this is hell.*

He forced himself to block it out, to compartmentalize the compassion he felt for the innocent caught in the chaos. He had one purpose—find the vice president and end his madness. He exhaled and drove forward, fingers clenching the luxurious leather of the steering wheel.

"Moving . . . two down . . . one . . . vehicle . . . fire," said an ethereal voice from the radio.

"Doesn't sound good," Jack said.

"No. It does not," Logan replied, "but if we don't get out of this nightmare, our chances of success crash to zero like the hills around us."

A large green van had hit the median, and Logan navigated the Mercedes to the left around the wreck. He glimpsed the panicked driver still at the wheel, helpless and shell-shocked in the maelstrom of sound and destruction. He glanced in the rearview mirror and saw nothing but swirling dust. *Cole, you better be on our six, brother.*

"Try him, Jack," Logan said.

Jack depressed the button on the radio. "Bravo Actual, you back there?" Jack asked.

No answer.

Holes appeared in the cloud, and random beams of sunlight pierced the roiling dirt and dust, as if the Sun God himself were shooting at point-blank range into the mass. Moments later, the Mercedes escaped the clutches of the cloud, and Logan and Jack both breathed a sigh of relief—until they saw the scene of carnage in front of them.

The Mercedes had reached the curve and now faced the long straightaway to the east tunnel. Chaos reigned, as Logan realized the earth had finally stopped shaking, though he was all too aware that aftershocks would be coming at some point.

Out of the swirling dust, Logan saw the east tunnel entrances had collapsed like the west ones, sealing the stretch of highway off in both directions from the rest of Caracas. Dazed drivers emerged from their vehicles, the initial shock creating confusion and disorientation. Logan already knew there was only one way out of the kill zone—down the side of the steep hill through the mountain forest to the district he'd spotted earlier, if it hadn't been destroyed in the initial quake. Soon, the other drivers would figure it out as well, which shifted Logan into his next gear, and he accelerated through the traffic.

"You see it? We need to find him before more people start exiting their vehicles and this turns into a shooting gallery full of innocent bystanders," Logan said.

"Then go faster," Jack commanded.

Logan saw the second Mercedes emerge from the cloud, which had begun to dissipate, *which will also eliminate the concealment we have from the three Tiunas. More good news. At least Cole and Santiago made it.*

"Got it," Jack said. "Seventy-five yards ahead, in the right lane, his right lane."

Logan's eyes shifted and immediately landed on the target. He saw the silhouettes of four men sitting in the SUV, and his adrenaline surged as he closed in on his quarry.

"What the hell are they doing?" Jack said.

"Trying to figure out what to do next and likely calling backup of some kind," Logan said.

A sudden sustained burst of machine-gun fire reverberated across the highway, no longer drowned out by the trembling of the ground.

"Here we go," Logan said. "Now it really starts."

Jack didn't respond, as he understood the wave of panic that would soon course through the throng of disoriented drivers. A natural disaster was one thing, but man-made violence was another. Screaming and running were next on the morning's agenda, and both men knew it.

"Get as close as you can, and once they start to react, we go," Jack said, as he pulled up a black bandanna to conceal the lower part of his face, his eyes already concealed by dark Oakley sunglasses.

The last piece of the ambush had been simple, as well as Santiago's idea. Other than Jack's source and his assets, who were dressed as normal Venezuelan bikers, the ambush team was adorned in tactical black fatigues with black Kevlar vests with "SEBIN" written across them in white letters. On their heads were black baseball caps with the SEBIN emblem. They'd briefly considered wearing Venezuelan army fatigues, but Santiago and Hector had emphasized one point above all else: because of the current political environment and oppression, people feared the SEBIN more and would respond more quickly in the middle of a chaotic situation. Logan and his team were about to test that hypothesis.

Logan accelerated the SUV and moved to the shoulder in order to minimize the obstacles. He glanced out the window and saw the edge of the mountain drop away into the forest only a few feet to his left. Absent guardrails, random trees and bushes were the only barriers to prevent a vehicle from plunging to its destruction below.

He closed the distance to fifty yards and heard Cole Matthews's voice erupt from the radio. "You two take twelve to three o'clock. We've got twelve to nine o'clock."

"Roger that," Jack said, and added, "Radio silence until this is over. Happy hunting."

Forty yards to the Land Rover . . . thirty yards . . . *almost there.*

Logan's luck ran out, and the driver and passenger in the front seat of the Land Rover pointed animatedly toward them. A moment later, the left rear door opened up, and two men emptied out onto the highway. Logan recognized the graying hair of the vice president—acutely remembering that he'd been fooled once before by an imposter in Northwest DC, mere weeks ago. A middle-aged man in his late thirties holding an all-black short-barreled version of an AK-47 7.62mm assault rifle propelled the vice president forward away from the vehicle.

Logan slammed the brakes of the Mercedes and turned the wheel to the right so that the vehicle slid to a halt, angled and facing the Land Rover directly. Cole Matthews executed a similar maneuver behind them.

"Let's do this," Logan said with determination, and Logan and Jack opened their doors. Sounds of gunfire a few hundred yards behind them mixed with screams and shouts. *Hope Jack's guys are taking it to them*, Logan thought, and exited the vehicle, his H&K 9mm MP5 with its red dot reflex scope at the ready position.

Instinctively recognizing that the two Mercedes SUVs had not arrived to assist them, the driver and front passenger of the Land Rover had already exited the vehicle. The passenger held an enormous shotgun with a modular, distinctive shape and a barrel that resembled that of an assault rifle. *Great. An AA-12 automatic shotgun. This is going to get loud.*

The passenger pulled the trigger and a series of *BOOMs* tore across the parking lot of the highway.

From the driver's side of the Land Rover, a second gunman opened fired with an Uzi submachine gun.

Heavy slugs and 9mm rounds struck the front of the Mercedes SUV, as well as the door behind which Logan took cover. Whatever armor package the criminal who owned the SUV had purchased had been worth it, as the slugs failed to pass through the doors. After the eighth round in the box magazine had been fired, both Logan and Jack emerged from behind the doors.

Both the shotgun-toting gunman and the Uzi operator had ducked back behind their doors to reload, thinking the cover would provide relative safety.

Logan and Jack seized the opportunity and acted as the aggressors, quickly combat-walking toward the vehicle, an MP5 trained on each side, vertical sway minimized.

Steady. Steady. Wait for it, Logan thought, his right eye fixed through the red dot scope on the passenger door. He exhaled and moved, finger on the trigger, no longer on the side of the trigger guard. *Point of no return.*

The passenger stepped out and began to turn. He never completed the rotation as the first 9mm round from Logan's suppressed H&K caught him in the left temple, killed him instantly, and dropped him to the ground, the AA-12 clattering to the concrete.

Jack had similar results with the driver, although his target managed to complete his turn, and two 9mm rounds struck him in the face. He reflexively pulled the trigger in death, and the weapon discharged as its owner fell, sending a streak of bullets into the eastbound lane that struck a man who'd been running away from the sounds of combat.

Goddamnit, Logan thought in outrage. *Can't you fuckers just die without wrecking more lives? That's more blood on your head, Mr. Vice President, and your ledger is going to come due.*

The vice president and his escort were now forty yards away and moving quickly, using the shoulder as a running lane. The eastern tunnel entrance was still one hundred yards away, and Logan realized it wasn't fully blocked by falling rocks and debris.

"I've got the escort," Logan said, and broke out into a full-out sprint onto the shoulder, knowing Jack would be close behind him but at a slower pace.

Logan had only run ten yards when automatic weapons fire erupted much closer than the last time he'd heard the M60. Bullets pinged off the cars to his right, a windshield shattered, and another scream of pain rose above the chaos. Logan dove to the pavement and slithered behind a white Toyota Land Cruiser.

From underneath the rear bumper, he searched for Jack or the

Tiuna that had crept up on them in the aftermath of the earth-quake. *Guess Jack's source and his guys didn't fare so well against the technical. One damn job to do . . .*

Cole Matthews was right behind Logan's Mercedes when the earth-quake struck. When the hillside collapsed into the eastbound lanes, he was certain they were going to die. Yet he had pushed the SUV through the cloud amid the screams and panic and emerged behind Logan.

He had no view of the gunfight that broke out between Jack's band of criminal mercenaries, but he'd paid attention to the ebb and flow of the battle, noting when the M60 had gone silent. He'd assumed Jack's outlaws had done their job, which was why he'd been surprised when the M60 had opened up four vehicles away, targeting Logan as he ran after the vice president. *Assuming won't just make an ass out of you, it will fucking get you killed, genius.*

Cole looked through the rear and side windows of the SUV and spotted the Tiuna twenty yards diagonally behind them to the right. Cars were littered and parked in random directions, providing him with an idea. *No way. This is something better suited for Amira. She's the crazy one.* He'd seen firsthand Task Force Ares's lethal female operator drop down the side of a building under con-struction in Khartoum. *But she's not here—you are.*

"The gunner isn't paying attention to us. I'm exiting the vehicle and dropping down out of sight. Exit behind me, count to ten, and then light that fucker up. It will buy me the time I need," Cole said, and opened the door.

"Time for what?" Santiago asked, even as he grabbed his MP5 and prepared to follow Cole.

"To take them off the battlefield *and* not get myself killed,"

Cole replied, and grinned under the adrenaline rush he felt as he dropped to the pavement.

Within seconds, Cole scurried under the SUV toward the Tiuna, his Glock 17 9mm—no longer suppressed—held in his right hand. He'd left the MP5 in the Mercedes. He was either going to succeed or die trying, and the submachine gun would only interfere with what he had in mind.

The gunner continued to strafe the area where Cole had last seen Logan, and he hoped his friend had reached cover. While only a 7.62mm machine gun—it wasn't a .50-caliber Browning, thankfully; Logan had told him what he and John had done to the insurgents who had ambushed them in Iraq with .50-caliber mounted technicals—it was more than enough to tear large holes into metal, skin, and bone.

Cole left the undercarriage of the Mercedes and found himself under the white SUV that had turned to its left before stopping. Certain he was still unseen, he moved as quickly as he could, scooting forward on the pavement, his black SEBIN Kevlar vest scraping the ground under his chest.

Once he reached the end of the SUV, exactly as he had anticipated, he left the safety of the Toyota and slid beneath a brown station wagon. *Who the hell drives these things? It was like something out of* National Lampoon's Vacation. He half expected Chevy Chase to pop out and tell him he was on a quest. *One more to go.*

Halfway under the station wagon, he heard gunfire from behind him as Santiago opened up on the Tiuna. *Move faster.*

Cole picked up the pace as a sense of urgency spurred him on. He reached the bumper of the station wagon and avoided the muffler that hung down to the ground. *Didn't get that fucking thing at Midas. That's for sure.*

The last vehicle he needed to get to was a red Nissan Pathfinder a few feet away from the *National Lampoon* vehicle. *Don't think.*

Just move. He left the safety of the station wagon, crawled into the open air, and rolled to his left until he looked up and found himself staring into the Nissan's undercarriage.

Santiago's MP5 went silent, but the Tiuna's gunner continued to fire, this time toward Hector. Cole crawled as fast as he could in the confined space. He reached the back of the Pathfinder and looked up, exactly where he thought he'd be—less than two feet away from the side of the Tiuna, directly between the front and rear driver's-side doors.

Please God, let this work. Cole Matthews exhaled, felt the stillness from his training take over his mind and body, and acted like the trained killer that he was.

He low-crawled forward and stood up, raised the Glock with his right hand, brought his left up to meet it, and sighted on the gunner's head in one fluid motion.

The gunner sensed his presence, but it was too late, even as he tried to swivel the M60.

The Glock bucked twice in Cole's hand, both rounds striking the gunner in the lower part of his face, killing him and spraying blood as he crumpled down through the open turret into the Tiuna.

Cole was already moving, as the driver did exactly what he'd expected: he began to open his door. Cole switched the Glock to his left hand, and as he reached the opening door, he lunged his right hand under the left that held the Glock and pushed the Tiuna's door open. He fired with his off hand point-blank into the left side of the driver's head, adjusted the Glock, and fired two more shots at the passenger.

The driver had been killed instantly, but the passenger wasn't as fortunate: the first round tore through his neck and sent blood spraying across the inside of the Tiuna. The second round struck him in the jaw, destroying his features, but it still didn't kill him.

Cole raised the Glock slightly, squeezed, and ended the dying soldier's suffering. The Tiuna and its M60 would torment the innocent bystanders on the highway no more.

Cole inhaled deeply and scanned the surrounding environment. Chaos reigned across the road, but no more threats presented themselves, at least for the moment.

Once he'd emerged from under the last vehicle, he'd dispatched the three soldiers in less than four seconds. He admired his macabre handiwork and quietly thanked the instructors at Fort Bragg for years of relentless training.

Bedlam had fully consumed the enclosed mountaintop stretch of highway. In the initial aftermath of the earthquake, at least two-thirds of the drivers trapped between the tunnels had exited their vehicles and remained stationary and confused with nowhere to go. But once the shooting had started, the inherent fight-or-flight instinct had kicked in with ferocity, compelling people to run, even if they didn't know which way.

Once the M60 had ceased firing, Logan had launched himself into a full-out sprint, leaving the MP5 where he'd crouched for safety. Since most had seen the black-clad SEBIN officers and army soldiers engaged in a firefight, the bystanders—like cockroaches scattering at the appearance of light—fled before Logan as he pursued the vice president and the last remaining hostile.

The vice president was halfway to the tunnel entrance when the steady thrum of a deep vibration grew louder. Screams from people mistaking it for an aftershock increased in pitch. Logan smiled, even as he pumped his legs furiously. *Air support. About goddamn time something goes our way.*

Inspector Hector Salazar stared through the open starboard side door of the SEBIN Eurocopter AS532 helicopter as it skimmed the treetops on the left side of the mountain range. Once they'd received the radio call for assistance as the earthquake struck, the pilot had rocketed them out of the city toward the tunnels.

After the events at the Humboldt Hotel, he'd had the air maintenance crew install the door mount for the M60 machine gun and its box magazine of 7.62mm ammunition. He'd figured for the ambush they had planned, if things went poorly, a more precise weapon than the 20mm mounted cannon might be required. As he held the pistol grip of the machine gun, his forefinger straight and off the trigger, he realized his planning and preparation were about to be tested.

As the helicopter sped over the draw around the left side of the mountain that held the first tunnel, Hector spotted the first large plumes of dirt from the landslide. *Just a few more seconds.*

In the moments he had left before the Cougar arrived at the ambush, he prayed for Santiago's welfare. He thought about Camila and the emotional roller coaster she and her father—a man that Hector considered a blood brother, a truly good man in a country of corruption and chaos—had been riding since Santiago's beautiful wife, Maria, had succumbed to cancer. It was why when Santiago had approached him after he'd been enlisted by the SEBIN director and the president of the Supreme Tribunal, Hector had never hesitated. Whatever Santiago needed to help his daughter, Hector would help him do, no questions asked. The fact that they were now working with American agents had been a bit of a shock, but Hector was a man of practicality. And if working with agents of a foreign power would help their cause *and their country,* then so be it.

The helicopter dropped to one hundred feet above the mountain and flew around the end of it to reveal the scene below. *Mother of God,* Hector thought, and reflexively inhaled at the carnage on display.

"Target is moving toward the east tunnel exit," Hector heard through the radio headphones he wore. "Stop him any way you can. Avoid collateral damage at all costs. There are civilians everywhere. Target is in a dark-red shirt and khakis, and one armed gunman is with him."

"Solid copy," Hector replied into the flexible microphone that extended from the left earpiece down and in front of his mouth. "On scene. Stand by."

The pilot heard the same communications broadcast and sped around the exposed curve of the highway, past the landslide, over several bodies that Hector spotted on the pavement, and toward the far tunnels.

"Drop it to fifty feet and move off the highway over the side of the mountain so I can get a better view," Hector ordered the pilot.

Within seconds, the Cougar hovered off the side of the highway over the open air of the mountainside, moving down the length of the road. *Got you, puta,* Hector thought, a detached part of his mind recognizing he was looking over the barrel of the M60 machine gun at one of the most powerful and corrupt men in the Western Hemisphere. As he watched the unfolding pursuit below and in front of him, he realized what he had to do.

"Move halfway to the tunnel entrance, rotate so I have a full field of fire, and stop," Hector said.

The helicopter slid to the left, reached its new position, and turned, providing Hector with a clear line of sight from the partially collapsed tunnel to the initial point of contact where the two Mercedes were stopped. He thought about his goddaughter one last time, sighted down the barrel past the iron sight post, exhaled, and pulled the trigger.

Logan hadn't seen Jack since he'd been pinned down by the M60. He knew the retired Marine would find a way to come to his assistance: he just had to survive long enough to get it.

The vice president was fifteen yards from the tunnel when Hector opened up with the mounted M60 and sent a new wave of fear through the trapped survivors. *And you guys thought socialism was bad. Welcome to the new war.*

Rounds ricocheted off the tunnel entrance and tore chunks of rock from the hanging pile above the dark mouth, which had partially caved in. The vice president fell to the pavement, face to the ground, hands on top of his head.

Logan was fairly sure the vice president screamed in fear, but he wasn't positive over the combined roar of the helicopter and M60. *Good, motherfucker. You deserve a lot more,* he thought, as he closed the distance to less than ten yards and sprinted in furious harmony with the chattering M60.

The vice president's guardian realized the pilot's intent, and he turned to open fire with a black mini-Uzi machine pistol, although moments too late.

More rounds from the M60 weakened the dirt and rocks above the tunnel, and the pile of debris crashed down onto the roadway, blocking the visible half of the tunnel entrance.

The gunman opened fired on the helicopter, which shifted away and to the right, its job of containing the vice president accomplished. As a result, he never saw the charging figure of Logan West, sprinting at him like a raging fullback, focused on obliterating his target.

Logan lowered his left shoulder and struck the escort at full force in the man's left side. He felt several ribs crack, and the blow lifted the shooter off his feet as Logan sprinted through the man, driving him up and then slamming him onto the concrete. Logan landed on top of him and turned to his left to get leverage.

The dazed man still held the pistol, although his finger had mercifully come off the trigger once he'd hit the pavement. Logan scooted up, grabbed the shooter's wrist with his right hand, and yanked the mini-Uzi upward with his left hand. He flung the weapon aside, and lurched upward, coming over the top of the shooter's shoulder, and delivered a vicious elbow to the man's exposed head. Logan felt his opponent's skull connect with the concrete below, the sick thud reverberating through his left forearm, and he hit him again. He felt something crack in the man's skull, and he rolled off, satisfied that his target was either dead or unconscious for the foreseeable future.

He looked around for the vice president. He was gone. *What the hell?* And then he spotted Joshua Baker, fleeing toward the slope of the mountain on the side of the tunnel. Logan saw what was between him and the hill, and fear set in, but not for himself. *You evil motherfucker.*

He rose to his knees to pursue when Murphy delivered his second blow of the morning.

Once he'd accomplished his objective and collapsed the mouth of the tunnel, Hector had watched with respect and admiration as the ferocious American had blindsided and then incapacitated the remaining gunman. *Never had a chance. Good.*

But like Logan, he saw what the vice president planned instead, scurrying away like the dog that he was, and Hector looked at the pilot, motioning for him to slide the helicopter farther left.

Had he been looking out the side of the cabin, he might've been able to avoid the inevitable, but his thoughts were on helping the innocent bystanders about to be stuck in the crossfire. As a result, neither he nor the pilot saw the Russian Hind Mi-24 attack helicopter as it rose up from the draw below and moved behind and to the left of the Eurocopter. The Hind hovered for a brief second, as Hector's peripheral vision finally detected the flying killing machine.

He screamed into the microphone and urged the pilot to climb, but it was too late. Two flashes erupted from under the right wing of the helicopter, and the missiles streaked toward the Cougar.

Hector realized that the end of his life was near, and he closed his eyes and thought, *I'm sorry I won't see this through to the end, brother. I tried. I'll miss you, Camila.*

The missiles struck the Cougar within a half second of each other, the first obliterating the tail section, the second detonating inside the cabin and mercifully sending Hector into the next life.

The main body of the helicopter, its rotors still turning, spun crazily and then veered down and to the right in an uncontrollable nosedive. The helicopter crashed through the canopy of trees on the side of the mountain below the highway, struck the earth, and exploded in a fireball, ending Logan's air superiority.

While he was disturbingly accustomed to mayhem, gunfire, and explosions, the destruction of the Cougar and the subsequent shock waves of the two air-to-air missiles caused Logan to reflexively dive to the ground. Once the Cougar—with Hector in it, his brain reminded him: another death at the feet of the Organization—plummeted down the side of the hill, Logan was on his feet, pursuing the vice president . . . and the twelve-year-old girl he dragged behind him for protection as he plodded up the hill.

The Hind had already moved into position, thirty yards ahead of the vice president, sending loose rocks, dirt, and underbrush flying through the air in its powerful rotor wash. Logan was fifteen yards behind the vice president—*the real one this time,* he thought.

He'd seen the girl, dazed from the quake's aftermath, circling aimlessly near the shoulder of the highway, and he'd known right away that Baker would use her as a human shield. It was just the kind of man he was, even if he had a son of his own of a similar age. Desperation bred evil and cowardly acts, and grabbing the girl for his own salvation had been one of them.

The side door of the Hind had already been raised over the opening, the lower extension hanging just below the bottom of the aircraft. Before Logan could react, a rope was thrown out the door, connected to an arm that swung out from inside the compartment. Four Venezuelan soldiers—*not normal soldiers,* Logan knew, *operators of some kind of fucking special forces unit down here*—poured out in rapid succession and hit the ground just up the hill from the vice president, black AK-103 assault rifles trained on Logan.

Logan combat-walked toward the vice president, the Glock 17 9mm pistol trained on Joshua Baker's forehead. Out of the corner of his right eye, a figure appeared, a pistol held in his hand. He couldn't tell who it was, but he knew it wasn't Jack. *Must be one of his mercenaries.*

He concentrated on keeping the vice president between himself and the new shooters as his mind calculated his options. *No good ones. Can't risk hitting the girl.* He'd closed the distance to ten yards, but with the downdraft of the Hind, he couldn't risk even the slightest sway on his sight picture. He knew a millimeter shift of his barrel would result in a several-inch shift on his target, and he didn't want to be responsible for the girl's death.

Two operators with black neoprene ski masks reached the vice president, stepped around and in front of him, and aimed their AK-103s at Logan and his newfound partner. *You won't shoot. Can't risk me hitting the vice president accidentally. It's a goddamned Mexican standoff in Venezuela.*

There were no other options. Any action resulted in his death, the girl's death, or any variation of multiple deaths. *It's not worth it. You have to let him go.* His blood boiled at the thought, that he'd come so close a second time, only to let his target slip from his grasp. But Logan West wasn't like the vice president: he wouldn't put an innocent life at risk. He was here to *save* lives, not take them.

He turned to the motorcycle rider and saw a man a few years younger than himself, black hair swept back, eyes covered by black goggles, and a black bandanna that covered his lower face. He held a Glock 17 pointed at the retreating group. There was something familiar about the man, but Logan couldn't place it.

The noise from the helicopter was deafening, and Logan shouted, "Stand down! There's no play!" He prayed the masked man understood English, even though his only response was to look at Logan and turn back to the group.

The vice president and his new protective detail reached the rope as the helicopter descended, the pilot bravely hovering several feet over their heads. The man in front of the vice president shook his head from side to side, his message clear: *Don't do anything. There's no need for any of us to die, at least not right now.*

A small rope ladder was thrown out the side compartment, and the rear two men scrambled up and into the opening. The vice president released his grip on the screaming girl, her shock now worn away into panic at the appearance of more armed men and a helicopter, and started climbing. One of the two remaining shooters gripped her by the arms, while the second pointed his AK-103 at her head, causing her to recoil in terror. The two shooters pointed their assault rifles at Logan and the *motorizado* as the vice president was pulled safely inside.

The man holding the girl said something into her ear, and she managed a nod. He nodded at Logan, waved a finger in front of his face as a warning, and released the girl. Logan anticipated the next events, and in a blinding-fast reverse draw, holstered his Glock. Whether from adrenaline or panic, the girl ran forward and stumbled into Logan's arms as the two remaining shooters leapt onto the rope ladder and disappeared inside the Hind.

A second later, the Hind ascended, and Logan caught a glimpse of the vice president looking back at him. Logan's eyes blazed with outrage, but there was nothing for him to do. As he held the trembling girl, who began to cry, he exhaled and calmed himself for her sake. *Your time will come, and when it does, I'll be the one to make sure you meet it head-on.*

And just as quickly as it had arrived, the Hind sped away, flying over the burning wreckage of the Cougar and the dead men inside.

Logan turned toward the *motorizado* who'd come to his assistance and now lowered his bandanna, and for the first time that morning, Logan seemed permanently affixed to the ground beneath his feet. Before him stood a man he'd hunted once before—a disgraced former Seventh Special Forces Group soldier who'd washed out of selection school for the Unit and had chosen a life in the violent world of the cartels and the Organization. The man once known as Juan Black, real name Marcos Bocanegra, a former advisor to Cain Frost, stood before him.

In a moment of pure instinct, Logan reflexively raised the Glock, his left arm still around the sobbing girl, and sighted on Marcos's face as his finger moved from the trigger guard to the trigger. *I said if I ever saw you again, I'd kill you.*

CHAPTER 21

Marcos Bocanegra was a soul in pain, and when Logan West pointed the Glock at his face, part of him wished that the man who'd once captured him would pull the trigger and end his suffering. But then the image of his young wife, pregnant with their unborn child, flashed in his mind, an emotional dagger that reminded him that if he died, he wouldn't be able to destroy the men responsible for the heinous act committed upon her.

"They murdered my wife, pregnant with our child, and left her severed head on top of her belly in our bed," Marcos said flatly.

"They did what?" Logan asked. The image created in his head at his former enemy's words caused him to lower the Glock a few inches.

The girl in his arms cringed at the appearance of the gun, traumatized by the vice president's actions only moments before.

"You heard me," Marcos said. "I won't say it again. These men are evil monsters whose only moral code is pain and suffering in its most vile, base form. It's why I'm here, not for you, but to make them all pay for what they did. If that's not good enough for you, someone well versed in violent revenge, then do us both a favor and shoot me. Otherwise, put the gun down, and let's go see how

Jack and the others are doing. I'm not going to wait here all day while these motherfuckers get away. And will you please let that girl go find her parents. She's been through enough."

Logan released the girl, and Marcos spoke to her in Spanish, reassuring her and calming her down. Screams from the other side of the highway erupted, fresh panic on the air. *The sound of terrified parents. That could be you someday,* Logan thought.

The girl started to run toward their voices, stopped, faced Logan one last time, and nodded with an expression of gratitude and sadness, whatever innocence she'd had permanently ground away.

Hector died, but she lived, one life for another. No matter what, you saved her.

Marcos turned his back on the man who'd bested him on the side of a mountain in northern Mexico and walked away.

What's old is new again, Logan. You're really in it now. You can't just shoot him in the back. The realization that Marcos Bocanegra was Jack's source struck him with a myriad of emotions—anger, empathy, resentment, vengeance—all rolled up into one dense feeling that stuck in his gut. He holstered the Glock and caught up with Bocanegra.

An aftershock rumbled through the terrain, and Logan braced himself against an abandoned SUV. All of the vehicles' occupants had fled the stretch of highway where they stood once the battle had moved to the tunnel entrance.

"What happened after Mexico?" Logan asked Marcos, staring at the tanned, black-haired former US Army soldier.

"The Mexicans honored the agreement: they let me go, just like you asked them to, once Cain was captured," Marcos said.

"Honestly, I thought they'd keep and kill you, and at the time, I didn't care. No offense," Logan replied.

"So did I, but they didn't. I chalked it up to the honor of Commander Vargas," Marcos said, referring to the commander of the

Fuerzas Especiales, the Mexican equivalent of the US Navy SEALs, whose men had teamed up with the FBI HRT, Logan, and John Quick to raid the Los Toros compound where Marcos had been hiding. The raid had cost both the Mexican naval special forces unit and FBI HRT multiple lives.

Logan nodded. "It doesn't surprise me, although you are still lucky to be alive."

"At the time," Marcos said, the loss of his wife underpinning the statement. "No matter, I left Mexico, came to Venezuela, and stayed in Maracaibo, the way I had planned and prepared, with bank accounts and a house in one of the upper-middle-class communities just outside of the city. Nothing too fancy, but prosperous for Venezuela. I stayed under the radar, new identity and all, knowing that one day the Los Toros cartel would come for me. But then I met a woman, a banker, and everything changed."

It always does, Logan thought, thinking of Sarah back in the States, pregnant and worrying about his welfare. *It's not going to get better once the news of this earthquake gets out.*

"I could not help myself, even knowing I'd be putting her at risk. I finally told her who and what I was—all of it—and rather than leave me, she stayed, as if trying to redeem the things I'd done by being with me. And I let her, and her death, like so many others, is on my head, and mine alone," Marcos said, his voice thick with grief.

"When did it happen?" Logan asked. He needed to know how fresh the wounds were that weighed the former cartel enforcer down.

"Three months ago," Marcos replied. "The Los Toros cartel figured out where I was and contracted with the Wild Boys, which is what they call themselves—one of these midlevel syndicates that occasionally works *with* the Venezuelan government. They're violent, ruthless, and will do whatever they're paid to do."

The aftershock ended, and the two men walked on. Civilians stared as they passed, the sight of the armed men creating a barrier around them that the innocent bystanders didn't want to penetrate.

They were halfway back to the parked SUVs when Logan saw Jack, Cole, and Santiago waiting for them.

"But how did you find the ones responsible? And how did you end up here?" Logan asked.

"Easy. I did what I used to do for the Los Toros cartel: I hunted down members of the Wild Boys, tortured and killed them, going from one to the next like a trail of human bread crumbs," Marcos said.

Except instead of bread crumbs, you left bodies, Logan thought. *So much violence.* Most of the citizens in the US would never understand the staggering levels of violence perpetrated daily across the world, but it was an epidemic becoming more evident, with atrocities captured and shared on social media like selfies on a family vacation. *It's mind-numbing. But you know, and so does he.*

"I caught up only four days ago with one of the sons of one of the founders of the Wild Boys, and he told me about this operation, which is when I reached out to Jack and told him about it. After what went down in DC a few weeks ago, I knew he'd be hunting as well," Marcos said. "And here we are."

"Two questions. What happened to the son?" Logan asked.

"He was an aspiring Wild Boy, and I accelerated his career so that he reached the pinnacle now, rather than later," Marcos said.

"How so?" Logan asked.

Marcos stopped, looked at Logan, and said with no emotion, "I killed him, because the life he chose always ends in death."

You need to keep an eye on him, Logan. His personal vendetta is driving him, not your quest for justice. Logan didn't respond to the answer, but instead asked, "Second question. Did you always know about the Organization, even when we captured you?"

A half smirk crossed Marcos's face. "It was literally *the only* thing I didn't tell you. Now that you know about it, about how big the Organization was, you have to understand that I threw my lot in with Cain because of what was happening in the Middle East, pure and simple. I told you what you needed to know to stop Cain. I didn't want to compromise myself more than I already had."

It made sense. Logan couldn't fault the man for it. It was a practical decision, and one Logan likely would've made himself if he'd been in the same situation.

"I'm sorry about your wife. I truly am, more than you might think. Mine is pregnant, and I can only imagine what I'd do if anything happened to her," Logan said sincerely. "But understand one thing above all else: if you do anything that jeopardizes our mission to capture the vice president and bring that motherfucker to justice, I will put you down myself, Jack or no Jack. Are we clear on that?" There was no menace to his voice. He didn't need to threaten Bocanegra. The man knew who and what Logan was.

"Absolutely, but let me tell *you* one thing," Marcos said, reverting to the way he'd talked to Logan West on the phone more than two and a half years ago on the day Logan's life had changed. "I want these men to pay for what they did. As long as you understand that, we're in this together until the bloody end."

Logan knew that commitment was as good as anything he'd get from the man on fire.

"I can live with that," Logan said, as they finally reached their waiting friends. "Now, let's get the hell off this mountain."

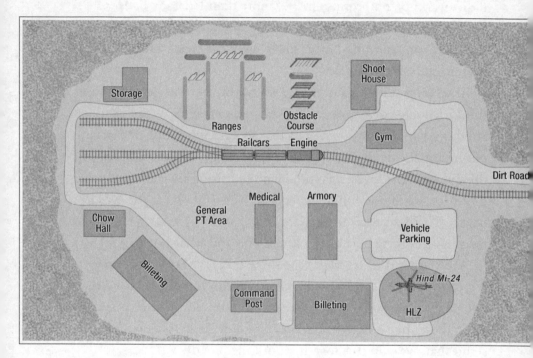

PART IV

LAST TRAIN
TO CARACAS

CHAPTER 22

The city was in chaos, and the citizens of Caracas had no one to help them and nowhere to go. Their government had abandoned them once the economy had collapsed, leaving the people to fend for themselves on a daily basis. The shortage of food and medical supplies was about to be exacerbated a thousandfold, and the coming days would test the survival skills of the average Caracas resident.

Large sections of the city had endured random power outages for months, but once the quake had struck, the entire valley had gone dark. Fortunately, most of the daylight hours that remained would be used for the city's search-and-rescue efforts to sift through the rubble of the hundreds of buildings—mostly older ones—that had collapsed.

The only chance of preventing a total human catastrophe of biblical proportions was aid relief. If the organizations that served the world's hardest-struck areas could establish the logistics to deliver supplies as quickly as possible, the postearthquake conditions of disease, malnutrition, and rampant crime might be mitigated.

But that meant US involvement, and the US and Venezuela hadn't been on speaking terms since the time of Hugo Chávez. Sanctions by the US designed to resist the autocratic rule of the current regime and countermoves by the Venezuelan government intended to aggravate the US had become the foundation of their international relationship.

But what was most relevant for Logan West was that the carnage from the earthquake had jeopardized the success of his mission.

Once the shooting had stopped and the vice president had escaped, Logan, his task force, and Marcos, who'd been the only survivor of the motorcycle team, had used a dirt service road to escape the closed-off section of the highway. Several other motorists and survivors had followed their lead, and like the Pied Piper leading away the town's children, the two Mercedes SUVs had led a small convoy of vehicles down the side of the mountain to a neighborhood less than a half mile away.

Santiago had found an abandoned warehouse and pulled in, but none of the other vehicles had followed, afraid to aggravate men they thought were the SEBIN and pay the consequences, even in the wake of a natural disaster.

It was how Logan, Cole, Jack, Santiago, and Marcos found themselves poring over the hard copy of the military maps Jack had provided exactly for a situation like the one they faced. *Thank God for Jack's preparation. Some habits never die,* Logan thought, as the speaker on the US government Iridium satellite phone Jack had provided chirped incessantly, waiting for Jake Benson to answer on the other end.

"About a mile west of here is a ridge and several dirt roads that connect all the way back to Caracas. It might take us a few hours, but we can at least make it to SEBIN HQ," Santiago said. He still hadn't fully processed the fact that his best friend and Camila's godfather was dead. He understood it to be true, but the constant state of agitation, panic, and uncertainty hadn't allowed it to sink into his psyche. He knew it would, but his grief would have to wait. *Otherwise, he died for nothing,* Santiago thought, and studied the map again.

"I'm good with the dirt roads," Jack said, "but I don't know about downtown Caracas. It's going to be a war zone, and it's only going to get worse with each hour."

The call connected, and Logan heard Jake Benson say, "This is Jake."

"It's me," Logan said. "I'm on an Iridium. There's no cell service here since the quake struck. Here's the number. Call me back when you're on another Iridium. Otherwise, we're talking in the clear." In order for the encrypted phones to create a secure communications pathway, both satellite phones needed to operate on the same Iridium network created for the US government.

Logan repeated the digits Jack had provided, and Jake said, "Call you back in five minutes. At the office and need to get upstairs," which Logan knew meant the roof of the FBI J. Edgar Hoover Building in Northwest DC.

"Understood. Out here," Logan said, and disconnected the call.

"What's going on?" Cole asked.

"Jake's finding an Iridium and calling me back, and then we'll go from there," Logan replied.

"Every minute we're sidelined here is another minute the vice president and General Cordones get to plot their next move, which won't be good for anyone, including this already ravaged country," Cole said.

"I know, but I need to talk to Jake. We need all national and theater-level assets the IC can get, and we need them now," Logan said, referring to the US Intelligence Community.

"Logan, whatever help the IC might be able to provide, it will take hours to move satellites, coordinate airborne ISR, and figure out how to route the intelligence to us directly. I know we're only in South America, but after the earthquake, we may as well be in the middle of the fucking Sahara desert with two cans and a string," Jack added. "By the time they set up what we need, it will be too late, and you know it."

Logan clenched his jaw in frustration. "What do you have in mind?"

"How badly do you want to capture Joshua Baker?" Jack asked seriously.

"You know the answer and shouldn't even have to ask the question," Logan replied sternly.

"I thought as much, but I needed to ask," Jack responded. "If you're all in, then there's only one option, since we're constrained by time and daylight and so many unknown variables it makes my head hurt."

"What's that?" Santiago asked before anyone else had a chance.

"We pull our own version of the great Clint Eastwood movie *Where Eagles Dare*," Jack stated, a thin smile on his face.

"What is this movie?" Santiago said.

"I fucking like it," Marcos said. "We hit the sonofabitch in his own house."

"It's bold," Logan stated, ignoring Marcos and Santiago. "And it's dangerous as hell."

"That it is, but think about it. Caracas is in chaos, we're on our own, although I can get us some reinforcements in the near term, but—"

"I bet you can," Logan interrupted, a tinge of disapproval in his voice.

"As I was about to say, so is General Cordones. I absolutely guarantee that whatever he had planned has been sidetracked by the earthquake. He's going to have to adapt, just like we are. I read the CIA's profile on him: he's angry, confident, and fueled by grief.

He lost his son to the protests in the streets. Whatever he's doing and needs the vice president for, I guarantee you one thing—it's personal."

"Which makes him unreliable and unpredictable," Logan said.

"No," Jack countered. "It makes him rash, hasty, and prone to make a mistake. But there's also one thing I'm certain of—he'll keep the vice president secluded on that base. Whatever he needs from him is so critical that he was willing to help the world's most wanted man sneak into his country *and then* defend him in broad daylight with a team of operators and a Russian Hind attack helicopter."

The minutes were ticking by, and Logan calculated the options. The only thing they knew for sure was that the vice president was at the general's base outside Caracas. It was possible he'd been flown elsewhere, but unlikely. *Fortune favored the brave. Step up or go home.* "Okay. I'm sold. It's the only play we have. We execute a raid on his base, late this afternoon or this evening, but there's one problem," Logan said, and looked around the warehouse. "We're a little bit low on manpower, and if the director of the SEBIN is right, the general has an entire battalion up there, ready to fight and die for him."

"You better have something good," Cole said to Jack. "I don't mind danger, but I prefer to avoid anything with suicide in the CONOP. You know what I mean?"

"Don't worry," Jack said, smiling. "I've got a *whole lot* of something good for this operation."

The Iridium phone in Logan's hand chirped electronically. "It's Jake. Let me update him, and then we use those dirt roads to get back to Caracas."

"Fine, but make it quick. We have to get back to my safe house to gear up. There's more there than just these SUVs," Jack said.

"Roger, but it better be good," Logan replied.

MATTHEW BETLEY

"Trust me. It is," Jack said.

"Whatever," Logan retorted, and hit the green triangle talk button on the Iridium. "Hey, Jake, are you secure?"

"I am, although I'm up on the roof. Hopefully, no one has a parabolic mic on me," Jake said semiseriously.

"Roger that. Then let me do the talking," Logan said, and updated the director of the FBI and one of the leaders of Task Force Ares.

CHAPTER 23

Vice President Josh Baker stood inside General Cordones's command post planning room and watched on Globovision the coverage of the aftermath of the earthquake. Scenes of death and desperation played on a continuous loop—children trapped inside a city school as rescuers scrambled through the rubble in a race against time; a four-story building that had collapsed inward, crushing the first two floors; a young, bloodied woman screaming for her husband in Spanish; and on and on the televised horror show went. *It's always the same,* Josh thought. *The never-ending cycle of misery and death.*

The planning room was empty, but soldiers scurried purposefully outside and across the plateau, loading several of the railcars with gear and vehicles. A shadow fell across the light from the hallway, and Josh turned to see the general enter.

General Cordones was dressed in a solid olive-green set of combat fatigues, black combat boots, an olive-green boonie cover with a tan stripe around the top, and a black Kevlar vest that held pouches for ammunition and other gear. A Browning Hi-Power .40-caliber pistol was strapped to the soldier's upper leg in a thigh rig. The resolute look on his face completed the ensemble, announcing one thing—*ready for war.*

"Are you sure this is going to work?" Josh asked. "Seems like a lot of unknowns right now. Too many things that could go wrong."

"Like I said, Mr. Vice President, the chaos will only increase our chances of success. This earthquake could not have happened at a better time for us," Victor stated.

"Not even the slightest bit of sympathy for all of the dead and suffering?" Josh asked, not accusatorily but as a matter of interest.

"This city—no, this *country*—is being run into the dirt by a failed system of government that doesn't work, that has *never* worked in the history of civilization. If it stays on its current course, more people will die of starvation and disease than were killed today," Victor said. "And it will be a long, slow suffering, the kind that permanently scars the psyche of the people with blood and loss." He paused and looked at the TV, which had been muted, while the image of a reporter standing in front of a burning building filled the widescreen HD monitor. "That may sound harsh, but it's true. I lost my son, and I can never bring him back. It took that kind of trauma to help me see clearly. And now because of the position I'm in, I can prevent others from losing their loved ones."

Josh appreciated the general's commitment; the image of his own eleven-year-old son filled his mind's eye. He'd felt that way once, even if it had been misguided, illegal, and often immoral. "I understand," he said, finally. "However, you still haven't told me what that has to do with me."

"How's your hip feeling?" Victor asked, catching Josh off-guard with the question and sudden change of topic.

"My hip?" Josh replied curiously. An incredibly devious and brilliant man, he realized instantly that something had been done to him during his surgery. Too much had been risked to orchestrate his escape and bring him to South America. *He knows something I don't, which gives him the advantage, at least for now.* "What is it?" he asked, ready to accept whatever answer he was proffered.

"This might sound a little like paranoid lunacy, but I've been assured it's true. Prior to your surgery, I've been told that an account number and password were etched into your hip. It's to a thirty-billion-dollar account for the Zürcher Kantonalbank in Switzerland, specifically chosen because of the country's lackadaisical approach to extradition. Once I'm done here today, you and I are going to fly discreetly to Switzerland, where we are going to link up off-site with a manager from the bank who was the Founder's personal contact, and ensure that the funds are available as needed. Between now and then, think about where you want to spend the rest of your life, because after today, not only will you be wanted in North America, but if word gets out about you down here, you'll never be safe here either. The hard truth for you, Mr. Vice President, is that your life becomes quite simpler. You only have one choice—leave with me," Victor finished.

It wasn't the shock of the secret hidden within his flesh that kept him silent, but rather it was the knowledge that he'd likely never again set foot in the Western Hemisphere once he left Venezuela. *You always knew this could happen, and now it has. Once you led your detail to their deaths, there was never any going back.* Josh crossed his arms over the black polo he wore and asked, "What do I do while you're in the city?"

Victor smiled. "You have the easiest job of all: you stay here, guarded by the head of my personal security detail and several of his best-trained soldiers. When we're finished, I'll call back here, and my pilot will fly you on the second Hind to an airstrip south of the city. If all goes as planned, we'll be wheels up toward a different fate by midnight, the stranglehold on my country will loosen, and my son will not have died in vain."

"And if something happens to you?" Josh asked, the idea of his fate intertwined with a high-risk operation unsettling.

"Then my pilot takes you to the airstrip, and you make your way to Switzerland with an itinerary on the plane for where to go and whom to meet when you get there," Victor replied. "I won't have your blood on my hands. I'm about to have enough as it is."

An honorable man about to commit what his country would consider treason. Sounds familiar. "I appreciate that," Josh said, and stepped across the chasm between the two men, extending his hand. "In that case, General, I wish you the best of luck, for both you *and* your country."

The two men shook, sealing a pact between the most wanted traitor in the world and another about to commit his own version of high crimes and misdemeanors.

God help us all, Josh thought, knowing full well that God would have no mercy on him for the deeds he'd done. His reckoning, when it came, would be with the one God had banished below. If nothing else, of that he was certain.

CHAPTER 24

Outskirts of Caracas
1500 Venezuelan Standard Time

The inside of the warehouse was in a state of commotion. Both Jack and Marcos had reached out to their local contacts, and twelve Venezuelan men from various disreputable backgrounds had arrived, no questions asked. No two looked the same, with ages ranging from late twenties to early forties, short or full beards, long hair—one even wore a man bun, but Logan wasn't about to criticize it, as the tattoo of a shattered skull on his cheek indicated he didn't care what the latest fashion critics had to say—bald heads, and numerous tattoos. All of them brought their own weapons and tactical gear, and they'd even managed to dress similarly in brown or dark-green earth-tone colors. Logan had watched the men assemble their weapons, and he'd been surprised by the dexterity with which they handled them. He'd commented to Jack and Marcos, "If I didn't know any better, I'd say this is like the Bad News Bears of mercenary work, but these guys aren't exactly mercenaries, are they?"

"Negative," Jack had answered. "Not even close. Four are the personal detail for a cartel leader the Organization had an arrangement with down here, four are individuals who work alone—usually—and handle wet work for the government in a nonofficial capacity, and four are personal friends of Marcos. You're right, it's a mixed bag of tricks, but they're more than adequately trained for what's coming," which was all Logan needed to know.

Once introductions had been made, Jack revealed the main reason they'd rallied at the warehouse: sixty Perdix micro drones wrapped and stacked in the back of an Austrian Pinzgauer high-mobility all-terrain vehicle.

"You've got to be kidding me," Cole said, gawking at the drones as they stood inside the secured warehouse Jack had purchased more than two years before. "Jesus Christ, Jack, is there anyone you don't know or anything you can't get? I read about these last year. DARPA has been developing drone swarm technology over the past few years, even putting out a call to engineers and drone experts to participate in what they call 'sprints.' A few years ago, they dropped a hundred or so from two F-18s, and the drones operated as one artificial organism, successfully executing several swarm maneuvers. There were several news stories about it."

"There were," Jack said. "It's why the Organization reached out to DARPA—remember, our resources aren't just monetary—and not only learned what they were doing but how. We obtained their software, and we purchased our own micro drone fleet to be used for a rainy day. When I realized I was coming to South America, I figured I might get a chance to try these little monsters out, and I figured right," he added with a sense of satisfaction in his voice.

"Great. You got some new toys, but how the hell are they going to help us? They don't exactly have Predator missiles on them. They're not much larger than my hand," Logan said. "And looking at the propellers, they're going to make a ton of noise." Logan paused, his mind solving the riddle before he'd barely thought of it. "But that's the plan, isn't it? Rather than quick and quiet, these things are going to be a diversion, aren't they?"

"They're going to do much more than that, Marine. They're going to cause *chaos*," Jack said. "And it's going to be beautiful."

"Okay, smart guy. I can't wait to hear this: what kind of Erwin Rommel master plan do you have up your sleeve?" Logan asked, referring to the brilliant German tank commander and tactical genius.

"The easiest one of all," Jack said, and actually smiled as he laid out the events of the upcoming evening's festivities.

CHAPTER 25

The convoy of six Tiuna military vehicles led by two black Range Rovers roared east through the middle of the crippled city down Avenida Sucre. Dust and smoke hung in the air like a cloak, as if threatening to suffocate the remaining buildings and infrastructure. General Cordones watched the wreckage from the earthquake as it passed by, a series of endless images with one thing in common— suffering. *But not for much longer,* he thought.

The convoy into the city had encountered fewer roadblocks and obstacles than he'd anticipated. Thanks to the continuous state of chaos, emergency personnel assumed the convoy was on some kind of official business, and the Caracas citizens assumed the convoy was on the way to help some unfortunate souls worse off than they were. *Just not in the way they might think,* he reflected.

The convoy exited the highway down a gradual ramp whose left side had collapsed to the ground below. A red SUV hung over the edge, its front wheels dangling in the air. Its passengers had abandoned it, a teetering carcass waiting to plummet to its permanent death at the next aftershock.

"Mother of God," Lieutenant Colonel Alfonso Gutierrez said as he navigated the exit ramp. He'd been with the general for the past five years, and like all of the men under his command, Gutierrez was committed to their mission. In Colonel Gutierrez's mind, there was no greater cause than the preservation of the country he loved, for all its woes.

"The darkness before the light," General Cordones said. The convoy reached the bottom of the ramp and turned left. "It will all be over soon."

"And you've confirmed it's going to happen?"

"They're in position," General Cordones replied. "Everything is in motion. We passed the point of no return before we entered the city. Are you having second thoughts, Alfonso?"

"Not for a second, sir," Colonel Gutierrez replied. "No nobler cause than this."

The general nodded slightly and turned to the two bodyguards of his personal detail in the back seat. The soldiers nodded at their commanding officer, intense looks of determination worn like battle masks. He nodded in return, satisfied with what he saw. *He'll never see it coming. He can't.*

A voice erupted from the encrypted portable UHF two-way radio the general held in his lap. "The press conference is underway. Just like you said, they're holding it on Avenida Urdaneta. We're in position and waiting for your mark."

"Roger," the general replied, and depressed the talk button on the side of the two-way radio. "We're less than ninety seconds out. Once we stop, you start. Maintain good fire and discipline until we leave. Then make your egress and meet us at the rally point. Radio silence until this is over. Good luck."

"You too, sir," the disembodied voice responded. "Out here."

"How did you know they'd hold the press conference outside the palace? Seems reckless," Colonel Gutierrez asked.

"Politics, Alfonso. Politics. His handlers want to maximize his exposure during this crisis to try and ingratiate himself with the people. He's no fool. He knows how unpopular he is, that people are fleeing Venezuela at an alarming rate, and that large segments of the population blame him. He might be a tyrant, but he's no idiot. He probably thinks this is the best thing that could've happened to him," the general finished.

Another left turn, and the convoy moved north on the east side of the palace. *So close to avenging you, Daniel.* He closed his eyes and remembered the boy he'd raised, pangs of grief and guilt penetrating the veneer of toughness he wore like armor.

The vehicles drove between the trees on the left side of the road and the buildings on the right, an urban canyon of wood, concrete, and steel. Victor glimpsed images of the palace through the dense canopy of foliage.

The Range Rover stopped at Avenida Urdaneta. To the left, the section of street in front of Miraflores Palace had been blocked off. Barriers had been erected and were manned by four men in dark suits and red ties—the president's personal bodyguards. Three hundred feet past the barrier were a throng of reporters and a podium that had been hastily erected near the main vehicle entrance from Urdaneta. Victor couldn't see the president, but he knew he was there, broadcasting live on the air.

Fortunately, every member of the president's personal security battalions knew General Victor Cordones, and he was about to take advantage of that fact.

"Let's go," General Cordones ordered, and the Range Rover accelerated as it turned, aiming straight for the point between the two barriers. The rest of the convoy followed close behind.

The four men raised their weapons instinctively, black assault rifles trained on the approaching Range Rover. But they didn't fire, as they recognized the four military vehicles as part of the Venezuelan army.

The Range Rover slammed on its brakes, and General Victor Cordones leapt out, already screaming in Spanish as the Tiunas behind him stopped and blocked the intersection midturn, a vehicular snake that stretched out more than eighty feet.

General Cordones rushed to the nearest guard, who lowered his weapon at the appearance of the army's commanding general. He didn't give the clean-cut man in his midtwenties a chance to respond, but instead started talking.

"You know who I am, I assume? Good. Move these barriers right now. There is an imminent threat on the president's life. I've been trying to get through to his personal detail for the last thirty minutes, but comms have been in and out. Now *move the barriers and let us pass,*" he finished forcefully.

The young man stared at the general for a moment and, to his credit, spoke into a microphone, relaying the information General Cordones had just provided.

Smart. Too bad he's on the wrong side of this, Victor thought, and cut the young man off. "The longer you delay, the greater the danger you place the president in."

The young man paused and opened his mouth to answer when the first shot rang out, echoing off the surrounding buildings. *Just in time,* Victor thought, and sprang into action, even as the first scream arose from down the street near the press conference.

"Too late," General Cordones said, and jumped back in the Range Rover as it drove through the barriers, trying to cover the distance before the inevitable panic ensued. The convoy accelerated, distracting the security, but more shots rang out, and the assembled crowd began to flee in all directions in hopes of avoiding a random bullet. Victor noted that the only ones who remained truly calm were the media cameramen, likely having been through worse.

The Range Rover skidded to a halt less than thirty feet away from the president of Venezuela, and Victor leapt out once again. As rehearsed, the vehicles stopped behind him, and the doors on all six Tiunas and the second Range Rover opened. The armed men within stepped out of the vehicles and began to scan the surrounding buildings with their AK-103s and H&K MP5s. In the middle of the bedlam, the effect was exactly as he'd intended—the cavalry showing up to rally to the president's side.

Victor ran up the stairs to the landing, even as the president's closest bodyguards held up black rectangles of Kevlar bulletproof fabric in order to shield the president.

Another shot rang out, and Victor heard a woman scream. He felt a pang of regret but pressed on, finally reaching President Ernesto Pena.

A slightly overweight man just under six feet tall in his early sixties who had somehow aged well, even under the stress and relentless pressure of his office, he looked at his chief of the army with concern—not panic—on his face. The current attempt on his life had not been the first.

"Sir, you have to come with me! I've been trying to reach you for the last hour since we picked up the threat, but I couldn't get through," General Cordones said quickly. "I can explain, but you have to come with me." He leaned in closer, his voice measured amid the pandemonium around them. As if the two of them were enclosed inside an invisible bubble, he delivered the last piece of information he knew would play into the president's paranoia. "It's not safe at the palace. They have men inside."

Another shot rang out, followed by another scream. Several of his guards fired indiscriminately toward a fifteen-story building two hundred yards away. The president's eyes flared for a moment, anger widening them. "Are you sure?" he responded.

"Yes, sir. I am. I have a safe location secured, but if we don't leave now, who knows what's going to happen," Victor said. "But it's your call, sir." The last part was intended to make the president feel like he had a choice, but Victor knew better. The second the shooting had started, his choices had narrowed significantly. And then, for good measure, Victor said, "Bring four of your men. There's room in the vehicles."

His decision made, President Pena gave instructions to the head of his detail who stood to his right. "Antonio, you and three men that you trust the most are with me. We're going with General Cordones, and we're going now."

The last footage the citizens of Caracas—and later, the rest of the world—would see of the embattled president of Venezuela was him being ushered into a convoy of military vehicles and whisked away into the heart of the city.

Within a mile of departing Miraflores Palace, the convoy split up, vanished, and swapped out Tiuna military vehicles for SUVs and sedans with tinted windows, which were nearly as common as the daily horde of motorcyclists.

CHAPTER 26

General Cordones's Base Camp
1915 Venezuelan Standard Time

The plan was simple in concept—a flanking maneuver from east to west with the drone swarm serving as a diversionary element cutting through the middle of the camp from north to south. A double envelopment would've increased the risk of friendly fire, which was the last thing Logan needed. The plan was to cause as much chaos as possible and use the bedlam to mask their movement until they'd infiltrated the camp from the two eastern corners. The base didn't have a perimeter fence, and Logan figured the remote location provided General Cordones with a sense of security, for which he was about to be proven wrong. Once inside the camp, all enemy combatants were to be treated as hostile, and deadly force was authorized for everyone except the vice president.

The sun had set thirty-five minutes ago, allowing the mountain and its plateau to be shrouded in darkness. Parts of the base were bathed in a harsh white light from the mounted floodlights, and the running generators sent out a low, thrumming sound that carried across the mountain. The nighttime noises had emerged, contributing to the auditory symphony.

Thirty meters below the northeastern lip of the plateau, Logan West and his Hunter Team waited. The decision on how to break up the assault force had been an easy one, and one that Logan had insisted upon. With Logan was Santiago, Marcos—whom Logan refused to let out of his sight—and six shooters, including the four cartel enforcers and two assassins. On the southeastern side of the mountain, Cole Matthews and Jack led the Killer Team, including the four friends of Marcos and the other two assassins. Everything north of the railroad was Logan's responsibility; the south was Jack and Cole's.

Marcos had asked Logan why his friends couldn't work with them, and Logan had replied, "Because I don't trust you. And the thought of you going rogue with four of your BFFs doesn't instill a real sense of security in me."

Marcos's only reply had been, "And I thought you were a big, badass Marine," to which Logan had answered, "Bad enough to take you once before. Don't forget that. And don't make me have to do it again, or worse."

Marcos had shrugged indifferently, and that had been the end of the conversation.

The communications plan was also simple—there was none, at least not until the shooting stopped. In the event of an emergency, Logan and Cole both carried a coyote-brown Motorola SRX 2200 Enhanced Combat single-band radio with a wired microphone looped over the front of the black Kevlar vest each wore.

Each man of the ad hoc assault force carried his personal preference of assault rifle and sidearm with a suppressor on each, with the intent to maintain the tactical advantage for as long as possible. The only downside of an assault force consisting of shooter's-choice weapons was that ammunition would not be interchangeable in the event that one man went down and another ran low on rounds. *Just another thing on the long list of things I'm not a fan of on this trip,* Logan had thought to himself.

In addition to the weapons, the men wore solid black tactical fatigues that Jack had provided, black boonie covers, black camouflage paint, black Kevlar vests with magazine pouches on the front and a medical pouch on the back. Some had knives on their belts, some had sheaths attached to the vests, and others adopted the minimalist approach with only firearms and ammunition—the essentials.

Once the raid commenced and the vice president was secure, the extraction plan was to use several of the multiple vehicles maintained on the mountain and drive them down the access road that ran alongside the railroad tracks.

If all went according to plan—although Logan and every member of the assault force, including the criminal elements, knew it never did—they'd be off the mountain in less than thirty minutes, depending on what they found.

Logan glanced at the dark, shadowy figure of Marcos on his right and wondered what the former cartel enforcer and onetime member of the Organization was thinking, although he suspected he knew—*his murdered wife, just like you would be if you were him.*

Logan felt a tap on his left shoulder and turned to see the outline of Santiago pointing up into the night sky, an outline against the black backdrop of the mountain forest.

And then Logan heard them, and for the first time of the chaotic day, he thought, *This might actually work.*

Josh Baker had remained in the command post since General Cordones's team had left. Two soldiers had provided him with dinner, and he'd watched news coverage of the president's rescue—in reality, a carefully staged and precisely executed abduction—since the event had occurred. Globovision—and he assumed the rest of the national and, likely by now, world media—continued to broadcast that the president was being held at a safe location until the extent of the attempt on his life could be determined.

General Cordones had told Josh he planned to permit the Venezuelan president to call his vice president and assure him he was safe in order to maintain the ruse, and Josh assumed that action had been completed. There was no sense of panic in the reporting, let alone a hint that anything was truly amiss. He knew the shock and chaos from the earthquake had contributed to their level of gullibility, and he was grateful for it.

A few more hours, and this will all be over. He glanced at his encrypted cell phone, a spare that only one person outside South America had the phone number to, and he hadn't heard from him in the past thirty-six hours. He knew that part of his plan was in position and prepared to be let loose like a precision-guided munition on the unsuspecting targets if General Cordones's plan failed. The presence of Logan West and his Task Force Ares had reassured him that he'd made the right decision in planning for that eventuality, though he knew it was his death sentence if he executed it. *But what choice do I have? They're down here, and I have to shake their resolve.*

After the events in DC at the National Cathedral nearly three weeks ago, the presence of Logan West on the field was the greatest threat. He'd told General Cordones exactly that, and it was also why his fail-safe was primed and ready to go. Once he was out of South America and over the Atlantic, he'd issue the stand-down order. Until then, every option was in play.

He was standing up to stretch his legs when he felt rather than heard a low thrum begin to vibrate in the wooden floor of the command post. He stiffened and listened as the vibration grew in intensity. He knew instinctively that whatever it was, it wasn't good for him, and he grabbed the black backpack with his extra set of clothes, his wallet—although he knew he'd never need his ID again—and a few personal photographs of his son, Jacob, and bolted for the entrance to the front foyer of the command post.

The double wooden doors were open, and four of his guards stood outside, AK-103s at the ready, scanning the night sky for the threat.

Josh stepped outside, where the thrum had become deafening. It was as if the plateau was surrounded by an enormous swarm of mechanical insects that moved and circled above, hungrily stalking them before striking. But he sensed a cohesion, as if they moved with one purpose, and he knew what they were. *Drones.* It also meant that the base was under siege, although the soldiers hadn't grasped that fact yet.

A figure appeared from behind him, and Josh turned to see Lieutenant Colonel Alvarez, the officer in charge of the protective detail. A man in his late thirties with black hair and brown eyes and a youthful appearance that belied his age, he processed the imminent threat.

Josh beat him to the assessment. "It's drones, dozens of them, by the sound. We're under attack, and we need to get the hell out of here, because they came prepared, *and they're here for me.*"

"Why do you say that, sir?" Lieutenant Colonel Alvarez asked, concern evident in his voice.

"Why else would they be here? Your government still thinks that General Cordones is protecting the president. And after the ambush on the highway, it's the same people—I know it. Somehow, they figured out I'm here, and they've come for me," Josh said. He paused for a moment. "Is there a loudspeaker system throughout the base? And if so, can you patch me through to it? I have an idea."

"There is, but we need to get you out of here, or it won't matter what you want to say," Lieutenant Colonel Alvarez said. "But there are several intercom stations throughout the base."

Josh's mind raced ahead of Alvarez's decision-making. While Alvarez might be an outstanding soldier, Josh was both strategic and tactical in his calculations, and he knew they were running out of time and options by the second.

"Is there one on that?" Josh asked, pointing 150 yards away at the parked, looming beast of the train and the two cars attached to it.

"Yes, but why?" Alvarez asked.

"Because we're never going to make it to the helo. It's the first thing they'll destroy to prevent us from escaping. I have an idea, and we can use that. In fact, if you want to survive, I recommend you stay close. They won't shoot me, at least not yet. Now let's go," Josh ordered, naturally falling once again into the role of commanding people around him. He started moving toward the train, and the four soldiers flanked him, two on each side, as Alvarez jogged ahead of him. *I hope he realizes he's going to take the first bullet, but better him than me,* Josh thought, his true nature on display, at least to himself.

CHAPTER 27

The drone swarm was surreal to Logan West. In all of the combat he'd experienced over the years, both in the Marine Corps and in Task Force Ares, he'd never charged into battle under the cover of a diversion like the micro drones that had descended upon the mountain. He'd run movement to contact ranges with machine-gun fire close overhead at the legendary Marine Corps Infantry Officer Course at Quantico, and he'd once had a Mexican navy helicopter fire 20mm cannon shells at the foothill he was on in Mexico—ironically, while he was locked in hand-to-hand combat with none other than Marcos Bocanegra. *But a swarm of drones operating as one artificial organism? That's a new one, even for me.*

The deafening hum of the drones turned into a full-pitched shriek, and Logan realized the swarm had entered the camp at a low altitude. He looked up through the canopy of trees, thought he saw a few drone stragglers veering away and then toward the middle of the camp. *Time to go, once again into the breach,* he thought, and sprinted the remaining distance up the hill.

Moments later, Logan West emerged from the darkness like a wraith materializing from the substance of the night. He entered the base first, leading from the front, and searched for targets with the same MP5 he'd used at the mountaintop hotel. A split second later, the rest of his assault team appeared from within the recesses of the trees, assembling on both sides of him in two lines that curved away from him at the center of the northeastern corner.

For the briefest of moments, Logan processed the scene before him. Between the two buildings in front of him—one a small rectangle, the other a larger upside-down L shape—pandemonium had broken out, almost at a comical level. Figures darted back and forth across the base, some of them firing weapons into the night sky, although the reports from their weapons were muffled by the sound of the drones. *Good luck with that tactic,* Logan thought, knowing that luck was the only way they might hit one of the machines. A quick glance left to the southeastern far side of the railroad revealed the dark figures of Cole and his assault team in the process of securing the helicopter. But the most important thing that Logan realized was that no one had detected the hostile threat now in their midst. *Time to work.*

Logan moved forward, and the rest of his lethal squad moved with him. Twenty feet from the L-shaped house, the formation split into three elements the way they'd planned. Logan, Santiago, and Marcos had the central avenue of approach, directly between the buildings. The three shooters on the right would move around the L-shaped house; the three men on the left, around the rectangular building.

A figure in combat fatigues appeared sixty feet away from behind the smaller building. He looked upward, his AK-103 held in one hand at his side. The soldier made a quarter turn, still looking up, as if trying to ascertain the size and scope of the drone swarm. He lowered his head and found himself staring directly into the path of approaching men, not realizing until too late that death had come for him on the mountain.

Without remorse, Logan fired a single shot into the soldier's

197

forehead, the suppressed *thwack* mostly inaudible under the roaring of the drones. The soldier crumpled to the ground, the AK falling uselessly to the grass.

Still, no attention was paid to the assaulting tidal wave of men and weapons. The chaos of confusion and disorientation continued unchecked beyond the two buildings. Logan saw five small black shapes dive toward a group of three soldiers. The men panicked and turned to run, reminding Logan of the victims in Alfred Hitchcock's *The Birds*, fleeing an imaginary horror in the sky, oblivious to the real threat on the ground. Unfortunately for them, they chose the wrong direction in which to flee, moving toward Logan and his team. A series of barely audible shots from Logan's left dropped all three men before they'd taken two strides.

This can't be that easy, Logan thought. *Four down, and no one seems to know we're here.*

As if an unseen enemy were attuned to his thoughts, automatic weapons fire erupted from the rectangular building in front of him. The muzzle flashes illuminated a barrel that stuck out of a cut-out opening that served as a window in the side of the single-story structure. Logan heard a groan from his left, even as he dove to the right and landed close to Marcos.

Santiago returned fire, and the barrage of bullets drove the shooter back inside the building.

Logan saw one man down, and another member of the team knelt beside him, looked toward Logan's direction, and shook his head from side to side. *Goddamnit. We can't start taking casualties this quickly.*

The plan relied on aggression and momentum, two intangible concepts that often determined the outcome of combat. Logan hit Marcos's shoulder and pointed to the set of wooden doors at the near end of the L-shaped building. Marcos understood, and the two warriors stood up in the grass and dashed toward the entrance to the building, even as the other two elements of the assault team moved forward toward the middle of the camp. But before Logan, Marcos, or Santiago could make any more progress, the shooter in the building had to be neutralized.

Logan studied the flimsy set of double doors, realized that they swung outward, and nodded at Marcos. In one fluid motion, the disgraced former Special Forces soldier dropped the MP5 against his chest, unholstered a Glock 19 suppressed pistol with his left hand, and grabbed the handle of the right door with his free hand. Logan nodded, exhaled, and waited.

Marcos yanked the door open, and Logan entered, the MP5 raised, even as he half expected to get shot. He moved quickly to the right side of the entrance and leaned up against the wall as Marcos entered and moved to the other side.

The wall against Logan's back was rippled, and he kicked his left foot back against the surface. He heard as much as felt a soft swishing, a sensation he'd felt countless times before—*sand moving*. Logan stared down the middle of this part of the L-shaped building as his eyes quickly adjusted to the gloomy interior. A silhouette appeared as his eyes adjusted, and Logan nearly fired, realizing just in time that it wasn't moving. Other shapes—a low-cut wall on the left, a doorway with no door on the right, a stack of tires near the wall—stuck out to him. *Oh no*, Logan thought, and recognized the purpose of the building, even as Marcos spoke it aloud.

"We're in a goddamned shoot house," Marcos said. "You've got to be fucking kidding me."

Logan had once heard a story about a squad of soldiers from the Philippine Army on a patrol in the jungle on one of the southern Philippine islands. The unit had inadvertently wandered directly onto the target area of an insurgent sniper range, *as the insurgents were training*. All twenty-four soldiers had died within a minute from precision fire. When he'd heard the story, his only thought was, *Bad luck can kill, almost as quickly as complacency.*

Logan and Marcos had just stumbled into an enemy shoot house in the dark. *Advantage, bad guys.*

"Good," Logan said with determination. "Let's beat them at their own game. We're better at this than they are."

"You're the boss," Marcos responded.

"You're goddamned right I am," Logan replied. "Let's move."

He didn't wait for a response and crept forward toward the low wall as the incessant drones screamed for blood and mayhem outside.

CHAPTER 28

Cole Matthews moved with purpose. The former Tier 1 operator emerged from the tree line less than one hundred feet from the HLZ. The Russian attack helicopter was exactly where they'd anticipated, parked parallel to the railroad track, its bulbous nose that earned it the nickname "the crocodile" facing due west.

Jack Longstreet was on his right, while the far left element of four shooters pressed forward to take up a position on the side of the large building adjacent to the HLZ. The noise was deafening and masked their movement.

Cole, Jack, and the two government assassins had one objective—secure the HLZ and several vehicles they could use for their extraction. No one was hiking down the mountain once the shooting ended. The four mercenary friends of Marcos were tasked with eliminating any threat that originated from within the large adjacent building.

The cool night air wrapped around him as he moved, calming his senses as he looked for targets. Halfway to the helicopter, the first two hostiles appeared—two soldiers in dark flight suits carrying helmets running toward the helicopter. For the briefest moment, Cole considered sparing one of them, but then reconsidered. The plan was the plan, and there was no point in altering it until necessary. The pilot on the left slid to a stop and looked in Cole's direction, even as his partner kept running toward the Hind.

Cole fired three shots from his suppressed Colt M4 Commando, and the pilot who had stopped short now fell to the grass as the three rounds caught him center-mass.

The other pilot kept running, oblivious to his friend's fate, at least until Jack fired several rounds, and he stumbled and rolled into the grass, his body still, the lone round that had struck him in the side of the head ending his dash to freedom.

Cole crossed the HLZ and reached the side of the enormous attack helicopter. It was the one used to attack them on the mountain after the earthquake. There were the same distinct markings on the nose, including an emblem of the Venezuelan army decaled just behind the forwardmost and lower cockpit.

Jack reached him a second later and said, "The exhaust port just below the propellers. Toss a grenade in there. It will shred the motor, and she won't fly anywhere."

Cole remembered the Mi-24 that had ambushed them seven months ago after they'd escaped a black-site Sudanese prison. "Believe it or not, this isn't the first Hind we've seen since I joined Team Logan. The fun never stops with this task force."

"Sorry. I forgot about Sudan," Jack replied, as he watched Cole grab an M67 fragmentation grenade off his Kevlar vest. "I read the after-action report you guys filed with the CIA when you returned."

"Of course you did. You seem to know everything," Cole muttered, reached for the safety pin, and paused.

"What is it?" Jack asked.

"I know we're supposed to disable this beast, but why not wait until the battle is over? You never know when we might need a quick ride out of here," Cole said.

"It's your call, but I support it," Jack said, and then suddenly changed the subject. "Targets, twelve o'clock. Get down!"

Cole glanced up just in time to see five more soldiers running toward their position. He reacted instinctively. His finger already near the grenade's pin, he pulled it, and threw the grenade as far as he could in the approaching hostiles' direction and dove into the prone position. He unslung the Colt Commando and sighted down the reflex scope.

The grenade detonated twenty feet short of the group of soldiers and sent shrapnel and clumps of dirt and grass flying in all directions. It was enough to stop the group in its tracks.

Cole Matthews and Jack Longstreet, side by side in the damp grass, opened fire at the disorganized group of men 120 feet away. Simultaneously, two of the Killer Team shooters who had taken a position on the side of the building stepped out from behind cover and opened fire on the soldiers at a closer distance. The five Venezuelan soldiers never had a chance.

In less than three seconds, the five men were on the ground, dead or dying.

The drones continued to swarm through the camp in a racetrack formation just above the buildings, bisecting the camp from north to south.

The shooters at the corner remained in position to provide cover as Jack and Cole stood up and jogged around the helicopter toward the parking lot and the four rows of military trucks and SUVs.

The explosion of the grenade from the direction of the HLZ sent a mild vibration through the shoot house. *Helicopter disabled. No way out, now, Baker,* Logan thought, unaware of Cole's tactical change of plan.

The inside was still dark, but with each passing moment, the black transformed into varying shades of gray, which seemed to shift back and forth. *As long as they don't have night vision, we should be good.* The drones had become a steady backdrop to the action, and the mechanical high-pitched whirring masked their movements.

Once Logan and Marcos had reached the low wall, they'd crept over it, Marcos covering Logan and vice versa. They found themselves inside a square room with two human-shaped metal silhouette targets. Another door—this one closed—stood between them and behind the targets. It was the only way out.

Logan realized they had to be near the juncture of the building where the two parts of the L met. They'd moved at least thirty feet into the building since they'd entered it.

Logan reached the door first and listened. No sounds came from the other side, although he wasn't sure he'd have heard them if there were any, due to the drones' death-metal screeching.

"Wait," Marcos said quietly, and yanked an M84 stun grenade off his vest and handed it to Logan. He stepped back against the wall out of the line of fire from the unknown room. "Use this, and I'll go in shooting."

Logan didn't argue and accepted the grenade. Crouched down on one knee, he secured his MP5 under his right arm, pulled the pin on the grenade, and held the spoon in place. He grabbed the door with his right hand, nodded, and yanked it open. Several shots rang out from inside and struck the door above Logan's head and the far wall where Marcos had stood moments before. He flung the grenade into the room, slammed the door shut, and moved back against the concrete wall, placing his hands over his ears and opening his mouth.

Even outside the room, the 180-plus decibel noise was deafening, and the flash of more than a million candela shot from under and around the door and then vanished, leaving an afterimage in Logan's retinas. A second later, Logan pulled the door open, and Marcos entered the room, MP5 raised.

The unfortunate soldier was on the ground in the far corner, one hand held against his right ear. His left hand was on his AK-103, which was all the justification Marcos needed: he shot the soldier once in the head, and the dead man slumped farther to the ground, falling sideways.

Marcos reached the next door, which was set on the left wall and led to the other part of the building. The window the shooter had fired from was toward the end of the building at least forty-five feet away, but they had no idea what was on the other side of the door.

"Use a frag," Logan said, and handed Marcos an M67 fragmentation grenade. Seconds later, their roles reversed, Logan waited as the grenade exploded, shaking the walls and floor of the building. Logan heard something split on the other side, and he thought he heard a low scream of pain that cut off abruptly.

Marcos pulled the door open, and Logan entered the unknown beyond. Smoke and dislodged dust filled the room, which was long and open, unlike the previous section. *Large area training. Great. Everything is a threat.*

Logan assumed, dangerously, that anyone within fifteen feet of the door was injured or dead, and he moved forward, reached a stack of oversized tires ten feet away, and crouched behind it. Several silhouette targets were set up in the space, but Logan couldn't see how far back they went, as the far end of the room was still swathed in an amorphous gray darkness.

Marcos appeared at his side. "Nothing to do but move forward," he said.

"I know," Logan replied. "Let's go. You first. I'll cover you. Shoot anything that moves, other than me."

"Funny," Marcos said, and stepped out, moving at an angle to the right side of the area, where a large desk stood.

Logan heard a shuffle directly in front of him and stood up. A soldier sat on the ground, his back up against a stack of tires. Logan saw blood, a black slick in the darkness, on the side of his face. His army boonie cover had been knocked off in the blast, and his legs were splayed out in front of him. As if in shock and disbelief at the sight of Marcos stalking across the floor, he tried to raise a pistol he held in his right hand.

Logan adjusted the MP5 and pulled the trigger once, striking the wounded Venezuelan in the side of the head. His head lolled forward, his chin rested on his body, and his pistol hand fell back to the floor. *Two down.*

He didn't know if there were any more, and he didn't care. He spoke to Marcos quickly. "Get down. Tossing an M67." Logan didn't wait for a response: his former enemy could fend for himself.

Logan grabbed a second M67 grenade from his vest, pulled the pin, and threw it into the middle of the room as far as he could. It struck something metal with a *clang*, landed on the concrete floor, and detonated a moment later.

The space lit up with a brief light, followed by the explosion and overpressure that filled the room and shattered targets and whatever other obstacles the darkness concealed at the far end. *Anyone down there is not having a good night.*

Marcos picked himself up, pressed forward, and remained close to the right wall. Logan emerged from behind the tires and crept up the left side, watching and listening.

Muffled shouts and the constant metallic shrieking of the drones entered the building through the cut-out window at the far end, but they were the only sounds either warrior heard. There was no one else in the space.

He must have moved down to this end when we took out his friend in the last room, Logan thought, as he reached the window and crouched to the left of it. He leaned forward and shouted, but not too loudly, "All clear. We're coming out."

He heard a subdued "Roger" and moved past the window to the double doors set in the middle of the wall.

The first bullet struck Logan in the middle of the back like a hammer, staggering him forward toward the middle of the room. Pain erupted in his back, and he felt his breath catch as his right foot struck the base of a metal target. He tripped and fell forward, which was the only thing that saved his life.

As he hit the floor, several more shots rang out and struck the doors above Logan. More shots erupted from the right side of the room, and Logan prayed Marcos's aim was true. He heard a grunt from his left as Marcos moved across the floor, firing three more times.

A second later Marcos said, "Clear. Are you going to live?" he asked, semi-concern in his voice.

Logan inhaled but didn't feel anything rattle in his side or back, just an enormous amount of pain, something he was accustomed to and could fight through. He gritted his teeth and said, "For now. Thanks for not missing."

"No sweat," Marcos said nonchalantly. "Now let's get the hell out of this funhouse death trap."

Logan staggered to his feet, regaining his strength with each breath, and pushed the doors open. "On that, we agree," he said, and stepped back out into the fog of war on top of the mountain.

CHAPTER 29

Cole Matthews turned the key in the white Toyota J70 Land Cruiser—called the Machito in Venezuela—and the 4.5L V8 diesel engine roared to life. *Unreal. Works perfectly, even in this third world hellhole. Honda would be jealous.*

Once Cole and Jack had elected to leave the Mi-24 intact, they'd moved north adjacent to the train tracks to the vehicle assembly area, where they'd both been shocked to discover not just Tiuna SUVs and cargo trucks but a row of twelve pristine J70 Land Cruisers. While no longer in production in Venezuela, the SUVs were the workhorses of off-road utility vehicles. And increasing their luck to the level of winning the Powerball, a small wooden shack had been erected that contained all the keys to the vehicles. Each set held a small aluminum tag that corresponded to a number on each J70's license plate. The vehicles were more than adequate to provide transportation off the mountain for their seventeen-man assault force.

While they'd secured five vehicles to be safe rather than sorry—in case one broke down—the sound of several explosions, which they both recognized as grenades, had reached them from the northernmost building in Logan's objective area. Cole just hoped it was Logan and his team delivering the punishment and not vice versa.

And all the while, the drones continued to swarm over the middle of the camp.

Leaving the keys in the ignition and the engine running, Cole stepped out of the vehicle, left the door open, and moved to the next one to prepare it in the same manner.

The other two elements of the team had proceeded onward with one objective—eliminate any remaining resistance. After the last five men had decided to investigate the activity at the HLZ and died doing so, no one else had appeared.

Moments later, all five vehicles were faced north and running with all four doors open, waiting to take their new owners down the dirt access road.

Cole stood on the passenger side of the far left SUV, his Commando resting on the hood in his right hand, ready to be put into action at the next threat. Jack joined him, and the two men watched with professional pride, absorbing the sounds and smells of combat and chaos, as the two elements moved around the buildings and toward the middle of the camp.

"Your guys are good, Jack. I'll give you that," Cole said with appreciation. Two hundred feet away, a soldier appeared from the other side of a central small building, started running, and was knocked down by a hail of bullets from members of Cole's assault team that he couldn't see. "Are they all Organization?"

"In one way or another," Jack replied.

"You guys built quite an empire for yourselves, and standing here, at this moment, I see the purpose," Cole said.

"It was built *long* before I joined Constantine," Jack said. "I just made it more efficient *and* more lethal."

"No doubt," Cole said. "But what happens to these guys when we're done here tonight? They just go back to their lives after attacking a Venezuelan army training base?"

"It's totally up to them. They can stay here, leave the country with us, or go somewhere else," Jack said. "The beauty of the Organization is that it truly does have almost limitless financing and resources, and every member knows it. They will get whatever they want and need. It's one of the promises we make when we recruit someone new. These guys aren't in it for the money, though. It's ideological for them, which, as you know, is a much greater motivation."

True believers were always more dangerous than mercenaries. Cole knew that to be gospel. Men willing to fight and die for a cause would always find a way, which is what made Islamic extremism and the rest of the radical brands of terrorism so dangerous. *But mix money and resources with a belief in a perceived just cause? That was a winning combination.*

"Well, then, I guess that's good for us and bad for the Venezuelan army," Cole said, ending the conversation as the two men watched the rest of the battle unfold.

With the initial contact and engagements over, Logan's Hunter team had reassembled on the far side of the shoot house and the smaller rectangular building. The pain in his back subsided a bit with each breath, but Logan knew that once the day's combat was over—*if I live through it*—his lower back would be discolored in deep shades of green and blue. He raised his right fist and paused the forward progress to assess the scene before him. From their vantage point, they had a full view of the center of the base all the way to the far side of the tracks into Cole's objective area.

One hundred feet past the shoot house, an enormous obstacle course ran from the north end near the edge of the forest and plateau to the south toward the middle of the camp, where the train tracks bisected the base. Parallel bars, several chest-high log obstacles, a cargo net wall, and a wooden wall with ropes that hung down provided several barriers to enhance the soldiers' fitness and athletic abilities. It reminded Logan of the Marine Corps' obstacle course, which every base had. The only thing missing was a rope climb at the end. *Lucky bastards,* he thought. He'd had enough ropes to last a lifetime, recollecting the recent debacle on a North Korean cargo ship when he fell from a helicopter to the deck below.

In the center of the camp on the railroad facing east stood a titanic General Electric 6000hp diesel-electric locomotive. Connected to it was a passenger rail car that reminded Logan of an Amtrak passenger train. The second and final car was some type of cargo carrier that had its sliding doors closed.

The drones continued to swarm the center of the camp, searching for new targets to terrorize. Several bodies were scattered between the buildings, but no other living thing was in sight. The Venezuelan soldiers were either dead or had sought shelter inside the buildings. *Which means the easy part is over,* Logan thought.

Logan estimated that they'd eliminated at least fifteen to twenty enemy combatants. The most recent series of US national-level imagery that Jack's intelligence network had provided had revealed at least twenty to thirty hostiles. If that assessment held true, there couldn't be too many more hostiles left. But then again, intelligence had proven to be wrong over and over throughout history. *Why should this be any different?* It was why the next phase was the most dangerous.

Once the Hunter and Killer teams had merged, they'd break up into smaller fire teams and clear the buildings of the base one by one. Wherever the vice president was, he'd be found: there was nowhere to hide.

Logan unclenched his fist and motioned forward. The assault line crept purposefully forward, with the far right element pivoting so that it faced inward toward the middle of the camp and the train.

A loud electronic squelching suddenly interrupted the metallic song the drones had established. It seemed to emanate from everywhere all at once.

They've got a loudspeaker system. But who the hell is going to broadcast right now? Logan thought, and instinctively knew it wasn't good for him and his assault force.

And then the voice followed, and a feeling of dread began to gnaw away at the confidence he'd felt seconds before.

"Logan West, are you out there?" Joshua Baker asked, his voice somehow clear, carrying over the incessant whine of the drones.

The gnawing dread turned into a fleeting moment of panic, but he squashed it, composing himself and stopping the forward momentum of the assault line.

"That's okay. You don't have to answer. I knew this was all you and your friends as soon as it started. It's why I had a contingency plan in place before I left the States. I knew that the president would send you or someone like you to find me. I don't know how you knew I was here, but it's irrelevant. All that matters for you, *at this moment*, is what I'm about to say," Josh continued. "And just remember, this isn't personal. It never was."

The dread was strong, a feeling of desperation and horror that uncontrollably insinuated itself into every fiber of Logan's being with every word that the United States' most-wanted traitor uttered. *Here it comes, Logan. Steel yourself for it.*

"But first things first. In case you're wondering, I'm on the train. It's armored, and you're not going to be able to take it with small arms. Good luck trying. Hell, give it your best. Part of me wants to see what you can do. You're a determined man, and I can appreciate that. But you're not going to do anything, and here's why," the vice president said.

Logan exhaled and waited for the proverbial axe to fall. *Whatever it is, you can do this, not for yourself, but for the men around you, for John, for Mike, and most importantly, for Sarah and your unborn baby. This is who you are,* he thought, not realizing that it was those very things he held dear that were about to be used as chips in a life-and-death poker game.

"Unless you let this train leave this base, your best friend, John, his new girl, Amira, and her father are going to be killed within the half hour. I have a team at her father's place in Owings, Maryland, and I just sent a text to the team leader with very specific instructions. If he doesn't hear from me in the next fifteen minutes, he's going to commence an assault on the house with the intent to kill each of them." Joshua Baker paused to allow the gravity of his threat to sink in.

Of course, Logan thought. *It made sense for the sonofabitch to use his friends as collateral.* Swirling emotions raged inside Logan. The anger that he'd kept at bay since Mike Benson's death suddenly erupted once again like a psychological volcano. He had to think clearly, to quiet his mind, or he knew they would surely die. He understood this was not a bluff.

"Here's your choice, Logan: Let this train leave. Do not pursue us, or *you* will cause your friends to die. It's all up to you. I don't want to kill any more people, but you know that if I have to, I will. I left the only person I cared about behind. Please don't test my resolve. We're leaving," Josh said.

As if on cue, the diesel locomotive roared to life, its engine thrumming and adding to the cacophony of sound on the mountain. Lights shot out of the windows in the engine and the passenger car, and Logan saw several figures standing inside the engineer's cab.

"Whatever happens next, just remember, it's all on you. I hope you make the right decision. Goodbye, Logan," former Vice President Baker said, and ended the one-way conversation.

There was a loud sound as the brakes were released, and the train suddenly crept forward, moving slowly toward its destination—the opening at the far end of the base that led down into the mountain forest and back to the city.

The hesitation was only a split second, but inside his head, it felt like an eternity. Emotions, memories, and images threatened to paralyze him. But then he remembered the sacrifice that Mike had made, giving his life in a way befitting a true warrior. He thought of what John would tell him right now and what John had risked in Sudan in the cemetery. And then there was Amira, who had proven to be as fearless and lethal as any of them, maybe even more so. *They would all tell you to hunt him down and end this, once and for all.* In a moment of clarity, he knew it was true, absolute in conviction. His friends were every bit as formidable as he was, and he owed it to them to let them fend for themselves. He knew it's what they would want.

As if a switch were flipped in his mind, all confusion was swept away by the harsh wind of confidence, singular in its purpose. The resolve that was his ally and enabled him to do the things he did was back in full control, replacing all hesitation and uncertainty with focus and intent.

As the train gained speed, the locomotive passed the obstacle course, and Logan West started running, with only one thought resonating in his mind, the memory of the chase in DC weeks ago still fresh: *You're not getting away this time, no matter what.*

He was halfway to the moving train—with Marcos and other members of the team following his lead—when the cargo carrier's metal doors in the center of the car slid open sideways, exposing an FN MAG 7.62mm machine gun.

Knowing he had no chance to reach the car alive, Logan dove to the right as the machine gunner opened fire, strafing from left to right as the train moved. Logan hit the ground and rolled to his right, finishing his evasive maneuver behind the obstacle wall. Unfortunately, the far left three-man element was caught out in the open ground, and the barrage of gunfire cut them down.

Marcos and Santiago, as well as the three-man team on the right that had already reached the obstacle course, were spared the quick and violent death.

"What now?" Marcos said in between ragged breaths.

The train slowly pulled away, the second car carrying the machine gun passing by the obstacle wall as Logan waited, ignoring Marcos's question. *One one thousand, two one thousand, three one thousand, four one thousand, five one thousand. Now.*

"Now, get off your ass and follow me," Logan said, stood up, and started sprinting, first around the right end of the obstacle wall on a line perpendicular with the train tracks.

Marcos sighed but stood up and followed, as did the others.

The machine gunner had lost his line of sight on the remaining members of the assault team and stopped firing.

Within seconds, Logan West and his Hunter Team had reached the tracks, sprinting at full speed to catch the escaping train. *Always running after someone or something,* Logan thought at the head of the pack, then concentrated on his breathing, and pushed his legs harder. The distance between the train and him grew smaller. The race between man and machine had started.

CHAPTER 30

As soon as the voice of Vice President Josh Baker interrupted the continuous cry of the drone swarm, Cole Matthews knew something had gone wrong. He'd listened as the vice president spoke, acutely aware that using Logan's friends against him was a dangerous gambit, which made Cole wonder why he'd done it.

If the train was bulletproof, as Baker claimed—and Cole had every reason to believe him—whoever was on the train could have rolled away, evaded pursuit, and ridden directly into Caracas unscathed. The dirt road branched off from the railroad less than a mile from the city and turned north before winding its way back into the city.

But something bothered Cole. Baker was a devious traitor, a master strategist, and devoid of any type of moral compass. He'd proven that when he'd betrayed his own security detail and led the Secret Service officers to their deaths, even if they were members of the Organization. They'd been pawns used to establish the kidnapping ruse, and their lives had been forfeit as a result. Baker had to know that Logan West, while a man who cared deeply about his friends and loved ones, was still a man who had demonstrated time and time again that he would not be deterred from his mission, no matter what the cost.

When Baker had finished his soliloquy, the train had started moving, followed by some type of heavy automatic weapons fire. As the train approached and picked up steam, Cole had seen several figures chase the last car, before disappearing behind it.

It was at that moment that it hit him. *Baker's counting on it, which means it's a diversion, just like DC, to conceal his escape. He wants Logan on that train because he's still here, somewhere, waiting for us to take the bait.*

"Logan's taking his team on the train. No way he's going to let Baker get away, no matter what that sonofabitch says or does. You and I both know that, but I think Baker knows it as well," Cole said to Jack, as the train neared their position. He moved to the back of the J70s, and Jack followed, on the off chance that whoever was on the train opened up on them.

"You think it's a decoy," Jack stated, rather than asked.

"I do, but in case it's not, grab Marcos's four friends and take two vehicles down the mountain after the train. No matter what happens, Logan is going to need a way off it," Cole said.

As Cole watched the train, the other six members of the Killer Team appeared from the buildings and sprinted toward the vehicle assembly area. *These guys are good. Knew to get back here once Baker threw the plan into tatters with the train.*

The engine of the train reached their location, and Cole saw silhouettes of several men inside the engineer's cab, as well as the passenger car.

"What are you going to do?" Jack asked.

The engine was already past them, picking up speed. The doors on this side of the second car were closed.

"I'm keeping the two wet-work government guys with me, and I'm going to radio your drone operators and ask them to call off the swarm—that was a great idea, by the way—but keep the ScanEagle on station," Cole said, referring to the mini UAV, small by UAV standards with only a five-foot-long body and ten-foot wingspan. It could loiter on the mountain, providing electro-optical/infrared imaging in real time, perfect for nighttime. "And then, we're going to wait."

"For what?" Jack asked, hopping into the front seat of a running J70, even as the rear of the train passed in front of the vehicles.

"If I'm right, for the sonofabitch to finally make a mistake," Cole said. "Just keep your radio on and channel open. Now get the hell out of here. He's going to need your help," Cole added, and pointed at the passing train.

On the back of the rear car, four figures stood on a railing that wrapped around the rear end of the cargo car and ran along both sides to the front of the car. Climbing up a ladder toward the roof of the car were two figures. As one reached the top of the ladder, the train disappeared into the darkness, engulfed by the tall mountain forest trees on both sides.

Good luck, brother, Cole thought. *Make them pay.* He grabbed the microphone, pressed the button, and issued orders to the drone operator in the mobile ground station several miles away.

Within thirty seconds, Jack Longstreet and his four mercenaries were gone, pursuing the fleeing train in two Toyota Land Cruisers.

Okay, you bastard, let's see what your next play is. Whatever it is, we've got it covered.

CHAPTER 31

Logan reached the roof of the boxcar and pulled himself up onto the top of the moving train. He found himself lying flat on a long, narrow walkway that ran the length of the boxcar. *This must be an old car,* he thought, remembering that most railroad boxcars had discontinued roof walkways decades earlier. *Or at least not subject to US laws and regulations.* His uncle, whom he hadn't spoken to in years, had once given him a brief history of the railroads in the US and the types of cars still in service. He'd been sixteen at the time, and he'd asked his uncle how it was that movie stars always seemed to have no problem standing on a moving train. His uncle had answered honestly: he had no idea, but it was likely Hollywood making the unbelievable believable, and then he'd told him about the walkways. *It's funny the things you remember. Now shut it down and figure out how to get into the car.*

The black forest roared by in a dark blur of shifting shapes. The only sound he heard was the train's engine and the thunderous *clack* as the wheels of the train lumbered down the tracks. He turned around and saw headlights in the distance from at least one vehicle, and he realized that his teammates had sent vehicle support for him. *God help me if I need it.*

His objective was simple—the midway point of the car on the port side. He knew that side was at least open, since that was the side from which the machine gunner had opened up on them. Before he'd started climbing, he'd told Marcos the plan, who'd then passed it on to the others on the back of the train. As long as one side was open, that was all he needed.

Logan was confident that Santiago and the other three shooters who'd hopped on the train with him and Marcos were in position—two covering a walkway on each side of the boxcar. For this evolution, Logan had the easy part.

He reached the midpoint of the train, rotated his body, slid himself carefully forward toward the edge of the roof, and braced himself against the edge with his hands. With his MP5 on his back and his Glock 17 in its gun clip to accommodate the silencer, he slowly inched forward until his head hung over the side and confirmed that the door was still open. A faint light emerged from the opening, the source dim and deep inside the boxcar away from the door. He knew he was safe since the other team members had a direct line of sight to anyone that stepped out of the car onto the walkway. If someone inside heard him, he'd just end up dead differently than Logan planned. *Now for the fun part.*

He pulled an M18 green smoke grenade off the left side of his vest, pulled the pin, leaned out over the edge, and threw the grenade like a hook shot into the open door below.

Even over the noise of the rumbling train and the roar of the rushing wind, he heard the *pop* as the fuse ignited, consuming the filler inside the grenade and creating a thick, acrid green smoke that instantly filled the car below. Within seconds, smoke billowed from the open compartment, and Logan waited from above like a hawk waiting to strike.

A figure suddenly emerged on the walkway below, coughing. Logan aimed with the Glock he'd unholstered, but as he squeezed the trigger, the train rocked from side to side. The Glock fired, but rather than strike the Venezuelan in the top of the head, the way he'd planned, the bullet shattered his left clavicle, drilling downward.

Logan heard the scream, but it was cut short as several rounds struck him from the back of the train and ended the pain Logan's wound had caused. As if suicidal in his last moments on earth, the soldier staggered forward and toppled over a short, narrow railing. His body struck the dirt road and bounced, disappearing from view as the train kept rolling toward Caracas.

Logan estimated the train had accelerated to at least fifty miles per hour, which meant—or at least Logan hoped—that the engineer knew the route and that they were on a relatively straight stretch of their journey back into Caracas.

Logan waited, counted to ten, but no one else exited the car, and the smoke continued to pour out, burning through its fifty-second payload. He scrambled forward, just past the left edge of the door.

The two shooters on this side of the boxcar moved up the narrow walkway and stopped at the right edge of the door. Santiago had point, and he looked up at Logan, waiting for his signal.

Logan nodded, clipped the Glock into its holster once again, and grabbed the edge of the roof that jutted up several inches, providing a decent handhold. He just prayed that the train didn't turn or hit a break in the tracks as he slid his legs over the side and allowed gravity to take control. He dropped to the walkway and retrieved his Glock in a lightning-fast motion, ready to engage the next target.

He felt a thud on the walkway behind him as Marcos joined the stack of men outside the open boxcar. The smoke dissipated, and Logan nodded at Santiago, holding up his left hand, the Glock in his right aimed at the compartment. Santiago returned the gesture, his MP5 raised, and Logan dropped his hand, and the two men peeled around the edges of the door and into the compartment.

Logan held his breath, waiting for the last of the smoke to clear the boxcar. A dim light bulb was mounted on the ceiling halfway down each end of the car, the light creating a green haze that hung in the air. Directly in front of Logan was the FN MAG machine gun, a fresh belt placed into the feed mechanism. Crates and other equipment were stacked along the walls on both sides, but he detected no movement. *Have to be sure.*

Logan turned back to Santiago, said, "Clear it," and stalked down the forward part of the boxcar. The Glock moved smoothly from dark crevices between the boxes to other areas that could be used for an ambush. He reached the front end of the car, uneventfully, and turned back to Marcos, when three loud shots rang out from the rear end of the car.

One figure went down, while the other dove to the back of the car. Marcos was already moving, his MP5 up and searching. A figure emerged from behind a stack of crates, and Logan realized what had happened. *The bastard waited until they passed him, and he shot the man behind Santiago in the back.*

As the soldier aimed at Santiago, who was on the floor of the car and lifting his own MP5 to return fire, Marcos squeezed the trigger, his aim true in the enclosed space. The round struck the man in the back of the neck, as Marcos hadn't fully elevated the MP5 when he let the first round go. His spinal cord severed, the soldier was momentarily paralyzed before the second round from Marcos's MP5, which was now on target, struck the soldier in the back of the head, killing him instantly. He crumpled to the floor and lay still, blood pooling less than a foot from where Santiago had landed.

"Nice shooting," Logan said, and before he could catch himself, he added, "Almost makes up for what you did two and a half years ago." He instantly regretted it, remembering why Marcos had allied himself with Logan and Jack. The hard truth inside the gray space that Logan and his task force had occupied for the past two and a half years was that battle lines had shifted, allegiances had changed, and people capable of committing great evil might also be capable of saving innocent lives. *What? Are you all of a sudden some kind of amateur philosopher? Who are you to judge, at least at this moment?*

Marcos looked at him, a flash of pain in his combat-drenched eyes. "Sorry," Logan said. Since he'd been sober from Day One, the day his wife was attacked, he'd gained the ability to realize when he was wrong and actually admit it, not just deflect or deny. "That was uncalled for. It won't happen again."

Marcos nodded, seemingly satisfied at the impromptu apology.

Santiago had regained his balance and joined them in the center of the boxcar near the FN MAG machine gun. The boxcar tilted slightly as the train hit a gradual curve to the right. Logan walked over to the closed set of doors, lifted the lever handle at the bottom of them, freed the locking mechanism that secured one door to the floor of the car, and slid the door to the left.

Standing outside, weapons raised, were the remaining two shooters, a former Venezuelan army special forces battalion soldier named Hernán, and a member of the SEBIN's Direction of Immediate Actions, which handled direct action and anti-explosive operations, who, for some reason known only to himself, went by George. The two men entered the car. Logan stepped outside and quickly looked toward the rear of the car. The headlights were still there, and one set had become two, their beams piercing the mountain forest at odd angles like random laser beams at a nightclub. *Good. At least we're not totally on our own.*

Logan went back inside, bent down, checked the 7.62mm ammunition belt—the gunner had inserted a new one as the train pulled away from the base—and picked the weapon off the floor, hefting the forty-plus-pound machine like Rambo. Marcos picked up the two-hundred-round ammunition belt, creating a two-man machine-gun team.

"What's next?" Santiago said.

"I think I have an idea," Marcos replied, and folded the ammunition into several long swaths that would feed smoothly into the FN MAG.

For the first time since they'd hit the base, Logan West allowed a subtle smile to break his black mask of camouflage paint and determination. "Now, Phase Two."

CHAPTER 32

Cole and the two government assassins had slunk back into the tree line behind the HLZ and assumed positions just inside the forest that afforded them a clear line of sight of the Mi-24 and the vehicle assembly area. He knew that if his suspicions were correct, the vice president would have to use one of the remaining vehicles to get down the mountain. Baker's choice was simple: the Mi-24 or one of the J70 Cruisers.

The drone swarm had finally vacated the airspace over the mountain and headed back to the clearing from where the mobile ground station had launched them. The drones would be recovered and taken with the team once the mission had ended. The silence that remained was nearly deafening in the absence of drones, gunfire, explosions, and a fleeing train.

The earbud in Cole's left ear erupted quietly, and the drone operator issued a status update, as he'd done every thirty seconds since the ScanEagle had assumed its aerial overwatch position. "No movement. Your three IR signatures are still the only things I see. Everyone else up there is dead, fading from white to gray on my monitor," he said, referring to the cooling bodies of the fallen Venezuelan soldiers and assault team members who'd been killed during the battle.

"Roger," Cole said. *Come on, Baker. I know you're out there, somewhere.*

"How long do we wait?" Frederico, the taller and older of the two assassins, asked.

"As long as it takes," Cole replied, as his eyes slowly tracked across the base, lingering for a moment on every object and every body. "He won't wait all night. He'll want to leave as soon as possible. If he's here and not on the train, once Logan discovers that, he has to assume we'll come back and tear this place apart. He won't want to be here for that."

"Makes sense," Frederico answered.

Cole only nodded in reply, keeping his real thoughts to himself. *Thanks. I'm relieved you approve of my plan. I was hoping to get in good with the local assassin's guild when this is over.*

The remaining five members of Hunter Team crouch-walked to the front of the boxcar out of the line of sight from inside the passenger car in front of it. The rear of the first car was a solid wall from the middle of the car down, except for the solitary door that swung inward. Set in the wall on each side of the door was a large rectangular window. The inside of the car was dark, where the soldiers waited safely for what they knew would come next—an assault. *But they don't know how,* Logan thought, counting on tactical surprise to clear the next lethal obstacle.

Santiago was positioned on the left corner of the boxcar's walkway, his MP5 ready for Logan's signal; the two surviving Venezuelan mercenaries posted at the right corner. Logan now lay *across the gap* between the two speeding train cars, and the FN MAG rested on the landing outside the passenger car, its barrel less than an inch from the door. His lower legs and boots lay on the boxcar, and as the train hit a subtle curve, he felt his legs move to the right as if an invisible force were rotating his hips.

Marcos crouched to the left of the door, reached across it with his left hand, and gripped the handle while his right hand held his MP5.

Logan exhaled, placed his left hand on the buttstock of the weapon, and rested his right cheek on his hand, looking down the length of the weapon and over the iron sights, his right eye waiting for a target. He was grateful the machine gunner hadn't mounted a scope on it, as it would've made it more difficult for what he planned next. He nodded, and Phase Two commenced as the train relentlessly rolled down the tracks.

Santiago raised his weapon over their heads and fired point-blank into the window, emptying an entire thirty-round magazine into the glass and the interior of the car. The window shattered into jagged pieces that tumbled both inside the car and onto Santiago. He ignored the glass and reached down for the next part of his plan.

In perfect synchronization, the two mercenaries on the right opened up as Santiago fired his last round. They fired blindly—every marksman instructor's worst nightmare—completely destroying the window in front of them.

Sporadic return fire from inside the car struck the boxcar at chest height and pinged off the corrugated steel. Santiago prayed that the wall he leaned against for cover was thick enough to stop whatever caliber round they were using.

As they fired, Santiago grabbed the M84 stun grenade he'd placed next to his boots, pulled the pin, and hurled it over his head and into the passenger car. Two seconds later, timed perfectly as the two mercenaries ceased firing and stayed down in cover, the stun grenade exploded with a deafening roar that was magnified inside the passenger car. It shot a brilliant flash of white through the shattered windows, briefly illuminating the boxcar with two blinding rectangles of light.

Marcos turned the handle of the door down and pushed inward, flinging the door against the back wall of the passenger car. He crouched down and covered his ears as Logan pulled the trigger on the FN MAG, unleashing a fusillade of 7.62mm lead that tore into the benches, the walls, and any unfortunate soul caught in the open aisle that ran down the middle of the car.

Logan strafed back and forth, adjusting the elevation of the barrel slightly each time to ensure he struck anyone on the floor, hiding on the benches, or standing up. The weapon chattered with its thunderous *clack-clack-clack,* a higher pitch than the M240G that the Marine Corps used as its crew-served 7.62mm death dealer of choice. The passenger car's windows exploded outward on both sides, sparks showered from the metal roof, benches were shattered under the barrage, and several cries of pain rang out, only to end abruptly a moment later.

Logan kept the trigger depressed, although he knew he might overheat the barrel. *But who cares? This is a one-time-use weapon.* He strafed across the car diagonally in both directions, creating an invisible X of machine-gun bullets, and the last of the ammunition belt fed into the weapon. The weapon went silent, and the sounds of the rushing wind and rolling train returned to the forefront of his hearing.

Marcos immediately entered the car, his MP5 up and searching hopelessly for any targets left alive, even though he knew Logan had turned the passenger car into a mobile slaughterhouse. Nothing moved. "I got to tell you, man, that . . . was . . . awesome," Marcos said at last, exhilaration still in his voice.

Logan understood the sentiment completely. There was nothing quite like the display of overwhelming firepower delivering death and carnage to one's enemies. It was primal, savage, and true. He'd just ended countless lives inside the passenger car, but he didn't feel guilty. This was war, and he felt pride and satisfaction that none of his men had perished in this part of the battle. *But it's not over yet.*

"I feel you, but we're not done yet," Logan replied, shoving the spent machine gun to the side. "One car—or should I say engine— left to go." He stood, unslung his MP5 off his back, and entered the car behind Marcos, who was already stalking down the center aisle.

Logan heard the rest of the team follow him inside the passenger car, the only sound they made that of boots crunching on shattered glass. But it was the devastation that captured his attention. It had been complete.

Several bodies lay along the walls, in between the benches, torn to shreds and missing large chunks of various body parts. Blood pooled on the floor on both sides of the car, and light twinkled on the shattered glass like diamonds in a dark sea of red. *They never had a chance,* Logan thought, followed immediately by, *which was the entire point of the plan.*

The team reached the other end of the passenger car. Marcos turned back to Logan, who'd already formulated the final phase of the assault on the train. "What's next? You're running this show, and not half-bad for a Marine," Marcos said.

His adrenaline still fueled by the carnage he'd wrought, Logan allowed a grim smile and accepted the compliment. "Now the real fun begins." He explained his intent and what needed to happen to take the cab of the train with minimal risk to them but the highest chance of capturing the vice president alive. When he finished, he asked, "Any questions?"

As he expected, there were none, but Marcos added, "You're a little crazy, you know that, right? Makes me wonder why we ever tried to go against you. Bad call on our part, I guess, but in our defense, you were still drinking at the time."

Taking it in stride, Logan replied, "Cain coming after me for the flag was probably the *best thing* that ever happened to me because I've been sober since that day. Probably never would've happened without the violent wake-up call. Regardless, I appreciate that, and now, the asshole at the front of the train is going to come to the realization you just had: he should've *never started this fight*." Logan stepped past Marcos and opened the door to the outside.

Several minutes had passed, and yet Cole and the two assassins waited, motionless inside the forest, just out of view and cloaked in darkness. Doubt had begun to creep into Cole's mind when the drone operator said, "Movement at the far end of the camp. Five signatures, moving toward your position from the large building south of where the track splits into three dead ends. They're walking, not running, but their weapons are up."

A brief sense of triumph coursed through Cole, but he abruptly squashed it. *Guessing right is only half the battle, and the smaller one at that, smart guy.* "Roger. I don't have eyes-on. Keep updating me every seven or eight seconds until I have them."

"Roger that," the drone operator replied.

Cole had assumed, correctly, that the vice president would want to leave as soon as possible. They had three choices for their escape—on foot, in a vehicle, or by air. He knew which one he would've picked if he were in Baker's shoes.

"I told you they'd come for the Hind," Cole said to the two assassins.

"We'll give you that one too, I guess," the second assassin, named Thomas, said.

"Jeez. Thanks. That means the world to me," Cole replied drily.

"Don't get all mushy about it," Frederico piled on.

Cole looked from one to the other, and said, "What? Are you guys some kind of stand-up tag team? I get stuck with the killer comedians. Fucking fantastic."

The next update interrupted the exchange. "They're approximately three hundred or so feet from you, passing the middle building."

"Roger," Cole replied, and looked over through the scope on his M4 Commando at the space between the helicopter and the vehicles. Five dark figures began to materialize in the murky light in the middle of the camp. "I have eyes-on," Cole said into the radio. "Go radio silent from here on out, unless you see something we don't."

"Roger. Happy hunting. Skybird out," the drone operator said.

"Just like I said, guys. We wait until they get as close as possible, and when we have a one-hundred-percent positive ID on the vice president, we take out his protection, and then we take him. But *do not engage* if you do not have a clear shot. He has to live, no matter what. Are we clear on that?" Cole asked imploringly.

"You got it, brother-man," Frederico said.

"No sweat, 'mericano," Thomas said, smirking as he said it.

Unreal. The fucking Abbott and Costello of hit men. "Okay, then. We shoot on my count," Cole said, and watched as the group of five men stalked quietly across the dead camp.

The jokes were over, at least for now. Cole looked through his scope as the other two did the same. There were two soldiers in front, one man behind them in the middle, and two men in the rear, creating a domino-five formation. "I've got the front man on the right," Cole said.

"I've got front left," Frederico said.

"I'll take rear left once you drop your guy, Freddy," Thomas said.

Freddy? Are these guys serious? Cole thought, and pushed it out of his mind as he focused on his target.

The group was now less than 150 feet away. *Gotcha, mother-fucker.* "I have positive ID on Baker. I say again, I have positive ID on the package." Dressed in khaki cargo pants and a dark shirt, the fugitive vice president wore a black baseball cap to conceal his salt-and-pepper hair, and shadows blurred his features. But Cole knew it had to be him, in the center. "On my mark," Cole said, waiting for the optimal moment to take the shot.

The group moved quietly and purposefully toward the helicopter, adjusting their direction toward the parked Mi-24. *Not long now. Wait for it. Wait for it. Three. Two. One.* "Fire," Cole said, and slowly squeezed the trigger. Frederico followed suit a fraction of a second later.

The front two soldiers dropped as if knocked to the ground by an invisible hand.

Thomas fired immediately, and the rear left soldier crumpled.

As the first three men hit the ground, Cole adjusted the dot on his reflex scope to center mass of the last soldier standing, squeezed quickly one more time, and sprang to his feet even as the last of the vice president's guards fell. He launched into a sprint, emerging from the forest with the ferocity of a wild predator, intent on its kill.

By then, the vice president had pivoted and begun to run toward the other end of the camp in the direction from which his group had originally emerged.

Frederico and Thomas were already moving, when the drone operator started shouting into Cole's ear. "Two more targets moving from the northwest corner toward the forest! I say again, two more targets moving into the forest!"

The hat flew off the fleeing figure, revealing jet-black hair. *Sonofabitch. He knew we'd be waiting, and he wanted to draw us out. This bastard is smart.*

In one motion, Cole stopped running, raised the M4 Commando, and shot the decoy vice president in the back of his right leg, the round tearing a hole clean through the right calf, missing his shin by inches.

"Damn, boss. I thought you said *not* to shoot the vice president," Frederico said, catching up with Cole.

"That's not him," Thomas said. "Keep up, will you?"

"Frederico, stay with this guy. Find out who he is. Do *not* kill him, or even hurt him, for that matter. In fact, try to treat that wound and bandage it up. We may need him. Thomas, you're with me. Now it's your turn to keep up," Cole said, and broke out into a trot, cutting a diagonal across the middle of the camp toward the northwest corner.

"Skybird, keep eyes on the two targets. We're on the move in their direction," Cole said into his microphone.

Shouldn't have run. You're only delaying the inevitable and pissing me off, and I don't anger quickly like Logan.

CHAPTER 33

Logan crawled along the top of the train's engine and worked his way forward, careful to avoid shifting one way or another. Unlike the boxcar, the GE engine didn't have a walkway. Instead, several hatches that swung upward to allow engineers and technicians access to the multiple engine compartments ran along the length of the engine. He didn't realize it until he'd climbed up to the roof, but the engine was actually several large components attached to each other to power the lumbering beast.

The noise and rushing wind were amplified on top and created the sensation that he was insulated inside a tunnel of sound, even though he was exposed to the elements. Logan felt as if the descent down the mountain through the forest had decreased in speed, albeit slightly. He wondered how much longer they'd be in the mountains, as the base was less than ten miles from the outskirts of the city in a straight-line distance. He crawled faster, protecting the small package in his right hand. He wanted to end the chase before the train reached civilization in order to prevent the further loss of innocent lives.

He glanced backward one last time and saw that the two SUVs had caught up to the train, one on each side of the tracks, inching forward. *I'm sure they have no idea what the hell we're doing, but they'll figure it out soon enough.*

Twenty seconds later he was at the front of the engine, and he grabbed a handle that jutted up at the edge, stabilizing himself on the swaying train. *Time to grab the golden ring.*

Logan pulled himself forward, looked over the edge of the roof, spotted the right half of the engine's windshield, and slammed the small package onto it. The extreme adhesive held the charge in place, and he quickly slid backward several feet, a thin filament wire trailing behind, connected to the small detonator he'd clipped to a loop at the top of his Kevlar vest.

One of the two remaining mercenaries had assured him that the small explosive charge was designed to breach only. It contained no shrapnel, and as the mercenary handed him the charge, he'd said, "They might get some cuts from the window, but they should live." Logan was about to test that hypothesis.

He grabbed the detonator, flipped the small curved cover protecting the switch, and flipped the switch upward.

Logan felt as much as heard the detonation, the explosive force sending a shock wave along the roof of the engine. He grabbed the last smoke grenade off his vest, scurried forward, pulled the pin, and tossed it through the shattered window. He'd considered a flash bang grenade to initiate a breach, but he realized that to send anyone into the engineer's cab would be tantamount to suicide. It was a cramped space with narrow doors, even if the occupants were temporarily incapacitated. *No,* he'd thought, *better to flush them out.*

As the smoke filled the compartment, Logan knew that Santiago and Marcos were moving up the port side of the engine; the two mercenaries, who had worked together previously, had the starboard side. Each narrow walkway was made up of three long sections like steps that led up to the narrow doors. Once the occupants fled the safety of the confined space, they'd run right into the welcoming arms of Hunter Team.

Logan's last choice was which side to cover from above. Trusting in the competency of Marcos and Santiago, he crawled to the edge of the roof on the starboard side, positioned himself several feet away from the narrow door, and unclipped the Glock once again. The two mercenaries were stacked up below him a few feet back from the door to provide a minimal standoff distance.

Smoke from the grenade curled over the lip of the roof, dissipating into nothingness in the fast-flowing air. Smoke obscured the glass of the small window at the top of the door. *Can't be much longer, now. It has to be suffocating inside, even with the window out,* Logan thought, knowing the grenade could last up to fifty or more seconds.

As if reading his thoughts telepathically, a soldier flung the door outward, allowing smoke to pour out of the cab. Unfortunately for him, he held a pistol in his left hand, raised at a forty-five-degree angle. Logan and the two mercenaries fired simultaneously, striking the Venezuelan in the top of the head and the chest, killing him instantly. He fell face forward onto the narrow walkway, his head resting near the top of the step that led to the middle section on which both mercenaries knelt.

The second man through the door realized the error that the first soldier had made, and he started screaming in Spanish. Logan assumed the two mercenaries understood him—Logan had never learned a second language—as they both shouted back authoritatively.

The soldier emerged, his hands raised in the air, and he stepped forward toward the mercenaries. He stopped near the feet of the dead soldier and waited for instructions. No one appeared behind him.

"Ask him where the vice president is!" Logan shouted down from the roof.

After a quick exchange, the mercenary in front looked up and yelled back, "He says he's the last one out. The other two went out the other side. There's no one else."

What? Bastard must have gone out the other side. "Zip-tie this guy up. I'll be back in a second!" Logan yelled over the roar of the wind.

Logan pushed himself up on his hands and knees, crawled backward, turned, and hurried to the other side. He looked down and saw Marcos securing the zip ties on a Venezuelan soldier. Further back, Santiago held the arms of another they'd already secured.

"Where's Baker?" Logan shouted.

Marcos looked up, shook his head, and said, "Not with us. Thought he came out on the other side."

Oh no, Logan thought, a sudden sinking feeling hitting him. He grabbed a handle on the side of the roof, hung over the side, and dropped to the top level of the walkway. Not uttering a word, he entered the cab, unsurprised at what he found—*a dry hole.* The cab had cleared of smoke, but the acrid stench lingered in the air. *Sonofabitch stayed on the base. This whole thing was a fucking decoy so he could slink away into the forest.* At that moment, Logan West detested Vice President Joshua Baker more than any other man or woman alive, and the fact that he'd been duped once again only added significant insult to injury. *He knew I'd take the bait because he knows what my friends mean to me.*

Logan hurried to the other side of the cab and said to the mercenary who'd already secured the smarter of the two soldiers, "Bring him in here."

Moments later, the Venezuelan soldier and the two mercenaries stood inside the cab. Marcos entered the impromptu meeting a moment later from the other side and realized immediately what had happened, cursing in disgust. Logan pointed at the stainless steel handle that jutted out of the control panel horizontally. He gestured as if pulling it toward him, and asked, "Does that slow it down?"

A mercenary translated, and the Venezuelan nodded eagerly.

"Good," Logan replied, and pulled the lever backward. He felt the train's brakes engage, screeching loudly, and the train gradually decelerated. The red digital readout ticked downward: *51 kmph . . . 46 kmph . . .* "Time to get off this ride and get back to the base."

"This was a major head-fake, wasn't it?" Marcos asked.

"Yup," Logan answered. "It's the sonofabitch's MO, and I should've seen it coming."

The earth began to tremble, increasing in intensity, as a major aftershock hit for the third time that day.

Logan looked out the ruined window of the cab. The train's triangular configuration of headlights illuminated the stretch of track in front of them. The ground shook violently, as if the earth were outraged at the train's presence and threatened to shake it off the tracks. A large mass of boulders and several trees tumbled from a hillside on the left and covered the tracks approximately one hundred yards ahead.

"You've got to be fucking kidding me," Marcos said.

"Nope," Logan stated matter-of-factly. "This is about par for the course." The train continued to slow, but there was nowhere near enough distance to stop.

Logan ran to the other door. "Santiago, get in here *now*! Bring those two if you can, but if you want to live, get in here now. We're about to crash!"

Seconds later Santiago dashed into the cab, looked out the window, and said, "Mother of God." He followed Logan's lead and sat on the floor of the cab, as the rest of the team followed suit, bracing their legs and holding on to any surface they could.

The first of the two prisoners appeared in the doorway, a look of pure panic on his face.

"Brace yourselves. This is going to hurt," Logan said, and dropped to the floor, his back snug against the base of the control panel.

The trained slowed a little bit more, and then it crashed into the boulders and trees with a deafening roar that stretched into the night.

CHAPTER 34

Cole and Thomas crossed the tracks at a sprint and angled toward the reverse L-shaped building Skybird had called out earlier. Cole glanced to his right and saw six weapons ranges from twenty-five to one hundred yards long. *These guys built this place with everything in mind.*

"They're at least twenty yards into the forest. I'm getting IR signatures, but the canopy is partially concealing them," Skybird said.

Cole increased his pace, and Thomas matched him. Twenty seconds later, they reached the edge of the forest. On this side of the base, it was eerily quiet, although Cole thought he could hear the tiny engine of the ScanEagle UAV several thousand feet above them. The sounds of the surrounding forest grew in intensity, as if the animals and insects had realized the battle at the base was over, and they were emerging from their hiding places to resume their nocturnal behavior.

"They're at least thirty-five yards ahead of you and moving at a steady pace," Skybird said.

"Roger," Cole replied, as he pulled a Night Owl iGEN night vision monocular from a pouch on the left side of his Kevlar vest. He pressed the top front button and looked through the monocular. The next-generation night-vision device used an infrared emitter on the side of the monocular, which filled the entire eyepiece with the view in front of them. The image lit up in the monocular and created a whitish scene with high contrast. The wall of trees was illuminated, and the path the vice president had taken was clear. A gap in the trees and bushes led into the darkness, and Cole had a large enough field of view to move forward. *Beats the hell out of the early generation of AN/PVS-14s,* he thought, remembering his infantry days before he chose to try out for Special Forces, ultimately ending up in the First Special Forces Operational Detachment–Delta, colloquially referred to as Delta Force. New names, including the recent Combat Applications Group and Army Compartmented Element, would never change it. Thanks to Chuck Norris and Hollywood, the Unit would *always* be called Delta Force.

"Going radio silent. Walk me on them. I've got night vision on."

"Roger," Skybird acknowledged.

Cole turned around to Thomas, and said, "Stay right behind me—and I mean *right behind me,* as in put your hand on my shoulder as we move. Stop when I stop, and be prepared for anything. This is going to get dicey."

The Venezuelan was unfazed. "After the day we've had? Bring it on, bitches."

Cole suppressed most of a laugh. "You're brave or crazy, but either works right now. Get ready."

Cole slung the M4 Commando around and onto his back and withdrew the suppressed Glock. With the Night Owl in his left hand, the pistol offered greater accuracy and maneuverability in the nighttime forest.

He stepped into the woods, and the world behind him disappeared. Instinctively, his senses heightened, a sensation as comfortable and familiar to him as breathing. He just hoped that Thomas wouldn't panic when things got intense, as he knew they would. The night had a way of amplifying *everything.*

Cole moved quickly, the Night Owl allowing him to navigate easily through the dense woods. He knew it was impossible to be perfectly silent in the woods, another myth perpetuated by TV and film. The trick was to minimize the noise and come down softly with each step.

"They've stopped. You're approximately twenty-five yards from them," Skybird announced.

What the hell? Why stop now? Cole thought.

"There's a third signature, ten yards from them. I can't tell who it is," Skybird said.

Cole moved quickly. *They're meeting someone in the forest, but who?* He knew that regardless of who it was, this wasn't good for himself and Thomas.

"Twenty yards out. Keep going in the same direction. They're still not moving. Third signature is a little closer but appears to have stopped," Skybird said. "I do not—I say again—do *not* have a good visual. The canopy is too thick."

No turning back now, Cole thought, and picked up the pace.

Ten yards farther he stopped and studied the forest in front of him. Less than thirty feet away, kneeling next to the base of a very large tree, were two figures. Cole couldn't identify from behind which one was the vice president. *Great. I can't shoot either one then. Need a better vantage point.*

With Thomas's left hand still on his right shoulder, Cole carefully crept to the right in an attempt to gain a better vantage point on the two kneeling men. In the whitish light of the monocular, the two men stared into the forest to their left. *Must be waiting for the other guy to join them,* Cole thought. Cole stopped, and both men now filled the field of view of the Night Owl.

The man on the right turned to the right, as if distracted by a noise Cole couldn't hear, and this time, there was no mistaking the features of Vice President Baker. *Finally have you in my sights, unfortunately for your partner*, Cole thought, and raised the Glock. He aimed it at the back of the Venezuelan soldier. He found the idea of shooting another warrior in the back distasteful, but there was no other choice. The shadow war in which they were engaged had forced all of Task Force Ares to make hard choices, and he knew this was just another one.

He moved his finger off the trigger guard onto the trigger, which was when the terrifying roar of an enormous jungle cat shattered the silence. *A jaguar. It has to be.* Panic flooded his system, and he froze, calculating his options. A second roar erupted from the right, no more than thirty to forty feet away. *This can't be happening. Jaguars don't hunt in packs . . . unless it's mating season.*

Thomas's hand painfully tightened on his shoulder. *I know. I know,* Cole thought. Like the vice president and the soldier, he knew there was nothing to do but wait to see what the jaguars did.

As if personally mocking them, Mother Earth added another variable to the intense standoff, and the ground started to shake violently.

Breaking his silence, Cole said, "Get ready." His panic turned to anger, anger that the target of their hunt was directly in front of him, and yet, as if the Fates conspired to stop him, one more obstacle had been thrown in his way: another predator had chosen to hunt the same target. The anger turned to rage, and clarity washed over him. *Either we get him or we all die right here. He doesn't get away from this one, no matter what.*

"Oh my God. It's not a person. It's an animal. It's moving right toward—" was all Skybird had time to speak into Cole's ear as his urgent warning was drowned out by the aftershock and the horrified scream of the jaguar's prey.

The engine shook violently back and forth, and Logan wasn't sure the train would reach the barricade of boulders and trees. *Just might fall off the tracks and die that way,* realizing a moment later he'd thought too soon.

The engine crashed into the boulders with a deafening explosion that sent a vibration rattling through every surface. Logan was pressed hard against the panel, but he held his hands over his head and pressed down, which prevented his head from whipping back against it.

Several grunts of pain and one shout mingled with the roar of the crash as the train rapidly decelerated. Logan couldn't distinguish between the aftershock and the trembling from the slow-motion train wreck. *Six half one dozen, or whatever the fuck that stupid saying is,* he thought, praying the ride would end. *This makes me actually want to ride Amtrak,* he thought, something he'd vowed never to do again considering how mismanaged and dangerous the public railway system was.

There was a loud crash from the back of the engine, and the train suddenly accelerated as the first and second cars broke free. More booms and crashes reverberated from behind the engine, and Logan realized the other two cars had derailed. *We're next,* he thought, and on that point, he wasn't wrong.

With the sudden burst in speed, increased by the decline of the tracks, the train hit a curve to the left and started to lean to the right. The train suddenly dropped as the front of the engine hit a patch where the track had been destroyed, leaving nothing but a ten-foot gap where the section of track had crumbled to the side. The nosedive was brief, but the engine struck the tracks and earth, taking an enormous gouge out of the forest floor and digging forward. As the forward momentum violently ceased, the engine fell to the right, and the rear of the car slid around, shattering small trees that lined the dirt road along the tracks. The engine landed on its right side and kept sliding, and dirt and debris shot into the cab through the ruined window.

Just as Logan thought the train wreck would never end, it struck something hard and stopped dead in its dirt tracks.

Logan's back hurt, but he knew it was a soft-tissue injury that he'd fight through until the day and mission were over. Santiago and Marcos were shaken up, but neither seemed to have suffered any major injuries. In fact, as Logan glanced around, by some miracle he'd thank God for later, *none* of the occupants was seriously injured.

"Is everyone alive?" Logan asked as he tried to stand on the right side of the engine, which was now the floor.

A series of English and Spanish responses confirmed they were, and Logan said, "Good. Now, let's get the hell out of this death trap."

Marcos stood up, a laceration on his forehead trickling blood down the right side of his face, creating a black line in the darkness. "Well, I can cross 'nearly die in a train wreck' off my bucket list."

"Keep hanging out with us, and this will become so commonplace you won't even notice it. Be just like riding a bike," Logan said.

"A bike that could tear you limb from limb," Marcos retorted.

"And I thought you SF guys were tough," Logan shot back, and moved to the rear of the cab and bent down. He pushed on the narrow door, which now lay horizontal near the floor. It opened slightly, but then struck something solid. "Not this one. I guess we have to climb up and use the other one," Logan said, pointing to the horizontal door at the top of the cab.

Santiago climbed up, using the back wall of the cab and its shelves as footholds. Within seconds, he had pushed the door outward and up so that it rested against the side of the engine, propped open. He looked back at the surviving men and said,

"See you hombres on the outside," and disappeared out the narrow door.

"I think that's the first semi-joke I've heard him utter since we met him," Logan said.

"I'm sure nearly dying in a train crash brought out the best in him," Marcos replied, quickly turning serious. "I just hope someone stayed up at the base in case Baker tried to make a break for it."

"Let's just get the hell out of this cab," Logan said.

Minutes later, freed from the confines of the cab and standing on the left side of the engine, which had become the top of the train in the crash, Logan surveyed the wreckage. The passenger car had flipped off the right side of the tracks, still attached to the box-car. *At least the front part of it,* Logan thought. The boxcar had split in two during the crash, and the rear half had tumbled off the left side of the tracks, smashing into trees before coming to rest.

"Hey!" a familiar voice shouted from below. Logan looked down and saw Jack standing behind the open driver's-side door, one leg still inside the running SUV. "Are you going to stand there all goddamned night and stargaze, or can we go?" Jack shouted. The two SUVs had navigated around the wreckage and parked next to the engine. "I assume the traitor wasn't on the train. Cole called it as you were racing to hop on. We need to get back up to the base. He stayed up there."

Logan looked at Marcos, a fresh intensity visible on his face. "Never doubt my guys. Ever," he said, and hopped off the train and dashed to the front passenger side of Jack's J70.

Through the night vision monocular, Cole saw the enormous beast in a dark blur as it pounced on Vice President Baker's sole escort. The cat had to weigh at least 250 pounds, was nearly six feet in length, and stood as tall as a Great Dane. To see a jaguar up close was terrifying, and as the big cat knocked the Venezuelan soldier to the ground, Cole could only imagine the man's horror.

The beast pawed at the man's shoulders, shredding his uniform and upper chest with its long claws. The man shrieked, but the noise was muffled by the squirming and muscular body on top of him. The cat opened its jaws, exposing four long teeth like vampire fangs with a small row of teeth between the upper and lower fangs. With one of the most powerful big-cat bites in the world, the jaguar gripped the struggling man's head between its jaws and squeezed with more than a thousand pounds of force. Cole imagined the sickening crunch as the large teeth punctured skull and brain, and the screaming ceased, the man's temporary terror permanently ended.

"Run this way or die, *now!*" Cole screamed to the vice president over the growling of the cat. "Shoot the other one, Thomas!" The chaos was pure and complete, exponentially exacerbated by the dark forest and intermittent illumination.

The vice president fell backward and away from the jaguar, which still had the dead man's head inside its mouth. He turned over onto his hands and knees, and in a pure panic, scrambled toward Cole and Thomas. It was all the window that Cole needed, and he opened fire with the suppressed Glock.

Several shots struck the jaguar in the shoulders and the skull, and releasing the soldier's ruined head, the cat howled in fury and pain. It looked up, directly at Cole, but then shifted its bleeding face toward the vice president. *Oh no you don't*, Cole thought, but it was too late.

In a dying attempt, as if to spite Cole and prevent him from obtaining what was rightfully the jaguar's prize, the cat lunged at the vice president. A huge paw dug into the back of Baker's right calf, but the mountain cat slowed, as if finally realizing it had been shot multiple times. Cole lowered the monocular, as a beam of brilliant light illuminated the scene.

Several shots rang out from behind Cole as Thomas turned on the high-power LED flashlight attached to his rifle and fired at the second jaguar, which had started to spring toward the fallen vice president.

Cole ignored the loud shots and stepped forward, sighting on the neck of the jaguar. In one last act of defiance, the jaguar bit down on the back of Baker's leg, and the vice president let out a shriek of pain. Cole fired several rounds into the neck of the dying beast. The animal roared in pain and fury, as if outraged that its life was being taken this way. Blood poured down the side of the animal and onto Baker's leg. Cole raised the Glock and fired into the side of the animal's head, stopping its cries and killing it. Its enormous head dropped onto the bloody leg of the vice president, as if resting on him instead of trying to kill him moments before.

The second jaguar nearly reached the vice president, but several shots from Thomas's AK-103 struck the cat in the side and in the head. Unlike its partner, the cat was stopped in its tracks by 7.62mm bullets, and it collapsed to the forest floor, its head several inches away from the vice president, who trembled in shock and pain at the sudden ferocity of the attack.

Silence once again reasserted itself inside the mountain forest as the aftershock ended, bookmarking the end of the sudden animal attack and brutal violence.

The vice president looked backward and found the strength to crawl forward, freeing himself from beneath the hold of the dead jaguar. He turned to his left and saw the second animal, and he moved a little quicker, eager to put some distance between himself and the dead predators.

"If you try anything, and I mean *anything*, what I will do to you will make you wish these two had got to you first. Am I clear?" Cole asked, anger in his voice. Not a hunter of animals, a part of him was disgusted that they'd had to kill two magnificent, endangered beasts.

"Yes," Baker replied simply.

"Good. I'm Cole Matthews, and I assume you know who I am," Cole stated.

Baker recognized the name from the brief he'd been provided with on Task Force Ares after the events in Sudan, and he understood, finally, that his long run had ended. There was nowhere left to go, no options to exercise, and no one left to help him. His future lay in the hands of the man who'd just saved him from a savage death, but he understood that what was in store for him might not be that much better, depending on how other events he'd already put into motion had unfolded.

"Thomas, can you please bandage his leg and then help him up? I'm not sure he's going to be able to walk on that. It looks like it hurts," Cole said.

"You got it," Thomas said.

He opened a pouch and pulled out a package of QuickClot Combat Gauze and a roll of medical tape. Within seconds, he'd placed the gauze over the bite and taped it in place. "It's hasty, but it will stop further bleeding until we can clean it out and sew it up. Now, let's get you up," Thomas said, and the vice president put his arm around his shoulder. The two men stood up, and Thomas gave Cole a thumbs-up with a huge grin. "What's next, boss?"

"Next, you're going to call off your dogs in Maryland," Cole said. "Where's your phone? In the backpack?" he said, indicating the black pack that had fallen off Baker during the attack.

"Yes," Baker said, and then paused. "But it doesn't matter."

A sense of dread fell over Cole, and even before he asked the question, he already knew the answer. *You're not going to live through the night if you did what I think you did.* But he asked anyway. "And why is that?"

The vice president looked at him, held his gaze, and responded, "I ordered the strike at the first sound of the drones because I knew it was you guys who'd come for me. And once I called, the team had orders to go silent and off the grid once the mission was complete, no matter who tried to reach them."

Cole looked at his digital watch. "Christ. That was more than twenty minutes ago. You better *pray* that our friends are still alive, because if they're not, Logan will try to find another one of these frisky kitties and *feed you to it piece by piece as you watch.*"

Baker didn't respond but only looked at the dark ground, leaning on Thomas as the two men stepped in synchronicity back toward the plateau.

"Sounds like you're in some serious trouble, my friend. Definitely wouldn't want to be you," Thomas said.

"Neither would I, especially at the moment," Baker replied.

Cole turned and marched up the hill, disgusted with the vile piece of human trash he'd just saved and worried over the fate of his friends. The only reassuring thought was that John Quick—wounded or not—and Amira Cerone were a lethal combination. If anyone had a fighting chance, it was the two of them. But then he realized that whatever was to be had already happened. It was just for Cole and Logan to find out. *What's done can't be undone, not now*, he thought, concern becoming the primary emotion. *Please, God. Let them be okay.*

PART V

A FATHER'S LOVE

CHAPTER 35

Rolling Knolls Subdivision
Prince Frederick, Calvert County, MD
Twenty Minutes Earlier

Thirty miles southeast of Washington DC, Calvert County in southern Maryland occupied the entire Calvert Peninsula. Bounded on the east by the Chesapeake Bay and on the west by the Patuxent River, it was a historically rural enclave with large farms and winding hilly roads with towns interspersed along the peninsula that ran from north to south, where the bay and river joined.

The main town, Prince Frederick, was the county seat of power, where the sheriff's office and county hospital were located. While the county itself was not well known outside Maryland, its most famous resident was a deceased, iconic international thriller author whose estate still stood on the cliffs on the bay.

Over the past few decades, though, the county and Prince Frederick had become known as an exurban area of DC, a prosperous area for those who worked in DC but chose to escape every day and on the weekend to a much more peaceful, rural-suburban setting. As a result, businesses, franchise grocery stores, and new neighborhoods were being built or planned throughout the county. Crime was negligible, with most incidents and continuing problems revolving around drugs, the one scourge that seemed to plague *every* part of the United States, no matter how remote or insulated.

The most attractive element of Calvert County was the cost of real estate. Four- and five-thousand-square-foot homes that went for upper six figures into the low seven figures just north in Anne Arundel County could be acquired for three and four hundred thousand, depending on the specific development. It was why Nicolo Cerone, retired Washington DC Homicide Branch detective, had fled the district to Calvert County after his wife of thirty-five years had passed away after a short battle with stomach cancer.

Bad Luck Nick—or just Nick to his friends—had started his career as a young patrol officer in the DC police department in the hard-nosed, crime-infested Sixth District on the wrong side of the Anacostia River. The nickname had been earned after a string of suspects had either fled or fought Officer Cerone, with each one suffering multiple broken bones, but nothing critical. His peers and desk sergeant had joked, "They have really bad luck," and the name had stuck and served him well later in the Homicide Branch. If Bad Luck Nick caught the case, the chances of it getting solved exponentially increased. In fact, it was the name that had drawn the attention of Amara.

Nick had met Amara Dinsamo in an upscale Ethiopian restaurant near Union Station. Unbeknownst to her at the time, the luncheon Officer Cerone had been invited to was actually an interview to be an investigator in the Sixth District's plainclothes vice unit. The sergeant in charge at the time, Frank Torres, had noticed arrest after arrest in the district's "drug book," the term affectionately given to the records log of arrests and confiscated material. Frank had researched the young officer, interviewed his superiors and peers, and requested the meeting outside the Sixth District. During that fateful interview that personally and professionally changed the course of Nick Cerone's life, Frank had asked him about the nickname, and Amara had overheard it.

She'd been so struck by his young, Italian, strong good looks and bright blue eyes—a rarity she recognized—that she hadn't been able to help herself and had interrupted their conversation, blurting out, "Why would they call you 'Bad Luck'?" She'd immediately apologized profusely, but the older officer had been amused, and Nick had shown no offense at all. In fact, he'd responded quite charmingly, "It's not for me. It's for the perpetrators that I come across."

"Why? Do you hurt them?" she'd asked, suddenly serious.

And Nick had laughed, not maliciously but sincerely. "Not intentionally, but when you run from or fight the police, it usually doesn't go so well, and bad things happen." His tanned features had hardened momentarily, and he'd added, "There are bad people in the world, and when they do bad things, sometimes karma comes back to them. They bring it on themselves."

And with that, he'd struck a chord deep inside her. She'd seen not just bad, but horrible, evil things in Africa, which was why her parents had fled after a particularly brutal battle between the Eritreans and Ethiopians that had destroyed her village. He spoke the truth, but more importantly, she recognized a man who believed it was his job—his *duty*—to protect others who could not do it for themselves. And if the bad guys got hurt? So be it.

She'd nodded and left them to their conversation, which had turned into an offer Nick had accepted. But one week later, when she'd thought about him often but hadn't expected to see him, he'd shown up at the restaurant and asked her out. There'd been no hesitation on her part. Every instinct in her being had reacted to his presence, and she'd answered immediately the moment he'd finished asking, joining their two lives onto one path that they shared until the day she died.

But when the lifetime together in DC had ended, Nick had needed someplace new, someplace fresh, to rebuild his life, which was how he'd found Calvert County and built the modern colonial home on two acres in a new subdivision surrounded by woods and undeveloped land. The Rolling Knolls subdivision had only twenty-five homes, but each one had anywhere from two to four acres, depending on the lot size and shape. Its residents were a mixture of DC elite, successful local business owners, and a few retirees, like himself. The pace was the extreme opposite of the violence and chaos that had consumed parts of DC in the nineties, and he'd been grateful for the sense of peace he'd found within himself.

But unfortunately, his daughter had followed in his footsteps, albeit in her own way. He knew it wasn't her choice, that she'd been called to the life inside the CIA, but no father wants his daughter to live a life of violence, even if it is for the greater good. While he didn't know the details, he knew she was lethal, and he knew she had killed. He couldn't explain how he knew, and they hadn't talked about it, but as her father, he knew. He'd seen something similar in the officers he'd known who had taken lives—as had he—on the job. They weren't guilt-stricken by it: every officer understood it could happen on any day at any moment, but good men and women did not *want* to kill others. Still, they had to be prepared psychologically and emotionally to do it, especially if they wanted to go home to their families at the end of their shift. It was the job.

He was proud of her, and he'd accepted her profession, but he took every moment he had with her to emphasize what was important in life—time spent with loved ones and friends. He'd had plenty of both, and he wanted to make sure Amira didn't get consumed with work the way young people tended to.

It was also why he scrutinized every man she'd been involved with, including the one that now sat across from him in his kitchen—John Quick.

The former Marine had been a constant presence in his daughter's life for nearly the past seven months. Older than Amira by several years, he was ruggedly handsome with short brown hair and brown eyes, fit, well spoken, and ruthlessly sarcastic, a trait that Nick as a former cop admired. He had a disarming, self-deprecating charm to him, and Nick understood why his daughter had fallen for him: John was as grounded as any man he'd met. But Nick also saw the trained killer, the professional Marine in him, and it gave him pause, although not much. Amira was strong-willed, and if she'd chosen John to be her partner, there was *nothing* he could do to stop it. Her happiness was paramount, and if the Marine made her happy in the life she'd chosen, then he supported their relationship, pure and simple. There was no denying how they felt about each other: it was tangible to anyone who spent more than a minute around them.

For the first six months after his daughter had returned from Sudan, John and Amira, as well as Logan West, whom he'd also met, had been intentionally vague about their experiences, mainly to protect him. He knew they were spies of some kind, although that didn't seem like an appropriate label for them, given their obvious physicality and capacity for action. But several weeks ago after the vice president had disappeared and multiple gun battles had erupted across DC and northern Virginia, they'd disclosed to him, without having to bluntly state it, that they were part of a task force and worked for the highest levels of the government. It'd been apparent whom they'd meant—the current occupant of the White House. With the knowledge came the realization that whatever Amira was involved in—which had nearly caused John to bleed out from his gunshot wound—was extremely dangerous, which only added to Nick's level of concern for her welfare.

The three of them sat around the ornate, heavy oak kitchen table in the sunroom that extended off the back of the kitchen. The sun had disappeared behind the dense wood line at the back of his property, and shadows fell across the flat backyard, even though there was an hour and a half before sunset.

As Nick Cerone looked at his daughter, Amira, a flood of memories washed over him, each and every time, bittersweet and nostalgic, full of love that he felt for his daughter and had felt for his wife. His daughter would always be his princess. It was why they'd chosen her name.

He looked back at John, and said, "How's it healing?"

"In all seriousness, *way* better than I thought," John said. "The doctor told me that I'm making a 'remarkable recovery for someone your age,' at which point I reminded him about the men I'd killed and the fact that age discrimination was still a crime."

Amira rolled her eyes, but Nick asked, "And how'd that go?"

"Fine, until they escorted me from the hospital and told me not to come back for another two weeks," John joked one last time, before mercifully losing the sarcasm. "Bottom line—I can start working out next week. The hole has closed, and both the stitches and pain are gone. Honestly, it almost feels like I wasn't shot at all."

Amira placed her hand on his. "You're lucky, and you know it. No heroics anytime soon for you."

"Yeah, well, we're not the ones in the field right now. So you're right. No heroics. Scout's honor," John said.

"But you weren't a scout," Amira objected.

"Does it matter?" John replied, and winked at her. He looked back at Nick and said, "She takes me so literally."

Nick only shook his head and replied, "You better be careful, lest you upset her."

"Tell me about it," John said. "I've seen what happens to people who do that."

I'll bet you have, Nick thought, not really wanting to know the violent acts his daughter had committed.

"Changing the subject, any news on the hunt?" Nick asked. The news continued to speculate as to the whereabouts of the vice president, but he knew that his daughter and John were two of the very few people in the country who might have an actual idea as to where the vice president had run. After the battle across DC while John was in the hospital, Amira had told her father what had happened, at least about Vice President Baker's real role as a traitor. She'd cleared it with Logan and John, who'd talked to Jake Benson about bringing her father into the fold, especially since families had been fair game in the past.

"Not yet, but I think they're getting close," John said. "We should know more within the next twenty-four hours." John suddenly smiled. "But enough about work. Here's the real question, the one that really matters." He knew one of them would bite.

Nick opened his mouth to reply, but Amira interrupted. "You know you're only encouraging him, right, Dad?"

Nick smiled. "There are worse things in the world. *And* we men have to stick together sometimes, especially if we have to combat whatever those millennial people think."

"It's 'millennials,' not 'millennial people,'" Amira replied.

"Who cares?" Nick said. "From what I hear on the news, sounds like they better stop complaining about how hard life is and start working. But what do I know? I'm only a retired cop."

"I'll drink to that," John said, and raised his Corona to clink bottles with Nick, who did the same.

"You two are insufferable," Amira said in mock disgust, although internally, she felt a deep sense of contentment at the way the two most important men in her life had connected.

Nick ignored her and asked, "What's the question?"

"Ah, yes. Almost forgot. The question is this—what's for dinner? I'm starving. Getting shot has a tendency to increase one's appetite. I think I read that somewhere," John declared.

"Unlikely," Amira replied. "That would mean you know how to read."

Nick laughed and pushed his chair away from the table. "Come on. I've got the grill going on the deck. I've been marinating fillets all day. They're in the fridge and ready to go."

"Sounds like a plan," John said, and stood up from the table. He looked back down at Amira and asked, "What about you?"

"You two boys have fun talking about how I'm emasculating you both. I'm going to go check the news in the family room," Amira said, referring to the two-story main room adjacent to the kitchen.

"Okay. But if you hear something explode, come check on us," John said, leaned over, and kissed her quickly on the cheek, sending a shiver along her spine.

"Wouldn't be the first time you caused a propane tank to explode," Amira said, the kiss still fresh on her skin.

"Hey, that's not fair! Logan is the one who shot it," John replied defensively.

"But *you* were the one who bought it, if I recall correctly. Proximate cause, babe. Proximate cause," Amira said, and smiled wryly at him, pale-blue gunslinger eyes sparkling.

"I had no idea you were so smart," John said.

"Shut up and go help my father," Amira said. "See you in a bit."

CHAPTER 36

Sixteen-year-old Anthony Buchman stared at the iPhone 8 display attached to the DJI Mavic Pro 2 drone controller. The latest generation of the Mavic drone was stunning in its responsiveness, 4K HDR video capability, and the fact that it could fly up to 44 mph. A quadcopter with four collapsible arms, the drone was so advanced it could automatically detect and avoid obstacles, track and follow high-speed objects, and automatically shadow its operator. The Mavic Pro 2 was a whirring blur of computing and audiovisual technology in the air.

An ambitious, lanky teenager with brown hair and blue eyes, Anthony had spent the entire summer mowing lawns with a John Deere tractor that his father had purchased for him but for which he was paying his dad back on a weekly basis out of his earnings. The rest of his money had gone toward the drone. It was more than a hobby: it was his passion. At the age of thirteen, he'd become obsessed with all kinds of drones—miniatures, quadcopters, fixed wing, single rotor, large, small, he didn't care—and his interest hadn't diminished with time. Instead, it had strengthened, and he intended to follow his dream with only one objective—the Air Force Academy and then an officer career as a remotely piloted aircraft pilot. His father had thought drones were a passing fancy, but then he'd realized his son was committed, and he'd encouraged him.

Anthony's current mission—this was how he already thought of everything in relation to the drone, in military terms—was to scout out the woods that ran all the way to the Patuxent River a few miles to the west of the subdivision. There was a random scattering of homes along the way, but it was mostly interconnected roadways and farmland. He also wanted to see what the sunset would look like in 4K HDR, taking advantage of the Hasselblad camera's processing power.

The drone rose into the air off his front lawn, and he watched on the screen as the ground in front of him grew smaller. He reached seventy-five feet in altitude, pressed the left joystick forward, and the drone shot out of his yard. Anthony looked up, a quick surge of adrenaline coursing through him as the small drone accelerated away and down the street. *It never gets old, no matter what.*

The sun was low on the horizon, and he didn't want the camera looking directly into it, even though he knew it wouldn't damage the lens. He was just overcautious, as he'd only had the drone less than a week. He kept the camera angled toward the ground, and the drone flew over the home at the end of the street. Anthony saw a second vehicle, a new dark-blue pickup truck—he couldn't tell the make and model—in the driveway, and the drone passed over it above the house.

A moment later, he spotted the large deck, a grill, and the big backyard that he'd mown several dozen times over the past two summers. Seconds later, the drone streaked over the woods, and bare spots between the trees provided glimpses of the ground below.

Movement flashed across the retina display. *What was that?* He pulled back on the left joystick, and the drone stopped its race across the treetops. He rotated the drone and lowered it, angling the camera to get a better view under the trees. *Might as well give it a try. It has obstacle-avoiding technology. Let's see how it works.* He navigated the drone through a large opening between two old trees, muttering, "Please don't crash."

Seconds later, the drone dipped beneath the canopy, and he adjusted the camera, finally spotting the source of the motion. His blood turned cold, and it took his brain a moment to realize what his body had already reacted to—*danger, and a lot of it*. Three men in some kind of camouflage fatigues were moving toward the far end of the woods, *toward his neighborhood*. They held what he thought were assault rifles, but it was the way they moved that spurred him into action. He'd played enough *Call of Duty* video games and done enough research into the military that he recognized a tactical movement when he saw one. These weren't hunters: they were men on a mission. And then he realized where they were headed, and he exclaimed, "Oh, shit!" His heartbeat increased furiously, and he thought, *I have to warn him*.

He looked at the controller in his hands, thankful that he'd purchased the Mavic Pro 2. He hit a small button on the upper left side of the controller that had an angled *H* inside a small circle— the return-to-home button. Knowing the drone would find its way back to him, he immediately disconnected the iPhone from the docking station in the bottom of the controller. He hit the phone button at the bottom, and his favorites list popped up. He scrolled down quickly, trying to control the panic, and found the one he wanted. He pressed the button and prayed, *Please, God, let him answer the phone.*

CHAPTER 37

Former CIA Special Operations Group officer Chase Grayson slowly stalked through the woods in Calvert County. The target's property was less than one hundred yards away, followed by a short distance across the backyard to the large colonial home the target occupied. A former Marine Special Operations team tactical element leader, he'd spent plenty of time in woods and forests across the globe, but for some reason, Maryland and northern Virginia always seemed especially uncomfortable in the summer.

The last thirty-six hours after they'd inserted under the cover of darkness into the woods from the Patuxent River had been uncomfortable, but Chase's team had made the best of it, setting up a small, concealed camp in the middle of the woods more than a mile from civilization in all directions. The only incident they'd had was the unfortunate encounter with the hunter.

Chase despised collateral damage, especially the loss of innocent life, but Vice President Baker—Chase still considered him to be the vice president, but if not that, he was still a Council member of the Organization, even if he'd gone off the reservation—had been clear about one thing: mission accomplishment at all costs. As a result, the hunter had been a human obstacle in their path, nothing more, and he'd had to be dealt with in a way that didn't jeopardize the mission.

The mission had started out as a simple kidnapping in order to provide the vice president leverage, but something had changed within the last twenty-four hours, escalation from kidnapping to direct action—eliminate the retired detective and anyone else with him. No prisoners. No witnesses.

When the vice president had called ten minutes earlier, he'd sounded frustrated but still in control. There was a continuous high-pitched roar in the background, but Baker had never wavered: terminate the targets with extreme prejudice. And neither Grayson nor the other two members of his team had an issue with it. There was a war underway, even if the general public wasn't aware of it. And like it or not, his mission and his job involved the taking of human life. While he didn't revel in it in the same fashion he'd seen others do, it was a necessity, pure and simple. Retired DC police officer Nick Cerone and whoever was with him had to die.

At the center of a three-man on-line formation, Chase carefully placed one boot in front of the other to eliminate any unnecessary sounds. The edge of the woods materialized, with spaces emerging in the wall of trees and underbrush.

Chase never heard the drone until it was close overhead, but by then, it was too late. The three men froze, and Chase prayed their commercial tree suits would hide them long enough for the drone to pass. But for whatever reason—karma, bad luck, or both—the drone stopped above and behind them.

Come on. Keep going. Whoever you are, you didn't see anything, he thought, which was precisely when the quadcopter descended through a gap in the woods' canopy thirty feet behind them.

No one moved, as if to do so would trigger some kind of alarm and send the drone screaming in their direction. The camera on the drone swiveled from side to side. *Damnit. We're made.*

As if sensing Chase's recognition, the drone suddenly ascended like a launched rocket through the treetops. Without hesitation, Chase said, "We're made. Let's move, and don't stop until we're at the house."

He didn't wait for a response, but instead, jumped into a sprint along the floor of leaves and twigs, no longer concerned about the noise. *Always has to be something. No matter. We'll overcome it. We always do.*

Amira stared at the photograph on the bookshelf in the large family room, lost in the memory of that day when she was eighteen and had just been accepted into the University of Maryland School of Theatre, Dance, and Performance Studies. Her parents had taken her out to dinner to celebrate and then walked along the National Mall, beaming with pride at their daughter, who'd received the opportunity to pursue her dreams.

Amira had been dancing since she was five years old, and she'd excelled at every level in every way possible. Graceful, fluid, and strong—the fact that she was stunningly beautiful helped, as well, with eyes that no one forgot—she'd pursued her goal with a relentless and fierce determination that her parents hadn't had to encourage. She was a natural fighter, which was why her father had also trained her in basic martial arts and boxing starting at age ten. The combination of dance and combatives had created the perfect synergy of power and grace, heightening her skills in the dance studio.

In the picture, taken by a passerby in what felt like a life lived by someone else, she sat on the steps of the Lincoln Memorial in front of the reflecting pool, obvious joy on her face. Her parents sat behind her, her mother's arms wrapped around her neck and her father's arms around both of them, leaning downward toward Amira.

The picture always affected her deeply, a reflection of a different time filled with hope and happiness, before the violence and the CIA had entered her life. All she'd ever wanted to be was a dancer, but life *never* worked out the way one intended. Of that, she was certain. Her mother had died five years ago, and her father was all that she had, a steady presence of support and love. *And John. You have John now too.*

Her father's cell phone on the kitchen island countertop suddenly erupted, the sound of police sirens wailing digitally from the device. *Seriously, Dad?* she thought, but also pleased at the knowledge that her father still had a sense of humor.

She walked into the kitchen, grabbed the phone, and looked at the screen. *Tony the Mower? Sounds like a mob boss with a penchant for yard work.* She contemplated letting it go to voice mail, but her curiosity as to who deserved such a ringtone and moniker won the battle in her mind, and she answered it. She'd reflect on that decision for days to come.

"Hello?" Amira answered.

"Is Mr. Cerone there? This is Anthony. I cut his lawn," a teen-aged voice said in a hurry. "Please. It's urgent."

Urgent? Does Dad owe the kid money? Definitely not a hardened criminal. "Sorry, but he's out back, grilling. This is his daughter. Is everything okay?"

The boy sounded panicked. "I don't think so. I just flew my drone over your house toward the woods, and there are three men in there with rifles in some kind of camouflage, and they're moving toward your dad's house. I didn't know what to do. So I called."

Amira's mind tumbled in free fall for a moment. *No. Not here.* But then the warrior inside her regained equilibrium, and the steel her enemies were familiar with appeared. "Call 911 and get back inside and lock the doors. Thank you."

Even as she ended the call, she started for the sliding door to the deck and shouted, "John! Dad! Get inside, *now*! Hostiles in the woods! *Move!*"

The shadow war in which they'd been engaged for the past two and a half years had just arrived in the rural suburbs of the Rolling Knolls subdivision.

"How is she doing?" Nick asked, glancing at his watch and waiting to flip the thick-cut fillets. He still preferred an old-school charcoal grill to the convenience of gas. The world might have moved on to pellets and propane, but he liked charcoal, nonetheless.

"As well as any of us," John replied. "For me, it's been the last two and a half years, but she just joined the fight. I won't lie. I know you can probably guess at a lot more than what we've told you. These are dangerous, violent people we've been chasing, people who would gladly undermine the Constitution and every other legitimate government for their own agenda. Hell, they wanted to pull us into a second conflict in the Middle East, which is how I got roped back in out of retirement."

"What happened?" Nick asked, knowing John might not answer.

"They came at me in my lake house in Montana, where I'd decided to hide from society after the things I'd done and seen in the Marine Corps. I'd been divorced, which was inevitable, considering the op tempo we'd been under for years, and I just wanted peace and solitude."

"What happened to the men who came after you?"

"Some of them died that night; the rest, the next day," John said, remembering the Alamo and the endless day that had started at his house.

"Good," Nick said.

John laughed warmly. "That's why I like you, Nick. You get it. So does Amira."

"I know, but as her father, there's a part of me that *loathes* the profession in which she works. I know most of what she does, and I can figure out the rest. I raised her to be the strong, independent woman she is, but I *never* wanted her to be immersed in a world of violence." His voice was strong with emotion. "I wanted her to be insulated from the world I saw every day on the streets of DC. I wanted her to be a dancer, to bring joy to others, but most importantly, to be happy for herself."

"You know she is, right?" John said. John didn't have kids, and he could only imagine what parents went through raising them, but he knew Amira was doing exactly what she wanted to be doing with her life. "What she does, there are *very few* people on the planet who can do it. All jokes aside, I'm good, really good, but your daughter, she's on a whole other level of warrior. But more importantly, she's on the *right side,* the side of those who can't fight for themselves. She's balancing the scales in the right direction, and no one can ever argue otherwise."

"I know. But it never turns out like we wanted, does it?" Nick asked, although it was more of a statement than a question.

"No," John replied. "It doesn't, but I believe she's precisely where she's intended to be and *wants* to be, and that's more than most can ask for." John paused for a moment. "Nick, you raised a warrior, a smart, beautiful, fierce warrior, and the world needs her. I absolutely believe there is no higher calling. Evil walks among us, and she's one of those who stand at the gate, refusing to let it in and crushing it when it does. It's why I'm crazy about her. So thank you for making her who she is."

Nick was silent, and then a smile crept across his tanned face. "I see why she loves you—and she does, you know. Who knew a

Marine could be so smart?" he joked, taking the edge off the conversation.

"Just don't tell anyone," John replied, and grabbed him on the shoulder in mock seriousness. "I wouldn't want people to get the wrong idea."

"Your secret is safe with me," Nick replied. "Time to flip the steaks," he said, and raised the lid on the stainless steel grill, which was when Amira started shouting frantically from inside and the first gunman opened fire from the woods.

CHAPTER 38

John yanked Nick backward and pulled him down as several rounds struck the open grill, pinging loudly like baseballs hitting a heavy sheet of tin. More suppressed shots rang out from near the wood line, but they sounded closer. *They're moving in. Need to get Nick inside.*

In addition to the composite railing around the deck, Nick had built a brick wall around the grill area to prevent the heat from causing the railing to blister and buckle. At the moment, it was the only thing providing substantial cover from the two weapons John heard firing at them.

Several rounds struck the back of the house, punching holes in the vinyl siding and tearing chunks of glass from the windows.

The grill was less than fifteen feet from the sliding door, but John realized that the brick wall wouldn't protect the last few feet. *Why did we have to leave our guns in the truck? Because you don't expect to get ambushed at Amira's dad's place. No one should even know who she or her dad are.*

"We have to get inside. Low-crawl behind me to the doors. It's either that, or we die out here," John said, and started squirming toward the back door. There were no other options.

271

Amira's shouts were interspersed with more shattering glass and thuds against the house. *It's going to have to wait until we're inside, babe,* John thought.

John reached the exposed gap and prayed that the railing would deflect the trajectory of any rounds sent their way. As if on cue, the door slid open to the right, and Amira shouted, *"Move! Now!"*

Here goes nothing, John thought, and scrambled toward the door. The two seconds of exposure induced a brief sense of panic, but he reached the door and pushed through as several rounds struck the right half of the glass doorway, destroying the large window and the glass door behind it.

Amira was just inside to the left of the open door, and John spun around. Nick was less than a foot from the door, struggling on his stomach. Fifty feet behind him in the middle of the yard, a man in a full camouflage tree suit with an AR-15 stalked forward. He couldn't see the second shooter since the brick wall obstructed his view. Two more shots destroyed one of the white posts, and the shooter's weapon emptied. *One small mercy,* John thought, as the man ejected the magazine, stashed it inside a cargo pocket on his pants, and pulled out a second magazine from a pouch attached to the front of the camouflaged suit.

John grabbed Nick by the arms and pulled him over the ledge into the kitchen, and all three scampered to the left into the family room.

"Where's your gun?" John asked.

"Upstairs, in one of those four-button gun safes next to the bed on the right side on the floor. It's my birthday and her mom's," Nick replied, breathless from the adrenaline surge and crawl to safety.

"What about ours in the truck?" Amira asked.

"They'll have someone covering the front. They came here to

kill us, and they won't risk letting us escape out the front," John said.

"Who the hell are these guys?" Nick asked.

"Welcome to the fight, Nick. It doesn't even matter, but we're going to take them apart, one by one," John said, a rage building in his voice as he spoke. "Let's get down the hallway and upstairs."

The shooting had stopped, but John knew the shooters had to be close to the back porch. He wasn't about to raise his head to find out: he knew it'd get shot off. "Amira, then you, then me," John ordered. "Now, move!"

Amira crouched and dashed toward the hallway that led from the kitchen to the foyer. The stairs were to the left just before the main floor powder room and the hallway itself. Nick followed close behind his daughter as she bounded up the first two steps and turned, waiting for her father. He reached her a moment later and stepped up, as the front door exploded inward, the lock destroyed by a small charge. The door slammed backward on its hinges, crashing into the wall on its left.

"Go," John said, and dove to the right into the kitchen as a third camouflaged shooter appeared in the entrance, a black pistol in his hands. John landed on the wooden floor behind the kitchen island, temporarily protected from the shooters in the back and the one in the front.

He heard footsteps as Amira and her father raced up the stairs, which turned ninety degrees up to a smaller landing. A short set of stairs led up to a rec room above the garage, and a second set led to the right up to the second floor, where the three large bedrooms were. Two of the bedrooms were in front, and the master bedroom was at the back of the house down a short hallway past the guest bathroom on the right. *At least they have options up there*, John thought, but he was down to one.

He scrambled forward past the island and through a small archway into the formal dining room. He just hoped that the gunman in front hadn't seen or heard him. A second entrance at the other end of the dining room led around to the front and formal living room. If he circled around and wasn't detected, he'd be able to take the shooter from behind.

He crept along the dining room, reached the door, and waited. John heard the gunman move a few steps into the house, and he stole a quick glance through the doorway just in time to see the back of his tree suit disappear into the narrow hallway. *Gotcha.*

He moved purposefully and as quietly as he could, trying to remain undetected in order to reach and neutralize the new threat. As he moved, the shooter spoke, "They're upstairs." A quick pause. "Roger that. Stand by."

John stopped at the far end of the living room near the foyer, exhaled, and leaned around. The shooter stood in the kitchen, his attention directed upward at the ceiling, and John realized with horror what he was doing. *He's listening for them.*

A creaking noise sounded from above, and the shooter raised the suppressed AR-15. *Oh no.*

John broke from cover and dashed down the hallway, screaming as he ran, "Move toward the back, *now!*"

The shooter heard him, but rather than turn to confront the threat, the discipline ingrained from years of training took command of his actions. His objective was to eliminate all targets in the house, and he opened fire a second and a half before John Quick crashed into him.

Nick chased after Amira down the hallway, only two steps behind. They passed the guest bathroom on the right as he heard John scream up at them, and his detective's sharp mind processed the warning instantly. *He's going to shoot into the ceiling.* And then the only, singular thought in his mind was—*Amira.*

Fueled by an all-encompassing primal need to protect his daughter, he reached her as she stopped at the entrance to the master bedroom and turned toward him to see how far behind he was. Concern and fear—*for him, not for herself*—shone on her face, but he didn't have the luxury of responding.

Loud bangs emanated from downstairs as puffs of carpet fibers and chunks of plywood kicked up behind him in the hallway. *God, forgive me,* Nick thought, extended his arms, leaned forward, and shoved his daughter, the last true love in his life, out of harm's way, backward into the master bedroom.

One more bang reached his ears, and he felt a punch to the right side of his chest. Even as he fell into the bedroom behind her, he knew instantly that he'd been shot, but he felt no pain, only the power of the blow. *Just a little too slow to save yourself, but she's safe,* he thought, and collapsed onto the carpet.

But then the sharp, burning, suffocating pain burst from his chest, and he realized the wound was serious, likely fatal. He felt weakness spread throughout his body, as if lulling each part of it to sleep.

A commotion ensued below them in the kitchen, and Nick realized John had engaged the attacker. *There's no time. She needs to help him, or I won't be the only one she loses today. She doesn't deserve that. She doesn't deserve any of this.*

"No!" Amira screamed, agony breaking palpably in her voice. "Daddy!" she cried in the voice of a panicked little girl, desperate to save the life of the man who'd raised her. She reached behind her and yanked a comforter off the bed and placed it under his head. "No. No. No," she repeated, as if denying the reality in front of her. Tears welled up in her eyes, and she felt the opening of a rift inside her, threatening to swallow her whole.

"Listen to me, honey," Nick said, and coughed, and he felt his breath rattle in his chest. "No matter what happens to me, you *have* to get the gun and help John. He's downstairs and fighting for his life. This is your world," he said, his voice sounding weaker by the moment. "You can't save me. You know it. I know it. I feel it. I know I don't have much time."

Amira wept, held his right hand in hers, and cradled his head in her left arm. She looked into the eyes of her father, and all she saw was love, the love of a father for a daughter. She cried harder.

"Listen to me," Nick said. "If I have to go, there is *no other way* I would've wanted than to save you and give you a fighting chance. Do you understand me?" he asked, his eyes burning brightly.

"Oh, Daddy . . ." Amira said between gasps of pain and tears.

"Stop it. Stop it right now. You *have to help John,* or you're going to join me, and I can't bear . . . the thought of it." He felt himself fading, fast. "Do you understand me? You need to do your job."

Amira was torn. The undying love for her father waged a war with the seething rage racing through her veins. She nodded, acknowledging that the man who'd given her advice, who'd taught her how to ride a bike, who'd encouraged her to pursue dance, and who'd sacrificed his time for her, *always,* was right one last time. "I love you, Daddy" was all she said. "I love you."

"And I love you, forever, no matter where I am. I'll see you again," Nick said, as blood ran from the corners of his mouth, his shirt already a thick, wet mess. His eyes fluttered, opened widely, and stared lovingly into his beautiful daughter's face. "Because you're my princess . . . my Amira," he said quietly as the life left his body, and his vacant eyes stared at the ceiling.

A guttural, tortured cry rose in her throat, hot tears mixing with her father's blood, but she heard a loud crash from the kitchen. *John,* and her heart raced once again in fear, not for her father, who was somehow *gone,* but for the other man she loved.

She placed her father's head on the comforter and closed his eyes. She kissed him on the forehead, only wishing to remain on the floor and hold him, but she knew she couldn't. There was no time. She inhaled deeply and allowed the rage and fury to soothe her broken heart. She strode to the gun safe on the floor and punched in 1-4-2-2 for her parents' birthdays. The door sprang forward, the top coming to rest on the carpet, and Amira reached in and grabbed her father's black Colt M1911 .45-caliber pistol. The weight, the heft of it, felt solid in her hands, as if begging her to use it to avenge its owner's death, a gunslinger's cry for vengeance. She pulled the slide back slightly, spotted the silver casing of the round in the chamber, and let the slide move forward. She cocked back the hammer with her right thumb, placed her forefinger straight and off the trigger along the trigger guard, and turned. As she passed her father's body, she said, "I love you, Daddy, until the end," and strode into the fray of the battle below.

CHAPTER 39

John struck the exposed left side of the shooter's face, and his knuckles left three white smears across the green and brown camouflage paint. He grabbed the barrel of the AR-15 behind the pistol grip and yanked backward as he pushed the gunman backward and slammed him into the granite island. He felt the jarring impact through the man's body, and the shooter's grip on the long gun slackened.

John reached up and grabbed the collapsible stock of the long gun, and with as much strength as he could summon from the off-balance position he was in, he yanked the weapon forward, extending the shooter's arms out, and then viciously slammed it backward like a rubber band contracting. The butt of the weapon smashed into the shooter's face, split his lip in half, and shattered his top three teeth.

John was fueled by rage, the thought that this mercenary had just tried to shoot the woman he loved fresh in his mind. Pulling the AR-15 toward him and to the left, he rotated slightly and delivered a short side-stomp to the man's left knee. The man dropped, and John wrestled the AR-15 out of the gloved hands.

The shooter landed on his right knee, but rather than yield, he shot his hand toward his right hip. *Oh no you don't, motherfucker,* John thought, whipped the AR-15 back around, and squeezed the trigger several times in quick succession as the man raised a black Glock from a drop holster. He only made it six inches before four rounds struck him in the left side of the chest, and he slumped against the side of the kitchen island.

More glass exploded as rounds from the backyard tore apart the remaining pieces on the left side of the sliding door. Several bullets struck the walls of the hallway, but John ignored the fire, raised the AR-15, and fired several shots in response.

Nothing more came from the backyard, and he heard screaming and crying from upstairs. *Amira. Please, God, let her be okay.* His immediate plan was simple—wait down here to prevent anyone else from infiltrating the house. Thirty more seconds passed.

He stared into the backyard, where shadows had fallen across the landscape like washed-out canvases of gray, ominous and foreboding. Nothing moved. *They're out there somewhere.*

John peered down the hallway and opened his mouth to speak when a second shooter in a camouflage tree suit appeared in the destroyed front entranceway. The man's AR-15 moved upward, tracking on him, even as John adjusted his own weapon. *This is going to be close,* he thought, and realized he might actually lose the long-rifle quick-draw contest in which he found himself. "Shooter!" he screamed, hoping that at least he'd warn Amira and her father upstairs.

Amira was cold, not from a sudden drop in the temperature, but from the way she'd compartmentalized her emotions less than a minute before. It'd taken every ounce of strength to resist the temptation to stay upstairs and hold her father, even though he was gone. Two things kept her moving—her father had sacrificed himself for her, and she was going to do everything in her power to honor that sacrifice . . . *as well as make the evil bastards who had brought this horror to them pay.* But to do that, she needed to focus, which meant removing herself emotionally from the situation. *For the next few minutes, Amira, you need to do your job. There will be time for everything else later.*

She exhaled and left the room, the Colt M1911 reassuring in her hands. She quickly and quietly headed back down the hallway. No sound came from downstairs. She'd heard more shots after her father had been struck, and she hoped John had been the one dealing death.

She reached the stairs and started down them, placing one foot along the edge of the carpet runner on each step to prevent the boards from squeaking. She passed the landing and turned left, descending a few more stairs.

The kitchen came into view, and she saw a body near the island and sighed in relief. *John, one; bad guys, none.* Two more steps, and she spotted the lower half of John, including the AR-15 in his hands.

She opened her mouth to speak, when a scuffle from the front porch sounded loudly in the foyer. John shouted, "Shooter!" and started to react, raising the AR-15 toward the front door. *He's not going to make it.*

With no other options, Amira Cerone, functioning on adrenaline and training, dove down the last two steps. She opened fire midair and struck the new threat in the right knee, which disintegrated in a red puff of mist and bone. She landed hard on her right side, which absorbed the impact, and fired two more times.

The .45-caliber reports thundered throughout the house and echoed across the front yard. Normally a world-class shot, her dive had dropped her aim, and the two slugs tore into the shooter's stomach, and he fell sideways and backward on top of the ruined knee. He shrieked from the initial agony of the crippling injury and gutshots, and then he began to moan incoherently.

Amira stood up, the M1911 trained on the writhing man. She turned around and found John staring at her. "Are you okay?" she asked.

He nodded, noticing the blood on the front of her green Under Armour shirt. "You?"

"Yes," she said, dreading the next question.

"Your father?" John asked, already knowing the answer.

For the briefest of moments, her features faltered, her eyes seemed to crumple inward from the pain, and she only shook her head, refusing to voice what he already knew.

"Amira, I am so, so sorry," John said quietly. There was nothing more to say.

"I know," Amira said, and regained her composure, turned around, and strode defiantly down the hallway.

She reached the dying shooter dressed in camouflage and stared down. He was suffering, and she considered letting him die slowly on the floor, his blood pooling under his ruined leg and torso. But after what he and his team had done, his mere presence and existence was an affront to her. *You deserve to suffer, but even more, you don't deserve to live.*

"Hey," Amira said firmly. "Hey."

The man opened his eyes and looked up into the merciless, beautiful face of Amira Cerone.

"Do you see me?" she asked.

As pain racked his body, the shattered knee a throbbing black hole of concentrated pain, he nodded, not daring to defy the warrior who stood over him.

"Good. I want to be the last thing you see before I send you to hell," she said calmly, raised the Colt, and fired three times into his chest, killing him.

It didn't make her feel better. She'd known it wouldn't, but at least she knew one more killer had been removed from the face of the earth.

"Amira, there's one more out there," John said. "Please step away from the door. I don't want him taking any potshots at you."

"Nor you," she replied, and smiled briefly. She started toward John, suddenly eager for his embrace, and he moved toward her.

Before they met in the middle of the hall, the sound of squealing tires reached them from down the street.

John's eyes widened in frustration. "Oh no. The cops."

"Let's go," Amira said, and the two of them exited her father's house through the ruined front door just in time to witness the second ambush of the night.

CHAPTER 40

Calvert County Sheriff's Deputy First Class Shea Jenkins was exhausted. He was at the tail end of his third twelve-hour day when the call came through his Motorola APX 8000 XE in-dash radio. "Be advised. We have a report of armed gunmen in the Rolling Knolls subdivision. The caller, a teenager down the street, states three men in camouflage with some type of assault rifles are approaching a home through the woods. He spotted them while flying a drone. He called the homeowner, one Nicolo Cerone, and his daughter answered and told him to call the police immediately."

Three men with assault weapons? What the hell? An eight-year veteran of the Coast Guard, Shea had spent his time conducting counternarcotics drug interdictions as a team leader on Tactical Law Enforcement Team South at the southern tip of the peninsula in Opa-locka, Florida. The last time he'd seen hostiles in camouflage, a four-man team from Cuba had evaded the cutter he was attached to, beached their powerboat on a small key island north of Key Largo, and tried to escape his team. Petty Officer Second Class Jenkins—he was amused by the fact that he'd moved up in class at the sheriff's office—and his team had pursued on their RHIB, landed a few minutes behind them, and stalked them across the small island of mangroves. It hadn't ended well for the bad guys—two dead, one wounded, and one surrendered.

"Seriously?" Shea asked, talking in plain language.

"The caller sounded serious and scared," the dispatcher replied, but promptly added, "Stand by." A ten-second pause ensued. "Just received another call from the same neighborhood. He's reporting shots fired. Scrambling all units to the location now, but you're the closest."

Jesus Christ. What the hell is popping off in Calvert tonight? Shea thought. Normally, a Wednesday night consisted of bar fights, drug overdoses, and traffic stops, but it sounded like someone had gone full Rambo in the rural suburbs. He flipped the light and siren switches on his console, checked the rearview mirror, and floored the pursuit-rated Ford Explorer into the left lane north on Route 4. "Roger. Rolling with lights and sirens but will cut them when I'm in the subdivision. Who's closest after me?"

"Deputy Phillips. Looks like he's thirty to sixty seconds behind you." *The rookie,* Shea thought. *Good to go. If I have to get into a gunfight, he'll do.* The twenty-three-year-old deputy was cocky and brash and not shaken easily, and Shea didn't think he'd cave under the pressure.

"Roger," Shea responded. "Will advise when I'm on scene. Out." *What a way to end a shift . . .*

As if reading his mind, the female dispatcher added, "Be safe. Godspeed." She ended the communication and started coordinating with the other eleven units that were on duty.

Deputy Shea Jenkins calmed his mind and exhaled, preparing himself for the unknown. *Never a dull moment,* he thought. It was why he loved his job. He just hoped tonight wouldn't be his last night on it.

The Ford Explorer raced up Route 4 in lane one, as the police referred to the left lane, passing post-rush-hour traffic. *Two minutes out.* The cars continued to move over ahead of him, and he hoped no elderly driver or subcontractor who'd started drinking early on a Wednesday afternoon held him up.

Ninety seconds later, he slowed down and turned left in a lane that cut through the grass median to enter the Rolling Knolls subdivision. The tires gripped the pavement, and he cut in front of traffic that stopped to let him through, their headlights in the dusk flashing across the interior of his Explorer.

Shea grabbed the microphone on the Motorola and said, "Entering the subdivision now."

"Roger, Unit 23," the dispatcher replied.

Shea cut the lights and the sirens and accelerated to 55 mph. The large homes sped by, and a half mile later he saw the street he needed to turn onto—Burning Leaf.

He turned left and slowed dramatically, although not enough to prevent the tires from squealing around the turn. *Sloppy. Get your shit together.*

The house was located at the end of the cul-de-sac, and as he approached, he saw the front door wide open with damage to the frame. *This is real,* he thought. *Not some prank or 911 hang-up.*

He stopped the SUV in front of the house two hundred yards away, grabbed the microphone once again, and said, "On scene. Parked a few hundred feet away. Front door wide open. No sounds of gunfire. Exiting the vehicle and moving in."

Shea reached into the back seat and pulled out a SCAR-H CQC 5.56mm assault rifle. The sheriff's office had established a relationship with the Belgian-based FN Herstal group that provided weapons to militaries and law enforcement agencies across the world. As a member of Calvert County's Special Operations Team, Shea was fortunate enough to have some serious firepower in the lethal form of the SCAR-H with a thirteen-inch shortened barrel for close-quarters combat. His heavy vest was in the back, but

285

he didn't want to waste the precious seconds to put it on. He hoped his standard black Kevlar would stop whatever was being used in the upper-middle-class neighborhood.

He stepped out of the vehicle, hoping Sam was close behind him. But Shea also knew that every second mattered. Unlike that cowardly sheriff's department in Florida, Calvert County was proud of its aggressive, confident, and capable force. *They never backed down, and they always went in hard.*

Deputy Shea Jenkins started running down the street, confidence building with each step. A man and a woman suddenly emerged from the front door. He saw blood on the front of her shirt. She held a pistol, and the man held an AR-15. *Oh shit,* he thought, praying to God that she was the owner's daughter and *not* a hostile.

Unfortunately, Shea never saw the real threat that stood near the bushes on the side of the house. He heard the loud *thwacks* from his left and felt two tremendous blows—one to each leg—followed by searing pain. He screamed in shock and surprise as he collapsed to the concrete.

Goddamnit. I never even got into the fight, he thought, and then his head hit the concrete and he blacked out, temporarily sparing him the pain of a shattered right tibia and a gunshot to the left quad, which missed the femoral artery. He wouldn't realize how fortunate he was until much later.

CHAPTER 41

Chase managed his frustration, even as the sheriff's deputy crumpled to the street and lay still. He hoped he hadn't killed him: that wasn't the mission, and he knew the deputy was only doing his job, but Chase had a job as well, and it had gone horribly wrong at the appearance of the drone.

He and his team had calculated multiple courses of action and response, but accidental compromise due to a small commercial drone had not been one of them. The plan had been a simple one—obtain clear fields of fire, wait until they had a direct shot at the target and whoever else was in the house, and then simultaneously take them out from the wood line and clear the house afterward.

But the drone had changed the calculus, and Chase had been forced to send in his men, and by the look and sound of it, neither had survived. He'd considered charging in himself, but he knew it was reckless, and as the team leader, he wasn't paid to sacrifice himself. He knew it wasn't what the vice president would want, and Chase didn't exactly relish the idea of confronting whoever was in the house in addition to John Quick and Nick Cerone. It was likely the daughter, who worked on the same presidential task force as

John Quick. And from what Baker's dossier had provided, she was just as lethal—if not more so—than Quick. He didn't think he'd win that confrontation, not against the woman and Quick.

As he stood off to the side of the house, he'd considered retreating into the woods, working his way back to the Patuxent River, and crossing it at night like George Washington on the Delaware. He knew he'd be vulnerable, that helicopters would be called in, as well as the K-9 units and God knew whoever else worked the woods in southern Maryland. His odds were not good, but they were better than his chances of survival if he remained at the house.

But then the first Calvert County Sheriff's SUV had arrived, and the plan, flexible until the end, shifted. *Steal the SUV, escape the neighborhood, ditch it before they can find it, change into the spare set of clothes in the daypack, and get the hell out of Calvert County.*

The first deputy down, Chase moved toward the Ford Explorer, jogging toward the SUV, a misshapen hunchbacked monster in camouflage. He needed to get the key fob off the deputy, since he knew the SUV wouldn't function without it.

A second SUV suddenly turned down the street from the right, its headlights briefly illuminating the scene—one SUV parked at an angle, door open, and the deputy unmoving in the street ten feet in front of it. *Damn it,* Chase thought, adjusting his avenue of approach, and moving toward the new arrival.

He didn't know if the deputy had seen him yet, but he didn't wait for a visual confirmation. The door opened, and a young, tall deputy with a short, military-style haircut stepped out, his eyes focused on the first SUV and the fallen deputy. Chase opened fire from less than eighty feet away, aiming for the legs once again. The collateral damage was mounting by the minute, and he hoped this was the last innocent bystander he'd have to engage.

The rounds struck the deputy as he stepped toward the curb, and his legs gave way under him. He fell forward, and the Glock pistol in his hand—he hadn't pulled his AR-15 yet—clattered to the street and bounced into the grass.

Chase ran hard, and loud pistol shots rang out from his left. Clumps of dirt kicked up behind him, and he ran harder. He needed to get to the deputy, who was crawling facedown on the pavement toward the grass and his Glock. If his instincts were right—*and he was betting his life on it*—Quick and the Cerone woman wouldn't risk hitting the deputy. *Just a few more seconds.*

He reached the deputy as the wounded man placed his hand on the Glock. Chase delivered a kick that broke two of the deputy's fingers but sent the pistol tumbling away and out of his grasp.

"Motherfucker!" the deputy shouted, and rolled over onto his back, pain and anger mixed as one on his young face.

"Sorry about all this," Chase said evenly. The shots from the front porch had stopped—as he'd expected—but he raised the AR-15 and fired six quick rounds toward Cerone's front porch. *That should buy me a few seconds.*

Chase looked back down at the deputy, who still showed no fear, even as spent 5.56mm casings now lay next to him. "Two things: I need these," Chase said, reached down, and yanked the key fob off the deputy's gun belt, disconnected the microphone from the Motorola radio, and grabbed the radio. "Second, you'll live. I didn't want any more collateral damage, and I know you're only doing your job. Tell your friend the same. Finally, there's a man buried about a mile and a half toward the river. His grave is marked by an orange flag. He deserves a proper burial."

Chase stood up, and the deputy said, "Who the hell are you?"

"Doesn't matter, and all of this, it doesn't involve you, which is why you lived. Be grateful," Chase replied, strode over to the second Explorer, hopped in, and shut the door. Seconds later, he spun the car around and fled the street, lights and siren off.

CHAPTER 42

John and Amira ran toward the fallen sheriff's deputies. "I'm going after him," John said between breaths as the two ran. The gunshot wound to his stomach had healed, but he felt a throbbing, as if the wound were threatening to reopen.

They reached the first, unconscious deputy and knelt down beside him. Blood ran from a small cut on his head, but a thick pool of it lay on the street near his legs. "Need to stop the bleeding," Amira said, rolled the deputy over, opened the IFAK kit on the back of his gun belt, and grabbed the contents, which included scissors, a tourniquet, bandages, and several packages of QuikClot.

John looked back at the second deputy, who had propped himself up into a sitting position, his legs out straight before him. His wounded right hand lay on his lap. "Hey!" John shouted. "How you doing over there? How bad is it?"

"A couple of broken fingers, my legs are fucked, but I think I'll live," the deputy replied. "How's Shea? Also, you call this in yet?"

Amira grabbed the Motorola microphone from the unconscious deputy's lapel, yanked the key fob from his belt, and handed the key to John. She stared at him fiercely, the anguish and rage burning brightly in her eyes. "Go. Hunt him down and end him. Please."

"I will," John said, leaned in, and kissed her fiercely on the mouth. "I'm so sorry about your father."

Amira only nodded. "I've got this. Now go," she said, and pressed the microphone's talk button. "This is Amira Cerone. There are two officers down in front of fourteen-oh-four Burning Leaf Court. I say again, two officers down with severe leg injuries from multiple gunshots. The shooter fled in one of the police Explorers, and my partner is pursuing him in a second Calvert County SUV. There are two enemy KIA on scene. Send medical and multiple units. How copy?"

There was a brief pause, and then the dispatcher replied, more calmly than Amira had expected, "Roger all. Scrambling EMS and additional units. Who did you say you are again?"

As John jumped into the front seat of the Explorer, which was still running, he heard Amira say, "We're with the FBI."

Well, that's kind of true, he thought. *They did give us badges, after all.*

He closed the door, whipped the SUV around, and floored it off Burning Leaf and onto the main road that led out of the subdivision. He grabbed the Motorola handset from the SUV's radio, pressed the microphone, and thought, *This should be fun.* "Calvert County Dispatch, is this a dedicated channel for only you and me?"

He waited until a female voice, calm and confident, with a twinge of a southern accent, answered, "Roger. It is. Who is this?"

"This is John Quick. I am in the SUV that was the first deputy's on the scene. I'm in pursuit of the shooter, who fled in the second SUV that arrived. I'm a federal law enforcement agent with the FBI. Please contact the FBI director's office at the DC Field Office for verification. More importantly, I assume you have a GPS on these vehicles, I need you to guide me to the one that just left the scene. That's our shooter. Also, keep the other units away until I can engage him. I don't want to spook him until I'm on him. Over." *Let's see how that goes over.*

"Stand by," the dispatcher replied. "Unit 172 is northbound on Route Four, approximately three-quarters of a mile ahead of you once you make the turn."

"Roger that," John said, looked from the radio and computer to the console between the two seats, and smiled. *Oh yeah. Now we're in business.* Two rows of buttons ran horizontally between the seats. He flipped two of the switches, and the police lights started flashing, and the sirens started wailing. *You're living every kid's fantasy right now. Damn straight.* But then his reverie was broken at the thought of Amira's father, killed by an unknown gunman who was now dead himself. He gripped the steering wheel tighter, accelerated, and reached the entrance to the subdivision at the intersection of Route 4.

Traffic stopped from his left, and he crossed into the median. The vehicles approaching from the north from his right slowed, and he entered the left lane and pushed the pedal to the floor. The specially designed shift point engaged for instant power, and the Explorer rocketed forward.

"You're gaining on him. Looks like he's maintaining his speed at fifty-five miles per hour. Half mile," the dispatcher said.

"You try to radio him?" John asked, as an idea formed in his head.

"Negative. You want me to?" the dispatcher asked.

"No. But I may have you connect me directly or broadcast in the open in a few minutes. I just need to catch up to the bastard."

"Roger. Standing by," she said, and went silent.

So this is what it's like to have working comms in the middle of a crisis or combat, he thought ironically, recalling the days in the Marine Corps when acquiring a clear communications signal was like searching for alien life in space—futile and endless.

A white Mercedes SUV moved into the left lane, and John pushed past the SUV, creating a pathway that utilized the left half of the lane and the shoulder.

"You should see him shortly. Looks like he's at a light or stuck in traffic," she said.

John scanned the traffic in front of him. *He's going to see and hear me coming.* "Can you put me through to him or broadcast in the open?" John asked.

Seconds later, "You're in the clear."

"To the asshole in the SUV, this is John Quick. I'm betting you know *exactly* who I am," John said, and slowed for traffic at a light one hundred yards away. "This is your one and only chance: stop the SUV and surrender. Otherwise, I promise you it's not going to end well for you," he finished, and released the talk button. He flipped the siren and light switches and crept up the shoulder toward the intersection.

A calm voice replied, "I don't think so. And you're right, I know exactly who and what you are, but I'm not stopping. Not for you or anyone. Just know that if it weren't for that drone, you'd be dead right now."

"I assume you're former military," John responded, ignoring the failed threat. "All you Organization types are. And that means you should be used to things going wrong on an operation. Things went south for you and your little team. They're dead, but you have one chance left, and this is it."

Gotcha, motherfucker, John thought as he spotted the Calvert County SUV in the left lane, third in line at the light, eight cars in front of him.

"No thanks," the shooter replied. "The only chances I need are the ones I'm taking on my own."

"Kind of figured you'd say something like that," John said, dropped the microphone, and floored the Explorer. The SUV shot up the shoulder, accelerating with each vehicle it passed. The Explorer reached 50 mph, and John braced himself for the impact.

The enemy in the stolen Calvert County Sheriff's Office Explorer must have realized John was close. As John bore down on him, the SUV suddenly pulled onto the shoulder to try and escape the traffic jam, but too little too late. *I have the advantage,* he thought as he slammed the crash gate of the Explorer into the left front quarter panel of the other SUV.

The two vehicles merged for a brief moment before the other SUV was pushed to the right. Its driver did the only thing he could to minimize the effects—floored the accelerator in a futile attempt to evade his pursuer. Chase's SUV separated from John's Explorer and was pushed right. It ricocheted off a dark-blue Nissan Pathfinder and careened left, striking the passenger side of John's Explorer. Both vehicles shot into the intersection.

John glanced out his passenger window into the enemy vehicle. A man in camouflage paint and a digital camouflage tree suit looked at him, the whites of his eyes in stark contrast to his outfit. But it was what he saw *through* the front seat of the other Explorer that made him smile and point quickly past the driver.

The other driver turned to look just in time to see a Chevy Suburban barreling through the intersection at more than thirty miles per hour.

The other driver was already halfway through the intersection before the two police SUVs magically appeared directly in front of him, as he'd recall later to the sheriff's deputies.

John yanked the steering wheel of the Explorer hard and to the left as the Suburban smashed into the passenger door and right-front wheel well of the second Explorer. The window shattered, and the impact flung Chase to the right as his vehicle was pushed left. Without his seat belt on, his right shoulder slammed into the corner of the mounted Toughbook laptop computer, and he felt a sharp pain in the joint.

Chase's Explorer was shoved sideways and struck the right rear corner of John's Explorer, whipping the end around as John unsuccessfully tried to avoid the collision. John's vehicle skidded across the pavement and rocked on its side as it came to a halt. The enemy's Explorer, slowed by the impact, wobbled slowly across the middle of the intersection on its ruined chassis before it stopped.

As soon as John's SUV came to a halt, he reached into the passenger seat where he'd stowed the dead man's AR-15 he'd taken from the kitchen and aimed over the dashboard of the Explorer. Traffic had stopped on the southbound lanes, and there were no vehicles behind the other disabled Explorer. *This is going to hurt,* John thought, and pulled the trigger.

The suppressor helped minimize the pain and saved John from permanent hearing loss, but the loud *bangs* as the weapon tore apart the non-bulletproof windshield still made his ears ring with each shot. He stopped firing after several shots, heard no return fire from the Explorer, unbuckled his seat belt, opened the driver's-side door, and stepped into the middle of the intersection.

The sounds of vehicles stopping, horns blaring, and people shouting assaulted him, but he trained the AR-15 on the other SUV as he circled around the front of his own vehicle.

"Last warning!" John shouted. "Come out of the vehicle with your hands up!" *Spoken like a real cop,* he thought, and dismissed it as he realized the front of the SUV was empty. And then he saw the passenger door, which had been blocked by his angle, ajar. *Motherfucker somehow made it out.*

Seconds later, he heard several shouts three or four vehicles back. John shifted his eyes and spotted the source of the commotion—a dark shape running in a crouch back down the shoulder of Route 4.

The figure suddenly bolted back through the northbound traffic and off the side of the road toward a small strip mall and several freestanding casual restaurants and the king of fast-food dining—Chick-fil-A.

John, with no clear line of sight on the fleeing figure, broke into a sprint down the right shoulder of the northbound lane. *No way you're getting away. No. Fucking. Way.*

CHAPTER 43

Beth Fritz was exhausted, counting down the hours until she could close the store and get home to sleep. A tall, thin, attractive twenty-year-old brunette who looked like she'd be comfortable in both rural southern Maryland and urban Washington DC, the Chick-fil-A assistant manager was enrolled in the College of Southern Maryland's Respiratory Therapy program.

She'd witnessed the decline of her father due to emphysema, which led to a condition called cor pulmonale, and ultimately heart failure and death. As a result, something had shaken loose inside, and she'd been compelled to research her father's killer. Someday she knew she'd be a doctor, maybe even a pulmonologist, but first she wanted to help those who suffered the same way her father had. It was why she'd also taken the position at the brand-new Chick-fil-A in Prince Frederick, Maryland. The money was good, the hours were flexible, and the company legitimately cared about her and the other employees. As advertised, it was a warm and friendly working environment. The free food was just an added bonus.

The restaurant was half full of families, construction workers, teenagers looking for a bite out on a Wednesday evening, and even six members of a girl's local lacrosse team. Lacrosse was revered in Maryland the way football was in Texas, although no one was making TV shows with Kyle Chandler about lacrosse. *Just another normal Wednesday night crowd,* Beth thought, at least until she heard the first scream, looked up from the register, and saw the *thing* holding some kind of rifle in his left arm as blood dripped from his right one onto the clean floor.

Her manager's hat on every minute of every shift, she couldn't help but think, *Damn. Someone's going to have to clean that up later.*

But then he spoke, and Beth's temporary transfixion on him was broken as other customers spotted him and screamed or gasped in surprise.

"I need everyone to remain calm," he said loudly, speaking across the entire restaurant. He looked at Beth. "You. I need you to lock the doors. We're going to be here a while." A boy no older than five started to cry, but his mother hushed him. The stranger spoke again. "I promise you that if you do as I ask and remain calm, no one, and I mean no one, is going to get hurt." He looked back at Beth. "Did you not hear what I just said?"

He's talking to you, Beth. As if forcing herself from a dream, she shook her head from side to side, walked behind the counter to the left end, emerged from behind it through the opening, and moved to the door behind the stranger. She passed through the first door in the small entryway, grabbed the outer door, pulled it toward her, and turned the lock, securing the door. Seconds later, she was back inside the restaurant and locked the inner one.

A scream rose up from the middle of the tables, and she heard a man exclaim, "Oh, damn. This is going to get bad." Beth Fritz turned around and found herself less than a foot away from the camouflaged intruder. He grabbed her with his wounded right arm and pulled her in front of him. She smelled blood and a musky odor as if he hadn't showered in days. But she forgot his grip on her as she looked at the door on the opposite side of the restaurant.

Standing across from her was a rugged-looking man in a blue T-shirt and khakis, holding the same kind of weapon her captor held, except his was pointed in her direction as the man stared through some kind of mounted scope at her. *Oh God,* she thought. *Please don't let him shoot me by accident.*

"This ends now, one way or another," John said firmly, the red arrow on the lens of the variable power reflex scope lined up on the Camouflage Man, as John thought of him. He ignored the noises to his right as the remaining patrons moved toward the front of the dining area and the door that led to the glass-enclosed children's playground. "You either surrender or die," John continued, his words eliciting a gasp from several of the customers, who'd grown quiet at the confrontation. *A modern-day Mexican standoff in a Chick-fil-A. Fan-fucking-tastic.*

The Camouflage Man slowly edged forward, and he swept the AR-15 toward the patrons. "You shoot me, and my finger, which is *not* straight and off the trigger but on it," he said, referring to one of the Marine Corps' weapons safety rules, "likely contracts, and some of them likely get hit or killed. I don't want that, I'm pretty sure you don't want that, and I *know* they don't want that. So I'm getting out of here, through the kitchen and out the exit in the back. This lovely young woman is coming with me, but she won't be harmed once I'm away from this place."

"Where the hell are you going to go?" John asked. "You got an Uber waiting out back? There's *nowhere* to run. Don't you get it?"

"That's not true, and you know it," the Camouflage Man replied. "There's always *someplace* to run, even if they're bad choices." He and his hostage had reached the open entrance to the area behind the counter. "No more talking. Just please let me do this, or it all ends badly."

John desperately yearned to pull the trigger. At this close range, he knew he'd hit his target and kill him instantly, but the thought of an innocent bystander taking a stray round sickened him. *There's been enough bloodshed for one Wednesday night.* And so he let him move, slowly, toward the back of the counter, hoping for something that might change the calculus of the standoff.

But neither John Quick nor Chase Grayson, the wounded and bleeding Camouflage Man, had accounted for Darren Nettles.

CHAPTER 44

Frustrated at the loss of another job to a new competitor in the area, thirty-three-year-old electrician and former army enlisted engineer Darren Nettles sat in the back of the small dining section near the restrooms of the Chick-fil-A. After another long day, he continued to struggle to build his fledgling business, the one-man electrician company Nettles Short-Fuse Electrical, a reference to his temper from his twenties. He brainstormed marketing and advertising ideas as he devoured the spicy chicken sandwich, extra pickles, and pondered his next move, at least until the gunman who looked like a hunter—except for the tactically modified AR-15 he carried in his left hand—stormed into the restaurant and ended his dinner.

A veteran of the Iraq War who'd participated in the rebuilding of Sadr City in 2008, Darren didn't panic. It wasn't the first time he'd seen an armed gunman, although it was the first time in rural southern Maryland.

As the crisis unfolded, Darren realized a second person had entered the restaurant and had engaged the gunman in conversation, of which Darren could only hear one side since the other entrance was around the corner from his booth and out of sight. *You need to do something, but you don't need to be a hero,* he thought as he reached for the concealed Glock G17 Gen5 9mm pistol he wore inside the waistband of his Carhartt khaki rip-proof cargo pants.

Notorious as one of the most difficult states in the Union in which to obtain a conceal-carry permit, Maryland did care about one criterion that fit Darren—small business owner. The fact that he was an army veteran had made the process easier. But even though he maintained his proficiency with his Glock, he didn't want to be responsible for an innocent bystander getting shot. He knew the state of Maryland would come after him if that happened, and he had enough problems. But he had to do something.

The gunman was distracted by his injury and focused on the other side of the restaurant. Darren pulled up his red T-shirt with a yellow dynamite fuse emblem on the left chest and withdrew the Glock, which he kept chambered. *What's the point of a weapon that's not ready to go?*

He quietly slid out of his booth, the Glock at his side, and crept forward, one work boot in front of the other. If he could get close enough, maybe he could distract him and get the AR-15 pointed away from the customers in the middle of the restaurant. He'd seen enough terrified, huddled civilians in Iraq to last a lifetime. He wouldn't tolerate it in Maryland, USA.

He was within eight feet of the gunman when he stopped, raised the Glock to the man's head, and said, "I have a Glock pointed at your head. At this range, I won't miss. I *do* know how to use it. Please don't make me. These people don't deserve it, and I pray that you know that."

Chase Grayson didn't panic: he was beyond that emotion at this point in his life and career. Instead, he suddenly felt exhausted, as if the weight of the past two days had just barreled into him harder than the bullet he'd taken in his right arm. He was a lot of things—mercenary, killer, and even a former Marine—but he didn't consider himself a monster. The retired detective had been a job, pure and simple, and the hunter in the woods had interfered with it, albeit unknowingly. But these people, they epitomized the definition of innocent collateral damage. His plan was to use them as bargaining chips, nothing else. But now some good Samaritan with a gun had blown that plan into oblivion as effectively as the drone had destroyed his original one. *I will not be remembered as a monster, no matter what happens.*

Chase exhaled, said to the young woman, "I'm sorry," and did the only thing left that gave him a fraction of a chance of survival: he dropped the AR-15 from his left hand and shoved her as hard as he could forward, propelling her into the area behind the counter. He lunged for the kitchen door and his last avenue of escape.

As soon as the tall, thin man in work pants had emerged from behind the corner from the other part of the restaurant with a Glock pointed at the Camouflage Man's head, John knew the situation had reached critical mass. *Oh, God. Please don't let him shoot anyone.* He placed the red upside-down V of the scope between the Camouflage Man's eyes, prepared to squeeze, and prayed his shot would be the only one fired in the next few seconds. It was precisely as his finger tightened that the Camouflage Man shoved the girl and moved toward the kitchen door.

John moved his finger away from the trigger, lowered the weapon, and took two steps toward the counter. He launched himself into the air, placed the AR-15 on the counter between two cash registers, and sprang over it like a gymnast over a pommel horse. He landed behind the counter as the Camouflage Man reached the kitchen door, slammed it inward, and disappeared inside. John hit the door a second later and entered into the secret world of the kitchen of Chick-fil-A.

The pleasant aroma of cooking chicken and french fries assaulted him. Brown cardboard boxes were stacked on the right just inside the door, and clear tubes ran up and through the wall to the fountain machine out front. The right half of the kitchen was a long, narrow walkway at least thirty feet deep with metal prep tables on the left, multiple cooking stations, standing ovens, and all sorts of restaurant equipment John didn't recognize. The Camouflage Man was only six feet in front of him and moved quickly, even with the wounded arm.

A metal rolling tray at least six feet tall with dozens of narrow slots to hold the cookie sheets stood to his left. *Too light. Won't do the trick.* Instead, John yanked a heavy box of soda syrup off the shelf to his right, tearing away the clear tube and sending a spray of thick liquid across his shirt. *Coke Zero?* he wondered, as he heaved the heavy box down the aisle. The packaged beverage struck the Camouflage Man in the back of the legs and sent him sprawling face-first to the kitchen floor.

John took several strides as his enemy scrambled to his knees, scurrying like a wounded animal trying to flee its stalker. John was suddenly filled with a pure black rage, overwhelmed by the primal desire to seek vengeance and justice for what this mercenary had brought upon them—the death of Amira's father, a good and just man who'd dedicated his life to protecting and serving those who could not do it for themselves. A low, guttural cry built up inside him and he roared, *"Nooo!"* as if the one word summarized all the hate, sadness, anger, and frustration he felt, channeling it toward one target—the Camouflage Man.

John grabbed a heavy wooden rolling pin from the table to his right, took one step, and swung downward as hard as he could, striking the Camouflage Man in the right arm, the one that bled.

He heard something snap, and he pulled the rolling pin back to strike again.

Chase shrieked in pain and fell to his left. He looked up and saw the merciless gaze of his attacker, brown eyes blazing with hatred, and he instantly realized there would be no quarter given. This man would kill him where he lay for what he'd orchestrated. There was nowhere to go, but he *had* to try. His attacker moved toward him, and Chase grabbed a bowl full of kitchen utensils and hurled it upward with his good left arm. He didn't even wait to see how effective the move was; he rolled over and scrambled away, grabbing with his left hand a small paring knife that had fallen to the floor.

John batted the stainless steel bowl away like a major league slugger, the contact creating a thunderous metallic clang that echoed throughout the kitchen like an ancient Chinese gong. The bowl sent its contents scattering across the kitchen like a utensil bomb, and John hoped for a moment nothing would impale the wounded Camouflage Man on the ground. He wasn't done with him.

The Camouflage Man reached the end of the aisle and crawled left into a small walkway that connected the right half of the kitchen with the left half, which had an additional extension to the back of the building and the exit beyond. John stepped forward and delivered a harsh kick to the man's exposed left side. He satisfactorily felt two ribs break under his blow, and he exhaled with the adrenaline and anger.

"I said *no*," John growled at the man, who writhed on the ground but kept moving forward, as if swimming slowly against a heavy sea. John watched the effort, a coldness comingling with his rage. He waited as the man reached the left side of the kitchen and staggered to his feet. Sweat smeared the camouflage paint on his face as blood dripped from his right hand to the floor. "I'm pretty sure that's not sanitary," John said, and nodded at the blood, even as he noticed the small knife in the man's left hand.

"I knew you'd be trouble," Chase said. He looked left and then right, calculating any moves that would turn the tide. There were none. This would be his last stand.

"You have *no idea* the trouble I am," John growled back. "But tonight, I'm not just trouble. I'm *death* come for you."

Chase nodded and said, "Well, come on, then."

John smiled, a mixture of malevolent glee and purpose, and stepped forward, wielding the rolling pin in his right hand like a baton. He feigned a jab with his left hand, and the Camouflage Man responded with a quick slash with the paring knife. John yanked his hand back and, like a windmill, slammed the rolling pin into his left forearm. The hand reflexively opened, and the knife clattered to the floor. With lightning speed, John reared back once more and struck the Camouflage Man on the side of the head, splitting the skin on his left temple. Blood flowed freely from the cut and mingled with the sweat and camouflage paint.

The Camouflage Man staggered sideways, and John felt the exhilaration of battle take control. John dropped the rolling pin and punched his enemy in the throat. The Camouflage Man began to choke, but John didn't care. He crossed his hands, reached forward, and grabbed his camouflage tree suit by the collar. He bent his wrists, and the motion applied pressure to the Camouflage Man's wounded throat.

John suddenly pulled the man close to him and hissed into his face. "No mercy. Damn you to hell, whoever you are." He suddenly took a step to the left, pulled the Camouflage Man with him, released his grip, pulled back his right hand, and delivered a powerful blow to the man's stomach. John felt him go limp, and in one quick motion, he held him up, spun him around, and placed his head in the enormous open pressure cooker he'd spotted once the fight had progressed into the left side of the kitchen.

Several feet deep by at least two feet across, a row of six of the behemoth cookers stood along the back wall of the left side of the kitchen. A wire basket lay in the middle of the cooker with battered and breaded chicken breasts ready to be lowered into the hot, bubbling liquid.

John didn't care about the basket, and he yanked it out of the cooker, flinging it to the side. He leaned in to the Camouflage Man's right ear and whispered, "Time to pay for your sins."

He shoved the Camouflage Man's head into the square hole and held his head near the scalding hot viscous fluid. The Camouflage Man screamed as drops of liquid exploded upward and splattered his face.

John grabbed the steel lid, pulled his left hand backward, and yanked down as hard as he could. *For Nick.* The commercial grade lid crashed down on top of the Camouflage Man's skull, and John felt the impact as it sent a tremor through the man's body. He lifted it up, saw the Camouflage Man still struggling, his left arm reaching backward to try and stop John. *For Amira.* The lid slammed down with a thud followed by the sound of something cracking. He raised the lid, which was covered in dark red, as the Camouflage Man's arm fell to his side. *For all the others you won't be able to harm,* John thought, and brought the stainless steel lid down one last time with a sickening crunch as the blow crushed the back of the Camouflage Man's head.

John felt the man's body twitch, and John knew he was dead or dying, but he didn't care. Emotion roared through him as he tried to regain control of himself, and he released his grip on the Camouflage Man. The weight of the lid kept his ruined head pinned inside the cooker while his upper torso rested on the edge of the machine.

John stepped back, and he felt the adrenaline begin to diminish. *You still got off easy, you sonofabitch,* he thought. He inhaled and exhaled, and his thoughts turned to Amira. He'd left his phone in the kitchen at the house and hadn't had time to grab it, but he needed to get back to the dining area and assure whatever patrons hadn't scattered that the situation was over, the threat neutralized, that they were safe.

He walked toward the front of the kitchen as one of the remaining workers came in through the door. John, exhausted from the hand-to-hand encounter, the chase, and the ambush, looked the blond teenaged boy squarely in the eyes and said, "You're going to need a new pressure cooker." He moved past the employee and through the door to wait for the police. He prayed that they'd get there soon. The physical exertion of violence had ended, replaced by the need to be with the woman he loved who'd just lost her father.

PART VI

JUDGMENT

CHAPTER 45

Caracas, Venezuela
Present Time

Logan West closed his eyes and briefly absorbed the peacefulness that had fallen over the ruined mountain base. He exhaled, opened his eyes, and looked at the man who'd caused all of the wreckage and death over the past month. *God knows what else he's responsible for.* Logan held the Iridium phone he'd carried into battle and listened to Jake Benson on the other end explain the events that had just transpired in Maryland at the order of the traitor who stood before him.

Cole, Jack, Marcos, and Santiago stood in a circle near the front of the abandoned command post. The surviving four mercenary members of the Hunter and Killer teams had recovered their fallen comrades and placed them in the back of two J70s for transport down the mountain.

Logan wanted to lash out—*physically needed to lash out*—at the monster in human clothing, but he knew he couldn't. Not just yet. Joshua Baker still had a purpose, and a plan was formulating itself in Logan's mind as he listened to Jake. Baker had already told them all he knew—or at least what he claimed was all—and Logan believed the man.

Baker was beaten, bloodied, and exhausted. He'd aged at least ten years since his last public appearance a month ago, and he wore his defeat like a medieval fur cloak around his shoulders, heavy and burdensome. There was no fight left in the middle-aged man in front of him, but Logan didn't care. His *very existence* elicited a feeling of unnatural outrage that the man still breathed after all he'd done. Baker would die for his sins and crimes. Of that truth, there was no doubt in Logan's mind, and he only hoped he'd be there to facilitate his demise or observe it. It didn't matter which: it just had to happen to preserve the natural order of the geopolitical world.

Logan had told Jake the reason General Cordones wanted Baker, as well as what the general planned for President Pena. There was a part of him that agreed with what the general was doing and why, but it wasn't for the general to do, at least not according to Venezuelan law. It's what it always came down to—men of power making self-serving decisions that exceeded their authority, always to the detriment of others.

"I'm so sorry about Amira's father," Jake said sincerely. "But I need you to hear me: you have to keep Baker alive. I need to brief the president, and then I'm going to call you back in five minutes. I'm about to step into the Oval Office. We'll figure out the next step. Trust me. I have to go."

"Understood," Logan said. "I'll let the rest of the team know. We'll stand by for your call, but I think I have an idea. I'll know for sure in the next few minutes."

"Logan, listen to me. Don't kill him. Please."

"I won't. And no one else will, at least not right now," Logan replied. "Go talk to the president. Out here."

Cole was the first to ask, "What happened? Are they alive?"

Logan scrutinized Baker and tilted his head to the left like a wolf studying a dying doe before he pounced to deliver the killing stroke. "They are," Logan said, his jaw clenched as he spoke.

"Thank God," Cole said, relief in his voice.

"Then why do you look like you want to tear him apart?" Jack asked, hesitant to hear the answer.

Logan stepped forward and lashed out before anyone could prevent him. He grabbed Baker's jacket collar and placed his face within inches of the terrified vice president's. "Because this *monster's* men just killed Amira's father, and I desperately want to end his life, right here, right now."

"Oh no," Cole said, sorrow and empathy for Amira hitting him all at once, a numbness that blossomed in the pit of his stomach.

"And it's all your fault," Logan spat accusatorily into Baker's panic-stricken face. Logan suddenly shot his right leg behind Baker and swept forward, struck the man's wounded calf, knocked his legs out from under him, and sent him to the ground. Logan stood over the cowering, wounded man and drew his Glock. He pointed it at Baker's face and said, "I want nothing more than to end your reign of terror and misery this very moment."

Baker instinctively held his hands up in front of his face, as if the skin and bones would magically stop the 9mm slug from killing him. "I'm sorry. I'm sorry. I'm *so* sorry," he pleaded.

"Your apology is *not* accepted," Logan answered quietly. "You deserve to die. You're a blight on this earth, and you contaminate everything you touch. But you're going to live, at least a little while longer, because I think you can serve a *higher purpose.*"

Logan holstered the Glock, turned on his heels, and walked away toward the command post in the middle of the base.

"You really have no idea how lucky you are," Cole said to Baker. "If Amira were here, I think she would literally cut you to shreds with her stilettos. Get up. We won't be here long."

Logan's Iridium chirped loudly, breaking the somber silence. He stopped in his tracks so that the rest of the group was within earshot, hit the talk button, and said, "Jake, what do you—"

"It's not Jake, Logan," President Preston Scott said.

Logan cleared his mind and forced his anger to abate, at least slightly, so as not to cloud his judgment as he conferred with his commander in chief. "I'm sorry, sir. It's been a little hectic here."

"That might be the understatement of the night, from what Jake told me," President Scott said. "I feel like I just said this about Mike, but I'm sorry for your loss. I've been told that John is with her. I've also been told that the two officers that were shot are going to be okay after some surgery and serious therapy. They're lucky that your friends were there."

Unfortunately, Amira's father wasn't, Logan thought, as the rage surged once again. *Get control.*

"That's who they are, sir. It's who *we all* are, even Jack," Logan said, referring to the retired commandant of the Marine Corps who'd joined their alliance after the events in DC weeks earlier.

"I know, and I'm grateful for it. But right now, we need to figure out what to do next, now that you have Baker. How fast do you think you can get to the airfield and get back here?" the president asked.

"We can be wheels up probably within thirty to forty-five minutes from now, if there's been no damage to the runway," Logan replied. *I can't believe you're going to say it, but you have no choice. You have to give him the option to do the right thing.*

"Sir, there's another play we can make here," Logan said, and left the words hanging in the digital space between them.

"What's that?" the president asked, his curiosity piqued. He trusted Logan West and his task force with his life and the highest level of national security of the republic. He owed it to him to hear him out.

"How bad is the coverage of the earthquake, sir?" Logan asked, changing the topic.

"It's bad. Hundreds, maybe a few thousand, dead. Power outages, food shortages—if that's even possible down there—violence, looting, you name it. The worst that humanity has to offer during a time of crisis, all exacerbated by a government that failed its primary mission—to care for and protect its citizens. Why do you ask?"

"Because as bad as it is on TV, it's that much worse in person," Logan said. The images of the shell-shocked bystanders from the earlier ambush on the highway were still fresh. Their eyes had a glossed-over, distant look—a look he'd seen in Iraq—and not just from the urban combat between the tunnels. It was the same look of desperation and hopelessness from the knowledge that their government couldn't help them. "What if there was a way to help the people in this country? I have an idea, and if it works, it might bring a little bit of light to the despair and suffering that's a constant condition down here. It's going to require a ton of coordination once it's over. But more importantly, I can't do it without your approval."

There was silence from the other end, and Logan waited patiently. *Come on, sir. I know you. You're a good man, even if you are a politician. Just hear me out.*

"Go ahead. Tell me," the president said.

Logan West did, instinctively aware of what the president's answer would be even before he was halfway finished explaining his bold and aggressive plan.

CHAPTER 46

Lieutenant General Victor Cordones stood inside the black cloth walls that had been erected in the back of the hangar to create an area for the execution. After the earthquake, he'd changed the location for the final phase of his plan to the secret airfield south of Caracas. Initially, he'd considered infiltrating the main Globovision studio on the north edge of the city, but he knew he'd never be able to successfully execute the president in the newsroom, escape the TV station via a helicopter from the rooftop, and then fly to the airfield undetected. As a result, he'd decided to minimize the number of moves that might potentially lead to failure. He'd had an epiphany that made significantly more tactical sense and increased his chances for survival. *Why not just do it at the airfield? You can fly away on the private jet the moment it's done, and they won't be able to stop you.*

The SEBIN security hadn't even scrutinized the black Range Rovers as the six vehicles driven by his detail entered the airfield. All wore civilian attire they'd changed into after the executive kidnapping, and the president and Victor lay concealed in the back of the third vehicle, never under the slightest threat of discovery. Clandestine locations served their purposes, and Victor was taking flagrant advantage of them.

A Globovision satellite truck was parked at the entrance to the hangar, ready to broadcast to the country and ultimately the world the fate of dictators that subjected their citizens to cruelty, poverty, and suffering, wielding them like social engineering weapons designed to preserve power.

His detail prepared the Gulfstream G550 for the trip to Switzerland. A Russian oligarch at the private request of the Russian ambassador had provided the luxury business jet for Victor's last trip out of Venezuela. Surprisingly, not all the soldiers on his detail had decided to leave with him and the American vice president. There were several who ideologically believed that once the president was dead, the country would escape the abyss into which it had already fallen. Victor wasn't so sure, but he didn't want to discourage their hope: it was all they had. Thus, he kept quiet and wished each of them well, thanking them for their patriotism and service. In his mind, they were all men of honor and nationalism, regardless of how the world would judge them.

Victor had borrowed the idea of the public execution from the extremists in Iraq, and he knew that the black background would mask their location, at least until he was out of the country.

"No matter what happens to me, you will never get away with this," President Pena said defiantly as he sat on the ground. His chief of security, Antonio, was bound and gagged beside him. "The people won't stand for it."

Victor couldn't help himself and snorted derisively in laughter. His voice rose in anger. "Are you listening to yourself? The people are fleeing the country in droves, starving in the streets, and rioting to overthrow you. If you think the people are going to mourn you when you're dead, you're more delusional than I thought. No one is coming to save you. Tonight, you pay for your crimes, for the deaths of so many, *for the death of my son*, and the whole world will watch and see you for what you are—a man whose only true guiding principle is power, power for its own end. But your run is about to end, and you'd better make your peace with it, because it's coming soon and it's coming fast."

Victor looked at Antonio, as if the presence of the man was an afterthought. "I know you're only doing your job. So when this is over, I'm going to give you a choice, and I hope you make the right one. Between now and then, think *very hard* about whether or not you even want a future."

He ignored the stare of the president, turned around, and walked away from the two captives, which was when he heard the sound of the helicopter approaching, low and in the distance. The distinctive sound of the rotors grew in strength and intensity, and he was relieved the Hind had arrived. He smiled to himself as he walked to the hangar doors, which two members of his detail had begun to slide open. *Right on time.*

He'd radioed the base to fly the vice president to the airfield. They'd been expecting his signal in his command post. Once the American had joined him, he'd execute President Pena and leave his beloved country, once and for all.

CHAPTER 47

As the Russian Hind helicopter approached the airfield, Logan studied the ground below, the multiple hangars awash in the glow of external floodlights, and the assortment of aircraft parked along the perimeter fence that surrounded the large, rectangular air operations center. *Too bad the US doesn't have something like this in northern Virginia, a way for external allies and adversaries to enter the country for secret meetings without dealing with US Customs and Border Protection agents.* But he knew risk-averse politicians would never go for it. It was practical, and they were political.

Logan glanced around the passenger compartment at the assorted raid force and figured they had a better than fifty percent chance of success. *Beats the house odds at a casino,* he thought. Logan, Cole, Jack, Santiago, Marcos, and the two assassins, Thomas and Frederico, were all dressed in Venezuelan army uniforms they'd found at the base. For Logan's plan to work, they only needed seconds to retain their tactical surprise, and he was confident the uniforms would provide it.

The only occupant in normal civilian clothes was Joshua Baker, his wounded leg wrapped and bandaged. The seven men—Santiago was in the cockpit with the pilot—sat on both sides of two small benches mounted in the middle of the passenger compartment. The design permitted troops to unload faster, from both sides of the gunship and from two doors rather than one choke point that an unseen enemy could target.

Logan tapped Baker on the left knee, leaned into the man, and shouted above the raging sound of the rotors, "If you do anything, and I mean *anything*, that jeopardizes this mission, I swear to God that I will kill you first. Even if someone else is shooting at us, I will take you out, step across your dying body, and then return fire. Do you understand me?"

Baker turned his head, looked directly into Logan's camouflaged face, and nodded.

Logan, satisfied with the response, sat back and waited as the ground rose up to meet the descending mechanical bird of prey. The target hangar was in the back of the airfield, and the nose of the helicopter lifted slightly on its final approach. The world outside tilted to the right as if on a gargantuan seesaw, and Logan anticipated the touchdown seconds away.

One last time, Logan. One last time, and then you can go home to Sarah and a new life, or so he hoped.

The Hind hit the ground with a soft thud, and the view through the side windows straightened. The compartment doors on the sides of the aircraft lifted out and away on their hinges.

First in line at the end of one side of the bench, Logan stood up and led the small chalk of men out the starboard side opening. He jumped down onto the tarmac and waited for the vice president and the remaining members of the elite raid force to join him.

Santiago remained inside with the pilot, the soldier that Cole had wounded when he'd realized the vice president was staging another diversion. The gunshot wound to his right calf hadn't hindered his ability to fly the helicopter, but someone needed to ensure he did as he was instructed.

The small force formed a bubble around the vice president, weapons held at the ready position, and waited. Logan stepped toward the hangar, less than two hundred feet away, and the armed band of men followed.

Victor stood in the middle of the hangar and watched the small group of his soldiers approach. The area outside the hangar was illuminated, but not enough to reveal the men's features, which were darkened with camouflage paint. *Camouflage paint? Why?* The men moved tactically and spread out into an upside-down V formation reminiscent of the fighter plan formation that originated in World War I. But something about the way they carried themselves set his nerves on edge, and he studied the group, which had closed to within one hundred and fifty feet of the enormous hangar entrance. Their weapons rose slightly as one in a barely perceptible motion, and alarm bells sounded in his head.

It's not my men. Whoever they are, they're not mine. After years of relentless training, the general recognized the moment—men seconds away from engaging in combat. *They're about to fire, which means they know why I'm here. They're waiting until they have a clear line of sight on everyone,* he realized, and he was forced to make a decision, one that ended in death no matter which way he chose. He could alert his soldiers who stood on both sides of the hangar, or he could grab President Pena, try to escape, and use him for leverage.

Anger soured with resentment taunted him. He'd been so close to avenging his son, but in order to fulfill his vengeance, he had no choice—he had to have custody of the Venezuelan president.

Victor suddenly spun on his heels and walked toward the back of the hangar and the hanging-black-cloth execution set. There was only one way out, and he needed President Pena as his human shield and battering ram.

Logan squeezed his grip on the 7.62mm AK-103. He'd swapped out his H&K MP5 submachine gun for the long gun since it was what the soldiers on the mountain had carried. As he moved toward the hangar, he calculated their odds against the assembled opposing force. *With a little bit of luck, not too bad.*

Four men stood on each side of the hangar entrance, weapons held but not as vigilantly as they should have been. A Globovision satellite truck was parked outside to the right of the door. Inside the hangar, a large private jet waited on the left side, and movement from inside the cockpit caught his eye. An additional four men stood inside the hangar, four near the plane on the left and four on the right near several parked black Range Rovers, once again the villain's vehicle of choice. But it was the main stage that had been erected in the back of the hangar that grabbed Logan's attention.

An area twenty-five feet long by fifteen feet deep was enclosed by hanging black cloths. Two men sat on the gray-colored epoxy floor of the hangar inside the black curtains, and Logan recognized the man on the left as President Pena. A professional camera was mounted on a tripod in the middle, just outside the enclosed three-sided stage, and cables ran from it down the right side of the hangar to the truck parked outside.

Memories of the torture and execution chambers in Iraq similar to this one sent shivers tumbling down his spine. *This is a thing of evil. The purpose is the same, just in a different country.* It reminded him of the barn in which they'd found the Iraqi flag, a moment that had kick-started a chain of events that would change the course of his life years later. He realized with a bitter sense of irony that everything had come full circle. What had started in Iraq would end tonight, one way or another.

Logan's assault force closed the distance to one hundred feet, which was when General Cordones abruptly turned around and began to move toward the execution area. The general glanced over his shoulder and picked up his pace, transitioning into a shuffle as he closed the final feet to the sitting Venezuelan president. *He knows. Somehow he knows, but he's not raising the alarm.* And then it hit him: *he's trying to escape with President Pena. He still thinks he can pull it off.* One word resounded in Logan's head in big, dark-red letters that matched his fury—*NO.*

Without breaking his stride, Logan raised the barrel of the AK-103 and snap-sighted on the first soldier in civilian attire on the right side of the hangar, just outside the doors. Like the precision drill team equivalent of an execution squad, the other five members of the team raised their weapons at preselected targets, coordinated beforehand and based on their position in the formation.

Logan fired first, initiating the attack on the airfield that was in reality a geopolitical struggle on a tactical scale. The 7.62mm rounds struck the soldier in the chest, and his black jacket flared up behind him as he fell. Even before he hit the ground, the remaining members of the team opened fired on their targets as the explosion of unsuppressed gunfire echoed off the tarmac and the hangar.

Before the Venezuelan security detail could return fire, six of General Cordones's men lay on the cold tarmac, cut down in the first volley.

Logan transitioned to a second target inside the hangar and squeezed the trigger, all the while stalking forward in a crouched combat walk.

Victor didn't even flinch at the sound of gunfire behind him, although he couldn't say the same for President Pena. Of the two men on the ground, Pena's head of security reacted appropriately, turned to the man who was under his protection, even while in captivity, and shouted, "On your stomach. Stay low!"

Victor was impressed with Antonio's dedication and concern for his master, but Victor didn't have time to commend him for it. A stray round struck the president's head of security in the side of the neck, and he fell over, blood pumping from the mortal wound and pooling on the epoxy floor. His eyes were focused on President Pena, the last image he saw before he died.

Victor grabbed the president, whose light-gray suit and white shirt—no tie—were splattered with Antonio's blood, and yanked him to his feet. More gunshots, this time from Victor's men—*About goddamned time,* he thought—rang out from inside the hangar. "Time to go," he said, and pulled the president to the back of the execution area, the Browning Hi-Power .40-caliber pistol in his right hand.

"You're insane, and you're going to get us both killed!" the president said with combined disgust and panic.

Victor reached the back wall of hanging cloth, and said, "If you really want to die right here, right now, I can make that happen." He reached down, pulled the bottom up, looked at the president, and gestured for him to go underneath.

President Pena fully grasped the deadly predicament he was in—die now, or pray for a miracle with every passing minute that he remained alive. In the end, it was no choice at all, and he ducked his head under the cloth and stepped behind the curtain.

CHAPTER 48

The second volley from Logan's team dropped the remaining two members of the security detail on the outside left of the hangar and three more inside, which left five shooters from the security detail alive and fighting. Unfortunately for Logan and his task force, those five men reacted the way Logan and his friends would've— calmly and smoothly.

They opened fired on the approaching force as the V formation split, a mitosis of men and weapons with Logan, the vice president, Marcos, and Jack dashing to the right to seek cover behind the satellite truck. Cole, Thomas, and Frederico broke left, angling toward two white pickups and a bulk fuel tank.

The last thing Logan saw as he reached the relative safety of the white satellite truck with the Globovision logo on the side was General Cordones drag President Pena under the back of the black curtains. *Where the hell is he going?*

Bullets kicked up puffs of concrete and punched holes into the side of the truck, and Logan hid behind the front left quarter panel, protected by the wheel and the engine block. The truck vibrated, not from the helicopter or gunfire, but from the engine itself. *It's still running. Must've been getting ready to film his award-winning executive snuff film,* Logan thought.

Logan glanced to the left and motioned to Cole and his team. He pointed at Cole, let his AK-103 dangle across his chest for a moment, performed a shooting gesture with both hands, pointed at himself, and then pointed over his shoulder to the back of the heavy-duty truck. Cole nodded in return and relayed the plan to the rest of his team. Logan gripped the AK-103 and moved past his teammates as he said, "Cole is going to draw their fire, and I'm going around the back of the truck to get a better angle. Feel free to open up from the front. Or not. There are only five of them left. It's almost a fair fight."

Cole watched as Logan reached his assault position. Cole raised his arms above the front of the pickup truck and opened fire in a spray-and-pray shooting position, a move that would make every weapons instructor the world over cringe in disapproval. Thomas and Frederico dropped to the pavement and delivered more concentrated fire from under the pickup truck.

All five soldiers—two on the left near the Range Rovers and three near the plane—returned fire on the pickup, which was Logan's cue. He emerged from behind the satellite truck and stalked forward, opening fire on the two men on the left. Several well-placed rounds hit the two closest targets simultaneously, as the two men stood with their profiles exposed to Logan, the second man just in front of the first from Logan's vantage point.

Jack opened fire from the front of the Globovision truck, and two men near the landing gear of the plane and the ladder dropped. The third man, in his late forties, his hair more gray than black, was the only one who made the smart choice: he fled up the ladder.

Can't blame the guy for trying, Logan thought, but still opened fire to prevent his escape. The first rounds struck the ladder and clanged loudly off the rungs of the metal rolling staircase. The man leapt up the stairs two at a time in the race of his life. Logan stopped his combat walk, raised the barrel slightly, and pulled the trigger. The man jerked at the top of the stairs and disappeared inside the plane. Logan waited for a two-count as the only remaining sound was that of the Hind gunship. The last man standing didn't reappear in the doorway, and Logan lowered the weapon.

He turned around and took three steps toward the execution area when a loud thump reverberated behind him. He recognized the sound, and thought, *Oh no,* and glanced back at the plane. The cabin door had shut, which meant Logan hadn't killed the last member of the security force. *Wonderful.*

Logan turned toward the plane, and as if taunting him, the two Rolls-Royce jet engines mounted on the main fuselage behind the wings near the tail roared to life. Logan turned away and watched as the high-pitched whine of the left engine sent a blast of air toward Logan that knocked the black curtains down and sent them twirling through the air like a magician's cloak. The black walls gone, Logan saw why the general had fled toward the back of the hangar: a single exit door stood halfway open.

The large business-class jet moved toward the open doors, a lumbering beast intent on escaping its metal pen. Logan didn't know who or what else might be in the plane, and he didn't care. No one else was leaving the hangar. *No one.*

He raised the AK-103 and fired at the rear set of tires. The 7.62mm rounds ricocheted off the landing gear and struck the side of the compressed rubber, but the tires remained intact and the plane kept moving. *What the hell?* Logan knew airplane tires were highly pressurized to withstand the weight and stress of landing and takeoff, but he thought for sure 7.62mm rounds would have done the trick. *Guess whoever owned this one anticipated getting shot at. Great.*

The jet pushed forward and taxied out of the hangar as Jack and the others opened fire on it from in front of the satellite truck.

With Logan's initial plan a failure, he was forced to choose—pursue General Cordones and the Venezuelan president or stop the plane. *Hell with it. They've got this,* he thought, confident in his teammates to do their jobs, and sprinted to the back of the hangar through the open door into the blackness beyond.

CHAPTER 49

The Hind's cockpit was the lower of the two bulbous spheres of glass that gave the gunship the moniker the Crocodile. Unfortunately, it was also physically separated by metal and the helicopter's frame from the copilot's cockpit above and behind it, which was how Santiago found himself cramped in the confined space with the pilot. In addition to the headset he wore to communicate through the noise and chaos, he had two other items—the Glock that was an omnipresent warning if the pilot disobeyed his orders and a medical kit to treat the wound to the man's leg where Cole had shot him.

The most critical decision Cole had made during the assault on the mountaintop base was sparing the life of the soldier who had impersonated the vice president. As fate would have it, that soldier was in fact one of the several pilots that General Cordones had recruited for his mission—and the only one left alive after Logan's task force had run through the soldiers like a buzz saw. Sparing the man's life had ultimately provided them with close air support for the raid on the airfield. *One small decision in the heat of battle with such significant unforeseen consequences,* Santiago had thought. Without the helicopter, the alternative options for assaulting the airfield were all in the favor of the general and his men. The Hind had provided cover for their arrival and dominance from the air, which was what Santiago needed as the white jet emerged from the hangar. As Logan and the others opened fire on the plane, he realized that whatever or whoever was on it had to be stopped.

"Take off right now," he ordered the wounded pilot, whose name was Gabriel.

A second later, with the rotors already turning, Gabriel pulled the collective up, and the Hind lifted away from the tarmac.

"Good," Santiago said. A practical, professional police officer, he'd realized over the past few days of spending time in combat with Logan West and his friends that while he was a very capable and dangerous man, they were inclined and almost enthusiastic in the way they dealt lethality and carnage to their enemies. He thought they'd be proud at how far he'd evolved in his thinking with what he had planned next. "Now stop that plane. I don't care how, but make it happen this instant. And *don't hit my friends.*"

Gabriel was exhausted, in pain, and still bleeding. But he was an excellent pilot, passionate about his profession to the point where he served the way of the helicopter and the exaltation from flying more than any ideology. And with a war machine like the Hind, he felt a special affinity for the weapons package it carried. As a result, when his captor ordered him to stop the plane, his response was immediate, and he thought, *Which one do I choose?*

The S-24 rocket was too large, as was the antitank missile. He'd likely kill everyone on the plane and several of Santiago's "friends," which wouldn't be good for his health. *No. It has to be the autocannon,* he realized, adjusted the control cyclic, aimed for the landing gear under the right wing, and unleashed a volley from the four-barreled Yakushev-Borzov YakB-12.7mm mounted machine gun under the nose of the cockpit.

Unlike the small arms fire, the 12.7mm rounds destroyed everything they touched, kicked up chunks of tarmac, punched holes in the back wall of the hangar, and most importantly, destroyed the landing gear and tires. *That should do the trick,* Gabriel thought with professional pride as he watched the chain-reaction destruction unfold.

Cole and the two assassins had been so focused on the plane that they didn't even realize the Hind had lifted off until the 12.7mm rounds tore into the landing gear and the inside of the hangar. The autocannon fire caused Cole to flinch, and he instinctively crouched down behind the pickup truck, although he realized, feeling rather foolish, that there was no point since no one was shooting at him. Thomas and Frederico stopped firing through the gap below the truck and turned their heads to watch the Hind unleash its stream of fire.

Please let this guy be accurate or he's going to shred us to pieces as well, Cole thought. After a brief eternity, the autocannon ceased firing, and Cole stood up to survey the damage, which sent a surge of adrenaline and panic racing through him.

The right front landing gear had been destroyed, and the tires were shredded. But somehow, the plane still rolled forward, the wheels disintegrating like the flat tire on a limping Nascar car. The plane had been knocked off-balance, the nose lowered, and as a result began a gradual turn to the right toward Cole and the two assassins.

"Get up and move!" Cole screamed at Thomas and Frederico, who were jarred from their reverie at the Hind's firepower. They scrambled backward, which was all Cole needed to confirm they'd heard his warning.

The jet was less than forty feet away and closing quickly. Cole waited for another second as the two Venezuelan killers reached their feet. While they weren't exactly CIA or Unit material, the two assassins had still fought valiantly alongside Cole, and he wasn't about to abandon them on the proverbial battlefield.

The three men dashed from behind the truck in a beeline toward the other part of the assault force. As they crossed the chasm between the pickups and the satellite truck, the jet lurched farther to the right, and the shadow of its left wing shrouded Cole and the two assassins in darkness, heightening the frenzied urgency all three men felt as they tried to escape. *Better run faster before it hits,* Cole thought, and emerged from the shadows with Thomas and Frederico close behind.

Jack stood next to the open driver's door of the satellite truck and yelled at them furiously to move faster. Marcos and the vice president, who was at his side after they'd exited the helicopter, had already sought cover at the back of the satellite truck.

What the hell is it now? Cole thought, but then realized it didn't matter. All that did was that the three of them reach safety. As Cole heard the collision, he realized they'd run out of time, and he dove into the air like an NFL player desperately reaching for the end zone.

The plane struck the pickup truck as the uneven nose, which had dropped a few feet, tore into the roof of the cab on the passenger side. The momentum of the jet drove the truck backward and turned it, grinding it along the tarmac with an awful wrenching sound. But it wasn't the pickup truck that had Cole and Jack concerned: it was the white jet-fuel tank behind it.

The pickup truck was lifted on its side, and the plane dragged it forward, sparks flying in different directions as the bottom left part of the chassis was torn apart.

Cole landed on his chest and waited for the explosion that he was certain would incinerate them all. Nothing happened, and panicked screaming brought him back to the moment.

Marcos and the vice president stood in the open back of the satellite truck among the communication equipment, computers, and monitors. Its doors hung open, and they motioned for him to get in the truck. Thomas and Frederico hadn't followed Cole's lead in his aerial antics, and still on their feet, they reached the back of the truck before he did. The truck's engine roared to life, and Cole realized Jack's plan—use the truck to escape the imminent conflagration. Cole got to his feet and was pulled into the back of the satellite truck as the last of its new occupants.

The plane slowed down with the impact and the increased friction of the vehicular weight it carried. Unfortunately, it didn't stop, and the pickup truck slammed into the 3200-liter bulk fuel tank that contained Jet A-1 fuel. The front of the truck punctured the cylindrical tank a few feet from the bottom, and the kerosene-based fuel poured out of the tank as the plane finally stopped its kamikaze run.

The Jet A-1 fuel splashed across the front of the ruined hood and covered the front of the pickup and the tarmac below. A normally inert liquid, it required a source for ignition.

Jack turned the satellite truck to the left and accelerated as it pulled away from the hangar. Flooring it, he prayed the inevitable would hold off for a few more seconds. *Another hundred feet and I'll feel a lot better about our chances,* he thought. The satellite truck reached the end of the hangar, and he veered to the left to place the building between them and the wreckage.

The impact with the pickup truck had completely torn away the jet's right-side landing gear. With no stability on the right side of the plane, its weight slowly crushed the cab of the pickup until it reached its breaking point, and the cab exploded inward. The plane dropped several feet, metal grinding on metal, and sent a shower of sparks across the pickup truck.

The Jet A-1 fuel was combustible with a low flash point of 100 degrees Fahrenheit, and the shower of sparks was more than sufficient to ignite the liquid. The truck erupted with a deep, thudding whoosh, and a second and a half later, the flames reached the inside of the tank, which detonated with a thunderous explosion. The resulting fireball consumed the pickup, the plane, and the inside of the hangar and illuminated the entire airfield as if it were bathed in the light of an enormous candle.

The satellite truck rocked forward as the shock wave slammed into the fleeing vehicle, and Jack gripped the steering wheel as he tried to maintain control. The truck's shadow created by the fireball swerved back and forth across the tarmac as if battling itself. The truck straightened out, and Jack breathed a sigh of relief, at least until he looked left and realized they'd reached the main course on the night's menu of death and destruction.

CHAPTER 50

When Logan had emerged through the rear exit door of the hangar, he found the back of the airfield shrouded in darkness. Beyond the edge of the tarmac lay a deeper pool of grayish black, and it had taken Logan's eyes a few seconds to process the fact that fifty feet beyond the back of the hangar was a steep drop-off. He had no idea what lay below or how far down the slope went. There was no fence line, and the Marine officer in him mentally commented on the fact that the builders of the airfield hadn't done the proper operational risk management assessment. *Then again, this is Venezuela, and I doubt safety is high on the list of national priorities at the moment.*

He'd looked right and been rewarded with the sight, forty feet away near the edge of the hangar, of General Cordones forcing President Pena, his wrists zip-tied together in front of him, into the passenger seat of a black Range Rover. Logan had raised the AK-103 and fired three shots, but the rounds had missed as the general ducked behind the front of the SUV. There was a thud as the driver's door had closed, and the taillights illuminated the vehicle with a reddish glow.

Even before the vehicle leapt forward, Logan had erupted into a sprint, launching himself at it. The SUV had sped away, although Logan had no idea what lay at the end of the airfield. He assumed there was an exit of some kind, but what the general's plans were after that, well, that was anyone's guess. But there was nothing left for Logan to do but run. It had come to this, and he prayed that his friends would help him sooner rather than later. *Just keep him in view,* he thought, inhaling and exhaling, his breathing deep and measured, as he operated near his VO_2 max, the maximum level of oxygen uptake his body could handle. He'd achieved the highest score in his entire Officer Candidate School class, and all these years later, his cardiovascular endurance was still that of a professional athlete. *Relentless training always pays off,* he thought as he ran like a college athlete at the NFL Combine, although the Range Rover was already more than two hundred feet away, and his run had brought him closer to the edge of the airfield.

A loud *brrpp-brrrppp-brrrppp* reverberated from the front of the hangar, the telltale sign that the Hind had entered the battle for the hangar.

Good, he thought, but less than a minute later, the world burst in a thunderous explosion, followed by a massive glowing fireball that illuminated the airfield and the drop-off behind it.

But he still ran, parallel with the edge, and he saw the tops of trees two hundred feet below. *Not a huge fall, but enough to kill you.*

The silhouette that had appeared in front of him with the explosion grew shorter as the fireball rose into the air and the warm rush of air surrounded him. Despair crept into his mind, and he wondered if his friends had survived the destruction behind him. But with nothing else to do but hope and pray, he kept running.

The sound of tires squealing across the tarmac turned his head to the right as the large Globovision satellite box truck sped in his direction. With a sense of relief that spurred him on, he kept running, refusing to lose any ground, not even for a few seconds. The satellite truck swerved around and behind him and screeched to a halt, the passenger door already open.

Logan leapt into the cab of the truck and landed on the bucket seat as Jack slammed the truck back into drive and floored the accelerator.

"Everyone still alive?" Logan asked seriously.

"All of our guys are," Jack replied, as he focused on the pursuit.

Logan glanced into the back of the truck and saw the rest of the team still in one piece as yellow firelight shone through the two back windows. "Glad everyone is still here" was all he said, and nodded at Cole and Marcos before turning back to follow the fleeing Range Rover more than three hundred feet away. It was closing in on another series of hangars and buildings.

"What now?" Logan asked. "He's got too much ground on us, and there's no way we can catch him in this."

"You're right, which is why we have that," Jack said, and pointed past Logan out the passenger window.

Logan turned his head as the Hind gunship raced across the tarmac less than fifty feet off the ground. "It's about time one of those things is on our side," Logan said, and watched as the Hind chased down the Range Rover, which never had a chance. *Fate is coming for you, General, and there's nothing you can do to stop it.*

CHAPTER 51

General Victor Cordones was desperate, exhausted, and furious at the carnage that his plans at the airfield had become. The only thing that drove him forward was the thought of his son, Daniel, and Victor's need to make his death a symbol that could change the future of Venezuela. As he drove away from the hangar, which glowed from the magnificent explosion seconds earlier, he glanced at President Pena, the source of his frustration and target of his wrath.

It wasn't just enough to kill the man. There was no question that he deserved it after the way his policies had plunged his country into chaos and despair. No. Victor needed to make an example of him, to show the world that the dictator's actions had consequences, that even though President Pena was the leader of a nation, he was still accountable for his decisions. And to do that, Victor needed an audience. The repayment of the blood debt owed to him wouldn't be complete until the citizens of Venezuela knew his son's name. But before he could solve the problem of how to broadcast the president's execution, he had to escape the assault force that had slaughtered his security detail.

"This is madness, Victor," President Pena said. "No matter how this ends, you have to see that this is madness."

Victor was acutely aware as his anger rose, and he troubled to control it. "You speak of madness? Look at what *you've done* to this once-great country. Your policies and inability to deal realistically with the collapsing economy brought us together on this night. It wasn't my madness. It was your inability to do your job, and people are starving in the streets and fleeing the country because of it. You lecture me again, and I may cut short what time you have left," Victor spat out.

The president remained silent after the verbal lashing and watched as the building up ahead grew closer.

As the Range Rover approached the next series of hangars, Victor spotted several hundred yards ahead the fence that jutted out from the edge of the abyss at the back of the airfield. The fence ran perpendicular to the edge to create the western perimeter. Once he reached the fence, he'd follow it north to the western gate and work his way through the city to the main Globovision studio. Since the studio could no longer come to him, he'd go to the studio and do what was needed to broadcast his message.

Victor pressed the accelerator, which was when two projectiles streaking from the right impacted the tarmac thirty yards in front of him. The ground exploded upward and large chunks of concrete flew lazily in his direction, as if taunting him in slow motion. He reacted to the destruction by slamming on the brakes of the Range Rover.

The SUV had reached eighty miles per hour, and by the time Victor slammed on the brakes, it was too late. He yanked the vehicle to the left as a several-foot-long section of concrete tumbled toward the Range Rover. The SUV swerved left and missed the huge chunk of tarmac, but Victor felt the vehicle threaten to control its own destiny. As the Range Rover skidded and swerved toward the edge of the airfield, no more than thirty feet away, he tried to course-correct it back to the right and released the brakes to regain a little traction. It was pointless, as a smaller, boulder-shaped section of tarmac with a flat top landed in front of the SUV. The Range Rover's right two tires struck the piece of tarmac and shot up the flat surface of the improvised launch ramp. The SUV tilted to the left, and as it flew off the surface of the improvised ramp, it was briefly suspended in midair. Victor wondered how bad the impact would be.

The SUV slammed down on its left two tires and struck a smaller piece of concrete, which violently decelerated the vehicle. The SUV was jerked to the left by the loss of speed, and the Range Rover toppled over onto its left side. The driver's-side windows exploded on contact with the tarmac, and the Range Rover skidded across the surface toward the drop-off.

Please let it be quick, God, Victor thought as the blackness rushed toward him.

Logan watched in amazement as the Hind fired two missiles and struck the airfield with destructive precision. No matter how many times he witnessed close air support, the firepower always sent an adrenaline rush and surge of confidence through him. *Damn. It's good to have air power.*

The Range Rover tried to avoid the chunks of tarmac that exploded in multiple directions, but it failed, and Logan enjoyed every second as the crash unfolded. The only occupant he almost felt sympathetic toward as the vehicle slid on its side toward the back of the airfield and the drop-off was President Pena. Then he remembered what the Venezuelan leader had done to the innocent people in the country, and his sympathy cooled. *But you still need him alive, no matter what.*

The Range Rover stopped short of the drop-off, and the satellite truck closed the distance to the crash, which the Hind gunship illuminated with a bright white floodlight as it hovered fifty yards away. There was no movement from the SUV, but Logan only saw the bottom of the wrecked vehicle.

Ten seconds later, Jack slid the satellite truck to a halt, and like a clown car of professional warriors, Logan and Jack emerged from the front, and the two assassins and Marcos—with the wounded vice president in tow—emerged from the back.

Logan left the AK-103 in the front seat, unholstered the Glock, and met Jack and the rest of the small team at the front of the truck. The faint sound of the scraping of glass floated toward them.

"Jack, you and the tag team go left. Marcos, stay behind me and maintain positive control of Baker. *No matter what, President Pena has to live.* Are we clear on that? I do the talking, and no one does anything until I tell you. You understand, Jack?"

"It's your show. Pena lives. I got it," Jack acknowledged.

"Good. Now let's go," Logan said, raised the Glock 17 in front of him, and crept along the bottom of the Range Rover toward the front.

In a seamless pincer movement, Logan and Jack, who'd circled around to the left, emerged at the roof of the Range Rover to find Lieutenant General Victor Cordones standing behind President Pena less than three feet from the edge of the drop-off. The general held a Browning Hi-Power pistol to the right temple of the president, whose face bled from several scrapes and cuts. The general had sustained a long gash down the left side of his face, and blood poured down his cheek near the back of his jaw. *I can relate to that,* Logan thought, reflecting on his own scar from a wound sustained in a knife fight more than two and a half years ago.

So this is how it's all going to go down. Okay. We can do this the hard way, Logan thought, and began to talk.

CHAPTER 52

"You're doing this for your son, aren't you?" Logan said. The CIA had provided a dossier on General Cordones once they'd identified him as the mastermind behind the events in Caracas, and Logan had studied it before the attack at the tunnels to understand the man responsible for orchestrating the chaos over the past few days. "Daniel, wasn't it? By all accounts, a good young man who wanted to serve and protect the people, a boy who grew up to be like his father, even if he served in a different capacity."

Victor crouched behind the president in order to minimize his silhouette. Logan had the sights of the Glock trained on the portion of Victor's face that he could see, but he hoped Jack had a better line of sight.

"Don't you dare speak about my son," Victor shot back, his voice tinged with a mixture of rage and sadness. "I know who you are. That man behind you, *your vice president,* told me all about you and your little task force, about whom you work for. There's nothing you can say that's going to change my mind. Nothing."

Logan nodded. *He's committed. There's no talking him down.* "In that case, you should also know I will stop at nothing to accomplish my mission, *what I was sent here to do.*"

For the first time, Victor looked confused. "But you have him? He's right there, behind you. So why come after me? Leave this monster to me."

"We're not after you," Logan said, and pointed at President Pena with his left hand. "But we are after him, and we need him *alive*."

"Why? He's the one who's created this desperation in Venezuela. You *know* that, don't you? He deserves to die. Don't you understand?" Victor pleaded, the muzzle of the Browning lifting away momentarily from the president's head.

There you go. It's working. Keep talking. "I empathize with your frustration, your anger, your grief, but I need you to hear me out. Just give me one minute. I'm begging you. For your son's sake." Logan paused. "I'm reaching into my vest for a phone. I'm not going to try anything. I swear to God," Logan said, and reached into a magazine pouch where he'd stored his Iridium. He pulled it out and held it up for Victor to see. While he held the Glock steady with his right hand, he called up the screen where the number he needed was pre-programmed and hit the green button. He pressed the speaker button, and digital chirping once again erupted from the speaker in the phone, audible over the sound of the rotors of the Hind, which had backed away to a standoff distance of more than one hundred yards.

"You have thirty seconds, and then I'm pulling the trigger for my son and for the people of Venezuela," Victor said, the barrel once again against President Pena's head.

"Logan . . ." Jack said quietly, inching slightly to his left to try and obtain a clearer sight picture.

I know. I know. I know. "Just wait for it, Victor, please," Logan said.

There was an audible click, followed by "Yes."

"Sir," Logan said. "I'm with him right now."

A brief moment of silence ensued, followed by "Very well." Another pause. "Mr. President, General Cordones, this is President Preston Scott. I have a proposal for you."

CHAPTER 53

For the first time in his entire career, General Victor Cordones was dumbstruck at the telephonic presence of the most powerful leader in the free world. *At least the world that most people understood, not the shadow one where the real power brokers linger in the dark,* he thought.

No one spoke, which was the only signal the president needed to fill the vacuum. "I don't know what's going on down there, but I have an idea."

"Sir, the general has the president with a gun to his head and is threatening to kill him momentarily," Logan advised. "I thought you might be able to dissuade him."

The president didn't even miss a beat. He was a veteran and A-10 pilot who'd seen combat, and the war with the Organization had dulled his sense of surprise. "Very well. General, you know why we've been hunting my own vice president. You know how he's betrayed *my country*, and by the presence of my people there, right now, you should also understand how determined I am to see him brought to justice."

"Then take him and leave the president to me," Victor replied. "I don't care about him. I'm no fool, Mr. President. I know I'm not leaving Venezuela alive, but neither is this man."

"You're not thinking clearly, Victor," President Scott said. "What if I told you there was a way to help the people of Venezuela, that out of all this chaos and destruction and *death*, not just from the Organization, but from the earthquake, we could truly *help* the people, the very same ones your son sympathized with. It would be a way to make his death and all the rest matter. What would you say to that?"

Victor's expression didn't change, but curiosity sparked in his eyes. The Browning once again moved away from President Pena's head, but Victor also shuffled backward slightly, moving inches closer to the edge of the drop-off.

"Logan . . ." Jack said again questioningly, his desire to pull the trigger on the Glock 17 he held trained on the general apparent in his voice.

"Wait," Logan ordered.

"How?" Victor asked. "How can you make such a promise?"

"Quite simply: it's all about the money," President Scott replied.

Of course, Victor thought, the simple brilliance of it gallingly apparent to him.

"You let President Pena live, and we use that thirty billion dollars of my vice president's to rebuild Caracas and try to restore some economic sanity to the quagmire Venezuela has become. It will take time, it will be painful, and there will be problems. But I believe it can be done. Otherwise, I wouldn't even be making this offer, and you'd already be dead. But for your son, I'm begging you to make the right choice," President Scott finished, and waited for a response.

At that moment, Victor was a man torn apart as a rift formed deep inside him, and the emotional pain that was his grief poured out into every cell of his being. His son's death was on the head of the man he held at gunpoint, a man who deserved a violent end for what he had wrought. Victor's thirst for vengeance consumed him, but he hesitated and lowered the gun several inches, resting the barrel on President Pena's right shoulder. *My son deserves justice.* But a voice countered in his head, *What about all the aid that money can bring to the people?* If it was an honest offer, he knew the money, if handled appropriately, would relieve the suffering of hundreds of thousands. But the pain was suffocating, a reminder of all he'd lost. There was one thing he had to know.

"What about Pena? What happens to him?" Victor said, the Browning dropping slightly from the president's shoulder to his upper back.

"Nothing," President Scott replied. "And here's why: your country has been through literal hell, and the last thing Venezuela needs is more instability. President Pena is the duly elected leader of your country, and I have no doubt that if you spare him, he'll do the right thing. Isn't that so, Mr. President?"

A moment of silence passed before President Pena answered, "Of course. If this is the best chance for the people, then I'll do it."

It was the briefest hesitation, but in that moment, it validated the suspicion, hatred, and rage that Victor felt. *He'll never follow through. He's not capable of change. He's a selfish, evil monster. My son deserves more than this*, he thought, and made his decision.

Jack had the only clear shot, and he saw Victor's posture change, his body stiffen, resolute in a decision only Victor knew. But Jack suspected what it was, and he readied himself.

"No. He won't" were the last words that Lieutenant General Victor Cordones, father, commanding general, and once patriot to the people of Venezuela, uttered. He quickly raised the pistol. The barrel had cleared President Pena's shoulder when Jack Longstreet, retired commandant of the Marine Corps, pulled the trigger on his Glock 17 and let loose one shot.

Jack's aim was true, and the 9mm round struck Victor in the right side of the temple. Blood sprayed across the back of President Pena's head and his right cheek, and he flinched at the wet warmth.

Victor stood still, suspended as his life fled his body, chasing his son into the afterlife, and then he fell backward, pulling President Pena with him toward the edge.

Logan leapt forward and covered the short distance in two strides as the dead man fell. Logan dropped the Iridium and the Glock as he moved, his entire being focused on one point feet away.

Victor's corpse toppled over the edge, as if plunging backward into a pool, and then he released his death grip on President Pena and disappeared below the edge into the real pool of oblivion.

President Pena was already falling when Logan dove into the air, his arms outstretched. The president's upper body kept falling, and his torso and buttocks disappeared below the edge as the president let out a terrified scream.

All Logan saw was black Italian shoes, kicking upward, as gravity pulled the rest of their owner down. Logan's hands shot out, and he latched on to the president's ankles. Logan's chest landed on the dirt, and he pressed down with all his might as if driving the president's legs into the ground to fix him in place. Logan felt the president's upper body strike the side of the cliff below the ledge, and Logan was jerked forward with the impact. *Oh, Christ. You've got to be kidding me.*

As the president shrieked in terror, reflexively swinging his arms wildly, Logan struggled to retain his grip on the man, and he wondered how much time he had left before he was pulled over the edge to join the body of General Cordones. "Stop moving or you'll kill us both!" Logan shouted. *Come on already.*

Two sets of hands gripped his legs and his belt, and the rushing figures of the two assassins blurred by Logan's face as he was stabilized. He watched in appreciation as the two men bent over the edge, one on each side, and reached down into the dark. Logan felt President Pena cease his flailing, and Thomas and Frederico squatted down and leaned backward, pulling the president up by his arms into a sitting position. Logan scooted backward, rolled off to the side, but still held on to the president's legs as the two assassins pulled the president forward to his feet.

For a terror-stricken moment, Logan envisioned the two assassins losing their grips and President Pena falling backward off the cliff, swallowed alive by the forest below. But instead, his body rose, and he reached the moment of inertia and fell forward, stumbling away from the edge. Marcos caught the president and held him steady as he regained his equilibrium.

Logan looked up from his back and saw Jack smiling down at him. "Always have to be the hero, don't you?"

"As do you, Jack. As do you," Logan replied, his body sore from the impact with the ground and the bullet he'd taken in the back earlier in the day. "Now, help me because you know we're not done."

The smile disappeared from Jack's face, replaced by a hard mask of determination. He bent down and pulled his former Marine up to his feet, and said, "Are you absolutely sure about this? I'm good with it, but you'll have to carry it. You know that, right?"

There was no hesitation as Logan replied with a hard edge to his voice, "Without a doubt. This ends tonight."

Logan walked over to his fallen Glock and the Iridium. He picked both up and held the Iridium in front of him. "Are you still there, sir?" Logan asked.

"I am," President Scott replied. "Who died?" He knew the shot had taken someone's life.

"Jack took out General Cordones, but President Pena is alive," Logan said.

"And everyone else, including Baker?" President Scott said.

"Yes, sir. We're all in one piece, banged up, but alive."

"Good. Then do what needs to be done, and leave the line open," President Scott said.

"Roger that, sir. Stand by," Logan said, and turned to face President Pena and Vice President Baker.

CHAPTER 54

"I really wish General Cordones had reconsidered. I truly sympathized with the man," Logan said, glancing back and forth between the traitor and the socialist dictator. Jack and Cole were on his left; Marcos and the two assassins, his right. "His son paid for your policies with his life, and I don't blame him for questioning your sincerity. In fact, I don't trust you either, Mr. President. Maybe you deserve to die for what you've done; maybe you don't. But that's not my call. We're giving you *one* chance to do the right thing. The details will come later, but what's important at this *very minute* is that you understand how serious we are, how *committed,* to ensuring you do it."

"I don't understand," President Pena countered, pleading. "I said I will do it, and I will."

"I hear you, and you sound sincere, but I think you'll be more convinced in just a moment. Just bear with me," Logan said.

Logan shifted his attention to Vice President Baker, the Glock steady in his hand and pointed at the man's chest. "I told you earlier this evening that I wanted you dead, that you deserved death for the crimes you've committed, for the lives you're directly responsible for ending. But I also told you that you had a higher purpose, and that purpose is about to be served."

Logan lowered his Glock and said, "Mr. President."

From the Iridium, President Scott said, "Josh, you chose evil and the wrong path, betrayed your oath to your office, the Constitution, and the country. Another innocent man died tonight, a retired DC police officer whose only crime was to be the father of one of this nation's greatest clandestine warriors. And that I cannot forgive." He paused. "For all that you have done, I—no one else— sentence you to death."

Logan turned to Marcos Bocanegra, who waited silently, and nodded.

"I know it was you who told the Los Toros cartel where I'd fled. Only Cain Frost knew my plan to escape, but I know he confided it to you, as you were the senior Council member in the Organization. I don't know why you were tying up loose ends three months ago, and I don't care. But they told me the order came from America, which means that it *had* to be you," Marcos said with a deep, seething rage.

"I'm sorry," Josh replied, staring back at his executioner. He knew what was coming, and he tried to compose himself, if only to convince himself he wasn't a coward. "I thought they'd kill only you. I was eliminating anyone who knew what I was, before the insurrection against the Founder. I only wanted you dead, but from what I heard after, you'd fallen in love. Don't fool yourself—you doomed her the second you became involved with her," he said, his voice rising in rebuttal. "Her death is on you. She was *your* collateral."

"No, you evil motherfucker," Marcos said with a pure hatred so thick Logan thought he could taste it. "She was my pregnant fiancée."

He raised the Glock and fired three shots that struck Joshua Baker in the chest. The onetime vice president collapsed to the ground and folded inward, his evil heart shredded by the bullets.

Marcos stared at the new corpse and lowered the Glock back to his side.

Logan noticed a slight tremble in the killer's gun hand, and he wondered if he'd ever find the peace that would steady that rage.

He knew that Marcos would be overwhelmed with guilt, and then he remembered that Marcos had once worked as an enforcer for a vicious drug cartel. Baker's last words, while cruel, had been like a thousand knives in the healing wound that was Marcos's pain because of one thing—there'd been an underlying foundation of truth to them. But that was for Marcos to handle as he saw fit. Logan had one last item to address.

No one spoke, and President Pena stared wide-eyed at the sudden execution of the second most powerful politician in the United States and one of the most powerful men in the world inside the Organization. Vice President Baker had waged a secret war, and he'd just lost to this assembled group of warriors.

Logan stepped forward, the Glock still held at his side, and stopped inches from President Pena. He wore a mask of merciless coldness when he spoke. "Now do you understand?" It was a simple question that explained everything, the future that could be or the alternative he could suffer.

"I do," President Pena said softly without a trace of hesitation or insincerity.

"Good, Mr. President, because I only want to say this one time, and I'm sure you'll understand why. If you do anything to undermine this arrangement, one that will give billions of dollars to your country and your people, then I promise you that you will suffer the same fate as that traitor right there," Logan said, and gestured to the dead body that bled onto the dirt. "Because there will be no place for you that is safe *from me*. No matter what, I will come for you. Do you understand?"

President Pena realized he'd never met a man as terrifying as the American that stood before him. His will was a force that emanated from his pores like sweat. The threat was so simple and sincere that he knew it would be done. *This man will hunt me down and kill me.* "I do. And I will do what's necessary" was all he said.

Logan's green eyes blazed, and then his features softened slightly, the merciless gaze transformed into something more human, and he nodded as he stepped back from the Venezuelan leader. "Good. Mr. President, did you catch all that?"

"I did. Then we have a deal, Mr. President, one that I will honor, and one that I sincerely hope will help the suffering people of your nation," President Scott said, turning his attention to Logan. "Logan, please return the president to his people and his palace. Once he's safe and secure, get back here as soon as possible and bring the vice president's body. We have a burial to prepare."

Logan understood the charade would continue, but he'd already resolved that internal conflict. The man was a monster and a traitor, but he would be mourned by his son and the country as a good father and a patriot. It was necessary to maintain the balance of power in the US. *Some prices are worth paying,* Logan thought.

"Mr. President, I'll make sure they have everything they need," President Pena said, eager to be of assistance to his new economic partners who had just saved his life.

"I appreciate that," President Scott said. "In that case, gentlemen. Your nation thanks you, even if they don't know for what, and *I thank you.* See you soon," he said, and the line went dead.

"Mr. President, it's time to get you back. I believe we'll all fit on the Hind, if that works for you," Logan said.

"I've never been on one, believe it or not," President Pena said. "I've seen them in demonstrations and now this, tonight. Just never flew in one."

"Well, sir, there's a first time for everything," Logan said, and allowed himself a small smile.

After the past few days, he realized no truer words could be said. He thought about his wife, their unborn baby, and an uncertain future. *There will be many firsts yet to come.* And he welcomed each one.

EPILOGUE

Logan sat in the suede rocking chair and gently pushed back and forth on the carpeted floor. He stared out the window over the expanse of the acre-and-a-half backyard to where the property dropped down into an area of dense foliage and the bluff beyond. At the bottom ran the Occoquan River, winding its way behind the Reilly's Bluff subdivision and to the southeast before emptying into the Potomac. The view reminded him every single time of the airfield in Venezuela more than seven months ago. *It was severe, swift, and certain, and more importantly, it had been the president's call, not yours.*

He felt no remorse over the execution of Joshua Baker. He was a traitor guilty of high crimes, murder, domestic terrorism, and the devil knew what else. It wasn't his death that bothered him, but rather the cover-up they'd all agreed to before returning his body to US soil. The vice president had received a hero's burial with full honors at Arlington Cemetery. The original story had miraculously stuck with the media: the vice president had been kidnapped by a militia in Montana upset about his blockage of an oil pipeline. His body had been found at an abandoned ranch owned by members of the Montana Freedom Movement, and the media had relished the idea of blaming a right-wing extremist group.

The only solace that Logan took in the entire affair was that Joshua Baker's son, eleven-year-old Jacob, would never know the true, treacherous nature of his father. As evil as Joshua Baker had been, Logan hoped that his son would grow up to be a kind, caring, confident man, the exact opposite of his father. *How he could do that to his son, I'll never know, especially now that I have her.*

Logan looked down into the angelic face of two-week-old Sophia Addison West, and he felt the warm envelope of love and protection fall over him. As a new father, it was a different kind of love than the one he had for his amazing and beautiful wife, and he was still getting used to it. From the first moment he'd held her after clamping and cutting the umbilical cord before handing her to his wife after twenty-seven hours of labor, he'd felt the bond that Santiago had told him about in Atlantis. "There are only two kinds of people in this world—those with kids, and everyone else." And somehow, he now found himself in that first category.

He smiled at the memory, not of Santiago, but of the last time he'd visited Venezuela, six weeks after the day of the earthquake. It was the knowledge that the CAR T-cell therapy had worked on Camila Rojas. The receptors that had been produced and infused into her body had eradicated her cancer. She was in complete remission, another sign that occasionally cosmic forces took mercy on the young and innocent. It was also symbolic, as the entire country of Venezuela seemed to be on a rebound, a partial economic remission, from the scourge of socialism.

In the immediate aftermath of the quake, aid had been flown and shipped in to provide food and medical supplies for the ravaged people. The bank in Switzerland, after a clandestine visit by a member of the CIA with all the appropriate account documentation, had transferred billions of dollars to multiple aid agencies, including several nongovernmental organizations that were "guided" by the US Treasury Department at the direct orders of President

Scott. In what many assumed was an act of mercy, the president had also lifted sanctions, allowing US investors to acquire Venezuelan debt. In return, President Pena had restructured Venezuela's national oil company in order to cut down on corruption and regulate production. The effect of such measures had been nearly instantaneous, especially with billions of dollars in aid rebuilding the infrastructure: the economy was slowly rebounding as hyperinflation began to creep back down. The mass exodus of millions of people had ceased, and the people were no longer starving. *All in all, I'd call that a win,* Logan thought, although he knew the country had years of rebuilding ahead of it.

Even the Russians seemed to be offering legitimate assistance, at least in a very Russian way. The Russian ambassador to Venezuela, the man who had befriended Victor Cordones in the hour of his spiritual need and had aided in the general's plans, had been killed two weeks after the earthquake in a single-car accident that reportedly had been caused by *motorizados*. *Those motorcycles can be dangerous,* Logan had thought at the news, satisfied at another loose end tied up neatly, albeit in blood.

Sophia let out a small gurgle, opened her baby-blue eyes, and stared up into her father's deep, bright-green ones. He knew she had no depth perception yet and couldn't make out more than shapes, but he didn't care. He was as much hers as she was his. The bond had been forged.

Logan grabbed the baby bottle from the cherrywood nightstand, absentmindedly noting that Pottery Barn would be depleting his funds for years to come. Sarah was asleep but had pumped several ounces for the bottle before lying down for a nap at Logan's urging. Like all new mothers, she'd barely had any sleep with nursing Sophia every few hours. Logan knew things would get better soon, at least from what he'd been told, but that place seemed a long way off at the moment.

He felt a hand squeeze his shoulder, and Sarah said, "How is she?" He hadn't even heard her approach. *Getting soft already? Losing that tactical edge now that you're a dad?*

"You were supposed to be sleeping," Logan replied softly. "That was the whole point."

Sarah laughed quietly. "I know, but I couldn't. It is only fifteen hundred, after all." She still used military time after all the years she'd spent with Logan and Marines. She leaned down and kissed Logan on the cheek. "She's an alert one, *aren't you, princess?*" she asked, transitioning into baby talk midsentence.

"Hey, that reminds me," Logan said. "Did you know there is an actual Disney Princess Sofia? I was looking for toys online and stumbled upon it. If nothing else, at least she'll have her own show."

"I'm not sure which is more disturbing—you waging war on very bad people or watching Disney Junior princess shows. I think it's a toss-up."

"That's not fair, babe. I can evolve. I might even learn a thing or two. I hear those shows are very informative. John told me all about them, and I trust anything he says," Logan added playfully.

Sarah scooped up Sophia and then settled into Logan's lap as he wrapped his arms around them both.

"How is Amira?" Sarah asked, worry in her voice.

"Since John moved into her apartment, you know how close those two have grown. They're nearly inseparable. I'm just glad he's there for her, to help her grieve. I can imagine what she's been through, but I don't want to. The only thing that seems to help is time, and even then, not always," Logan said. "At least she knows what happened to the man responsible, that he won't ever be able to do to anyone else what he did to her. For someone like Amira, I think that helps, even if just a little."

Sarah was silent, and then changed the topic. "I love you," she said simply.

Logan squeezed her tightly, inhaled deeply, the scent of the baby filling his nostrils, and let it out with a slow exhalation. "And I love you," he replied. "Check that," he interjected, falling into military jargon. "I love *both* of you." He kissed Sarah on the top of her head. *This is what it's all supposed to be about. Family.*

As the three of them rocked silently in the chair, lulling Sophia back to sleep, Logan found himself truly content and deeply calm for the first time since childhood. It was a sense of pure belonging and tranquility in the knowledge that he was exactly where he was supposed to be at this very moment in his life. He didn't know how long it would last. But what he did know was all that mattered was the present, and that was more than enough for now.

ACKNOWLEDGMENTS

Writing a series is a commitment to try to produce something better and unique each and every time. With *Rules of War*, I hope I've accomplished that goal. As the storyteller, I'm especially proud of the underlying themes of parenthood and sacrifice, but ultimately, you, the reader, will make that determination. Like with all things in life, the future is uncertain, but it has taken a team effort to get to this point.

First, Team Bestler, comprising my editor, Emily Bestler; her assistant, Lara Jones; my publicist, David Brown; and our Pocket Books mass market editor, Jen Long—thank you. Without your commitment, the world would not have known Logan West or his family of warriors and loved ones.

Second, my agent, Will Roberts, who dealt with the day-to-day of this grueling business and listened to my regular venting. This is a brutal business, and we've learned that together—thank you.

Third, to my wife, Amy, who has consistently supported me throughout this endeavor, managed my mania, and kept the Family Ship on course. You get the biggest THANK YOU.

A special thank you to the Calvert County Sheriff's Office in Maryland and to Assistant Sheriff Lt. Col. Dave McDowell, who facilitated my ride-along with the outstanding Sheriff's Deputy First Class Shea Rediker, who tolerated my sarcasm and endless questions. At one point, we rolled up to a 911 hang-up call after hours at a mosque surrounded by woods. I surveyed the empty building and said, "You know, if I were writing this story, we'd be about to get lit up from the tree line," to which Deputy Rediker replied, "Just make sure you shoot back." You guys are an amazing testament to what it means to serve and protect. Continue to hold the blue line.

Finally, to you, the reader, thank you for your investment of time and emotion. Without you, there is no series, no further adventures, no more tales to tell. You are why I or any other author does this, and you are what matters—thank you. It's been an honor. Until the next time.

Semper fidelis,
Matt

ABOUT THE AUTHOR

MATTHEW BETLEY is a former Marine officer of ten years. His experience includes deployments to Djibouti after September 11, and to Iraq prior to the surge. A New Jersey native who considers Cincinnati home, he graduated from Miami University in Oxford, Ohio, with a BA in psychology and minors in political science and sociology.